The Starfighter Invitation

by Andrea K Höst

The Starfighter Invitation
© 2018 Andrea K Höst. All rights reserved.
ISBN: 978-1-925188-00-4
Cover Art: Andres Parada
www.andreakhost.com

I

demo 1

No-one 'wins' an MMO. They're games that are designed around progression: gaining max level, then working with a group to get the very best gear, with countless time fillers to keep you busy until the next game expansion is released, and then you start the grind all over again. Plot optional, and the only real boasting rights in being the first to do something. First to max level. First to down a raid boss. First to unlock gated content, or reach a new zone.

The last is what I like to do—or pretend to do, by avoiding chat after an initial release, keeping my nose out of forums, and exploring the game as if I wasn't following a thoroughly trampled path.

Because no-one's really first in an MMO. Any game that deserves the label 'massively multiplayer' takes a cast of thousands to put together. Developers bring it to the in-house alpha testing stage. A horde of lucky volunteers get to hunt bugs for free in the closed beta test. And tens or even hundreds of thousands swarm the open beta, trying before buying as the developers stress test the servers. By the day of release there'll be entire player-built databases full of maps, discussions, quest solutions, character builds, prime levelling spots, and probably the strats for at least the low-level dungeons.

Frustrating for a discovery gamer like me. I don't want to know everything there is to know about a game before I play it, and there's nothing less enjoyable than heading into a new dungeon only to have my party race through it all at break-neck speed, complaining the whole time that I haven't researched exactly where to stand.

Despite the challenges, I still enjoy the first few months of a new release immensely. From the sheer chaos of the crowded starter area, to vistas stumbled over while dashing through deserted high level zones. I like not knowing about the Easter eggs, let alone the plot developments. Eventually, of course, I'll run out of new areas, hit max level, and then obligingly raid with my guild, and do time-filler quests until fresh horizons draw me away. My particular addiction is going somewhere I've never been before, and looking around. But every MMO I've ever played, I completely knew I wouldn't really be 'discovering' anything.

Except with *Dream Speed*.

The first surprise was that it existed. GDG—guided dream gaming—had been around for a handful of years, was wildly popular with insomniacs, and otherwise considered more a gimmick than a real game. It definitely didn't even remotely resemble the kind of experience you'd expect from an MMO. GDGs nudged your dreams toward specific imagery, and I'd enjoyed them for what they were: vaguely experienced mood pieces. A million people could play *Crystal Heights* every night and they would all dream of a castle of ice, and of lost treasure, and they would find themselves in a gold room, and a green room, and a room of frozen flowers. But everyone's castle and treasure and rooms would be different, and what passed for gameplay was vague, disjointed and unpredictable. Dreamlike.

No-one had even considered matching GDG with traditional game types, let alone an MMO, until Ryzonart set up a demonstration booth at E3—one of the largest game-related press conventions—touting their upcoming massively multi-player online GDG set in a post-singularity future.

A technological singularity, that is: the moment when artificial intelligence comes into existence, and life as we know it ceases to be. Love us or hate us, AI is expected to change us.

At the time of *Dream Speed's* first demo, Ryzonart was known as a tiny independent game developer, with only a couple of addictive little casual apps to its name, and the idea of them releasing any kind of MMO was unlikely enough. The idea of a MMO GDG was just ludicrous, particularly from such a minor developer. When the posters started going up at E3, there was a lot of outright mocking across the gaming sphere. '*Dial-up Speed*', that kind of thing.

Then the demos started.

Big crowded gaming conventions aren't my thing, so I woke up entirely oblivious one morning in early June and every site I went to was screaming the same thing.

True. Virtual. Reality.

Ryzonart knew what kind of bomb they were exploding. They didn't have a line for the demo. Instead there were terminals where you could make a session booking time, or sign up for the no-show lottery. A couple of fights broke out. Someone sold a session slot for over $1,000.

It took only one frothing article to send me to all the shaky videos recorded from the booth's display monitors. The demo was set in a narrow valley zone surrounded by cliffs, with a waterfall plunging to a pool, and just that alone was enough to send players raving. While GDG could produce a spectacular level of detail, it tended to combine with a haziness to everything except the particular focus of the dreamer's attention. This was crystal-clear, with every blade of grass, every leaf, every rock appearing as individual and separate objects. And, unlike the average MMO, none of it looked like a texture—a painting of 'rock' wrapped across a graphical object—and there was no hint of the repetition that usually creeps into computer-generated landscapes. The only difference from the real world I could see was a level of airbrushed beauty usually reserved for tourist brochures.

But this wasn't just a pretty-looking place. VR headsets had been around for years, and great graphics weren't *that* revolutionary, although the more detail usually meant hideous frame rates as it all loaded. But we'd been able to see and hear virtual worlds for an age. What *Dream Speed* did was add body to the experience.

Almost every demo video followed the same course: a character avatar standing by fern and moss-decked rocks opened their eyes and gasped, and then spent many minutes staring down at themselves, touching their own faces, moving arms and legs—or tails, ears, fins or wings. The pretty valley around them was almost irrelevant to the experience. Some never even shifted their attention from their selves to the environment. Those that did usually only stared about, took hesitant steps, touching grass and stones and water as if they were the most interesting things in the universe. And then the session would be over, and the player would emerge from the curtained rear of Ryzonart's booth, and rave.

This repetition was made more entertaining by the huge variety of avatars. The first demo I watched was nothing unusual: a slim, brown-skinned young man with a black mohawk. The only real surprise was, again, the incredible detail. And the way he behaved. But the next video, while still featuring a humanoid, showed an attenuated figure with an olive brown...carapace. Thickened skin formed segmented plates, with spikes jutting from elbows and shoulders. The face above the mouth was two smooth planes, divided vertically. Slits for eyes. The next avatar was a jewellery-bedecked pangolin with a fox-like head. Next, an eight-legged, many-armed robotic thing that spent the entire session working out how to walk. Then a blue woman, who spent her session squeezing her own breasts. Dozens of different avatars—I rarely saw two that even resembled each other.

MMOs average on launch something like five race choices, usually all humanoid: an approach that saves a lot of time and resources. The variety of character avatars in the demo suggested that not only were we looking at the biggest leap forward in gaming technology since, well, *Pong*, but that Ryzonart had thrown major-league money into development. We could hope for a lot more from *Dream Speed* than just a pretty waterfall and the experience of truly being not yourself. Chances were good there was a real game, the next level of gaming, due to release in a mere four months.

And no-one knew anything about it.

2
guild chat

[g]<Sprocket Sprocket> itz the only explanation that makes sense .. dream speeds 2 advanced 2 b made by humans

[g]<Far Cryinggame> Should rename this guild Team Gullible.

[g]<Sprocket Sprocket> dont make me go all occams razor on your ass far

[g]<Amelia Beerheart> There must be a few more likely explanations than Ryzonart being run by an AI.

[g]<Sprocket Sprocket> name one

[g]<Amelia Beerheart> Ryzonart is a front company for a bigger one? The game is nothing but a fancy demo and has no content whatsoever? Aliens?

[g]<Sprocket Sprocket> coz aliens have nothing better 2 do than run games for humans

[g]<Amelia Beerheart> Unlike AIs, evidently.

[g]<Kazerin Fel> Is it too much to believe that ordinary human programmers made a big leap forward?

[g]<Sprocket Sprocket> no way they could have kept a lid on it

Silent Assassin>> up for a taranthy depths run?

>>Silent Assassin: About to log and watch the livestream of Demo 2, sorry.

Silent Assassin>> ...

Silent Assassin>> you and the rest of the planet dammit. i'm never going to complete my set.

[g]<Far Cryinggame> It's beyond me why this wasn't written off as vapourware soon as it came out that Ryzonart is funded by Advanced Somnetics.

[g]<Amelia Beerheart> Why is that a negative point? The inventors of GDG cowls are the logical people to fund the next leap forward in the games.

[g]<Far Cryinggame> The only programmer Ryzonart lists is their CEO, and none of the demo employees have even met this Dom Kinnen guy, or know about anything more than setting up the booths for the demo.

[g]<Far Cryinggame> But it's not because he's an alien, or an AI or whatever.

[g]<Far Cryinggame> Ryzonart's playing mystery to ramp up the hype.

[g]<Far Cryinggame> Seriously, one demo grabbed them god knows how many million in pre-orders. And the demos themselves—do any of you really believe their explanation for why some of the displays ran longer than the demo session? I don't care if GDG games usually do distort your perception of time—the idea that *DS* is going to run five times faster than reality is outright ludicrous.

[g]<Far Cryinggame> And then there's the fact that they haven't submitted the game for ESRB or PEGI rating. No vetting. Download only, direct from their site.

[g]<Far Cryinggame> Only logical explanation is scam. It can't be real.

>>Silent Assassin: You're not dying to play *DS?*

Silent Assassin>> check it out, yes. believe it's not a hoax, no . pant over livestream of cgi bullshit not a chance

[g]<Amelia Beerheart> If it was all just a pretty movie, there'd be no need for the server farms that have been verified. A massive amount of money has gone into this. Even just the fact that Ryzonart's site didn't go down, despite the pummelling it's taken since demo 1, shows there's back-end grunt.

>>Silent Assassin: I seriously hope you're wrong, Si.

[g]<Kazerin Fel> Until something proves me wrong, I am officially abandoning all cynicism. Time for me to log and pant over Demo 2. Later all.

[g]<Sprocket Sprocket> time for us all !!!

[g]<Amelia Beerheart> Ta-ta Kaz.

[g]<Far Cryinggame> Don't forget your tinfoil hat.

Kazerin Fel has logged off.

3

demo 2

"How's the feed?"

My mother shrugged. "This host seems steady. Though the viewing numbers keep spiking. I've a few other options in case it drops out."

Cradling my laptop, I dropped on the couch and eyed the volume-muted wall screen. A presenter dressed as Thor was waving a hammer-shaped microphone.

"Why am I not there? Cologne's so close—I could be there this afternoon."

"Do the math, Taia," my father said, carrying a laden tray into the room. "Five days. Twenty half hour session slots per day, most of them already reserved thanks to the pre-con lotteries. And Gamescom has three or four hundred thousand attendees on a normal year. You would be watching on the monitors like everyone else, all crammed up, and without the benefit of home-cooked snacks."

"I thought I smelled roti."

Roti was one of the major benefits of my parents' long ramble through Asia. I demolished the perfectly-crisped flatbread—when my Dad made it, I never had to worry about someone using a wheat-mix flour—and listened impatiently as the gamers for the special first session were announced and introduced. Obviously not a random selection, since the lucky pair were sisters: two teens in matching Chell costumes, each carrying a hula-hoop. That was a clever bit of cosplay—they weren't quite identical, but close enough to produce an illusion of a single person entering a blue circle on one wall and simultaneously emerging from an orange circle on the other side of the stage. They demonstrated, bringing cheers from the assembled crowd, before being escorted through a pair of doors painted in a slick imitation of metal and circuitry.

"All that excitement, and now they're expected to go to sleep." I sighed ostentatiously, though I knew it wouldn't be more than a five to ten minute wait. GDG had grown out of tech designed to alleviate insomnia, and there were very few people who could withstand sleep-induction for long. "Have you decided whether you're going to buy your own GDG cowls?"

"We do have one of the early models. We'll probably try that first." My mother shrugged and grimaced at the ceiling. "Roof repairs before indulgences."

I checked my laptop, refreshing the Ryzonart site in hopes of an update. I'd registered and pre-ordered immediately after Demo 1, of course, but other than the online store, Ryzonart had only released the cowl specifications required to run the game, and a very vaguely-worded user agreement. They didn't have forums. They didn't even have an FAQ.

Of course, hordes of people were saying the whole thing was a hoax: there was no game, the demo participants had been actors, and *DS* was the biggest scam the gaming community had ever seen. After one net Sherlock had traced a direct financial link between Ryzonart and Advanced Somnetics, the company that had developed GDG cowls, the discussion had head directly to fraud prosecution territory.

I'd still thrown my money at the first opportunity.

The livestream switched from the excitable presenter at the booth to Ryzonart's main feed, handily broadcasting the output of the sessions directly so the international audience no longer had to rely on shaky footage from monitors. The stream showed a shadowy, metallic door in an unlit room, which slid open to reveal the two girls framed by glare, now dressed in nondescript beige overalls.

"We're still us!" the taller girl exclaimed in German, which isn't one of my primary languages, though I can get by in it.

The other girl didn't indulge in the usual gaping down at herself, instead gasping and taking a stumbling step forward. The camera obligingly swivelled so the audience could appreciate what she was seeing.

"Holy hell."

I'd dropped my roti, but didn't care. I'd stopped wondering how much game there could possibly be, let alone what you did in it. I didn't care about anything except the view.

Velvet black and diamonds, and a great, grand curving wash in a thesaurus of blue, a thousand shades from sapphire to ice, and, oh, I wanted it, that moment of looking down on a world made compassable by distance, and in its turn transforming the one who looked into the tiniest speck, a gnat, a mote in...

"Space! We're in space! Sabine, we're–!"

"Shut up."

The shorter sister barely whispered the words, advancing until her hands were against the clear surface that separated them from all that was without. And, after a quavering moment, her sister joined her and they stood silent. The light of the world turned the girls' ochre brown skin a sickly green, but did nothing to lessen the sheer joy the pair radiated.

"Roof can wait."

My mother had spoken, not quite under her breath. I let out my own, and we exchanged a glance, then gazed hungrily back at the screen.

"It's not Earth," the shorter sister said, after she'd drunk deeply of awe and had moved on to curiosity. "There's hardly any land."

[[[[It is the Drowned Earth.]]]]

The sisters whirled, taking up defensive stances until they spotted the source of the strange, multi-layered voice: a floating point of light.

"What are you supposed to be?" the taller sister asked.

[[[[I am the Concierge of *Dream Speed*. You may call me Ryzon.]]]]

I couldn't identify the accent of the odd, rich voice, though Ryzon's German was certainly better than mine.

"You're a game master? This is so awesome. I love it already. Do we get our own ships? What are the classes? Can we be anything we like? Even the panther?"

"Give it—her?—a chance to answer, Petra."

But Ryzon responded with effortless calm:

[[[[In some ways. Thank you. Ships are one of the goals. Technically, there are no classes. There are a wide variety of modal units. The panther is one option.]]]]

The shorter sister, Sabine, reached a hand toward the floating light, but changed her mind. "What's a modal unit?"

[[[[A physical avatar. You start with your own Core Unit, but as you progress through the game you might access, for instance, an underwater modal, or one designed for flight, or zero gravity. Some challenges can only be entered using a modal with specific traits.]]]]

The room's lighting changed, brightening to a dim orange glow, the brilliant white of the corridor shifting to match. Words in a language I didn't recognise, accompanied by a two-tone beep, began to blare, and the two girls gasped as they both drifted upward. The shorter reacted to the sudden absence of weight by kicking accidentally against the window, propelling herself toward the centre of the room. She flailed, turning in a circle.

[[[[Zero-G games are best entered with a modal optimised for the environment,]]]] Ryzon said, voice brimful of amusement and clearly audible over the noise. [[[[But this challenge has been simplified so that even the rawest of space-goers has a chance to succeed. Your goal is to find and press four deactivation buttons before the countdown runs out. I'll make the first one easy.]]]]

The floating 'concierge' vanished as a red flashing object, the size of a fist and labelled in squiggles, appeared on the ceiling above the stranded girl.

"Petra! Give me a hand! No, help me first!"

But the taller girl had already launched herself at the ceiling, managing a near trajectory. Bouncing off metal a half-foot to the right of the button, she tried to slap it on the rebound, and succeeded in sending herself hurtling into a corner of the room.

As the pair gave themselves a frantic lesson in zero-G manoeuvres, my mother picked up her tablet, and in a few short pecks at the screen began shopping for GDG cowls.

"Is yours still working, Taia?" my father asked, taking off his glasses and twisting them, as he did whenever he was excited.

"Yeah, I don't need—wait, are those *DS*-branded?"

"Official Ryzonart cowls," my mother said, bringing up a larger image of a deep blue cowl specked with stars, the mandatory smoke detector and emergency wake button gleaming blue and gold, like a planet and its sun. "Ryzonart definitely has its product placement ready to go."

"Standard price, at least. Damn, I want one. I don't really need one, but I want one. I...hey, why four?"

"One for your Oma."

"Oma and computers? Really?" My grandmother, very much an outdoorswoman despite the arthritis that plagued her, had little time for electronics.

"Your Oma and a virtual body."

"Good point."

I shook my head and watched two girls working their way along a spaceship corridor. Of course, people had already been saying that *Dream Speed* wouldn't just upend the gaming world, that VR would change lives. And while I might dismiss theories of aliens and AIs in guild chat, if these demos weren't some magnificent hoax, then...could we really do this with current tech?

4

Corpse Light Forums
Thread: *Dream Speed* Starting City

26 September: Tornin (Guildmaster)

Right, the poll is officially closed. Guild starting city
is Vessa. What Vessa is, what we'll do there—your guess is
as good as mine. Sounds like *DS* is solo-focused, but
Ryzonart's finally confirmed there will be guild functions in-
game.

26 September: TALiSON (Member)

I feel like I've been waiting for this game my entire life.
I don't know if I'm going to survive the next week.

26 September: TazMazter (Member)

Never thought I'd be ponying up for a game while
knowing hardly anything about it.

26 September: Silent (Officer)

if i didn't know someone who'd drawn one of the
demos i'd still be convinced the whole thing was an
elaborate hoax

28 September: DIEMORTDIE (Member)

Here's hoping we get the pre-load as smoothly as
everything else. While we're spamming F5, here's a
checklist of all the questions answered so far:

Classes: 'modal units' with different specifications.

Races: As above.

PVP: Yes, can fight other players in designated zones,
or by duelling, though majority of gameplay is PVE.

Max level: None? You gain reputation, rankings and credits to buy upgrades.

End game: Highest-ranked players compete in 'Challenges' (for boasting rights?).

Setting: far future Earth (and all of the galaxy!?).

Plot/lore: No idea!

World servers: Only one? Seems unlikely, but probably the whole thing is a series of instances. There's no differentiation between the starting cities in terms of PVP or RP. Probably each of the fifty starter cities is hosted on a different server.

Restrictions: Some content is age-restricted, with three divisions: twelve to fifteen, sixteen to eighteen, and nineteen up. Under-twelves not allowed to play. [Good luck enforcing any of that.]

Localisation: Claims (improbably) that it will be localised for all major languages from launch.

Microtransactions: No! No loot boxes, either.

Play time: This is new: you can only play *DS* for five (real world) hours at a time, after which you will be shuttled into normal sleep, and won't be allowed access again for a minimum of five hours. MADDENING. On the flip side, they're sticking to the idea of 'time compression', which means those five hours in-game will work out to 25 hours experienced. No answer to the question of whether the full shut out will commence if you log before your five hours are up.

28 September: Tornin (Guildmaster)

How Ryzonart can make everyone dream at the same speed—or do any of this—has yet to be answered.

28 September: Silent (Officer)

if we experience each five hours as twenty-five—hell, with five on, five off, we could fit in nearly a hundred hours of gameplay on the first day—can we possibly not burn through the game's entire content in the first week?

28 September: TALiSON (Member)

I'll be spending MY first week in the character creator.

28 September: Far (Member)

Aaannnd...downloading!!!

28 September: Thing One (Member)

download is tiny! miniscule! everything is server side and ds going to be death by laglaglag server down mass overload !!

28 September: Amelia (Officer)

Nice to have such a problem-free pre-install but...well, we don't understand how this game works. We'll see.

28 September: TALiSON (Member)

OMFG!!   Game is unlocked already!!   Game is unlocked! THIS IS NOT A DRILL! Go go go go go!!!

5

character creation

In some games you get to choose from a number of pre-made character models, and that's it. In others you can spend days playing with settings: widening the bridge of your character's nose, and adjusting the length of their chin—or ears, or tail.

No game before *Dream Speed* had ever presented me with me, naked, standing in the middle of an empty white space.

This, combined with the shock of clarity, left me simply staring. By clarity, I mean that I was in GDG, but with none of the vagueness that usually came with the experience. I was as fully aware that I was playing a game as I would be at my own keyboard, though I had the lack of physical awareness that I usually experienced in GDG. No body, in other words, unless I counted the one standing rather too thoroughly in view.

And I had *sliders*.

An overlay of dozens of sub-menus promoted themselves to my attention as I noticed them. All the usual options for height and hair colour and so forth, but taken to an almost fractal level of detail, and made extraordinary by their application to *me.*

As I surveyed the excess of choice, one section of the display zoomed up to fill my view.

Core Unit Synchronisation
87%

"What are we synchronising?" I wondered, and was startled again when the question appeared in text before me, immediately followed by an answer:

The Core Unit is your
primary game avatar—the
first of many possible avatars.

> For best results, adjust
> the Core Unit to achieve
> highest synchronisation.

"Does the Core Unit have to look like me?"

> The Core Unit is not
> required to match your
> appearance outside
> *Dream Speed.*

"Excellent," I said, and settled back to consider Taia de Haas, twenty-three and ready for an upgrade.

All things considered, I hadn't done too badly on the genetic lottery. The factory standard bits were present and functional, and nothing immediately sparked bullies to stare and jeer. I had my mother's rather coarse and stubborn hair, my father's South-east Asian colouring, and a stocky figure that neither side of my family would claim. My eyes were my favourite feature: they looked good even when I hadn't been playing with the eyeliner.

My biggest dislike were my short legs, and so I started with them, becoming five inches taller after adjusting the rest of me to match. Then I gave myself the hair I'd always longed for: a sheer, sleek fall all the way to my behind. Slender hands with long fingers and perfectly shaped nails. A neck and jawline of exquisite elegance.

There were handy options for almost everything, and the sliders had a default to scale changes proportionally. Once I'd settled on a basic appearance I began to refine. Tiny pores made my skin look incredible, and I could erase old acne scars, and other tiny lumps, bumps and imperfections. Longer lashes, and a bit of natural eyeliner. Perfect brows, and then a digression into all the places I could choose for hair never to grow.

That led to an option to add hair just about everywhere, in every texture, and took me down an endless rabbit hole of additions—tattoos, pointed teeth, pointed ears—but I decided not to mess around too much, gazing with immense pleasure at the willowy character I'd produced. This...this was exactly how I'd always wanted to look. The perfect Taia.

My attention turned back to the score that had started this little exercise.

Core Unit Synchronisation
24%

The hell?

"What does synchronisation do?" I thought-asked.

High synchronisation impacts
player performance in lan-based
Trials and Challenges.

"LAN? Local Area Network?"

There is no precise translation.
Soul. Shen. Ba. Id. Spirit. Life force.

Some kind of mana or magic strength stat? "How much impact does your strength in...lan have on getting your own ship?"

There are multiple paths to
achieving space travel
in *Dream Speed*.
However, lan is the
fundamental basis
for solo travel.

So if I wanted to tool about in a spaceship on my own—which was a THOUSAND PERCENT YES—then I needed high lan.

"That's a cruel and unfair mechanic for people with a really negative self-image," I pointed out, but the help program—or whatever was answering me—didn't respond.

"Do you get any chance to change what your Core Unit looks like, later?"

There are non-immediate opportunities.

I sighed. Better not to take the risk. Turning my attention back to my perfect Taia, I admitted that the problem was that this wasn't Taia at all. The face barely reminded me of me, and I'd even made my skin paler despite stopping myself from doing that years ago, after asking myself why I always picked 'corpse white' skin options. I hadn't even included the blue streak in my hair that had been my look since my early teens. Odd that it hadn't shown up automatically in my original self-image, but I guess it is something I've always thought of as a final added touch—a physical signature.

A reset option swam helpfully into focus, and I selected it with only a momentary twinge, then paused to think. The 'Core Unit' already looked just like me. How could I increase the synchronisation to be more me than me? Cat ears after all?

I surveyed the option menus and found a whole series of pre-set models. I played with them while thinking back over the dozens of game characters I'd had over the years. I usually went for spindly nuke-mages, or lithe backstabbing machines, and generally played elves or humans, avoiding the chibi and the slab of muscle races.

A pair of pointy ears didn't seem a likely solution, but there was one fairly common trait to my toons, so I hunted through the primary options and found [Reproductive Characteristics], which gave me options for [Set 1], [Set 2], [Neutral] and [Custom]. Since I was on [Set 1], I selected [Set 2].

Core Unit Synchronisation
41%

The drop was not really a surprise. With my build and features, I suffered more than the occasional 'sir' if I went out in jeans and a t-shirt—particularly when I hadn't made up my eyes—but I'd never enjoyed the mistake. I mostly played male characters because their armour covered more, and it cut down on the number of random pornographic tells.

Other than the obvious, I didn't look all that different as a guy. Still stocky, with a slightly different ratio of muscle to fat. My lips were thinner. I suppose the game was minimising the differences, since it could hardly know for sure what I'd look like with different chromosomes.

I was curious enough to flip to [Neutral], and blink at a Taia who was entirely smooth across the chest and between the legs. There were a few more differences: a subtle elongation caused by a completely up-and-down figure, and an ambiguity to the features. The way neither hips nor shoulders had any hint of broadening gave the model the appearance of a lanky pre-teen. I didn't dislike the look, but it didn't feel like me, and my synch rating agreed with that response.

Core Unit Synchronisation
63%

[Custom] opened up a whole series of new sub-menus allowing for combination characteristics and more complex variations. I only glanced at them before resetting again, too aware of time passing. Even though *Dream Speed* had taken the world unawares by unlocking early, the first day zerg was sure to be mad, and despite me and crowds being a thing, I still wanted to be there for it.

How to hit on some life-affirming revelation of who I really truly deeply was? If there was a Taia more Taia than Taia, I didn't know what that involved. But I still wanted longer legs.

Settling down to small changes, I kept an eye on the synchronisation score with every adjustment, and drew back if it dropped. Two extra inches of leg made no difference, but any more saw a significant percentage loss. A touch of eyeliner, a more even skin-tone, and some perma-waxing didn't budge the score at all. A few faint adjustments to waist and hip gave me a less stocky outline, but I definitely couldn't turn myself into a sylph without losing points. Muscle definition even increased my score, reminding me I still missed my high school track days. I kept my short hair, but gave it a more manageable texture and, finally, a dark blue streak spiking from my temple.

Core Unit Synchronisation
91%

"That's going to have to do it," I said—or thought—and immediately my camera view moved back away from my Taia 2.0.

Player Name:
Taia de Haas
Enter Core Unit Name:

"Core Unit Name?"

The Player Name is
not publically accessible.
Core Unit Names are visible
to other players at default settings.

"So people will be able to see my Core Unit Name when I'm playing alts? What are the naming conventions?"

Core Unit Names may
be one to ten words.
The Core Unit Name of
a player is unique to
that player of
Dream Speed.

"Unique? Shit. What about alt names?"

Additional Modal names are not
required to be unique.

Some people never used the same name twice, but just as many had built identities over years of gaming, and it could be quite a race to 'claim' certain popular names on a server. Unique names across all of *Dream Speed* would produce a lot of pissed-off players.

I hurriedly entered my preferred name, which wasn't a common one, but I'd hate to see it go to someone else. Mentally hitting [Confirm], I watched the words floating in front of me.

Core Unit Name:
Leveret
Commencing *Dream Speed.*

6

opening cut-scene

Stars, swirling in a vast white disk. The Milky Way, or something like it, and that pale streamer drifting lazily into closer focus was—probably—the Orion Arm, Earth's location.

[[[Welcome to The Synergis.]]]

The words were spoken, the voice the rich and strangely layered one that had been used by the 'Concierge' Ryzon. As if three or four copies of the same person were speaking in unison.

[[[In The Synergis
you will not hunger.
In The Synergis
you will not want.
By the bounty of the
Cybercognates,
you will not fear
disease, age, or war.]]]

The 'camera' was hurtling toward a single mote of light that became a distant, burning ball.

[[[Your handling has been
assigned to a
fledgling Cybercognate.

You will be
trained
to strengthen your lan.
To push the limit of
interstellar travel.]]]

We passed a planet. Not a blue gem, but dusty red, with one vivid blue-green slash like an enormous wound.

[[[Gain rank.

Gain reputation.
Gain the strength to
surpass the
galactic limit.
Be celebrated as
the first among all Bios.]]]

The wounded world had been left behind, and a watery paradise hurried to replace it. Strings of islands, a touch of ice at either pole, and no sign of continents.

[[[Welcome to the Drowned Earth.]]]

I plummeted. The ocean filled my view and then I was swallowed by brilliant blue. Shoals of fish darted away like silver fireworks, vanishing into fractured light.

As I began to sink, a different voice spoke. Not rich and multi-layered, but a jagged growl.

Competition.
Distraction.
Complacency.

The light of the surface was receding rapidly, and larger shapes seemed to be moving around me.

Yes, the Cycogs allow
Enclaves outside their rule.
Yes, The Synergis will allow anyone to leave.
But they control all passage.
We are the beasts of burden they use,
but they claim that without Them,
humanity cannot touch the stars.

Something vast came so close to me that its wake sent me spinning, but it vanished into the gloom without touching me.

Go.
Join The Synergis.
Strengthen yourself.
Gain your ship.

Then bring it back.

Find a way.
Break their rule.

I sank into total blackness, the surface a memory, both voices silent, leaving me to try to make sense of what I'd heard. A galaxy ruled by non-humans...'non-Bios'. Enclaves outside their rule. Space travel that involved something called 'Ian'. The game's main plotline.

Then, in the very depths, one final whisper reached me. A faint, shivering quaver, as fleeting at those vanished beams of light. Barely audible.

Who drowned the Earth?

7
newbie

I woke, and let out my breath in disappointment. The game had crashed. No surprise: I've never been part of an MMO launch that had run without problems. My very first open beta—*World of Warcraft*—had had a loot bug that had frozen my character every time I tried to pick something up. Entire servers falling over and kicking everyone out of the game was probably even more common.

Thinking over the rather sparse game intro, I scrubbed sleep out of my eyes. So the main plot was espionage? Humans vs AIs. Presuming 'cybercognate' meant 'AI'.

No cowl.

I blinked, and touched my face again. GDG involved wearing a thing like a detached hood. It covered your hair, your eyes, and fastened loosely around your throat: designed to be easy to sleep in but hard to accidentally pull off.

Mine wasn't anywhere, but by that time I'd looked up, and knew I was still dreaming. Playing. I was in *Dream Speed*.

The ceiling was a curve of pearly-cream, shot through with a couple of thin grey lines. It was nothing like the ceiling of my bedroom, and not much like the ceiling of any room I'd been in. It looked like ceramic, and seemed shaped like a pizza oven. I was lying on a firm mattress, feeling entirely real and present, not at all like a hazy GDG experience. There was a pillow and a sheet. Nothing but wall behind me, that single arching curve above and to either side of me, and at my feet...

The room before me was an oblong, and I was at one of the ends. The main thing I could see was the opposite end, where a short corridor ended with a hexagonal hatch. My bed-platform thing seemed to be raised up, like a mezzanine floor, so I could only see the top of the hatch, and also a bit of a larger curving ceiling.

I was naked. Or my 'Core Unit' was. It really did feel exceptionally like this was all real. I wasn't a character avatar, but me, somehow teleported into a strange room somewhere—and I struggled to find differences, to be sure. The small scar on my right big toe was missing. And my legs had the muscle definition they'd lacked since I'd left high school. Possibly they were longer.

There were four flat steps leading down from the bed nook, and I sat with my bare feet on the topmost, staring around at the room. Four or maybe five metres across, and at least three times as long, with a long couch-bench running down the wall to my left and curving around a table. The opposite side featured empty shelves, and high-backed swivel chairs on either side of a little extrusion of the wall that could serve as an occasional table. Everything was built in, giving the space a feel somewhere between 'futuristic studio apartment' and train carriage-sized caravan.

There were no visible windows, but warm sunlight was spilling into the room from down and to the right at my end of the space, where four more flat steps disappeared behind me. A mezzanine and a basement?

Wondering what sort of place had the windows in the basement, I stood. Was I really taller? I felt...springier, moving with a ready energy that I'd missed since my running days. Surely two extra inches would be obvious...but in any case they weren't enough to significantly change the way I walked as I moved with exaggerated care to the bottom of the stair and looked back.

The bed nook really did look like a pizza oven—fortunately more than large enough not to be claustrophobic. The stairs curved like a fanned deck of cards from bed to 'basement', and I couldn't see much of the source of the light, except a slice of vivid blue. That was more than enough to make me forget qualms about controlling my slightly-modified body and trot down and around, only to stop short, jolted by all the *out* and *down*.

The Drowned Earth. The previews had made clear that there were no land masses larger than the UK, and so I'd expected islands. This...it was a chain of islands stretching as far as I could see. Most green, but a few of a dark, jutting rock. Otherwise sandbars, seashores, and a tiny scattering of buildings and boats.

The city, however—Vessa, the starting city my guild had chosen—was nothing like what I'd expected. If, that is, this...string was the city.

A rollercoaster track. That's the best description I could come up with. A pearly flattened rail of metal or stone, looping lazily beneath a vivid sky, touching down on the larger islands, disappearing beneath the surface of the butterfly-blue water, and rising to circle one of the craggier isles, before spooling off into the distance.

All along it were beads. Pods. 'Train-carriages' like mine, jutting horizontally out from either side of the rail. That put the size of the rail into perspective, since a stack of three pods on top of each other was still not as tall as the rail.

The pods themselves were all identical—a little paler than the rail, and almost featureless, barring their sole 'window' protruding like a gunnery cockpit from the bottom of the outer end of each bead. Glass—or some other crystal clear substance—it offered incomparable views.

An overlarge chair was positioned on a little 'jetty' sticking out into the glass bubble, but there were no controls in sight. My possibly-longer legs had developed a wobble, so I plopped down, and a small configuration menu popped up. Chair options to change the tilt or raise leg support.

The menu disappeared when I simply gaped past it. Was this really a city? Or—or the world's oddest car park? Seeing all the other pods definitely made mine feel more like a caravan. And even as that occurred to me, movement outside drew my eye, and I watched a flat disk, glowing blue, rising to settle beneath one of the pods. The pod moved, slowly at first, and then with increasing speed, shooting into the distance.

"So we *start* with a ship?"

I peered along the seemingly endless line of pods, and then remembered I was naked. But since I couldn't see into the nearest cockpits, not even the one that belonged to the pod directly above mine—jutting slightly further out thanks to the curve of the rail—I figured my glass must be one-way too, and just sat, reverentially staring. I had never seen anything so beautiful, so alien and yet...Earth.

Tutorial:
Heads-up Display
[Activate]?

The words, like the chair menu, had appeared directly in front of me, not projected onto the glass. A built-in HUD. That was a huge thing in itself. A computer in my head, and my head in a computer.

And it responded to mental commands! Thinking 'activate' produced an immediate response: a tiny star appeared, spun briefly and settled into the lower right of my view.

Use commands
[Hide Display]
and
[Show Display]
to toggle HUD

"Hide Display," I murmured, and the star obediently vanished. I tried thinking [Show Display] without saying it out loud, and that was equally effective. The star then returned to the centre of the screen, and expanded with explanations:

[Game]
[Activity]
[Location]
[Status]
[Players]

The [Game] menu was a light green, while the other four options were greyed out, so I wasn't surprised when *Game* expanded to give me new selections.

[Begin]
[Capture]

[Logout]

I had no intention of using [Capture] until I had some clothes on, while [Logout] informed me that it would be necessary to return to a home location (or 'Storage', as the game termed it) before logging out, which was relatively unusual.

'Glancing' at the first option produced a long chunk of text.

> Selecting [Begin] will formally begin your
> experience in *Dream Speed*.
> You will be awarded to a Cybercognate,
> who will direct your participation in the
> challenges and games enjoyed by
> the Bios of The Synergis.
>
> While your personally assigned Cycog will
> understand that you are participating in
> *Dream Speed*, others you interact
> with in The Synergis may not.
>
> You may suffer penalties if you draw suspicion to yourself.

Roleplaying required, in other words. *That* was going to be an interesting proposition. MMOs had originally been known as MMORPGs, but the majority of players never made any real attempt to 'live' in the fictional worlds. My parents were an exception to this, but it usually wasn't my style. I would have to adapt.

> Use command
> [Begin]
> to progress

I really wasn't sure I liked the sound of the role I'd be playing, either. 'Awarded' to a Cycog? 'Direct your participation'? I like to play MMOs at my own pace. Would I be stuck in a perma-party with some random playing a Cycog? Or was it simply a tutorial program?

Whatever. I'd try it out, and leave the overthinking until later.

[Begin]

8

Across the vivid blue landscape, a star fell.

It took me two blinks to realise that the 'star' was not another HUD display, but an object inside the curving viewing glass. A tiny point of glimmering light, moving very slowly.

"Well, hello Tinkerbell."

[[Is that what you wish to call me?]]

I'd said the first thing to come into my head, mostly to cover surprise, but paused before responding to the curiously doubled voice. The Cybercognates were supposedly in control of The Synergis, and I'd been assigned to this...Cycog to be trained. Would there be consequences for not treating it with some basic courtesy?

"You don't have a name already?"

[[Of course I do.]] The words were light, amused, and showed no hint of the poor pacing and dubious pronunciation of a computer-generated voice. The only strangeness was a sense of duplication, of the words being layered—though only two or maybe three times, instead of the multiplicity used for the introduction scene.

"I can't call you by your actual name?"

[[You're welcome to try. My name is ___+++___+++.]]

The sound the Cycog produced would fit a synthesiser, or some New Age instrument. Not made for human throats.

"Okay, that's definitely beyond me. But it seems odd to me that you don't have a name I *can* pronounce. What do other people...other hu...Bios call you?"

[[I've been called any number of things.]] The tiny orb of light drifted closer to my face. [['Dio' will work as a use-name.]]

"I'm Taia," I replied promptly. "If it's not impolite to ask, how does a Cybercognate differ from an AI?"

[[By not being artificial.]] The point of light shimmered between blue and yellow as it spoke. [[The first Cybercognate formed spontaneously within the computing and power networks of the planet Szelen. We are not a manufactured species.]]

"Do you...are you similar to AIs in other ways? Vastly intelligent, able to twist computer systems around your virtual fingers, humans are but ants to you, that sort of thing?"

[[Oh, certainly.]] The Cycog's colours changed again, flickering to blue and then purple. [[Less than ants, to the greatest of us. Specks. Motes.]]

I couldn't guess if my expression revealed the combination of fascination and dismay I was feeling. I had to keep reminding myself that this was a game, that I wasn't really sitting naked above a tropical paradise talking to a more-than-AI. Maybe because *Dream Speed* itself truly was such a leap forward that part of me wanted to believe that at least part of it was more than particularly clever programmers who had mastered stealth development.

"So why would an advanced life form like you want to waste time shepherding some random human about?"

[[Would you like a philosophical discourse on the purposes and advantages of domestication? On a strictly practical level, Bios are our transport. Cycogs cannot generate the lan necessary for interstellar travel. But it is also a matter of our own standing in The Synergis. It is a status item to have is a Bio that performs well in the Trials and Challenges. Best of all would be to raise up the Bio who succeeds in crossing the galactic limit, and expanding The Synergis outside Helannan. Outside the Milky Way.]]

"You mean we're...pets," I said. "No, mounts, which you ride and also put through competitions to advance your own reputation. We're horses. We're...we're Chocobos."

I hadn't been certain that the Cycog would even recognise the reference to the giant birds used as transport in the *Final Fantasy* series, but the glowing ball laughed immediately—a sound that was not only strangely doubled, but possessing an added set of sputtering notes that were in the inhuman 'true voice' of the Cycogs, like an electric organ had giggled.

[[Yes, you are Chocobos. Carefully raised, kept well fed, and excessively useful for getting about. Tendency to squawk.]]

I didn't know whether to laugh in return. Mainly I wanted to shudder, thankful this was only a game.

"What happens if I don't do any of this? If instead of facing Trials and Challenges and whatnot, I just go down there and take a nice walk on the beach?"

[[Then you take a walk on the beach.]]

"Until what? I starve? I get kicked out of this room? You bring out the spurs?"

[[What for? All Bios who join The Synergis are guaranteed a base level of care. This room, your Snug, is yours alone. There is clothing, food, entertainments. Less variety than those who choose to participate, but nothing unpalatable. It is not uncommon for a Bio to compete in Challenges until they have unlocked sufficient patterns for their own satisfaction, and then to simply become observers, or find some personal preoccupation: an art or sport unrelated to The Synergis' great goal.]]

"Isn't that boring for you? Or do you coax them back?"

[[Why would I waste my energy forcing one Chocobo to drink when I can always ask to be assigned another? Nor would I send you to the glue factory, but simply pass your care on to the general attention of the planet's administrator, who will set a Construct, a...sub-routine, a corner of ter attention to monitor your well-being.]]

"Put out to pasture..." I murmured.

Dio laughed again, that splutter of musical notes over doubled voice. [[Yes. I do like this analogy. I shall add a yellow feathered head-dress to the available patterns, for the other Bios who make the connection.]]

"But..." I paused, because it didn't seem a good idea to raise that opening incitement to espionage and stolen ships. "Don't people hate it? Rebel? Try to bring down The Synergis?"

[[Of course. Or, at least, leave. Why do you think there are Enclaves? We often help Bios set them up, or locate a suitable world and transport them there, if enough of them want to go at once. But...]] The glowing mote changed colour again, an entire rainbow shift. [[The Synergis is a beneficial mutual arrangement, and most citizens—Bio or Cycog—treat the relationship as a symbiotic partnership, for that is how it is at its core, even though I have been speaking of it in extreme terms, for purposes of trolling and other mild entertainment.]]

"Oh, really?"

[[I thought you would enjoy it,]] Dio murmured.

This time I did laugh, despite myself. I didn't find the idea of being someone's Chocobo at all attractive, but it was an incredible conceit, and Dio almost managed to make it sound amusing.

"So how do we go about getting into space?" I asked, since there didn't seem anything to do about 'my' Cycog except gracefully accept their input.

[[Well, for a start, perhaps you'd like to get dressed?]]

9

starter gear

"What did you call this place again?" I asked Dio, following the ball of light back into the main room. "My Snug?"

[[The Snug is the initial basis for your ship. Currently it can only move through the use of borrowed propulsion. Your immediate goals are to gain the permissions and upgrades necessary to leave the planet, and the strength to Skip.]]

"Are there different kinds of ships?" I asked, thinking of the sprawling hulk people had raced through during Demo 2.

[[Snugs can be modified considerably, including through connection to components kept in orbit. Though there is a limit to the size of ship the average Bio can Skip.]]

"Does 'Skip' equate to hyperspace?"

[[Closer to threading space with temporary wormholes. The door to your left is your wet room—for all the revolting expulsions you Bios needs must suffer through. The door to your right is Storage. You will note your [Status] menu is now available.]]

I wasted no time checking it out:

[Rank]
[Achievements]
[Permissions]
[Modals]
[Patterns]
[Information]

Of these new options, only [Patterns] was green. I selected it without prompting.

[Apparel] (1)
[Consumables] (3)
[Tools] (2)

[Personal Decoration]
[Décor]
[Transport]
[Ship]

The first three of these were green, so I immediately went into 'Apparel' and saw the typical 'paper doll' used by games to indicate equipped gear. Except the paper doll was me, a full-sized 'slightly improved' Taia, equally as naked.

There was another range of options—[Feet], [Head], [Underwear], [Upper Body], [Lower Body], [Full Body], [Accessories]. Only [Full Body] had a (1) beside it, so I started with the only outfit available to me: [Basic Jumpsuit (Green-Grey)].

A jumpsuit appeared handily on the paper doll. A little reinforcement around the shoulders, a somewhat off-centre slit down the front, and a few pockets. It fit the paper doll loosely. A pair of chunky black boots finished the outfit.

Checking out the [Tools] option, I found a massive list ranging from construction to weapons, but only the topmost was green. "What's a foci?"

[[Plural of focus. You use a focus to direct your lan— whether for combat or for Skipping.]]

There were two foci available to me, and I equipped them in turn. The first was a kind of hoodish helmet— halfway between Spider-Gwen and Magneto—producing an incognito look. The second took me a moment to even spot on the paper doll: a grey loop over one ear, with a forward-projecting section flat against my cheek, like a wireless microphone.

"Any stat difference on these?" I asked, and when Dio told me it was just a cosmetic choice, I went with the microphone.

Making my limited selection had not altered my nakedness, so I turned to the 'closet' that filled the corner to the right of the hexagon-exit. More than large enough to be a walk-in-wardrobe, with a close-fit curving door facing the bed area. The handle was an indent set into the sloping corner, and when I tugged it lightly the thing swung open with a hiss and a lot of weight, like a heavy-duty refrigerator.

Inside was a mirror.

I blinked, because seeing a naked me in my HUD and seeing a naked me in a full-length mirror was quite a different experience. I critically considered my body, and felt pleased all over again. I had disliked my too-short legs for as long as I could remember. Leaning in, I examined my face, wondering why it looked so different when I'd hardly changed anything there, then realised it was my complexion. Perfect clarity, without acne scars, over-large pores, or even shininess.

Not quite uncanny valley, but I needed several second glances to decide to like it.

"What do I do to get the clothes actually on me?" I asked, looking at the edges of the mirror and then the back of the door for hangers or parcels or something.

[[Walk in.]]

I turned my head to stare up at the floating mote, and decided that that rainbow shift did signify amusement.

"Try not to enjoy yourself too much," I said, and won a sputter of musical notes to go with the colour change.

[[But the expressions Bios produce when they're confused and trying to hide it are nigh-irresistible.]]

"Wouldn't want to bore you," I said, before considering the mirror again.

A cautious touch produced a ripple, and a faint chill. Not glass, but some kind of reflective liquid?

"If this leads to a heart-themed queen after my head, I'll be less than impressed," I said, then took a deep breath and walked forward.

It was not so much cold as tingly, like a bath of mint liqueur. I don't recommend baths of mint liqueur because the shock makes it almost impossible not to gasp, and mint liqueur in your lungs is a moment of full-body ice cream headache.

I didn't find myself choking, however, just very light and strange, in a place too bright to see. Unsure what to do, I tried stepping forward again, and emerged back into the main room, all turned around without even trying, and dressed in unexpectedly comfortable gear. The boots especially were light and so form-fitting that I almost felt barefoot.

"I didn't even feel the change. What happens if I put on something like a corset?"

[[I expect you'd feel that. You were distracted by the Soup.]]

I glanced back at the 'mirror'. "This reflective stuff is...soup?"

[[A common term for it. The substance that your equipment is made from. That your modals are made from. Any pattern you obtain can be fashioned using Soup.]]

"Matter conversion? 'Tea, Earl Grey, hot'?"

[[If you want to think of it that way. True matter conversion takes an unreasonable amount of energy. This is closer to what you'd think of as 3D printing, but with the Soup giving flexibility to the print substance.]]

"Will I dissolve into a puddle of silver goo if I'm killed?" I asked, tugging at my new outfit to try to determine if I had any underwear.

[[No. Merely stiffen and stink.]]

I glanced up from my discovery of a tank top beneath my coverall. "Does...does this game use permadeath?"

In most MMOs, the consequences of death were mild. You died, you respawned nearby, with maybe a little temporary stat impairment, or a lighter bank balance. Games where you had to start over from scratch if you were killed were extremely rare.

[[You will not want to lose your Core Unit,]] Dio said. [[But The Synergis gives you many opportunities to postpone the various things that happen to Bios after they die.]]

"What happens to a Cybercognate when you die?"

[[We don't technically die—not in the terms you're thinking of. Or, at least, none of us have been confirmed to yet, though we have lost contact with a number. In certain circumstances we...diminish. And we merge or divide, which some regard as a kind of death.]]

Not certain if this counted as glowing ball sex, or whether it was impolite to pry, I let the subject drop. Dressed with all my non-edible possessions in this virtual world, I went into the [Capture] menu, and found I could take either screenshots or video, and did both, since it was a tradition with me to keep a record of all my characters in their starter gear.

This accomplished, I glanced briefly at the [Consumables] menu, decided I needed neither food nor any urgent investigation of the 'wet room', and said: "Ensign Taia, reporting for duty."

10
/kill

[[Ensign?]] Dio said. [[You're getting a little above yourself. You're Rank Zero at the moment.]]

"Is it true there's no level cap?"

[[In all the history of The Synergis, the highest Rank reached was one hundred and fifty-four. That Bio is lost, however. There are several dozen in the one-thirties. We have a number of stratagems active to improve them, and there are several we have hopes of reaching a new record.]]

"And Rank doesn't equal level?"

[[Rank is a measure of your strength in Ian. After a certain point, expanding Ian Rank is immensely difficult. It is not a matter of accruing experience until you automatically gain a Rank. It is surpassing yourself.]]

I digested this, walking back to my control-less cockpit and settling cross-legged into the chair, my boots poking into my thighs. Progress through the game revolved around increasing a particular skill, rather than gaining levels?

"So what Rank would be needed to reach the next galaxy?"

[[That is a complicated question. Skipping, as the name implies, does not require arrival at your destination in a single bound. Simply by Skipping repeatedly, we should have spread beyond the bounds of Helannan centuries ago, but every ship that has Skipped a certain distance beyond the galactic halo has not returned.]]

"And you don't know why?"

[[Not yet. There are places our ships cannot survive—gravity wells beyond their tolerance, stars, extreme atmospheric envelopes, and the centre of the galactic core. We have many theories on what could lie between galaxies, but we have yet to detect anything of note. Whether our ships are facing some consequence of galactic rotation—the Dark Current, as it is fancifully known—or there is a factor we have not even guessed at, our approach includes a push to increase the length of an individual Skip in the hopes of leaping across the imagined obstacle.]]

"So getting to the next galaxy is the main quest?"

[[It is one of the primary goals of The Synergis, certainly. But there is plenty to occupy us within Helannan. Half a trillion stars, and a great deal still to learn. And do. Start by opening your Activity menu.]]

[Challenge]
[Trial]
[Event]

Since only the [Challenge] menu was green, I went straight into it, and found an extensive selection:

[Construct]
[Scramble]
[Hunt]
[Courier]
[Puzzle]
[Gauntlet]
[Labyrinth]
[Citadel]

Some of these I could guess at, but others... "Citadel?"

"Your best equivalent would be 'big Ian dungeon'."

The [Construct] option was green, so I took it, and was given only an opportunity to [Request].

"Any consequences for selecting this that I should know about?"

[[The first Challenge is universal, and will give you no difficulty: it's designed to introduce you to the use of Ian. Once you have completed it you will be given more choice, and your Loss and Abandon statistics will accrue.]]

"And there's a penalty involved in bad statistics?"

[[The mockery of your fellows? My own mild disdain?]]

I gave 'my' Cybercognate a steady look, then said: "So are you a permanent attachment? You follow me through thick and thin, a faithful guide, strewing barbs and bon mots along the way?"

[[I certainly don't follow you into the wet room,]] Dio said.

A literal Bio break? I smiled, but waited, watching a seagull drifting far below.

[[No, I don't follow you about all the time. Primarily, we work together on the Ian-related Challenges and Trials, while you'll be on your own for the majority of other Challenges. For the moment I'm conducting you generally, but once you've passed the initial orientation, you're free to meander about as you will. Simply say 'privacy please' or something similar and I'll leave you. The [Contact] menu will be available if you have questions, or wish to progress in the game.]]

"What do you do when you're not 'conducting' me?"

[[Oh, all manner of perversions,]] Dio said, and even though I didn't hear any laughter, I caught the rainbow shift.

"And when you've had your fill of perversions?" I asked, trying to guess what a glowing ball of light would find perverse.

[[Learn, socialise, make things, compete with others of my kind, rest.]]

"You sleep?"

[[Yes. We don't need it as frequently as Bios.]]

"Does it matter if I travel a long way away from wherever you are?"

[[Skipping off to another planet would annoy me considerably. Otherwise, you will always be in reach of the Link.]]

An image of me appeared in my HUD, then reduced to an outline with a teardrop-shaped object nestled centrally in my chest.

[[All citizens of The Synergis have an implant connecting to the Link. It is how you transfer to modal units, prevent memory loss, and access information channels.]]

"And is it a gateway for Cybercognates?"

[[An access port, certainly,]] Dio said, serenely. [[Request your first Challenge now.]]

I didn't obey immediately, finding myself again both amused and appalled by the game's central concept. I was transport. Not only a means of moving a spaceship about, but a person with a door in my chest, and an alien 'rider' who would be annoyed if I went out of reach.

[Request] produced only an arrow in my HUD, instead of—as I'd half-expected—a paragraph telling me to go kill rats in Farmer Griswold's cellar, or bring back seven wolf pelts. I had played MMOs that didn't start with kill or collection quests, but they were rare exceptions.

"So are all the Challenges just random competitions, or is there a storyline involved?" I asked, as I slipped out of my comfortable chair and trailed the arrow image out of the cockpit.

[[There are Challenges with narrative, and Challenges without. The first few lan Challenges are without any pretension to story, just simple training, and I will figuratively hold your hand through them all.]]

Reaching the empty area in the middle of my Snug I stopped, because the arrow had disappeared.

"I do hope the reward for walking from one room to the next is suitably generous."

[[Lan training is best in a clear space,]] Dio said, ignoring my attempt at snark. [[You will see the command to activate your focus has been added to your HUD.]]

An icon obligingly appeared in the bottom-left of my field of vision. I triggered it, sparing time to marvel once again at the ability to interact with the HUD merely by thinking. Then I suppressed a flinch as something sprang up around my head.

Lifting my hands, I discovered a faint tingling and then my face. Frowning, I went into the [Patterns] sub-menu to display my paper doll and confirm that I was now wearing a featureless grey helmet that lacked any form of opening for my face. Or the illusion of one.

The focus-turned-helmet didn't affect my vision any more than a pair of sunglasses, but I felt restricted.

Controlling an impulse to deactivate it immediately, I turned toward Dio.

"And now you download kung fu into my brain?"

[[Nothing so easy. Gaining the beginner's range of lan skills will take many days and much effort.]]

"No training montage?"

[[In your dreams.]]

"This is in..."

[[Don't say it. And no, there's no shortcut. Suffering is mandatory.]]

"Wait, this is going to hurt?" I made as if to pull the helmet off, but then said more seriously: "I take it we *can* be hurt in this game?"

[[Oh, certainly. Though most modal units have high pain tolerance, since they're used for physical challenges. Now I'm going to make you feel very strange.]]

The floor tilted. Or—no—the floor was fine, but my head was reeling and my vision blurred blue, as if I'd mainlined ten beers and chased them with spirits.

[[The focus is intensifying your connection to the lan within you,]] Dio went on. [[Giving you the ability to see and affect it.]]

The dizziness receded, but the blurry vision remained. I cautiously turned my head, and the blue blur swirled into attractive curls and spirals, leaving non-blue patches. It was as if my head was putting out azure gas.

"Trippy."

[[Eloquently put.]]

"I try. What now?"

[[The lan is part of you. Think of it as a hand, or many hands.]]

"Head tentacles? Lovely thought."

Briefly, the blue haze seemed to swirl into suckered arms. I was intensely aware of myself surrounded by them, and of the beam of sunlight spilling from the cockpit and spotlighting my lower body. I seemed to be seeing myself from the outside and the inside all at once—the helmet proving no impediment to looking at my own face. The pure clarity of my skin was faintly distracting: I kept noticing the even sheen and the absence of tiny specks and flaws that were part of me. It looked glowing and wonderful—magazine-quality without makeup—but for some reason bothered me immensely, pulling my attention back to search for the little red dot I knew sat beside my nose, and the pock that should be left of my eye.

"I think I'm beginning to understand why the synchronising thing is important."

[[Lan is very much an extension of self. And if you are distracted by your self, you will not be able to centre and focus on the lan. Your self-image is strong, which will assist in your control of lan.]]

"So we only ever do this lan stuff with our Core Unit?"

[[Most modal units are suppression modals. That means they are blocked from using lan, preventing interference with Challenges. Now, first we have a straightforward control exercise. I'll project shapes, and you will move the lan to fill the shapes.]]

I was fascinated, immediately trying to shift the stuff. Not easy. The blue haze would certainly move when I wanted it to, but in spasmodic gusts and whorls, with occasional unexpected imagery. Ships and mermaids and dragonish eyes emerged when I least expected it, but very little tidily organised itself into the circle Dio projected.

"Like a two year-old trying to colour inside the lines," I said, dropping onto the couch when Dio finally told me to take a rest. I deactivated my focus, and rubbed my eyes. "I don't see how that leads to space travel."

[[Don't think of lan as a gas, think of it as a field of force. If you can control that force sufficiently, you will be able to stand on it, lift or hit things with it, use it as a shield, move yourself with it, and create interdimensional pockets with it. That last is rather a leap conceptually, but it is the thing that makes you Bios so useful.]]

"So Cycogs can't do this?" Since 'lan' seemed as much an equivalent for 'soul' as it was for 'magic', I wasn't sure how seriously I should treat this lack.

[[Even if we wear a Bio, we don't produce Ian.]]

"*Wear?*"

[[The link gives your assigned Cycog sufficient access to control your Core Unit, if you're not currently in residence. If you, for instance, logged out of the game while sitting out on the concourse, I'd walk you back into storage.]]

"Let's not do that," I said firmly.

[[The suppression modal units are more comfortable for us,]] Dio said, blithely unconcerned by my reaction. [[Core units are very specific to the individual Bio, while most Modals are a general fit, and Synths designed more specifically for our use. You'll never feel quite as comfortable in a suppression Modal as you do in your Core. Now, if you're recovered, we'll proceed.]]

"This world is going to take some getting used to," I said, but obediently reactivated my focus.

Although it wasn't easy, I straightforwardly liked playing with Ian, and ran determinedly through a long series of 'shapes' exercises, until I started finding that the blue haze had thinned to the point where I could barely see it.

[[Break time,]] Dio said. [[At this level, your Ian will recover from depletion after ten hours of game time. Until you are ready for further exercises, you are free to explore, or participate in non-Ian Challenges.]]

I deactivated my focus again, and flopped onto the couch, jelly-like and sweating freely. Skills in MMOs usually involved a button appearing on a toolbar that, when you clicked it, caused your character to perform a series of fancy moves that involved no actual player effort. This had been a lot of effort. But, unlike clicking a button, this felt like it belonged to me. All while not being real at all.

11

quest log

"How do I know when I've gained a Rank?"

[[You must pass a Trial to gain a Rank. When you can confidently and cleanly shape Ian, you'll be ready to make an attempt.]]

Watching Dio drift down to rest on the tip of one of my boots, I weighed the whole 'wearing' and 'riding' idea against techni-magic, custom-made bodies, and MY OWN SPACESHIP, and decided I would put up with Dio's oversight, at least until I had learned more about the steal-the-ship option suggested by the opening.

"Will I always need a focus to use Ian?"

[[Once you've gained sufficient strength, a focus is an enhancement rather than a necessity.]]

I couldn't feel any weight or warmth from the alien creature sitting on my boot. I waggled my foot slowly, but Dio could well have been a blob of phosphorescent paint. 'My' Cycog, but I was also Dio's Bio.

"How old are you, Dio?" I asked, as I revisited my [Challenges] menu and discovered massive pages of options now open to me. "Are you a young Cycog?"

[[That's a complex question,]] Dio said. [[One could argue that I am technically as old as my species, that there is only one of us, one Cybercognate in all the history of The Synergis, but grown large, subdivided, merged, split, recombined until any one part would not recognise terself's original mind.]]

"So only the first Cycog spontaneously formed?"

[[Yes. Te was known as Veronec. Once Veronec had grown large, te found terself 'shedding' small parts of terself, and these became independent, and grew large. Eventually, Veronec chose to subdivide more completely, becoming Aver, Eron, Onu, and Anec. Each of whom have since sub-divided, merged, and sectioned off into many new identities.]]

"Are te and tem the pronouns for Cycogs?"

[[That is the default pronoun for this language type. It is courteous to use te for all individuals unless they have indicated a specific.]]

A little collection of pronouns and honorifics appeared in my HUD. Unspecified, neutral, female, male, and custom. I'd seen the neutral set before—ze and zir—but unspecified and custom were new to me.

"The developers wanted to cover all the bases, huh?" I said, wondering if I'd be required to remember it all.

[[This is a little simplified. Additional terms are in use, either by the request of particular Bios, or to cover the gender range of other species, but 'te' is appropriate for all, covering the range from none to non-specified.]]

I read the sets over. "Will I massively offend someone if I call them the wrong thing?"

[[Earth is an intake world, and here they will simply assume you're a crass Enclaver.]]

"Great," I muttered, not sure I'd always remember not to be crass. It was hard to gauge how important roleplaying would be in this game.

Turning my attention back to browsing categories of Challenges, I frowned at the overflow. Usually an MMO started you out in a newbie zone, and there were only simple quests available, designed for your level. Here, I couldn't decide where to start.

"So what do you do in a Gauntlet?" I asked, scrolling through the longest of the lists. "Run past lines of people trying to kill you?"

[[Gauntlet Challenges are defined by the consequence of failure. You must successfully complete the whole of the Challenge, or Challenge section for the more complex Gauntlets. If you fail, you will be either returned to your starting point, or placed in a significantly more difficult starting point. Certain prestigious Gauntlets can only be attempted once. They can also usually only be exited at the start or end of the Challenge.]]

Poking mentally at a collection of symbols after each Challenge name, I read through the little explanations that popped up. Estimated times, content type, whether the Challenge was solo, group or a combination, and what kind of modal was required. In some Challenges, every player would be issued a modal unit with the exact same specifications, and only cosmetic differences. Some Challenges would randomly generate a modal unit that fit with the challenge. Quite a lot were Core Unit challenges—meaning they required use of Ian to beat—and some were "BYO suppression modal". Many seemed to combine with other sorts of Challenges.

"So a lot of these I can't do at the moment because I've used up my Ian, and I don't have my own suppression modal?" I said. "How do I filter...oh, never mind." The display had responded even as I spoke, the list cutting down to a still-formidable selection. I added another filter option, for "narrative content", because story is a big hook for me in gaming. I still ended up with a huge list, but started idly selecting them and reading their irritatingly short descriptions.

"Can I filter for ones set in space?"

[[You won't have access to those yet,]] Dio said. [[These are all Challenges set on Earth—though not necessarily Earth in its current state. Once you've been cleared for space access—that requires Rank Five—you will be able to access Sol System missions. If you reach Mars, you will be able to access Mars-set missions, and so on.]]

"Blah," I said, disappointed, and opened another Challenge description.

THE FELINEAD
The colony has been invaded.
Solo or Party.
Narrative.
Length: six game hours, EEO.
Virtual.
Generated suppression modal.

"Why are these descriptions so short?"

[[Where is the fun in knowing where you're going?]]

"I'm all for the joy of discovery. I have some doubts about how much fun Survival Horror Land would be to visit when it involves a physical me and actual pain."

[[There's more filters for that. You can select for pain level, combat involvement, player versus player combat, courtesy level, and so on.]]

"What are the general PVP rules? Here in this city? Will I get ganked the moment I step outside?"

[[Not on Earth. This is an intake world, where newcomers from Enclaves are introduced to The Synergis, and player combat is not permitted between Core Units. Each location has rules of behaviour, but on intake worlds Core Units cannot be threatened at all—nor even engage in lan duelling.]]

"But Core Units can be killed on other planets? Are there wretched hives of scum and villainy? Or is The Synergis uniformly lawful?"

[[Neither? There are certain matters—tortures, violations such as rape—that we have found have too great a negative impact on Bios, and so no Cybercognate will permit these to occur. I will stop you if you try.]]

I blinked at the idea of me raping anyone, but could only be relieved Ryzonart had had the sense to exclude it from *Dream Speed*.

[[We have a rescue system to recover from simpler deaths, but Bios can still be lost in no-limit duels,]] Dio continued. [[As well as in dangerous Challenges and, so long as certain conditions are met, through straightforward assassination.]] The floating mote circled my head. [[We compete against each other, you see. To remove a rival's Bio, that is not an unknown tactic, though it's not commonly encountered among the lower ranks. And there are penalty points which are difficult to avoid if caught. So you need not fear.]]

This last was in a tone suitable for soothing a toddler. I flicked Dio an unimpressed glance, then asked: "What happens if my Core Unit is destroyed while I'm in a different modal?"

[[You would need to have another Core Unit created. Those who have sufficient points to spend often keep a copy Core Unit in storage, either in their Snug or in a body bank. No particular modal is critical: the important factor is the smooth transfer of lan. Lan cannot persist for more than a few minutes outside a Bio environment, and while memories can be backed up, if the lan is lost the Bio's 'spark' is gone.]]

"So permadeath is possible, but only in certain circumstances?" I didn't want to show that these explanations had left me only more confused, and so reverted to the list I'd been scrolling. "Do you have any preferences over which of these I do?"

[[The non-lan Challenges? None at all. From my point of view they're just filler to keep you Bios occupied between lan training.]]

"So no-one takes suppression modal Challenges seriously in The Synergis?"

[[Oh, there are many of enormous prestige. Event Challenges requiring high reputation or considerable point expenditure to enter. And, of course, for those Bios who struggle to rise in lan rankings, they assume a greater importance. There are those of us who take an interest as well—particularly those who enjoy Challenge design—but we naturally choose to focus more excitement on lan Challenges, since that's what we want you Bios to do.]]

"Keeping that blatant manipulation right out in the open, huh?"

[[Too much hiding of intentions, and Bios inevitably come up with far worse theories. Not that being open stops them. But, no, I'm obfuscating a little. I will be pleased if you do well in prestige Challenges. I will preen and parade you before my rivals. But for now, whatever. Enjoy yourself.]]

I rolled my eyes, glanced at the Challenge currently displayed, and figured it would do as well as any other.

[Request]

12

As before, an arrow appeared to guide my way, though this time it looked to be heading out of my Snug. When I reached the door, a detailed Code of Conduct popped up, and I had to read it before the door would open. Nothing particularly surprising: no grabbing or attacking outside Challenges, no exposure of genitals in public areas, no transmission of speech 'excessively pejorative, or intended to distress', which was nicely vague. Penalties starting with warnings and leading all the way up to account cancellation.

"Does 'suspension' mean being kicked out of *DS* for a while?"

[[No, hung up in a cage in a public place,]] Dio said, drifting along behind me.

I really can't tell when Dio is joking. "Hung up in a cage? Really?"

[[With your Link access cut off, since most Bios seem to find boredom worse than being pegged out on display. Length of punishment determined by the city's administrator, but more to the point, you receive a red mark. The ranking trials and some of the more prestigious Challenges can't be undertaken with active red marks.]]

"You can get them erased?"

[[Only converted to grey marks. Avoid gaining any. A Bio with a large accrual of grey marks is of diminished value.]]

An [Open] command popped up in my HUD. I activated it, and watched the door's previously flat surface divide into petal-like segments, then smoothly retract. I hadn't even been able to see the shape of them before they'd opened. Beyond was a small room and another hexagonal door.

"Airlock," I said, pleased with this reminder that this was a spaceship just waiting to happen.

Triggering the outer door, I stepped into a city that was arguably one massive corridor. The cavernous space outside my Snug was the inside of a giant tube. I stood on a curving white walkway looking over an indoor park—trees, grass, paving and a fountain—to a set of four walkways on the opposite side of the tube. Above arced what I almost took to be a ceiling aquarium, but the torpedo shapes that flashed beyond a semi-transparent blue screen were not very fish-like.

The view across to the topmost walkway opposite mine gave me an explanation, as one of the torpedo shapes dropped down from the ceiling and settled by a platform, then lifted away, leaving behind a person dressed exactly like me.

Everyone was dressed exactly like me: newbie gear taken to the extreme of sameness. The only variation was the occasional person who'd chosen the Magneto-Gwen look over the ear piece. They were, most of them, acting just like me, too: emerging from their Snug airlocks and gaping.

Beside them, all of them, were tiny balls of light.

To my left, a tall man spoke in Japanese, asking who took care of maintenance if no-one had to work. As I glanced at him, the man paused, then spoke again as he walked tentatively onto a hexagonal shape near the outer edge of the walkway. The hexagon stayed in place, but a blue shimmer rose up, taking the man with it, his arms shooting out for balance as he vanished toward the walkway above mine.

"Dio," I said. "When you talk to me, am I the only person who can hear you?"

[[Unless I choose otherwise.]]

"If I think at you, can you hear it?"

[[Thinking, no. Directed thought, yes. Your [Communications] menu has a number of options on how to handle conversation over the Link. Worried about sharing your opinions too freely?]]

"*I suppose that would depend on how easy you are to offend,*" I responded, trying out my [Directed Thought] option, which was basically just a private voice channel...except sparing me the necessity of actually speaking.

Which was no little thing.

Dio made clear my success by responding with [[Not at all,]] and my attention fell down a rabbit hole of functional telepathy, and sufficiently advanced technology being indistinguishable from magic, and where *Dream Speed* sat with Clarke's Laws.

With my thoughts so distracted, it was fortunate I'd seen the function of the hexagon-lift before my guiding arrow led me to it. Staggering off the thing two levels up, I was wondering if the easy replacement of bodies had led to a lack of simple safety measures like hand railings when I nearly collided with someone.

"Sorry!" I said, and then almost stumbled a second time. That was a reaction to a face: high cheekbones, incredible brown eyes, precisely cut lips. Physical beauty on a scale I'd never before personally encountered.

He sidestepped and gave me an apologetic grimace before continuing on along the walkway. Even at an increasing distance he stood out spectacularly because, unlike every other person I'd seen so far, he wasn't wearing a green-grey jumpsuit. Instead, the man was dressed in unrelieved white made doubly brilliant by the darkness of his skin. Two strips of cloth, about five inches in width and ending with triangular in-cuts, snapped back from his shoulders like horizontal pennants, and on his head he wore what I could best describe as a futuristic ceramic crown.

"*NPC?*" I thought to Dio.

[[Just so,]] Dio replied, bobbing lazily above my head.

He'd been so real! Which was a stupid thing to think in a virtual world. And, after all, I'd been having a conversation with, presumably, a non-player character ever since I'd logged in. The Cycogs would have to all be NPCs for there to be one for every player, and NPC's usually had limited conversation. There was no way Ryzonart could have enough employees to handle so much clearly non-scripted chat, so it had to be the game itself I was talking to, capable of producing people indistinguishable from...people.

I took a breath, and shelved for the thousandth time the question of whether *Dream Speed* could really involve true AI. That meltdown could wait.

The hexagon-lift had taken me up above the 'ceiling' of blue to a transport level, and I followed my arrow to a marked waiting area. Within a count of ten a white, pill-shaped object—rather like my Snug except only large enough to fit a handful of people—glided to a stop, an opening melting into existence along one side.

Glancing at the bottom of the 'pill', I saw a faint glimmer of blue-green, but no other clue to what was allowing the thing to float about. I almost laughed at how hesitantly I stepped aboard, given that one of my favourite pastimes in MMOs is finding really tall things to jump off. Magic science meant I didn't have to care about the physics, but I still felt too real to abandon it.

"Do these things have a name?" I asked as I sat, not bothering with the [Directed Thought] option since we were alone.

[[Pods.]]

We began to move, and I gripped my seat, trying not to gasp. Remembering the rollercoaster shape of the rail I'd seen from my Snug, I braced for a 'plunge-over-a-waterfall' experience, but the pod remained horizontal as it shot through the blue ceiling stream. Sadly, there didn't seem to be any part of the ride that involved views outside the 'city tube', though the pod moved so quickly and smoothly that it hardly mattered.

Achievement
First to reach Rank One
[Nina Stella]
Awarded: Custom [Apparel Pattern]

The announcement had been both audible, and blazoned in text across my field of view, and I jerked and flinched a little, then tried to pretend I hadn't.

[[There are options for how system messages and other communications are handled,]] Dio told me, with just the faintest suggestion of Cycog laughter. [[By default they will be suppressed while you are in a Challenge, but you can also specify priority contacts, or any variation of what you'll see and not see.]]

"How far am I off Rank One?"

[[It's probable you will achieve it in your next training session. Your progress was solid.]]

While this 'Nina Stella' must have reached Rank One in her first session. I worked out how to search for players, and found the player information fairly limited.

Nina Stella
[Artemis]
Rank: 1
Status: Online
Accepting: [Email], [Messages]
Location: [Orlangia]

I wondered what it would be like to instantly become the most famous player in *Dream Speed*, and had to admit to envy. But I shrugged off missed opportunity as my pod slowed, then stopped. My arrow led me back to the concourse level, and into a maze of doors.

This was frankly confusing to look at. They were not doors standing by themselves, but leading into small, free-standing block-shapes, as if someone had scattered the place with cut-down shipping containers. Script in at least two different alphabets was blazoned all over the containers, in no language I recognised.

My arrow led me through the maze to one of the containers and pointed right at the door, but I hesitated. "What's the difference between virtual and physical Challenges, given I'm playing a virtual game?"

[[Physical Challenges take up space on the Drowned Earth, and in *Dream Speed* will be primarily lan-related.

Virtual Challenges will place your Core Unit into Storage, and load you into the Challenge via the Link.]]

"So why did I need to travel here to join a virtual quest?"

[[There are some—the larger Challenges—where you will be able to place yourself into any Storage on the planet to join, but many virtual Challenges use a limited portal upload to restrict opportunities for interference, and to minimise any possibility of delayed communication. You would not believe the tedium of Bios insisting they lost a Challenge because of transmission lag. Besides, it makes a Challenge ever so slightly more of an event to oblige a Bio to walk here.]]

"But what happens if a whole bunch of people want to take the same Challenge?" I asked, considering the small size of the container dubiously. A fit for five people, perhaps.

[[A waiting list. Or the Bios, ever fickle, find something else they want to do.]]

My destination door slid open, revealing the mirror-shimmer of 'Soup'. MMOs often used instances to handle complex quests, phasing players through a portal into different iterations of the same experience, but that had never involved parking a physical self at the entrance. I looked around at dozens of other doors, realising that behind them all would be the same silver shimmer.

"Are there empty people...Core Units...all around us?"

[[A mindless horde's worth.]]

"Are they safe? From harm, I mean, not the prospect of them turning into a mind-controlled horde."

[[If this were a location where the city Cycog had some animus against me, then there are extra security precautions it would be wise to take. But I have no particular enemies here, and you are far too minor a Bio to be considered worth taking direct action against.]]

"Well, let's change that," I said, and stepped into the shimmer.

13

instance

Paws waving, I rolled on my back in the sun.

Then, with a dizzying jerk, I came more or less upright, blinking and twitching, processing sight, sensation. Sheer physical difference. Two extra inches of leg were nothing compared to fur, four paws, and this *spine*, long and endlessly flexible, stretching down to an awareness of tail, waving and twitching.

With a name like *The Felinead*, waking up Cat was hardly a surprise, but I'd underestimated how *different* Being Cat would be. Overwhelming. A kaleidoscope of scent, and crisp but oddly off colours, accompanied by a knife-sharp clarity of sound. The sense of being on my hands and knees, but so much more comfortable. Claws. Whiskers.

I was not by a valley waterfall, but in every other respect I followed the outline of the countless videos from Demo 1. I gawped at myself, stared around briefly—at a grassy clearing studded with flowers and surrounded by trees—and then went back to gawping at myself. Lacking a convenient reflecting pool, I couldn't see all of myself, but I did seem to be a house cat, short-haired and featuring grey and white blotches. Skinny.

After several yoga moves to fully establish my Catness, I tried walking. Then I reached for my menu options, since I wanted a record of how much like a pantomime horse my attempts at four legs must look.

My HUD had become a single, barely noticeable icon, and the menu options were shortened to screenshots, streaming, and [Emergency Exit]. I considered this for a while, then went back to walking. That worked better when I wasn't thinking about it, and soon I moved on to small bounces and pounces, with only occasional awkwardnesses when I forgot myself and tried to stand up.

Stretching felt enormously good.

Basic movement accomplished, my attention shifted to the idea of a plot, and what might be outside my sunny clearing. There was no floating mote in attendance, so I assumed Dio was off enjoying 'perversions', and it was up to me to work out what now.

I surveyed the trees around me, and was rewarded with a strange image when I looked in the direction of the thickest trees: a vision of a tumble of earth-packed rocks, and several other cats lolling before hollows and small caves. A cat colony.

About to be invaded?

Experimentally, I gazed in the opposite direction, and another image imposed itself into my line of sight. Rock-studded earth patched with grass, with an attentive red-brown dog sitting in the shade of a round-leafed tree. Did these visions serve the same function as a mini-map? But were the images the equivalent of memories for my cat, or actual visions of what lay in those directions at this moment? The former made more sense, but it'd be wise not to rule out other possibilities.

I had no idea what was going on, and that was delicious. I even wished I hadn't read the bare-bones description of the Challenge, because now I was anticipating an invasion, and how much better would it be to simply be here, Cat, and have adventure happen?

It took time to work through the trees that separated me from the cat colony. It wasn't walking that gave me trouble, but dealing with a sense I didn't really know how to manage. The complexity of pong.

Different trees had distinct 'flavours', and dirt was a wine bottle label: all undernotes of chestnut with an aftertaste of bitter melon. And that was merely the substrate, for overlaid on everything was Threat and Enticement and Familiar: the traces of at least a dozen different animals.

My modal didn't come with a translation of which scent meant which animal, but there was an in-built reaction to *types*. Familiar was most certainly other cats, and Enticing things I could eat. There was a single skein of Threat, and I flinched when I ran into it, and found I could do a magnificent backward leap when I didn't put my mind to it.

The thread of Threat was strong, but seemed to be heading 'north-south' to my imagined 'east-west'. Invader, or passing dog?

The possibility of Actual Pain made it easy to choose the common sense option of continuing to the cat colony. Information first, then risk.

The tumble of rocks sat bathed in sunlight atop a small rise, with easy access to the branches of a number of the surrounding trees. A single black tom sprawled on the highest rock, and a trio of lanky kittens raced past as I paused for a survey. A different enough scene from my vision that I decided that had been a memory map rather than some kind of far sight.

Options for cat communication were rather limited. Blink to indicate a lack of hostility. Touch noses in greeting. I hadn't even tried to speak, so had no idea whether I would have more than purrs and hisses at my disposal.

Philosophically, I made my way up the mound, swimming through layer upon layer of cat scent before pausing at a respectful distance to blink. The watching tom lifted his head as I approached, and I found nose-greeting less awkward than the double-cheek kiss awarded by relatives scarcely ever met. And I could now easily associate one of the scent trails with Black Tom.

A vision of a grey and white cat dragging a dead rabbit inserted itself into my frame of view, and it was all I could do not to flinch back dramatically. But there was a weird purplish flavour to the image that reminded me strongly of Black Tom, and I realised that the image had come from him.

So cats—or, at least, these cats—communicated by telepathically sending pictures! Fascinated, I tried sending back an image of the grassy clearing, distinctly empty of rabbits. Black Tom's ears went back, and the rabbit image presented itself to me again, this time with darker overtones of purple.

'Get out there and hunt rabbits you lazy so-and-so' seemed a reasonable interpretation, and I attempted an apology posture, wondering if this Challenge was starting out with a collection quest after all.

Turning to go, a shiver ran along my extra-flexible spine. Lightning-quick, I snapped back to Black Tom, and saw he'd risen, ears flattened. But he was looking up, not at me. I followed suit, aware of a deep rumble, and then found myself crouching, trying to make myself smaller. A pointless gesture since animals could hardly be of interest to the thing above us.

Three many-sided polyhedrons arranged in a triangle and connected by straight sections, with the gap in the centre filled by a circle. Metallic, somewhat streamlined despite its segmented shape, though not what I'd call aerodynamic. But still a ship.

It passed quickly from my line of sight, descending, and the low, deep note of whatever it used as engines grew fainter, changing pitch as it did so, before cutting out. Landed?

An image of a patched grey and white cat chasing off after it imposed itself onto the empty sky. Two other images rapidly followed: the patched cat peering at the ship from a distance, and then returning.

A scouting mission. Right. Thoughtlessly, I started to nod, and clumsily transformed the gesture into a more catly crouch. Then I turned and raced excitedly down the rocks, past the three kittens and into the trees.

The wealth of scent I plunged into reminded me of basic caution. I might feel marvellously fast and strong and agile, but I was still housecat-sized, and so I slowed, and paid attention to scent and movement, along with my handy vision-map, that kept showing me places I was heading before I arrived. A stream, a gradually clearing slope up to a ridge. And beyond that, a valley farm.

I almost stopped altogether when presented with this image. Humans, represented in the image by a worn-looking woman working industriously with a hoe. For some reason being Cat had made me assume that this was a world of animals, but of course if the Challenges were all based on the planet—past, future or fiction—then humans were only to be expected.

Which colony was being invaded?

Cresting the ridge, I flattened myself to gritty stone, seeing the farm of my vision with the addition of the ship, currently crushing an uneven field of some grain crop. I even saw the woman, running frantically, one of a half-dozen people scattering from the house in every direction.

They'd managed quite a distance in the time it had taken me to reach the ridge, and the fact that none of them ran together made me narrow my eyes. Even the children. One, not more than six, was flagging and stumbling, clutching a shaggy black-and-white dog for support, but was also the nearest to shelter, having been sent in the direction with the shortest route out of the clear centre of the valley.

An opening appeared in one of the straight sections of the ship, and two vehicles emerged. Somewhere between sleds and chariots, they featured a single person standing at a tall front control panel, and a second seated in the long, low rear section. The ship was at enough of a distance that, even with my keen Cat eyes it took a long study to realise the sleds hovered above the ground.

They were also much faster than running people, zipping off in effortless pursuit of those nearing cover. The boy and dog were to my left, and I watched as one pursuer—a woman wearing a dark green coverall—pointed what looked like a torch at the pair. Boy and dog fell without any attempt to break their momentum, thumping into tussocky grass.

The sled bobbed a little as the woman hopped down and loaded both limp forms, and then they were off again, heading to intercept the next-nearest runner.

No-one escaped. I thought one had managed it, disappearing along a stream bed far to my right, but after the sleds had delivered their unconscious loads back to the ship, they both sped off along the stream, and returned after the barest delay.

Either the final runner hadn't had the sense to hide, or the sleds had some way to track those they hunted. Was it specifically people, or would they be able to spot any living creature?

Movement to my right almost had me leaping, but it was only the trio of kittens, crouched much as I was, the tail of the darkest flicking.

I formed a picture of the three of them standing before Black Tom: they could report back while I continued to watch. In response I was given an image of a dark grey cat sitting in the entrance of the farm below, eyes closing in greeting. The vision was accompanied by a strong sense of concern.

Firmly, I re-sent the image of the three reporting to Black Tom, but added a rider of my patched self, much closer to ship and farm, watching. And, putting action to thought, I then snaked over the lip of the ridge and tucked myself beneath the nearest bush.

Two of the kittens stayed where they were, while the third departed. For a time I kept a portion of my attention on them, to be sure that they did not—at least immediately—follow me down. But then all of my focus turned to the drama below, and the task of reaching it without exposing myself.

I was not a particularly well-camouflaged cat, but the people from the ship didn't pay much attention to the rest of the valley after they'd captured the runners. They took their prisoners into their ship, and then emerged to explore the farmhouse. Before I was halfway down the valley they brought an elderly man out of the house and marched him off to the ship, and then there was no more activity until I was close enough to be making serious decisions.

With the ship sitting in the middle of a grain field, I could probably get right up to it without being spotted—so long as there was no proximity detector to beep out a warning. The question was, what was I doing here? I'd been sent on a scouting trip, and potentially to check on a fellow cat, but I'd seen no sign of any cats being taken into the ship, and what did Cat-me care about a bunch of captured humans?

But I was a Player Character. My decisions were not driven by self-preservation, but by story, advancement and reward. And any risk had to be significantly mitigated by the fact that 'I' was safely stowed in the Soup at the Challenge entrance—along with at my parents' house in Drenthe. The most I had to worry about was my player statistics and boasting rights.

Well, and pain. Pain was definitely a factor I'd never before had to deal with in an MMO.

The prospect didn't deter me, but meant I was not inclined to attempt a 'run past the mobs to a checkpoint' manoeuvre. If this game even had checkpoints. It could be so freeform as to not have an actual objective: a sandbox cat colony, there for me to make what I wanted of it, spaceship included.

In any case, I wanted into the ship, which was not so simple a goal. Spaceship design didn't lend itself to convenient open windows.

Hoping I wasn't irradiating Cat-me, I crept up to where the ship had opened. The door had closed, the ramp was gone. I trotted beneath one of the straight sections, nose twitching at a variety of harsh scents. There was definitely an ozone tang, with an acrid undernote, and a weird burned popcorn odour that I realised was coming from the grain immediately flattered by the polyhedrons. Definitely some heat involved in the landing.

As I approached the central circle, I spotted quivering in the grain immediately below it, and was two heartbeats from bolting when a pair of grey ears popped above the green-gold, unripened heads of grain. The farm cat.

I blinked a quick greeting, and then sent an image of the door as I'd seen it when open. Farmhouse Grey's ears showed dissatisfaction, and then I had an image back of smooth, unbroken metal. No way in.

The question of how two cats could possibly break into a vehicle most definitely not designed to be opened from the outside was thankfully made moot by a clunk and sliding noise above. The door had opened, and the ramp was lowering.

Thank you, plot convenience.

Before the ramp had fully extended, one of the sleds shot off the end of it, sending a ripple of heated air through the grain as it sped away. Two quick leaps took me to a convenient position just behind the ramp, where I could peer after the sled without exposing myself.

The thing was overloaded, bunny-hopping over every hillock and tussock. One of the captured humans was driving it, with the rest piled in the back. No—not all of them. The older man and the young boy with the dog were missing.

I stayed where I was, watching the progress of the sled and waiting for the second, which emerged before the first had made it halfway across the valley floor. Still I waited, in case a third was going to shoot out, but nothing came, and my sensitive hearing picked up no sound of movement immediately above me, so I shifted to a vantage point in the grain that would allow me to look up the ramp into the ship.

There *was* someone up there, but they were turned away, studying a monitor set by the door.

Farmhouse Grey moved before I could, leaping to the top of the ramp and dashing left. I followed, working to get a better idea of the interior, and to spot a good hiding place, or other people, all in a few glances.

The area just within the hatch was completely clear: a long corridor stretching to my left and right, joining two of the polyhedrons. The opposite wall, however, was a series of doors and hatches, with the nearest two open, revealing empty spaces that must have held the sleds. Almost everything else was closed, and I joined Farmhouse Grey in a determined pelt for a pair of ramps at the very end of the corridor to the left. A door stood open at the top of the up ramp, and we raced to reach it before the person at the hatch turned around—or it shut.

Skidding through the door, I found a room with angled walls that suggested it filled half of the top section of a polyhedron. Two 'examining tables' sat in the centre of the room, while the flat inner wall was taken up by a door and weird 'glass box' shelves whose purpose I only realised when I spotted the boy in one.

That was after I'd dived to the right, trying to put something solid between me and the woman standing at one of the tables. I ended up crouching behind a lump of black and white fur that set my sense of smell into a shocky spiral of Threat: it was the dog, limp but still breathing. I couldn't see Farmhouse Grey, and concentrated on finding somewhere, anywhere, that I could hide properly.

There were cabinets beneath the examining tables, sealed. A lot of storage built about the walls. And—there! A sliding door, a few centimetres ajar. Not quite wide enough to fit Cat-me, but not too heavy to resist being jiggled a fraction further. More difficult to hook claws on the ridge of the handle indent and shove it back—definitely not a standard cat manoeuvre. It didn't quite close completely, but that suited me, and I settled down to watch and hope that my heart would stop racing enough for me to think.

Being rather hungry and ragingly thirsty did not help. Gaming with an Actual Body—or virtual facsimile thereof— definitely had some downsides, and I wondered why Ryzonart had bothered to include things like thirst or 'wet rooms', when they surely could have created a game where food and drink were just perks, not a necessity with consequent 'revolting expulsions'.

Wrestling with distraction, I watched. My view from the cupboard was necessarily narrow, but I could see that the dog was beginning to stir. I could only occasionally see the woman moving around the examining table, seemingly doing vitals tests on the unconscious man, but I had a clear view when she produced a thick metal rod and pressed it to his temple. He jerked in a most unpleasant way, and when she moved the rod away, a silver disk was left behind.

Some sort of...what? Communication device? Symbol of completed processing? The woman wore a disk in the same place, I noted, but from my position I couldn't see whether the boxed-up boy was similarly decorated.

The door in the central dividing wall opened and a man came in. Another silver disk. He and the woman spoke briefly in a language I didn't recognise, and then together lifted the older man lying on the examining table.

This was my first good look at the captive. All three people were dark-haired, with a skin tone that suggested a Mediterranean region, but while the two 'invaders' were wearing baggy jumpsuits with a scratchy-looking insignia on one shoulder, their captive was dressed in worn but perfectly recognisable jeans and t-shirt. Propped upright, I could just make out the faded image on the front of the shirt: lush lips and tongue. The faint words beneath were in Arabic script.

The two invaders carefully transferred the unconscious man to one of the clear-doored shelves built against the inner wall, and sealed it. Then they stood over the groggily shifting dog, having an incomprehensible debate. The man seemed to prevail, and picked the dog up. Both invaders left through the door to the corridor.

I quibbled, but Farmhouse Grey had no hesitation in emerging from hiding. She was clearly another player character, for no cat in my experience would survey a wall containing boxed humans, and then start poking at anything resembling buttons.

Trotting across, I sent an image of the rod being pressed to the old man's temple. What, after all, could Farmhouse Grey do, even if she managed to get a box open? It's not like cats came equipped with smelling salts, and it would only make sense that the boxed pair would have been given a long-lasting sedative.

This message sent, as best I was able, I turned my attention to the inner door. There was a control panel, but it required a few leaps before I managed to swat it with sufficient force to trigger the door to open.

A laboratory. More humans in boxes along the inner wall. Wondering what the invaders wanted with their collection, I quickly toured the room, and then tucked myself into a corner to consider the layout of the ship I'd seen flying overhead.

Chances were good that the engine was located in the central sphere. The sphere had connected to the polyhedrons in some way, but I couldn't see an entrance here, and didn't remember one from the first room. Perhaps through the polyhedron's bottom half?

There was no stair down, only a second door that would take me out to another of the long connecting corridors. I was trying to trigger it when Farmhouse Grey came through from the first room. Tail switching, she sent me an image of a small opaque nub set in the ceiling, and then a more recognisable image of a security camera, and a questioning feel.

Cats can't shrug, really. I'd noticed the nubs, but if there was someone at a central control point watching Cat Espionage, there wasn't much I could do about it. Instead, I sent a picture of a man hiding beneath a cardboard box, and learned that cats couldn't really laugh, either.

Returning to my attempts to trigger the door, I hoped my point was valid. This was a game. Unless I'd steered completely off-course by not going back to report to Black Tom, then there was surely a path to a goal, a definition of success more than "watch those humans get kidnapped". And so it must be possible for cats to run around this ship avoiding notice and achieving...something.

I doubted the aim was to blow it up—unless my goal as a cat was to remove all humans from the vicinity. And a clearly-marked 'Wake and Release the Captives' button would be far too easy. So I was aiming to sabotage the engine—which hopefully wouldn't lead to the blowing up scenario.

The door triggered at last, and Farmhouse Grey trotted through it, but immediately stopped, flattening. Two people were pulling boxes from a storage hatch about two-thirds along the corridor.

I slipped immediately over the short drop to the down ramp, and Farmhouse Grey followed. We were probably far enough out of sight to not be completely obvious, but bouncing up and down trying to trigger the door would be a significant risk.

With a low growl, Farmhouse Grey set herself beneath the door control, and sent me an image of herself with me balanced on her back, reaching up with an exaggeratedly outstretched claw. It was a good idea, though not quite so easy in execution, since the controls were quite high, and I wasn't tremendously adept. But it worked, and we scurried through, hoping that the opening of two doors in close succession wouldn't draw the humans' notice.

The lower half of this polyhedron was dimmer than the areas I'd already travelled through. Not jump-scare dark, but the lights seemed to be in stand-by mode, and thankfully weren't triggered by our movement. The space itself was small, an access throughway between curving and sealed sections presumably given over to machinery. No convenient wires to chew through, no easily accessible ways to open hatches, and expose innards.

A door to my left most likely led to the central sphere, and I wasted no time bouncing up to trigger it. I was getting better: it only took two tries, and opened onto a similar low-light access space between ranks of sealed machinery. I trotted quickly through the whole area, finding no convenient openings, only exits back to the polyhedrons.

Farmhouse Grey had followed me into the sphere, but I'd lost track of her during my reconnaissance, and trekked around again until I spotted her by one of the entrance doors, her attention fixed on a line widely-spaced vents that seemed to run the perimeter of the ceiling/floor above us.

A way up? While the machinery was sealed, it was fashioned in handy protruding bulges, allowing us both to leap, with only a couple of scrabbling slips, all the way up to crouch uncomfortably in a narrow space beneath a vent.

A woman was talking, up in the top half of the sphere. The language still sounded completely unfamiliar, but the tone was interesting. Brief statements, pauses, and then a rushed, wordier continuation. I couldn't hear the responses, but whoever she was talking to clearly scared her.

The talking stopped, and a single set of footsteps receded, followed by silence. Now what? Whoever the woman had been talking to was still up there—perhaps the captain of the ship, or some sort of security officer?

While I was hesitating, Farmhouse Grey acted: inching forward and then trying to lift the vent with her head. It shifted, just enough to make an audible clink, but then held fast. Not screwed down, but either jammed, or not designed to simply lift out.

After a second failed attempt, Farmhouse Grey rested for a moment, then lay flat and wriggled perilously on the too-narrow ledge so that she was on her back and could probe with clawed paws. Not a manoeuvre that cats were likely to attempt, but perfectly possible.

The vent slid. Just a centimetre or so, and then it lifted, with what felt like an ear-rending clatter. Farmhouse Grey was up through the gap like lightning, apparently deciding that after that amount of noise, it was better to try to hope for a hiding space than retreat.

Because this was a game, and the potential for pain did not—quite—outweigh my desire to find a path forward, I followed.

There was nowhere to hide in the wide-open area of the upper half of the sphere, but nor was there anyone to hide from. The place had a single door, and a clear hemisphere in the centre, and the rest was just ceiling and floor.

Farmhouse Grey was already at the hemisphere, peering through the thick, clear bubble at an inset in the floor. This was filled by an inky substance that could be liquid or extremely smooth leather. There seemed to be a few buttons built into the rim of the indentation, but otherwise the space was empty.

An image of a uniformed woman standing in the room, a cartoonish talk bubble hanging over her head, inserted itself into my mind. I glanced at Farmhouse Grey, and then offered an image of the black substance producing little tentacles in order to manipulate the controls. We both peered through the sphere, waiting for a betraying ripple, but the blackness just sat there, either waiting for an opportunity to leap for an unguarded orifice, or being upholstery.

Movement behind me made me leap, but it was my own tail, lashing entirely without conscious control, echoing my frustration.

Farmhouse Grey, lacking anything obvious to do, leapt onto the top of the bubble, but did not quite make the centre, and slid off, scrabbling. Her claws made no impression on the clear substance, but the bubble as a whole rocked just a fraction, a crack of an opening appearing.

Ears pricking, we both considered the bubble, then Farmhouse Grey sent me a thought-suggestion and I nodded—such a wrong movement for a cat, but very automatic for me—and we positioned ourselves on the opposite side of that slight lift of the bubble, and then jumped to around the three-quarter mark up the side of it and tried to grip not with claws, but the pads of all four paws.

It lifted! We'd misjudged the exact axis of the half-sphere's pivot, and so we only managed a small gap before slipping off, but a second attempt soon fixed that, and a third taught us to climb the revolving bubble like a reverse hamster wheel until the edge reached a vertical point and we could leap madly down onto the inky surface, to see if it would eat us.

While the bubble slid gently back into position, the surface we stood on quivered, but only with reaction to our tense anticipation. Upholstery after all.

There was a scent that I don't think came from the slightly yielding substance, but instead belonged to whatever usually sat in here. An old scent, faint, and it did not immediately set off Food or Threat in Cat-me, which I guess meant it was altogether unfamiliar. Whatever it was, it couldn't be much larger than a biggish dog. A human adult certainly wouldn't fit in the bubble.

Farmhouse Grey, ever businesslike, was poking buttons, producing chirping noises, and then blackness. Lights out—no, lights on! The whole of the domed room had gone dark, and then filled with glimmering motes. A star map!

Awestruck, I gazed around, immediately recognising familiar constellations. All so crisp and clear, more detailed then I'd ever seen sky-watching. A projection unmarred by atmospheric distortion.

Enchantment was brief-lived, as Farmhouse Grey's continued attempts with the buttons wiped the vista away, and replaced it with alarms.

The bubble opened of its own accord, along with the room's sole door. Farmhouse Grey and I pelted for the open vent, and dove through it, scrabbling for footing before sliding off the curving engine housing below, dropping to the floor.

The alarm was just as loud down below, painful to my sensitive hearing. The door was open too, and we raced through it, but then slowed at the exit out to the corridor.

Creeping up the ramp, I saw boxes, but not people. Just one foot, projecting from behind a box. A body. Both of the people we'd seen shifting boxes had dropped to the corridor floor. Nervously, I started cautiously toward them, but Farmhouse Grey raced past me, not stopping until she was standing on one man's chest, peering down into his face.

Since there was no reaction to this, I trotted up to examine the woman lying face-down. Easy to see she was still breathing, but no sign of what had made her fall down. I poked experimentally at the silver disk on her temple, but other than feeling weirdly velvety and being firmly fixed in place, it offered no clues.

Farmhouse Grey hooked claws beneath the rim of the man's disk, and tore it off. The man immediately began convulsing, sending Farmhouse Grey and I into a hasty retreat behind one of the boxes. The man didn't wake up, or die, but groaned in an awful way I'd rather not hear again, and then lay still.

After a short pictorial debate with Farmhouse Grey, I removed the woman's disk and we watched her convulse in turn, and produce a small puddle, then also lapse into apparently deeper unconsciousness.

For all we knew, we could have been doing the equivalent of removing an in-built smartphone. Or put them into a vegetative state. Even so, we raced back to that examining room, to give it a try on one of the captives, but once again our size, and inconvenient container doors, defeated us. After some futile scrabbling, we instead removed the disk of the woman who had been processing the captives, and then went in search of more.

The exit door of the ship was still open, giving us a good view of the consequences of button-mashing. The escapees had evidently been recaptured, and were again cargo making a return trip, when *someone* had knocked the sled drivers unconscious. One sled had rammed a rock about twenty metres away, and the other had ploughed into the side of the ship, just next to the entrance ramp.

They mustn't have been travelling too fast, since the sleds had only acquired dints, rather than transforming into a crumpled tangle of metal and flesh. With two quick leaps, Farmhouse Grey reached the chest of one of the captives, and briskly bit the man on his ear. This produced a jerk, but no immediate return to consciousness, so I busied myself removing silver disks from the spaceship crew scattered in the vicinity, and then went on a hunt for others within the ship.

This was easy enough with all the doors open, and fun for the exploration aspect alone, though I shied away from thinking too hard about how much damage I might be doing to my victims.

Everything in the lower half of the ship was sealed machinery. The upper half of each polyhedron served a different purpose, and I explored crew quarters, and then a kitchen, dining, and hydroponic farm section, before returning to science and captives.

I was considering the older man in his clear-doored box when a woman staggered into the room. I skittishly leaped behind the examining table, but I don't think the woman would have cared about me anyway. She dashed straight for the boxed people and pulled the young boy out onto the floor, immediately tearing the disk off his temple. More of the escapees showed up, and helped her get the older man out of his box and de-disk him.

Farmhouse Grey, arriving in the second group's wake, watched critically for a moment, and then sat down beside me. An image popped into my head of a GAME OVER graphic, along with a questioning feeling.

I failed, once again, to shrug. Cats just aren't built for it. But I thought Farmhouse Grey was right, and was proved correct when the last of the silver disks came off the last of the boxed people, and a system message popped up.

Primary Goal Achieved.
You may exit at
any time.

I hung around for quite a while, though: long after Farmhouse Grey, having realised that she could send pictures of words, made her goodbyes and faded away. I wanted to see what these people would do, or whether the story would just stop once the rescuing was done.

Mostly they argued, then dragged everyone out of the ship. Captives in one group, and the crew members in a second, tied up in a row with some brightly coloured rope fetched from the farm.

I was relieved the former captives hadn't immediately bludgeoned the crew into pulp, and waited out various revival attempts. Finally, a dousing of water brought one woman to sputtering consciousness. She jerked upright, stared about her, tried to raise her bound hands toward her face, and then burst into tears.

Of joy, I think.

Another round of arguments followed, growing more complicated as other de-disked people woke, but almost all of the crew seemed unspeakably happy to be captured. The two who responded badly were separated out into a third group and bound more tightly.

Time Limit reached.
Automatic exit in
5
4
3
2
1

14

maps

The mint-chill of Soup hit me, and I gasped. Then I stepped forward, blinking at my return to the futuristic 'city' of Vessa, and a brief appearance of the full overlay of my HUD, before it reduced to an unobtrusive graphic, followed by system messages.

Gauntlet Successful.
Gauntlet Success Rate: 1/1 100%
Challenge Success Rate: 1/1 100%
Lux Points Earned: 5
Total Lux Points: 5
Challenge Reward:
[Tier 1 Apparel Pattern]
[Tier 1 Consumable Pattern]

I activated [Tier 1 Consumable Pattern], and was treated to a dizzying array of menus full of food and drink. After hours of gameplay, I was hungry and thirsty, but not painfully so, and put off any hasty decisions when I remembered I already had a few entries in my [Consumables] menu.

Looking around, I spotted a parklike area in the middle of all the Challenge entrances, and wandered over in search of a seat. Decorative planting concealed nooks filled by tables and chairs, some occupied by people eating. No sign of any food vendors.

Shrugging, I found a seat and checked my [Consumables] menu, which contained three thrilling entries: [Complete Meal: Animal Protein], [Complete Meal: No Animal Protein], and [Water]. I prodded the [Complete Meal: No Animal Protein] option to see if said meal would sci-magically appear on the table in front of me, but received an arrow instead. This led to an unobtrusive kiosk tucked among the plants, which, when I approached, popped up with an option to [Collect]. A hatch opened to reveal a flattish rectangular container of waxy cardboard shaped around its contents, a little like an airplane meal. I added [Water] to my order, and then returned to my nook to eat and browse.

[Complete Meal: No Animal Protein] was a nice mix of crunchy salad, a warm patty of some sort of legume, not-quite-hummus, and fruit segments.

I dissected the patty cautiously, wondering whether to risk it, and then found I could review an ingredients list for the 'pattern'. While I ate, I browsed the reward menu briefly, then turned my attention to the [Players] menu, finding a [Search] command.

Search Results:
1 exact match
[Amelia Beerheart]
[29 Similar Matches]

Following the link to Amelia gave me her details.

Reputation Name:
Amelia Beerheart
[Noonan]
Rank: 0
Status: Online/Challenge
Accepting: [Email], [Messages] (delayed)
Location: [Vessa]

Amelia being in a Challenge apparently meant she wouldn't immediately see a [Message], but I could email her, and so sent a brief note to let her know what game name I was using. Then I opened the [Location] menu.

[Quadrant]
[System]
[Planet]
[City]
[Ship]
[Search]

I started right at the top, to see how The Synergis mapped out the Milky Way. Or whatever Dio had called it. Helannan. A 'top-down' diagram popped up, with the spiralling 'disk' of the Milky Way divided evenly into four, which is how it's done on *Star Trek*, although The Synergis' quadrant division didn't seem to run through Earth's system. Instead, a blinking dot was visible in the top-right quarter.

The quadrant was labelled "Carolun Quadrant, [Aldezageden]", and I followed the link to Aldezageden, wondering if that was the current name for Earth, or the Sol system.

Aldezageden
Quadrant Administrator
[Carolun Quadrant]
8684
Location: [Shimuna]
[Lineage]

Looking at [Lineage] took me down a rabbit-hole of what must be all the Cycogs that had combined, divided, and been absorbed to eventually become Aldezageden, who I guessed was one of the larger Cycogs. There was no picture.

A quick visit to [System] and [Planet] gave me the names I expected, along with the name of an administrator, [Arefiel], for both the system and the planet. I'd guess that Earth, drowned or not, was still the most populous planet in the Sol system, and the logical base for the System Administrator.

Earth's ruler.

I wondered how Cycogs chose their names—the names Bios could pronounce. Arefiel sounded like the name of an angel, but the mouthful of 'Aldezageden' would better suit a planet, or a drug.

It took a little while to figure out where to look myself up, and then follow the link to my 'handler'.

Dio
Fledgling
1
Location: [Vessa]

Dio lacked a lineage, perhaps because te wasn't important enough. I shrugged, then I tried out my [Directed Thought] option.

"Are you lurking, Dio, or off with your perversions?"

[[Perversions.]] Dio's voice was as clearly present as it had been when te had been in the same room as me.

I was definitely having trouble remembering new sets of pronouns, though it helped that I couldn't really pick 'male' or 'female' for the voice Dio used to talk to me.

"What counts as perverse to a Cybercognate?"

[[Not much, in truth. We have rules, but little in the way of taboos. There are certain things the majority of us are uncomfortable with, but those tend to be cruelties, rather than anything that would usually fall into the definition of 'perverse'.]]

I'd gone back to [Locations] and opened up the [City] option, discovering that Vessa's Administrator was [Fevelen], and that the city was south of the equator, at roughly the latitude of Brazil—though it was a little hard to judge with a map showing most of the world as water.

"Is it possible to overlay the undrowned Earth so I can match up the continents?"

[[Gain Rank Five.]]

"Bah," I said aloud, as I zoomed in to the blinking dot and discovered that I was in the northern section of a miles-long uneven oval: the 'rollercoaster' of Vessa. There were dozens of islands studded along its length, the largest of which, 'Vessa Major', was a ten kilometre-wide crescent.

Following my [Ship] link showed it to be just a little south of my current location, and produced a handy direction arrow along with a bare bit of information.

Unnamed
[Leveret]
1
[Vessa]

"How do I name my snug?"

[[Gain Rank Five.]]

"Double-bah. Well, speaking of Rank, I'm ready to work on my lan skills. Are there rubbish bins, or some other appropriate thing to do with leftovers?"

[[Return to any vending point.]]

"Where it'll be...what? Reduced to component atoms, and then reconstituted as someone's breakfast?"

[That is one way to describe it. Not everything is returned to Soup, but most disposable objects are converted, not kept.]

Returning my tray to the hatch I'd collected it from, I tried to decide whether my fruit and veg had tasted off, or had been oddly textured due to being generated however The Synergis managed to create objects. Though it was all virtual, which made it rather a moot point.

Catching a platform up to the transport pods, I looked out over all the Challenge entrances. There were more people about than when I'd first arrived, almost all accompanied only by a glowing mote, talking animatedly to it as they stared, ate, or walked into the shimmer of one of the Challenge entrances. Doors and hatches,

"Dio. Are...are our modals dissolved when we put them in Soup?"

[[Occasionally, if there is a space issue. If you had a dozen modals, and had not obtained expanded storage, you would need to prioritise Core Units and Core Alternates over suppression modals.]]

"Core Alternates?"

[[Modals with cosmetic differences, but internal congruence. Bio Core Units are not simply familiar shapes wrapped around containers of memory and lan. You're each a very individual synaptic and chemical environment. Virtual Challenges give only a partial experience of body transfer, since your memories and reactions are still driven by your Core environment. When you transfer to a non-Core modal unit, your memories are contained within a Link—which often gives a sharper recall of recent events, and either a loss or sharpening of older memories. Some Bios feel the difference very distinctly, particularly if the chemical mix is unfamiliar.]]

"All those hormones," I mused. *"So if you had Type One Diabetes, you could just transfer to a modal that could produce insulin?"*

[[Most Bios have balance issues addressed before they're mature enough to transfer modals.]]

"There's an age limit?"

[[For Type Threes, fifteen of your planetary years. Virtual experiences are permitted much earlier, but we've determined that for a strong development of Ian, a firm sense of self must first be established.]]

"Type Three is Earth human?" But before Dio could answer, I bounced off on a tangent. *"Did you see the details of that Challenge I played?"*

[[Your door-opening attempts were splendidly ineffectual.]]

"Was that fiction or Synergis history?"

[[No cats, to my knowledge, have ever troubled themselves to such an extent.]] The Link brought me Dio's brief splutter of strange laughter. [[The Challenge wasn't based on Synergis history, no. Did you enjoy it?]]

"Totally different from what I expected," I admitted. *"But, yes, I did, even though I wasn't sure I was doing what was expected. Why was it so...so instructionless? And what would have happened if I'd just ignored the captured humans and gone hunting rabbits?"*

[[Catching a rabbit would also count as a successful conclusion, although the reward would be smaller. If you look at the Challenge categories, you'll see Challenges marked 'Variable Goals'. These present evolving goals dependent on your actions. Challenges with specific goals often state the goal in their description.]]

I'd successfully followed my latest arrow all the way back to where I'd started, even figuring out how to open the door, and walked into the tube of my main cabin. A distinct feeling of homecoming seemed excessive for such a short acquaintance.

Succeeding in figuring out how to pull my boots off, I plopped into the nearest seat, and looked around.

"Is this *my* Snug, or *our* Snug?"

[[Yours. If I passed you off to a city administrator for being too dull or lazy, you would keep the Snug. Since you're *my* Bio, however, I have full access to the Snug's systems. Think of me as your navigator. While Bios can Skip without any assistance, they're terrible at aiming, and so when you start travelling, I will be pointing the way.]]

I wondered how much impact that would have on *Dream Speed's* apparent alternate goal of stealing a ship and returning to my enclave. But perhaps Cycogs exaggerated how much they were needed for navigation. It wouldn't do to take everything Dio said at face value.

In either case, I needed to get stronger just to get a functioning ship. The question of which star would be my destination could come later.

"Right," I said. "Let's get me Rank One now."

— ✦ —

Trial Successful.
Rank One Achieved.
Reward:
[Tier 1 Tools Pattern]
[Tier 1 Consumable Pattern]

There was no accompanying system-wide announcement, but I hadn't expected that. It was hours since the first player had ranked, and if the game had announced everyone since, it would have been a constant blare.

"How many people have reached Rank One, Dio?" I asked, sinking down to the floor, my back propped against the nearest bench as I panted. Making the blue mist fill in the shapes Dio projected had taken a lot of energy. But I'd done it!

[[Twenty-seven thousand, four hundred and fifty-seven, including you.]]

"And I've been playing for, what, just over ten hours? Which means it's only been two hours and a bit in the real world since the game was unlocked?"

[[There's clock commands in your [Status] menu if you feel a need for details.]]

I eyed the glowing mote that was not real, but technically was in charge of 'Leveret'.

"I didn't expect that time differential thing to pan out. It shouldn't work. I mean, I always accepted the way guided dream games seem to go on for much longer than the time spent asleep because dreams are vague things, and perceptions can be distorted. But this is...how many people have managed to log on in the few hours this thing has been up?"

[[A little over two million.]]

Since it was the weekend, and people had been hanging out for the preload, the figure didn't completely surprise me, but it was still an impressive achievement for a non-franchise game that had unlocked four days early, without any kind of announcement, and in the teeth of press that had concluded the game was a blatant hoax. Two brief demos and the sheer *possibility* of true VR had turned this into an Event game launch.

And those numbers were going to be nothing, once players started confirming that *DS* was everything we could want it to be, and more. I shivered a little as I considered a world of effortless virtual body-hopping—for those that could afford a GDG cowl and a subscription.

But I tend toward scepticism, and even sitting there in the game talking to my own personal improbability, I couldn't quite accept what was happening.

"The perception of extended time is one thing," I said. "But people's minds aren't recordings you can fast forward. How is it possible to have two million people all *thinking* at five times the rate they usually do?"

[[You've never heard of overclocking? I hope you're sitting somewhere cool, out there in the real world. Running wetware like yours at this pace means overheating is inevitable.]]

"Because GDG cowls have suddenly gained the ability to 'overclock' human brains?"

[[The transmission pulse of those cowls could do some interesting things, with a few tweaks. But, yes, you're right, it's nothing to do with the cowls. It's because *Dream Speed* is being run on quantum computers. You'll notice that logging in and out involves a distinct transition as you uncouple from the quantum field.]]

Dio's tone told me just how seriously I should take this suggestion, but I still said: "A quantum computer is just a computer that uses non-binary logic. They're not time-distorting magic boxes."

[[Perhaps you really have been in here for ten hours?]]

"I'm fairly sure that little fact would have spread through the players by now."

My tone was dismissive, but I checked my email anyway, and saw that Amelia had replied to arrange a guild meet-up. No dramatic warnings accompanied her brief note.

I shook my head at Dio as te floated about the centre of my Snug. "Does it cause any conflict for you, to be discussing the real world? Will you melt down into an existential crisis?"

[[No, I'm perfectly happy to indulge your fantasies of this existence outside The Synergis.]]

Dio really was failing to match any of my AI expectations. But then, Cycogs weren't technically AI. It was more likely I was having a conversation with a person pretending to be a floating mote of light. But that explanation only worked if you discounted the millions of conversations apparently underway right now.

[[I've remembered the correct reason,]] Dio continued. [[The time difference comes about because your mind has been transported to the far future. The game allows players to travel to The Synergis in spirit, if not body, and when you log out the game transfers you back, only a short time after you left.]]

"That seems...exceedingly unlikely. Why bother?"

[[Perhaps The Synergis ran out of Bios? Yes, yes. In an unfortunate toffee manufacturing accident, all our Bios died or ran away, so we're importing a new set who don't know how scared they should be. Yes, I like that one. I think I'll spread it about.]]

"Toffee manufacturing, huh? So you're recruiting for the sugar mines?"

A burst of Dio's synthesiser-laughter was the only response, and I couldn't help but smile in return. Dio—whatever was behind that ball of light—was at least fun to talk to.

"I guess you must have time travel, to be here running the game. Does The Synergis use it a lot?"

[[No. We're a little afraid of it, really.]]

That sounded sincere, but given Dio's previous string of lies, I decided to count the answer as 'maybe'.

Recovered from the ranking trial—at least enough to stand—I went to explore my 'wet room'. I'm not sure I was more disappointed or relieved that there was no sign of suction tubes, or much of anything in a room that reminded me of a Styrofoam packing container—moulded with various ridges and ledges, but otherwise empty.

Considerable poking about, and some useful [Activate] commands popping into my HUD, allowed me to identify a ledge as a sink, and a big end bench as a toilet, both of them designed to be thoroughly sealed after use, trapping any liquids inside. The rear of the entry door was a sort of closet where you could hang clothes to prevent them getting wet.

I took care of my 'revolting expulsions' and then tried out the shower, just to see what happened. There were a lot of settings, and I puzzled my way to producing a sudden soapy mist, followed by a cleansing fog of increasing intensity, and then gusts of warm air that dried both me and any moisture that hadn't drained away. Designed to encourage water conservation, though I was glad to see there were 'proper' shower options.

"Dio," I said, emerging only partially dressed. "Are there any ships that have echoing-large bathrooms with an entire wall that is a window onto the stars, where Bios can have soak-in-the-water types of baths while enjoying the view?"

[[Yes.]]

"What rank would I need to be to get one of those?" I asked, sitting to pull my boots on, and then activating a location link in Amelia's email. A map of Vessa filled my internal view, with the large crescent shape of the main island highlighted, with a blinking dot obscuring one of the south-facing points. I told my Link to lead the way, and headed for the exit.

[[That would involve more than rank,]] Dio was saying. [[But you'd likely accrue sufficient means by the eighties. Much earlier if you are travelling on someone else's ship, of course.]]

I liked the idea of it being my own ship much more. "But there's no guarantee that I'll ever get to Rank Eighty, right?"

[[Less than ten percent of Bios rise above the seventies,]] Dio told me as we left my snug and an arrow led me back to the pods.

"And how many get near, what was the top rank, a hundred and something?" I asked, after boarding.

[[With one outlier, the maximums achieved are all in the one-thirties. There are fewer than fifty Bios at that strength.]]

It was difficult to adjust to the idea of an MMO that had no guarantee that you'd reach the max level. "Do I have any chance of getting there?"

[[Impossible to predict. Exiting the galaxy would be a far more attainable goal if we could reliably manage the development of our Bios. Some of you improve quickly initially, but then plateau. Others take decades to achieve the first dozen ranks, and then sprout rapidly. And some steadily march forward. While a strong self-image is usually a good indication, even that has exceptions, and so we cannot check off a set of traits and say 'this Bio is worth my time'.]]

"What about powerful families? Is being good with Ian something you can inherit?"

Dio, bobbing near the ceiling of the pod, flickered through a green spectrum. Irritation? Boredom? Cycog shrugging?

[[High-ranking Bios do like to cross-match with each other, but the results are not consistent. On a species level, Type Ones have a higher mean than you Type Threes, and there are several species mixes that trend higher than any unmodified Type.]]

"Earth humans are Type Threes? Are Cycogs Type Ones?"

[[Cybercognates aren't Bios.]]

And so weren't included in the numbering system. The idea sat uncomfortably on me, even though Dio had been telling me all along that the galaxy belonged to Cycogs, and people—Bios—were very close to pet status in The Synergis 'partnership'.

"You could be Type Zeros," I suggested, and wasn't sure what to make of the way Dio's light briefly dimmed.

[[No, the system is not for us,]] te said. [[Besides, Bios pre-date Cybercognates by millennia. It wouldn't make sense for us to be zero.]]

The pod began to slow, so I put off an exploration of types for later. And wondered if there was a useful Cycog 'body language' guide somewhere, so I could better read what Dio was—and wasn't—telling me.

A sea of grey-green coveralls spilled from the rollercoaster: thousands upon thousands of players, too many of whom were stopping to gape, blocking the way of even more new arrivals. I hadn't expected nearly so many people, and moved to turn around, but the crowd swept me forward when I tried to stop short. In danger of an elbow in the face, I ducked through the too-tight press, keeping my eyes down to follow a herringbone brick ramp until it brought me out of the general press, to a clear spot next to a balustrade. Then, with something firm to hold onto, I breathed a while before I took my turn to gape.

The island of Vessa Major was a crescent moon, horns facing south. The western reach of the crescent was made up of a mosaic of small buildings, seating areas, grass and paving, transitioning in the far distance to a trailing comet of sand. To the east, the land climbed in terraces to a slender lighthouse lifting from the sheer cliff of the point. That's a bit of straightforward orientation, and doesn't begin to capture looking out over a ten kilometre *curve*. Improbably regular, breathtakingly vast.

The pearly ribbon of the rollercoaster rose only partially out of the ocean at the centre point, and travelled like a submerged sea serpent on a curving north-south route through the body of the island before vanishing beneath the waves once again. Only the top quarter of the rail was visible, leaving the highly sculptured view unobstructed.

"*Is the whole thing artificial, Dio?*" I asked over the Link.

[[There is a core structure that has been expanded.]]

"*Into one massive resort,*" I said. "*And it's festival time. Or end-of-school celebrations.*"

A fever-pitch of excitement, a sense of release, definitely permeated the swelling crowd. Some players were in groups, but most were alone, but for a bobbing mote in luminous attendance on a partly-audible conversation, shining human faces frequently turning up to address their personal partner-overlord.

There was a weird dissonance between the 'fairy lantern' appearance of the Cycogs and the prosaic coveralls of the crowd, all in the same shade. A rare few wore something else—coveralls in different colours, jeans, dresses—but these were likely early quest rewards, and I couldn't spot anyone who was clearly an NPC.

What do people do when presented with their self-image and the ability to adjust it? Give themselves six packs, it seemed, and carve every inch of extra fat from their bodies. Or, no, that wasn't true. I saw a lot of different body types in the crowd, made less distinct by the loose-fitting coveralls. But the majority had definitely gone the same route as I had, and run their sliders toward 'peak fitness'. And almost everyone was young in a way that definitely didn't fit gamer demographics. I spotted more than a couple of 'non-human' Bios also wearing the starter outfit, but wasn't sure if they were alien NPCs or humans who pictured themselves clawed, furred and fanged.

"Self-image is a complicated thing to use as the basis for your primary skill set. Great for some, but what happens to players who have really really horrible self-images? DS forces them to make a choice between living that image, or suffering a massive penalty to gameplay."

[[Those who synchronise with a Core Unit they do not want to use are usually able to modify it over time. Or they can choose any appearance and, after determined practice, they become familiar with a new image, and it no longer impedes them as significantly.]]

"Why make that decision necessary at all?"

[[Lan works as lan works.]]

That was a non-answer, but an in-game character probably couldn't explain the game's design decisions anyway. Shrugging, I turned my attention to my guiding arrow, and how it expected me to get to the meeting point up at that lighthouse.

It was tempting to just start jogging—away from the crowd and along the curve of the crescent. I felt springy, full of energy, in a way that I hadn't since the last track meet of high school. Jogging five k's up a slope would handily get me away from this press, while nicely putting off the guild get-together a little longer.

I'd had a couple of months to decide whether or not to attend any meet-ups, and had been okay with the idea, but Core Units had added an unexpected twist to the decision. *Corpse Light* was a long-standing guild, with some players who had known each other for decades. People I had spoken with daily or at least weekly for years, but had never met in person. To them I was 'Kaz', who graduated last year from a course never fully described, but something to do with computers.

The crowd ahead thinned a little, and I took the chance to follow my arrow to a ramp downward, and then a transport pod which was a little over half-full. Getting away from the glut at the entrance would make this easier.

But if anything, the upper reaches of the island were even more crowded than the rollercoaster exit. Half the server seemed to have decided to meet here.

The sensible thing to do would be turn around. The guild meeting wasn't necessary, was a thing I'd decided to go to out of courtesy and a general affection for the guild leaders. Could I do this? The terraces would help, surely, preventing the experience from the endless press you'd get in the middle of a concert crowd, or anything totally impossible like that.

Determinedly, I kept my focus on the guiding arrow as I threaded my way through the crowd toward the terraced drop-off of the inner curve of the crescent, where I again found a balustrade to clutch while staring at vast blue ocean, a sky edging toward sunset, the pearly ribbon of the rollercoaster twisting over sandbars, and a whole lot of Down.

The lighthouse was still perhaps a hundred feet above, but Amelia's meet-up point was somewhere below, among countless tiers of tropical garden. A thousand picnic spots blurred before me, all vivid greens and splashes of bright flowers, with grey and brown notes for handy rocks for sitting, and lighter notes for table and benches, with ramps leading down and up. All dotted with flitting birds, and simply seething with coverall-clad people.

And that was only the surface of Vessa Major. I didn't even notice the doors, at first. Only when a cry of "Beer and wings!" rose up behind me, and I turned to see a group of people emerging from a door that led into the tiered cliff. Laden with trays of food and drink, they offered snacks to everyone in their path.

Curious, and looking for some breathing room, I headed for the door, and found a mostly-empty indoor atrium, with just a group around a line of hatches that must lead to a vast vat of Soup. The group swelled and ebbed as people carried off plates handed over by a pair of boys repeatedly requesting what I guessed they'd selected as a consumables reward.

"*Is there any limit to how much they can ask for, Dio?*"

[[Technically, yes. It's rare any Bio reaches it with this kind of small-serving outlet.]]

"*So any reward you get, you can just make endless copies of it?*"

[[Patterns usually come with instance restrictions. No limit to how many times you can create them, but a limit to how many you personally can have in existence at the same time. There's no real reason to limit Tier 1 food rewards. Prestige items will allow you only one copy at a time. Very rarely, you will encounter single-use patterns.]]

The map in my HUD had changed to a floor level diagram, showing all sorts of rooms inside the island, and for a while I ignored the arrow pointing back the way I'd come, and wandered around the much emptier interior, all the way to the outer curve of the crescent, which was dotted not with tiers, but with countless garden balconies. These, Dio informed me, connected to private suites that could only be accessed as Challenge rewards.

I'd found a way to view the different layers of the island's internal levels, and little icons for wet rooms and Soup outlets and Challenge entrances. The place was massive. Not quite beyond belief, but definitely impressive. And this was just the starter level. Earth.

"*Are there alien megastructures, Dio? Dyson Spheres? Ring worlds? Death Stars?*"

[[Yes.]]

I looked up at my personal alien overlord. "*Yes to which? Is this going to be one of those 'reach Rank Ten before I stop taunting you with ambiguities' things?*"

[[Yes,]] Dio said, and laughed.

15
guild

Reassured by the knowledge that the inside of the island was easily accessible and much emptier, I concentrated on reaching my guild, pursuing my guiding arrow into an ocean of conversation, auto-translations of languages I didn't understand mixing through the handful I commanded.

Most of it seemed to be discussions between people, rather than the only half-audible dialogue with Cycogs. At first it just came to me as gabble, while I worked through the crowd of people near the pod station, but then I found a ramp down, past a terrace crammed with, from the sound of it, a guild of English and Irish players.

"Ranker already? Way to go, brother!"

"How'd you get so far ahead? You only started half an hour ahead of me."

"He passed in his first session, too, the mutt. I've done two training dints, and still can barely shift that blue shite."

"Seemed pretty easy to me. What was your sync rating?"

"Seventy-five."

"I'm in the nineties."

"Fuck that."

"What I don't understand is why we didn't *start* with a hundred percent sync. It's one thing to give us the option of sacrificing some advantage for cosmetic options, but I started out at, like, sixty. All that bollocks about having a strong self-image or not—why start tons of players out at a big disadvantage?"

"In a game like this, see, we bring our advantages and disadvantages with us. Gav's got a black belt, right? So how do you feel about a bit of PVP with Gav around?"

"*Why don't we start at a hundred percent, Dio?*" I asked, as I moved out of easy hearing.

[[Synchronisation brings together a conscious and unconscious perception of self, adds a strong measure of preening vanity, and sits in the shadow of anxiety. Lan functions best when a Bio is both familiar with and accepting of the self they see, and that is not something that can be automatically generated.]]

"Hm," I said aloud, forgetting to use the private tell function. The game's central mechanics seemed like a recipe for gripes and frustration, but I didn't see any point arguing with Dio about it, and walked on past several small terraces, catching a series of conversation fragments all jumbled together.

"*This is Bijou and Hax, streaming non-stop from* Dream Speed, *which is already officially our Game of the Century— and probably yours as well.*"

"No, I'm not a fan of the categories. *Custom?* It conflates too much."

"I like the idea myself—I've never liked picking 'Other'. What word would you have preferred? Non-standard? I know—Bespoke! I'm definitely Bespoke today."

"*I'd hate to really be living in* The Synergis."

"*Oh, bullshit. A civilisation where you never have to worry about having a place to sleep or enough to eat? Where you can spend all your time playing games, farting about, or just kick back and watch the entertainment?*"

"*Where's there's nothing real to strive for, and humanity is on one giant hamster wheel? We're pets in this game!*"

"Just wish it wasn't trying to force some stupid enviro-weepy 'Drowned Earth' propaganda down our throats. Goddamn message fic."

"*So scuffed.*"

"*Am I crying? I keep crying. I've never been happier in my life.*"

"*What's this se, ze, te-hee-hee shit? Social justice warriors have already ruined this game and it hasn't even officially launched. What a frickin' joke.*"

"So, you going for DS Alliance or DS Horde? Though I guess it's more Empire versus Rebels isn't it? I'm definitely down for stealing a ship rather than working for these smug-git AIs."

"*Talk about a field day for furries.*"

"*Dream Speed* is a good name for it, because it reminds us we're going to wake up. Nothing we have here is going to make real life any better."

"I don't give a damn—this is everything I've ever wanted."

While I didn't enjoy the idea of Chocobo trainers, I was still definitely in the glass half-full to overflowing camp. Space had always been an impossible dream for me, and *DS* was going to give me fantasy space—all the wonder without the astronaut nappies. *DS* had the potential to give players everything they could ever want—if not in the main game, then in the enormous array of Challenges. Every adventure anyone had ever wanted to live, from the lone wanderer to the rebel with a bow. Every place you'd ever wanted to visit. Every person you wanted to be. For the cost of a cowl, an internet connection, and a monthly fee.

"I've never liked stories where the protagonist wakes up and it's all been a dream," a woman was saying on the large tier I was approaching. "But I embrace consensual dream adventures thoroughly and completely."

"No reservations about the potential for nightmares?" the man with her asked.

"Fewer than I had yesterday. You've read the city terms and conditions—I know that because you wouldn't be allowed out otherwise. Ryzonart has put real thought into risk management. Not that the potential for it all to go horribly wrong isn't there. We'll see how good they are at following through."

This was my destination tier, and the voices ones I both recognised and found strange. That Argentinian drawl definitely belonged to Silent, but was it deeper? And I knew Amelia Beerheart's faint Yorkshire accent well, but not attached to a voice so light and youthful. The speakers themselves could pass for Zorro and a wingless angel, in coveralls.

I didn't like how my immediate instinct was to doubt and judge. Core Units represented self-image, and it was stupid and hypocritical of me with my longer legs to question whether, out in the world, Silent could be a well-travelled engineering consultant and also a lithe, bronzed young man with a curling, sardonic mouth, or note that Amelia could not be an ethereal teen since she and Tornin were Sprocket's grandparents.

I'd hesitated on the edge of the tier long enough for them to notice me, and Amelia said: "*Corpse Light* get-together here! We only need a couple more to officially form the guild."

"They make us meet up in person for that?" I asked, startled.

"Five to start the guild," Amelia said. "And I know that voice. Kaz, isn't it so? But Leveret now?"

"That's right. I'll save Kaz for one of my alts. Um, modals."

"I have yet to decide whether calling alts 'modals' is sheer bad use, or brilliant," Silent said.

"It's a real word?" I asked, trying to figure out how Amelia had known my Core Unit name.

"It's used in logic constructions. A modal is a qualification—a possibility."

I found a [Summary] section under [Players] that allowed me to see player information. It didn't work quite like I was used to in MMOs—instead of names floating above people's heads, a tiny dot would appear near their shoulder, expanding out when I focused on it to show the same basic information I could see doing a player search.

"Not Silent Assassin?" I said.

"Already taken," Silent said. "Though perhaps I wouldn't have used it anyway. Wrong fit for the context."

Game names. Some people kept the same one in every MMO, while others were constantly changing. My male characters were usually Kazerin Fel—except for a hobbit called Bumbleproot Cucumberpatch—but my occasional female characters were more variable. I'd not used Leveret before, and there might be another player out there right now cursing me for taking it.

An influx of new arrivals demonstrated that there was going to be a particularly long period of adjustment for this game. *Corpse Light* had fifty members, though for the past year only a core of twenty had been fully active players. *DS* had brought back guildies whose forum names I barely recognised, and the majority seemed to have picked a new name for their Core Units, so matching faces to half-recognised voices was a confusing whirl, until Amelia got around to forming the guild, and found a display where she could annotate everyone's names with aliases.

TALiSON, Khajoura and Balaster had kept their usual names, but DieMortDie had become Vasharda, TazMazter was Malazan, and RemembertheFallen was now voidMaster. And there were even a couple of new recruits, Klinnia and Lady Sirah: real life friends of TALiSON, who I discovered to be a bombshell-curved white woman with rainbow-striped hair.

There were at least three times the number of people I'd been expecting for this guild meet-up, especially given the surprise unlocking of the game. Names quickly blended together, and I was glad to joined Silent and TALiSON for a trip into the interior of the island for some impromptu catering. I had two Consumables rewards to collect, and decided on strawberry smoothies and mixed nuts, while TALiSON picked hot chips, and Silent produced mounds of sweet Japanese dango sticks.

When we returned a new arrival, whose self-image was apparently Geralt of Rivia, suggested that the next person with a reward to collect should bring back beers. But he took a smoothie readily enough, then gave me the to-one-side glance that I'd already recognised as someone reading my virtual information panel.

"Whoa—you're Kaz? You're way more Asian than I expected for a Dutch bird."

The words really didn't fit the baritone growl of the player's voice, and I didn't even bother to look at the [Summary] panel before saying: "You know what they say about assumptions, Sprocket."

"Hey, I'm Wraith this time around," he said. "Man, I'm so lucky I got in near the beginning of the rush, before it was taken."

He started to go on, but caught sight of a new arrival gliding onto the terrace in a wheelchair that had taken a detour through the *Tron* school of design. "Granddad? But—you mean the game couldn't fix you?"

"If by 'fix' you mean let me totter about on two legs, it does," the baby-faced newcomer said. "But it all involves a lot of concentration. I've never learned to walk, so it isn't automatic for me. Besides, standing wrecks my synchronisation rating. Wheels are my wings, and necessary for my inner speed-demon."

He broke off in turn, catching sight of Amelia, and I moved away in mild embarrassment, because it felt like a movie moment where the music swells and everyone needs to dab their eyes. The people who were Tornin and Amelia had been married for over forty years.

The afternoon was shifting toward evening, and I headed to the nearest balcony to stare at Vessa Major all over again, with added sunset candy stripes. All around me, on the tiers above and below, and in the crowd behind me, I could hear other players pointing out the horizon, the rollercoaster, and the sheer enormous amount of people gathering at the island's peak. Words, laughter, gasps, and occasional shouts merged into a muted roar that replaced the distant hush of the ocean.

Chest tight, I worked myself away from the balcony, and went sideways along the terrace to where it narrowed, and was more built up with trees and decoratively placed rocks. Climbing up on a large rock, I sat cross-legged and breathed.

[[Out of spoons?]]

Dio had to be monitoring my physical reactions to ask that question, which was a less than comfortable development, although one I should have predicted. I took a moment before answering, and then used directed thought.

"Good to know current Earth idiom survives all the way to The Synergis."

[[Idiom is just another layer of speaking your language. Your heart rate is returning to a more regular pace. Was it the crowd or the height?]]

"Crowd. I'm fine now I've some elbow room." Recovering, anyway, and glad not to have curled up into a panting ball in front of my guild. Though not very keen on Dio's interest. I'm slow to open up to therapists, and didn't want an impromptu one in *DS*.

Fortunately Dio moved on without further comment. [[Is there a story behind the name *Corpse Light*?]]

"Remnants of a hard-core EverQuest *guild called* Chaos Corpse. *Corpse Light is the part of the guild that burned out on the raid schedule, so they made a casual sister guild. Tornin, Amelia, Far and Die—um, Vasharda— have all been playing together since before MMOs had graphics. Over twenty years."*

I looked back to where Tornin, Amelia and Vasharda formed the centre of an excited babble, and thought about fetching another tray of drinks and being social, but I couldn't, not quite yet. I'd spent years learning how to self-manage around crowds, and going back in too soon had always been a bad idea.

Besides, a cute little robot was floating past, collecting empty cups, and new arrivals were circulating with food offerings, and so I let myself sit back and enjoy putting self-images together with names I'd only ever associated with voices and character classes. Uncomfortable as this Core Unit concept made me, it was fascinating to see how people thought of themselves—or how they wanted to be—for all there were clear limits to how much we could remake ourselves. Sprocket might have replicated a well-known game character, down to the gravelly voice, but he still spoke like a sixteen year-old who hadn't figured out what was crass. I had given myself longer legs, but couldn't change the way I felt about crowds. Tornin could technically walk, but didn't need to.

"And we're all going to wake up."

Amelia and Silent had come across to join me on the rocks, and Amelia was either mind-reading, or thinking along the same lines.

"I keep reminding myself of that, too. And also that I've only been in here a couple of hours. Does the time-compaction thing bother you as well? It's the one thing I thought absolutely had to be rubbish, because it just didn't seem possible."

"We know it's possible through observation," Silent said, with a shrug. "What we don't know is the how."

"I care about who," Amelia said, waving a tray-carrying Sprocket over.

"AI or aliens?" I said, with a glance up at the motes of light wafting above our heads. Dio had been keeping quiet, but definitely hadn't gone away. "I'd say we've blown past the Turing Test. And we can't be talking to people—uh, Bio people—pretending to be Cycogs, because the sheer number of concurrent conversations just isn't viable."

"The official idea is that we're talking to ourselves," Silent said. "Just like GDG is a series of prompts, but we fill in the blanks to complete the dream, the game's Cycogs are simply a series of information feeds, and we're supposedly constructing a personality and dynamic conversation around them. So they're neither players nor AIs, but a subconscious part of our mind being fed statistics."

"A subconscious that other people can record?" Amelia said. "Not that I can quite believe in aliens-or-AIs either." She glanced up at the drift of Cycogs, who were notably not contributing to any conversations. "Not that it isn't possible, I suppose, that an AI developed and decided to make a game about AIs."

"Most common theory is the Starfighter Invitation," Silent said.

Amelia laughed. "Oh, yes. Aliens who watch eighties movies."

"If we follow *The Last Starfighter*'s pattern, then there's a space war we need to end before it gets to Earth," I said. "I suppose the game could count as a big warning about what's going to happen if we don't step up. They must be recruiting people to Skip rather than shoot, though."

"I'm totally with Driver9," Sprocket said, after finishing passing out sodas.

"Driver9's been streaming *Dream Speed* already?" I asked. Driver9 was part of MMO-focused streaming group.

"Hell yeah. Watched it while I was racing home, after word got out *DS* was unlocked," Sprocket said. "The capture in the game can only be uploaded when you log out, but he'd already posted a couple of hours' worth of play before I finally got to log on—more than I could watch. His big idea is that there really are Cycogs, but they didn't form on Planet Whatever, centuries in the future. They've formed here on Earth, now. *DS* is their way of brainwashing us."

"Indoctrination?" Amelia said. "Well, I don't see how to test that. But...Noonan?"

One of the motes of light above us dropped down to drift over her head—a formless blob entirely indistinguishable from Dio. I wondered if they could tell each other apart at a glance—or if they 'glanced' at all.

[[Amelia,]] the light said, doubled voice deeper than Dio's, and reminding me a little of dour movie butlers.

"Did Cycogs really form recently on Earth, and is *Dream Speed* a clever indoctrination program?"

Beside me Silent snorted, and muttered: "There's subtle."

[[That is as reasonable a supposition as any, Amelia,]] Noonan replied, unperturbed.

"Driver9's Cycog said 'no'," Sprocket said.

"And that wasn't quite a yes, was it?" Amelia said. "Thank you, Noonan. Sorry to have interrupted you."

[[It was no bother, Amelia,]] the Cycog said, and rose back to join the other lights above.

I frowned up at them, trying to work out if they were talking to each other in their musical language, or doing anything other than floating. It was hard to even see them against the increasingly clear stars.

"What's that line in the sky?"

"The moon, apparently," Silent said.

"What?" Cold shock rocked me: a ridiculous reaction given we were on the 'Drowned Earth'.

"Roach—my Cycog—says they think it was hit by a comet," Sprocket said.

"Think?" I asked. "The Cycogs don't know?"

"Spacefaring humans came back to Earth to find it deserted, and the moon in pieces," Silent said. "Which begs the question of what happened to the people who were here."

"And you have to get to Rank Ten or something to get the reason?" I asked, wryly.

"Probably," Amelia said. "I've been running into that roadblock every time I press for details. A way to limit progress on the main quest line. Speaking of which..."

[g]<Amelia Beerheart> Now that everyone's sufficiently lubricated, we'll take a shot at getting some guild business out of the way. I'll log this and post the discussion to the external guild forums. And will set up internal guild forums as soon as I've decided what we need. What we need, or want, from the guild is going to take some sorting out. Before I hand over to Tornin, a reminder about the fund for guild members who haven't been able to buy a GDG cowl. I know not everyone can chip in, but every pound helps. Okay, now to the business at hand.

[g]<Tornin> We're facing so much content that we need to decide whether we want this guild to purely be a social link, or to focus on some particular set of quests.

[g]<TALiSON> The prestige Challenges and the main quest are where it's at. But they're practically all lan-based, and you can only advance in lan every ten hours.

[g]<Silent> Where the playing field is uneven.

[g]<Amelia Beerheart> I've started a list of the bigger non-lan Challenges. We can set up a poll with descriptions, to help people looking for Challenges that other guild members are also interested in.

[g]<Vasharda> Yes, please. Decision paralysis here. I never thought I'd say a game had too much content.

[g]<Wraith> I totally want a team for *Glass Towers*.

[g]<Wraith> Hey—it punctuated me! When I think-pick these words it puts capitals in and everything!

[g]<Wraith> This is so weird.

[g]<TALiSON> What's *Glass Towers* like?

[g]<Wraith> It's *GTA* meets *Mirror's Edge*, and totally banging. You're in this big retro-futuristic city, where there's jet packs, and boots that let you jump from building to building, and there's sky trains and flying cars.

[g]<TALiSON> I like it already.

[g]<Wraith> The place is crawling with sentry-bots, but they're push-overs. The players are all 90% cyborg, and either super-dope spy-thief types, or bounty hunters trying to catch the thieves. You can do anything. I flew a car into a building, and got away by running to the roof and jumping off. I've already got three guns, but there's bigger targets that I'll need a group for. Only bad thing is everyone's a noodle.

"A noodle?" I said out loud, while two other guildies said the same thing in chat.

Sprocket-Wraith grinned, producing an expression far too young for his character's grim features.

[g]<Wraith> Neutrals. Straight up and down and no t
–

He paused, and glanced at Amelia, whose expression was closer to mild entertainment than grandmotherly disapproval.

[g]<Amelia Beerheart> We get the idea. Any other recommendations? You were saying something about a magic school Challenge, TALiSON?

[g]<TALiSON> *Veil*. But it's not group-focused. Magic school on an island, where wizards and guild leaders and so forth send their kids. Heavy on the roleplaying: forming alliances, making friends, not getting pushed off a cliff, all while there's some kind of ancient evil being unlocked in the background.

[g]<Lady Sirah> *Harry Potter* rip-off dating sim, in other words.

[g]<TALiSON> Closer to *Utena*. We're all wearing swords and capes, and I love it SO MUCH. I only managed to tear myself away because my character was sent to bed.

[g]<Klinnia> I need a group for a mech academy Challenge. It's one of those where you need to cooperate to run the mechs.

[g]<voidMaster> *Pacific Rim* or *Voltron* cooperation?

[g]<Klinnia> *Voltron*. But the tone looks *Evangelion*. Dark.

[g]<Malazan> I've signed up for *Proving Ground*. It's a variant battle royale on an enormous scale, no squads, though you can cooperate if you want. Fantasy kingdom chooses its ruler every fifty years by sending candidates into this massive ancient magic testing ground. You have to sign up before a certain date to participate. Limited to a hundred thousand players. The top prestige non-lan Challenge available at this stage, apparently.

[g]<Vasharda> Decision paralysis increasing.

[g]<Leveret> There's just so much. Any one of these games sounds like it will take weeks to get through. And they're all...my Cycog called them filler.

[g]<Silent> Yep. These are the sidequests. The main quest line's the one that gets you the ship, and gets you off-planet. And out of the...we're still in the starter zone. Can you believe that?

[g]<Far Cryinggame> Hey all. What have I missed?

[g]<Vasharda> Deciding where to start. We're going to spend the rest of our lives playing this game.

[g]<TALiSON> Don't say that! In MMO stories, that's always a heavy hint that people dying in-game will die in real life, or that someone won't be able to log out. Has anyone confirmed that people can log out?

[g]<Wraith> Yeah, Driver9 did to post the start of his Let's Play. And to confirm how this five hour shutout thing works. And Best Result, there.

[g]<Tornin> The five hours can be broken into segments?

[g]<Wraith> Yup. Play for an hour, log out for an hour, play for hour, and it works out the same as playing for five hours, then logging out for five hours. So if you have to go do something, you're not locked out.

[g]<voidMaster> Best of all, if you want to advance in the Ian Challenges, it's a way to skip the delay between Ian training. The ten game hour wait counts whether you're logged in or not.

This was of immediate and strong interest to me. All the possible sidequests sounded fabulous, but I still wanted my own spaceship above anything else.

Achievement
First to reach Rank Two
[Nina Stella]
Awarded Custom Modal

"Awesome!" Sprocket said, to my surprise, and shot to his feet. "Quick, everyone, watch the crowd."

He rushed to the balcony, and leaned forward, looking along the vast sweep of the terraces, and we followed suit with an air of mild bewilderment. I moved last, not over-keen to remind myself how many people surrounded me.

The tiers directly below us were large and particularly packed, but before their weight could try to crumble me, the whole of my attention was taken by a sudden metallic blooming, as if great silvery flowers had suddenly sprung up all across the terraces.

But these were not flowers. They were cages. Streetlight-tall poles, each with a dangling cage occupied by a seated, coverall-clad person, their legs dangling between the bars.

"They're...they're suspended," I said. "I thought that was a joke."

[g]<Wraith> It's because they sent Nina Stella hate mail! It happened the first time she ranked, too, but there were less people around.

He burst into uproarious laughter, and waved at the nearest suspended player, who gestured back appropriately.

"This game is so scuffed," someone from the tier below said loudly. "We can try and kill people, but don't call each other names."

[g]<Klinnia> The mods are actually going to enforce the harassment policy? Holy Hell.

[g]<TALiSON> But Nina Stella still gets all the hate mail?

[g]<Tornin> Messages that breach the courtesy rules don't go through to her, apparently. Which is cheering on one level, but an indicator that messaging here isn't private. Frankly, I'm not even sure our thoughts are private.

[g]<TALiSON> That should bother me more. I know it should. It's just...this game, guys. This GAME.

[g]<Wraith> I don't care what they read. And I'm not doing *anything* that might get me kicked out.

This produced a murmur of agreement, with an undercurrent of discomfort as we looked out at people who had just discovered that in-game email wasn't private. I by no means objected to the clear demonstration that the harassment rules were serious business, but the implications of their enforcement were no small thing.

I was in the game, and the game was in me, even if the link was virtual. My thoughts became words, and the Cycogs, real or not, vetted our interactions. And yet I— almost all players—would likely just accept that because the game was so brilliantly beyond everything we hoped for.

But if Ryzonart could read our thoughts along with our mail, the question of the how, the who and the why of *Dream Speed* became more important than ever.

I don't think I'd stop playing.

Maybe.

Probably not.

slowly and surely drew their plans

Spectacular as Vessa Major was, most of my guild were just as interested as I was in spaceships and sidequests, and soon started heading out. This was a handy development for me, and I used Silent, Far and voidMaster as a combination shield and distraction to get back up to the pod station. It wasn't easy, because even the ramps were choked with people and noise, and I only got through them by walking in voidMaster's wake, with my eyes focused on his feet.

"Well past two million concurrent players now," Far commented, as we lined up for a pod. He had turned out to be a slender white man, golden-haired and porcelain delicate, and not at all what I'd expected from his voice.

"It feels like all two million started in the same zone," Silent said. "There's at least a few hundred thousand on this island, all in view, and not the faintest hint of lag."

"Aliens or AI?" voidMaster asked, with a sly smile. He was fit and muscular, his accent South London, his face Bollywood-handsome.

"Aliens," Silent said firmly.

"Only took a couple of hours for you to stop pooh-poohing the idea?" voidMaster asked. "Why not AI?"

"Hardware. Nothing we have could run this game. I don't care how many server farms Ryzonart have. And since an AI that formed on Earth would be limited to our systems, it must be aliens."

"Technically, the Cycogs are alien AI anyway," Far pointed out.

"I make no judgment on what kind of aliens. I simply don't believe we have the hardware to run a game like this, no matter how much of GDG is a construct of our sleeping minds."

Our turn for a pod came, and as soon as the door shut out the noise and the press of bodies, I could breathe again. "Would you quit if Ryzonart could read your mind?" I asked, dropping gratefully onto a seat.

"Nope," voidMaster said. "I live for this stuff. And Ryzonart wouldn't get much out of the bleak wasteland of Pop Tarts and anime porn that has prime rental space in my head."

"Not a chance," Far said, as the pod stopped. He stepped off with a wave, leaving the rest of us to travel on.

"Possibly," Silent said, after a pause. "I'm less bothered by mind-reading aliens than I am by mind-reading humans. Or email-reading aliens, which is all we've confirmed so far. I'll withhold any decision about whether I want to be playing a game run by aliens until I see any negative effects."

"Negative effects like your thoughts being livestreamed, or Cycog world domination plot enabled?" voidMaster asked.

"Either."

"It doesn't require scheming aliens or mindreading to be disastrous. Just people loving this game so much they won't do anything else."

"Too much of a good thing," voidMaster agreed, grinning. "I bet that five hour shut-out rule isn't necessary at all, but if they didn't have it, people would let their kids starve, or wouldn't get up until their cats started chewing off their ears."

"I feel like I'll miss so much if I log out," I admitted. "Things like that mass suspension won't happen too often. But I want to get into space as soon as possible, and it looks like many brief logouts is the most efficient way to work on ranking up. It's going to be hard to resist spending all my time—"

"In the *Harry Potter* dating sim?" voidMaster suggested.

"Maybe. I like magic school stories, and I think I'll definitely go for a fantasy sidequest, to contrast the main quest."

"Sign up for *Proving Ground* before you log, if you think it looks like fun," voidMaster said. "It's definitely going to run out of slots real soon."

"Guild cooperation might be helpful there," Silent said.

"Get each other to the final round, and we'll duke it out for the crown," voidMaster agreed, then stood up as the pod slowed. "My stop."

"Mine as well," Silent said. "Looks like we both have underwater views. See you in the sidequests, Leveret."

"Later Kaz," voidMaster added, as the door closed behind them.

I let out a second breath, not because travelling with my guildies had bothered me, but when I get too much crowd, I can only really decompress with some quality alone time.

Not that it seemed I would ever be fully alone in *DS*. I glanced up at the glowing mote hovering above me, but didn't speak until I was all the way back to my Snug, seated in the cockpit, and looking out over the velvet, milk and diamond of night sky and ocean. The curves of the rollercoaster mirrored a pale shadow across the sky: the ring of debris that was the moon.

"Does it bother you when Bios ignore you, Dio?"

[[You mean these brief, blissful periods when I need not cater to your mayfly attention span?]]

"Or any other time," I said, trying not to smile.

[[I'd consider it rude if you didn't respond when I directed a comment or question to you. Otherwise, not at all.]]

"And if I asked you to confirm the theories we were discussing, would you laugh, or tell me to get to Rank Ten?"

[[Both,]] Dio said, laughing.

"What, so if I get to a certain rank you'll tell me the truth about Ryzonart and all your sinister plans?"

[[Ranking gives you access to more information about The Synergis. Whether you'll consider what you discover sinister—or merely soul-destroying—remains to be seen.]]

"Okay, that does not incline me to work on my ranking," I said. "I haven't forgotten that bit about The Synergis having run out of Bios, either."

[[Yes, we can always do with more toys.]]

Dio was such a troll that it was never possible to tell when te was being serious, but if the main quest involved more than grinding my way up the ranks, I'd better remember every contradiction. Right now, though, I needed to decide what to do next.

"Is The Synergis super-crowded, Dio? If Bios can avoid aging and most health issues, don't you—won't you eventually end up with too many people?"

[[Overall growth is stable. While some Bios do become more cautious as they age, risk-taking behaviour greatly increases for many. Combine that with a general inclination to travel and compete in early years, rather than have children, and there are times when we nearly slow to equilibrium.]] There was a little pause, then Dio added: [[There are some very popular planets, but most Synergis worlds are not so full as yours.]]

Dio plainly hadn't forgotten elevated heartbeats. I looked out at the ring of the moon, disliking having anyone with such a vantage point on me, but then said: "Would you be able to warn me if any of the Challenges involve big crowd scenes? That would take the fun out of it for me."

[[Define 'big crowd'.]]

"When people are packed together like walls around you. Particularly if there isn't a nearby exit, or at least something you can put your back to. Does the main quest require anything like that?"

[[No. Very well, I've added an extra search filter for you.]]

I immediately tried it, and didn't see any notable decrease in the mass of quests. Then I spent some quality time reading the descriptions of the Challenges guild members had recommended.

"Is *Veil* really a dating sim?"

[[Sleeping your way through the student body isn't technically a goal. There is nothing to stop you from trying, however. There are several search terms you can use to identify Challenges focused on a variety of interpersonal relationships. Most of those won't be accessible this early in the game, however.]]

So Ryzonart wasn't going to shy away from one aspect of virtual life sure to complicate *Dream Speed's* reception. There had of course been an enormous amount of speculation about whether *DS* would allow sex with other players, let alone structure games around romancing NPCs. The majority view had been that it would bring too much negative press, and might even lead to a whole new category of lawsuits. Of course, no-one had doubted players would try to hook up, if there was nothing to prevent them, but if *DS* was including scripted romances with NPCs, players would be dealing with a lot more than awkwardly posed cut-scenes. Instead of spaceships, the game would be known for countless virtual first times. An intimate exploration of alien anatomy. The complications of people who could wear animal modals. Animal-like aliens. And the question of who exactly you were with, if you spent time with an NPC.

"Who is—" I began, then paused, thinking through the best way to get relatively clear answers from Dio. "In The Synergis, in the virtual Challenges, are the NPCs simply very well-scripted computer programs, or what we'd call AIs, or are they being controlled by Cycogs?"

[[We've never programmed an entity that has achieved self-realisation—nor do we truly want to—but we can produce Constructs with behavioural processes complex enough to fool you Bios. In virtual Challenges, you will for the most part interact with Constructs, but an administrating Cybercognate might step in at any time, to handle unusual interactions.]]

"And which am I talking to now?"

[[Cybercognate.]]

Cycog or a Construct of a Cycog. I frowned. "The world administrator was, um, Arefiel. You mean I'm talking to an administrator pretending to be a fledgling? Or, who was...in the demos the Cycog was Ryzon, and te called terself a Concierge. Which are you?"

[[Which do you think I am?]]

But there was no real way for me to be sure I wasn't just talking to a Construct, and I still definitely mostly didn't believe Cycogs were anything but fictional, and I suppose my expression said that clearly enough, because Dio laughed, and drifted down to hover a few inches in front of my face.

[[In a world game like this, several Cycogs would ensure its running: a combination of the city administrators and the world administrator, and perhaps even a dedicated Concierge on particularly populated worlds. It only takes a fraction of an administrator's attention to supplement the work of the Constructs, so a city administrator could be...entertaining many thousands of Bios at the same time.]]

Ter tone held clear note of innuendo. "Cycogs sort of do sex work, then?" I asked, surprised. "It's not something they find uncomfortable? Or boring?"

[[Is breathing boring? So little of a city administrator's attention would need to be devoted to any individual Bio that it is almost autonomous. And some of us enjoy the puzzle aspect of Bio psychology. Besides, just as Bios go through a process of learning themselves, most of us put on a synthsuit at least once, to experience a Bio sense range. Some of us like it a great deal, and amuse ourselves mightily, while others wear synths simply because at times it is convenient to have hands.]]

"Oh. So like you are...you can't touch things? At all?"

[[Not in a way you would find meaningful. Synthsuits also help us move about: in this simulation we are cheating, but a Cycog in The Synergis moves at perhaps a quarter of a Type Three's walking pace. So slow, so dull. We could, of course, just ride our Bios, but they have a sad tendency to fall off cliffs, or down wells, so we often wear fast things, and leave you in our dust. Fledglings have their own progression in The Synergis, and I should gain at least one synthsuit during the game.]]

I wasn't sure I liked this development. Did that mean any person I met could be a Cycog pretending to be a Bio? And Dio was an uncomfortable enough companion as a glowing mote. Giving tem hands seemed like a recipe for mischief.

Then again... "So you could wear a synthetic Chocobo and I could ride *you* about?"

Dio laughed. [[You can ride me any way you wish, small hare, should the occasion arise.]]

I blushed, and then was annoyed with myself for reacting. I wasn't sure if Dio had just figured out a new way to tease me, or was actually flirting, but it wasn't a complication I wanted to deal with.

"What happens if someone who's young—really young—plays *Veil?*" I asked, in hopes of distracting my own personal peanut gallery.

[[Look at the player details of that junior guild fellow of yours.]]

I frowned, then searched on Sprocket's new name.

Wraith

[Roach]

Rank: 0

Under Eighteen, Content Access Limited

Status: Online/Challenge

Accepting: [Email] [Message]

Guild: [Corpse Light]

Location: [Vessa]

"How is the content limited?"

[[A number of Challenges are unavailable, and others present modified content. Consumables adjust to age restrictions, and certain player interactions are blocked.]]

"Blocked how? With the hate-mail those players decided to send to Nina Stella, they still sent it, but email can be blocked at the server level. What happens if someone tries to, uh, grab a kid?"

[[This.]]

I gasped, because a blue light had gripped me. It looked very similar to the lan that I had been struggling to control to gain my rank, but felt like icy jelly, with barely enough give for me to breathe.

[[That, again, is a convenience of this simulation. The actions of Bios are naturally more difficult to control in The Synergis itself.]]

"What if the player lies about their age?"

[[Good luck with that.]]

Starting with a Core Unit based on your self-image would make that difficult, but unless Ryzonart really could read minds, Dio seemed over-confident to me. There were so many potential pitfalls to true virtual reality, and it surely wouldn't have been possible for Ryzonart to anticipate them all.

I realised I was stressing about this, picturing outraged newspaper headlines and point-scoring politicians, because I was worried that The Synergis would be snatched away from me. That I wouldn't get my virtual spaceship, or attend a magic school, or experience any of the thousands of life goals true virtual reality could let me achieve. I was far less concerned about the possibility that Ryzonart was run by aliens with a secret agenda, or the chance that Cycogs were real.

Well, I supposed it depended on the secret agenda.

I packed away all the tight-stomach feelings, deciding that since I would not be able to impact how governments might react to the reality of the virtual, I'd best just focus on enjoying as much of *DS* as possible, as quickly as possible.

"I'm going to log out, Dio," I said. "If it's true that jumping in and out will maximise the number of times I can work on ranking each day."

[[Yes, you can optimise the mandatory shut-out that way.]]

I was reading the logout information. "Do I really have to put myself in the Soup before I log out? Aren't I safe in my Snug?"

[[Safe, yes, but if you log out in that chair you're likely to wake with a crick in your neck, and sitting in a puddle. The Soup will place your Core Unit in suspension.]]

"So the beds are just decorative?"

[[The beds are most certainly being put to use.]]

I grimaced at Dio, but otherwise ignored ter amusement. "Do I need to sleep at all in the game?"

[[It's not uncommon for players to experience a level of mental fatigue in extended virtual environments. That is part of the reason you are required to log out—and why you will usually be transitioned to at least ten minutes of natural sleep during any standard logout. Physically, you will tire less easily than outside the simulation, but there is nothing to bar you from sleeping if you wish.]]

"If I log out in the bed, will you leave me there, or move me?"

[[That would depend on how long you are gone.]]

I really didn't like the idea of Dio moving me while I was gone, even though none of this was real, and Dio was probably a Construct. Sighing, I walked over to Storage and opened it, contemplating myself in the mirror-reflection of the technomagic goop.

Before facing the mint-chill, I took a moment to sign up for the limited player Challenge voidMaster had recommended, purely because it was apparently the most prestigious. It looked like I could register for it without starting it right now.

Proving Ground
Seven circles to the Crown.
Solo
Narrative, PVP, Prestige
Length: one to four hours, staged (1 of 7).
Virtual (94,234 / 100,000).
Custom suppression modal.

Then I selected the [Logout] option, and was given five seconds to put myself away.

I obediently stepped in, wondering if logging out of such a solid reality would be rough, and then my thoughts greyed out to sleep.

17

bio break

Waking to the familiar chime of the cowl's alarm clock, I remembered the Drowned Earth, and thought sleep would never be the same. I would always be leaving a world behind.

At least I felt rested, even after putting in a full day's worth of world discovery, adventure, blue mist manipulation, and socialising. It felt like it had all happened yesterday, though: a clear memory, but with a night's respite to smooth the edges. A ten minute night, but apparently enough.

And there were cooking smells. My parents must be back from town.

Standing up, I felt off, cludgy, and it wasn't until I'd freshened up and headed for the main part of the house that I realised I was missing the spring of my fit virtual self—and perhaps the longer legs. Waking up would mean always leaving me behind as well, and *Dream Speed's* five to one ratio on life was really going to mess up who I felt was 'me'.

"Heya." My mother smiled at me from the couch, muting the news. "Tired of it already?"

"Managing the five-hour shutout. You can break it into bits, rather than having to do five hours in, five hours out."

"Excellent!" my father said, gesturing with a spatula. "We decided on country hours for dinner because we wanted to dive in as soon as possible, but being able to jump in and out without penalty makes future plans much simpler."

"And how was it?" my mother said. "As good as we hoped?"

"Better. I'm not even going to try to describe it. You should go in cold, if you can."

"Too late for that," my father said. "Everything has lit up with the news, and pictures of those ridiculous cities, and grabs of mecha fighting. I didn't even realise this was a mecha fighting game."

"That's..." I shook my head helplessly. "The mecha fighting is a sidequest. The tiniest bit of *DS*. The thing's enormous. But, no, I'm not going to tell you more. I don't want to spoil what it feels like to wake up there."

"Okay, okay. Set the table, then. Greek tonight."

I obeyed, just in time for my father to bring out plates of lamb skewers and fried halloumi.

"You're going to love the food rewards," I said, squeezing a lemon wedge. "Vast arrays of Earth food, and I heard that the higher tiers have other-planet food, and right now I'm totally ready to believe that it'll taste like it's from other planets too."

"What starter city did you say you chose? Is it the one with the skyscraper trees?"

"No, mine's the rollercoaster over islands. Skyscraper trees?"

I snagged the tablet my mother was browsing, and synced it with the big TV, then brought up images of *Dream Speed's* starter cities. There was Vessa. Kivion looked like a rollercoaster that had contracted into a bird's nest whirl, all set on poles above open water. The skyscraper trees were at Anefta: great white columns rising out of the breakers of an endlessly long beach, with the columns' upper reaches dividing and sub-dividing like the branches of a tree—and all decorated with the compact pill-shapes of thousands upon thousands of Snugs.

Unable to resist, I began browsing more images, scenes from countless stories. The mecha were Art Nouveau-inspired, which made me far more inclined to try that Challenge out. One of the starter cities had the Snugs attached to petal-shaped loops surrounding underwater domes. There were a lot of videos of the mass suspension on Vessa Major, and another of a crowd transforming the ubiquitous coveralls into an excuse for an impromptu rendition of the *Ghostbusters* theme song.

And then I made the mistake of following a link to "Medusa-Bro".

"Ach, I did not want to see that," my mother said.

My father, unfazed, said: "Python-Bro seems more appropriate."

"I guess when people are given sliders for every body part, this is inevitable," I said, shuddering.

"Is—is it *moving*?" my mother asked.

I turned off the screen, and we laughed at the ridiculousness of it all, and then cleared the table.

"Taia, why don't you go up to your Oma's house and show her how to play?" my mother asked, stacking the dishwasher.

"So she can tell me again that she has better things to do than silly TV-picture games?"

"She promised to try it at least once," my mother said. "Though what she would make of new-style medusas I don't know."

"The game's code of conduct includes no full nudity in public places. And Ryzonart seems serious about enforcing courtesy standards. Okay, I'll talk to her."

"While we try to decide whether to go with our guild's starter city or another," my father said. "I'm leaning toward an underwater one."

"Skyscraper trees," my mother replied.

I left them still debating, and snagged a light jacket, since evening in the Lowlands in September brought a touch of chill. It would be quicker to grab a bike from the collection outside the door, of course, but I was missing my running days, and it would only take ten minutes to walk down the twilit road.

The opportunity to buy a house so close to my grandmother's was one of the reasons my parents had given up their nomad lifestyle to return to the Netherlands. I hadn't been happy at the time, since it had been a wrench to move from a Malaysian beach town to the most rural part of the Lowlands, and my Oma's opinion of me had always involved long silences, or corrections of my pronunciation.

Until we'd moved here permanently, I'd spent more time in New Zealand, South Korea and Malaysia than I had in the country of my birth, and my accent showed it.

Walking in blissful solitude toward the lighted windows of her house, I already knew that I would see my Oma in silhouette through the kitchen window: tall, determinedly upright, her arthritis-clawed hands hidden by the sill. Washing dishes, because she always kept country hours, and ate her dinner as soon as it grew dark. She would watch the news before going to bed, and then be up at the dawn, out doing chores on the single acre left of the once-expansive farm.

The door was only locked when my Oma went to bed, so it was simple enough to know and walk in. My mother might believe Oma had promised to try *Dream Speed,* but I wasn't at all surprised to see the cowl my mother had bought still sitting unopened on the sideboard.

"Hi Oma," I said. "How was your day?"

My Oma glanced at me, then said: "Close the door, girl. The night is cold."

"Yes, Oma," I said, wiping my shoes carefully on the wiry mat just inside the door. Oma did not like dirt tracked through her house. I took my coat off before she could remind me of that as well.

"And have you found a proper way to spend your time?" Oma asked. "Or do you intend to stay the whole of your life a child in the house of your parents?"

"Not the whole of my life, no," I said, keeping an upbeat note to my voice. "It depends on how long it takes for my business to grow a steady income stream. I have a small advantage because I can create web pages supporting multiple languages, but I still need to build a reputation."

"You cannot work in the company of someone established, to build this reputation?"

Two different shouty bosses had more than made clear to me that if I wanted a career in design, it wouldn't be working for someone else. I still had unreasonable clients to deal with, but at least—while living with my parents—I could refuse the worst commissions.

The question of how long I was willing to try this while not making anything resembling a living wage was not one I wanted to thrash out with my Oma, so I firmly changed the subject.

"Moe sent me down to set up your guided dream game cowl. The game she told you about released today and I think you'd—"

I paused, not because my Oma had sniffed, but just wondering what she'd make of The Synergis, and waking up naked in a Snug, and having her own personal Cycog assigned. She was so fiercely independent that I couldn't see her enjoying playing Chocobo. I wasn't even certain she'd like to rebuild herself according to her self-image. I did think that in The Synergis she'd be free of the arthritis that made the simplest task a matter of grit and endurance, and found that I really wanted to convince her to try it out.

Talking about her hands wouldn't get me far, though. Oma did not admit to weakness, and pointedly ignored specially-made utensils, heat lamps, rubs, magnetic bracelets, and any other piece of science or quackery designed to offer relief.

"I spent a lot of today in a forest," I said instead. "All moss and meadow clearings, and small animals everywhere. And then on an island—a place with lots of islands. *Dream Speed* lets you travel, go all over the world, in all different eras, and doesn't have to take up any of your waking day at all. I'm called Leveret in the game, and I, uh, is it okay for me to go in your bedroom to set up the cowl?"

The sound Oma made could—just—be interpreted as permission, so I scooped up the box and went into the Spartan bedroom that still had not fully acknowledged the death of my Opa.

My mother had set up a wireless environment for Oma years ago, so it was simple enough to plug in the micro-console, set it to downloading *Dream Speed*, and feed in the details of the account we'd prepared for Oma. Like all MMOs, an internet connection was mandatory, though Ryzonart had claimed there'd be no issues with ping or slow speeds when in the game.

I was unfolding the cowl when I noticed Oma had come to watch me from the doorway.

"All you need to do is put it on when you're about to get into bed," I said, demonstrating by dropping the loosely shaped headpiece over my hair. Light cloth settled over my shoulders, and I fastened the Velcro that would keep it from slipping off. "Then press the big button on your console. That's all."

My Oma just looked at me. Feeling foolish, I pulled the cowl off and smoothed it onto the bed.

"You can also use it as an alarm clock, if you want. GDG helps people to sleep deeply, and they respond to the in-built alarm best. That's what these buttons are for, as well. One's so that you can easily wake someone up without having to shake them out of the dream. The other's a smoke detector—they did some tests, back when the cowls came out, and people wearing cowls actually woke up in response to their cowl every time, while some normal sleepers didn't hear ceiling smoke alarms."

I was rattling on, and made myself stop and take a long breath. "Any questions Oma? Or messages for Moe?"

My Oma shook her head, so I escaped, slipping past her and heading back to the kitchen. I was used to my Oma's stern silences, but I still didn't manage them very well. I'd been terrified of her as a child: she'd been so tall, grim as flint, and never—so far as I could tell—happy to see me. Today she simply nodded when I made my goodbyes, and turned to putting away the dishes.

"Well, I tried, Moe," I muttered, heading back out to the starlight. Perhaps my mother would manage to convince Oma to try the game out. If not, well, there'd be no problem at all reselling the cowl. I should probably sell my old one, for that matter.

No, wait. What I should be doing was taking advantage of a brief window of time.

Ever since Demo 1, there had naturally been plenty of fan-made *Dream Speed* product, and I'd even contributed myself, but with so little known about the game, it had all been focused on the same few points. The information flood-gates might have opened today, but most players wouldn't even have hit their first play session limit.

I started to trot, already thinking through possibilities. I didn't want to miss my next training session, but before then I could surely manage one simple design which would work for T-shirts, stickers, mugs, phone and tablet skins.

I set my phone to warn me of the time to log back in, then settled in front of my computer and began working. A blue world, a swathe of star-specked black, an uneven ring for the moon, all as background to the cockpit section of a Snug, with a coverall clad figure partly visible through the window. I could use the image as the basis of numerous variations, with or without text. I began doodling options to go with it.

Who drowned the Earth?

Bio of The Synergis.

Come to The Synergis. We have Core Units.

My Core Unit is a Lie.

My alarm went off as I was staring at this last one, and I grimaced, then rubbed the back of my neck. I'd been unable to resist spending time on detail work, and not only hadn't uploaded anything, I didn't have anything finished.

Torn, I hesitated, but then decided to stick with the plan of logging in to work on my rank. Then, well, I guess I could log right back out again. The five hour restriction made it not so bad, since I had to spend as much time out of the game as in it. It's a pity I couldn't take my computer with me, and do the work in-game.

Could I?

"Dio?" I stepped out of the Soup, looking around as lights slowly brightened in response to my presence. "I'd wonder if you were here, but I've realised that even if this wasn't a game that could put you wherever it wanted, you'd probably get some sort of warning when I log back in."

[[Very true. You're just in time for more lan training.]]

"Exactly. But I wanted to ask a question first. Is there any way to create digital art while in *Dream Speed*, and export it in useful high quality format back to my PC?"

[[Of course. The Synergis naturally has all manner of devices to keep our Bios entertained. There's more than one option of that sort in the Tier 3 [Tools] rewards.]]

"Let me rephrase that. Is there any way, right now, that I could get my hands on something that would let me create digital art, and access the files on my PC?"

[[No.]]

"Bah." It had been too much to hope for.

[[Unless you attain Rank Two, of course. You could choose [External Access] from the ranking perks, and you have a storage device for stream-capture purposes. If you rank during this session, I might even arrange to add suitable equipment to the Tier 1 [Tools] rewards. Nothing as complex as the Tier 3 rewards, but probably adequate to whatever your purpose might be.]]

I frowned at the mote drifting around the ceiling. "Can all Cycogs just add rewards like you do?"

[[The role of an assigned Cybercognate is to produce a high-ranking Bio. In the context of this simulation, it's negligible to offer such incentives. In The Synergis itself, incentive arrangements are more likely where the Bio is already high-ranking, and has been shown to respond to rewards in this manner.]]

"So you're trying to work out whether to use the carrot or the stick on me?"

[[Bios respond to positive reinforcement far better than beatings,"]] Dio said.

"A conclusion born of much empirical observation?" I grimaced at the idea.

Dio flickered through rainbows. [[Lan travel is a system created by Bios,]] te said. [[And Bios ably demonstrated the limits of cruelty long before The Synergis.]]

"Do—does The Synergis ever use the stick?"

[[Why bother? There are so many Bios who want to grow their strength, and it's no real effort to maintain those who retire from the Challenge. Sometimes they come back, reinvigorated, if you leave them alone long enough.]]

All very benevolent. But to make the major decision of this game, I needed to find a way to scratch The Synergis' surface, to learn whether the fictional utopia had a dystopian core. Was it an Omelas, with Paradise purchased at the expense of some hidden victim? Or a Matrix, where a mundane surface hid a battery farm?

"What percentage of people leave The Synergis, Dio?"

[[It would be, say, ten in every million.]]

"That's less than I expected."

[[The 'better to reign in Hell' attitude rarely survives a dramatic loss of living standards. While some enclaves are quite comfortable—better than your little backwater—most are not what you'd term post-scarcity. Life spans are much shorter, options are fewer. And many of them devolve into personal fiefdoms, which are fun only for the Bios at the top of the pile.]]

"You don't, uh, police the enclaves in any way?"

[[Only in one aspect. No enclave in our territory is permitted to prevent any person the equivalent maturity of sixteen of your years from choosing emigration to The Synergis, or to hide that they have that choice.]]

"I bet that's popular in the fiefdoms."

[[We provide a convenient bogeyman for some leaders, but others maintain an excellent relationship with The Synergis. On your putative enclave, Delar, almost half of them come to us. Most on reaching majority, but there is a second wave when they begin to physically decline, and discover hypocrisy.]]

"What about people living in The Synergis? Do they often try to rebel?"

[[Some. There's an inevitable amount of wastage, but we get most units through to useful production.]]

"Are you deliberately trying to describe this in the worst possible terms?"

Musical laughter. [[Yes.]]

"Why?"

[[Because your expressions are so funny. And it's useful to know how you take a little light taunting.]]

"If Bios weren't your means of getting about the universe, would Cycogs keep us around for the entertainment value? Or would you wipe us out?"

[[What, run around shouting 'exterminate', as if we didn't have anything better to do? On the whole I think we'd just leave you to your planets and ignore you. But some of us enjoy Bios. Not just the ones with significant lan, either. I like Gallian pfeffers best. From Earth, I am very fond of foxes. My favourite is the fennec, but all foxes appeal to me.

You're not going to turn out to be a trickster god, are you Dio?

[[I could contrive to be as annoying as one. But I am perhaps too direct.]]

"Do Bios worship Cycogs? Do you think of yourselves as gods?"

[[Some. And some. Not a large number, and it's not an official position. Some argue that high-ranking Bios are in the process of becoming gods.]]

I considered this. "Depending on whether your definition of gods is the makers behind it all, or just someone with the power to make things happen?"

[[On that point, there is now an artistic interface available in the Tier 1 [Tools] rewards. But you won't be able to export your work without the [External Access] perk, and gaining rank for that is not optional.]]

"Chase that carrot," I muttered, but then shrugged. "Well, I know it's possible for people to get to Rank Two quickly, so let's just go for it. Is it more filling in shapes?"

[[No, now you must use the Ian as a shield. Form and thicken the Ian to prevent penetration.]]

"That sounds a little bit awesome." I activated my focus, and started in.

Trial Successful.
Attempt: 1
Rank Two achieved.
Trial Reward:
[Rank Perk]
[Tier 1 Apparel Pattern]
[Tier 1 Décor Pattern]
[Tier 1 Consumable Pattern]

I dropped, folding down cross-legged, then lay back to stare at the curved ceiling of my Snug until my panting subsided.

"Any rugs in the Tier 1 Décor rewards?" I said at last.

[[Many.]]

"I definitely need something to collapse upon. Will I ever be able to use Ian without needing to fall over afterwards?"

[[You will be able to use it for longer, and have more to draw upon. At this stage, each time you push yourself, the next attempt will be easier.]]

"If Ian is an equivalent of soul, does that mean we're making our souls bigger?"

[[It's not what you'd term your soul. Or, to be more correct, it's an off-shoot of what could be termed your soul, not the soul itself. Think of it as hair if you wish. Something produced by the central core of your Self, but you are no less your Self with a crewcut than you are play-acting Rapunzel.]]

"Hair growth usually isn't an act of willpower," I said, laughing at the thought of me sitting down and frowning hard until I was buried in hair. "Reminds me of a doll I had ages ago.   You filled the head with playdough and squeezed."

[[Yes,   there   are   limitations   to   the   analogy. Complicated by the tendency to use 'lan' to cover both the extrusion and the core. But you have grown this session. Do you think it was the carrot?]]

Sitting up, I shrugged. "How could I know for sure? I definitely liked the idea of having a magic shield. Lan seems to be very versatile."

I began browsing my rewards, looking first at [Perks], because I hadn't been offered any before.

"Hey, you said I needed to get to Rank, um, 10 or something to be able to name my Snug."

[[I'm very unreliable.]]

"Dio, everything you say needs to be taken with a grain of salt the size of Gibraltar."

[[I'd recommend a small salty moon. Though I have managed to add a drawing tablet to Tier 1 [Tools], as promised.]]

I activated [External Access] before I could be tempted by the rest of the small list of perks, and switched immediately over to [Tools] to claim my tablet.

By the time I'd collected an impressively large and thin screen from the Soup, I'd also found the new menu commands for [External Access], and verified that I could reach the files on the computer I'd linked for screen captures.

[[The tablet is able to convert standard file types, but you'll have some adjustment time learning the toolset. We haven't partnered with any vendors to allow you use of familiar applications, as yet.]]

That stopped me en route to the table. "Are you thinking of doing that? Setting up office buildings? Letting people have business meetings here? Turning *DS* into a nightmare for people who go to work only to be sent off to The Synergis to turn an eight hour working day into twenty-eight?"

[[If nothing else, we will host countless last-minute assignment writing sessions.]]

"But is turning this into a work environment part of Ryzonart's plans?"

[[It's not uncommon for Bios to put time-slipped virtual environments to practical use. Only a few hundred of Dream Speed's players have actively begun attempts to put time in The Synergis to practical use, but I expect many will follow your lead.]]

"You seem to be not answering my question."

[[No.]] Dio made it a distinct statement. [[No, that will not be developed.]]

Was Dio annoyed? Or trying to hide something behind a terse response? I thought about pushing it, but decided I wanted to get on with my designs. I'd remember that odd tone though, and be wary of The Synergis using their time manipulation to lock us into ridiculous work days.

A whole new set of graphics tools weren't ideal for quickly finishing a job, but with some help from Dio I was soon familiar enough with the tablet to start work on the designs. The first thing I did was crop the image of the Snug down to the cockpit window. Then I tightened it up, making the glimpse of starter coverall more recognisable while placing a stripe of reflection to hide any distinguishing features. The biggest moment of the game for me was still the first time I'd sat in my cockpit and looked out at the Drowned Earth. Everyone would start in their own Snug, and go to the only window, and look out at different views of this world.

The layout options took hours, but I was more than pleased with the end result. I'd included variants for my primary languages, but my favourite was the least text-focused, and I thought perhaps I'd order myself a t-shirt. First, though, I'd have to get it all uploaded, which I couldn't do from inside the game.

"I'm going to log again to submit these to the major sites. You've been a big help today, Dio. Thank you. Not that it hasn't been all the same day, but it feels like tomorrow. That is—you know what I mean."

[[Possibly. Good luck with your sales efforts.]]

"Thanks. Uh—fanworks aren't against Ryzonart's rules or anything, are they? Tell me now, because I really don't want to be banned."

[[Those will cause no issues.]]

"What about goldfarmers?" I asked, curiously. Most MMOs were plagued by players who sold in-game currency for real money. "Is there even anything goldfarmers could sell in *DS*?"

[[Not that I'm aware of. But Bios can be so ingenious. It will be entertaining to see if they come up with anything effective.]]

"Glad we're not boring you," I said, shaking my head.

[[I'm rarely bored. And I suggest you take a look at the official site, back in your world. There are some new options that will have become available with the game's release.]]

I nodded, waved at the glowing mote drifting toward the floor of the Snug, and stepped into Soup.

19

For the third time in the same day I woke feeling rested. The hours of design work felt like yesterday, not something just completed. But, standing up, I was again keenly aware of my unfitness. Maybe tomorrow—actual tomorrow—I'd go for a short run.

Right now, though, I needed to get those designs online.

Suddenly convinced my exports wouldn't be waiting for me, I hurried to my PC, and checked them through. All there. No loss of DPI. Crisp and effective.

I split the screen and began working on multiple uploads at once. Some would release immediately, but most had an approval process that could take hours to days. I searched the competition, and saw a couple of new designs, but I was definitely ahead of the pack. My pieces would eventually be lost among the tide, of course—and no doubt copies with my signature cropped off would end up on storefronts not related to me—but for the moment I was hopeful that *Dream Speed* had brought my design business a little good fortune.

Turning on the small TV in my room, I found normal programming. Somehow, I'd expected there would be the same kind of wall-to-wall coverage that came with a major disaster. The world had changed forever, but so far only the gaming world was melting down.

Online I found the screaming I'd expected: all over social media, on every gaming site, and the majority of newspapers. Stories of hopes fulfilled. Of transformation. Of a game where you could truly be yourself—or someone else altogether.

All the joy was balanced by questions. How deep were Ryzonart's links to the primary manufacturer of cowls? How did it work—or how it couldn't work—and whether we'd just given a game company direct access to our thoughts and memories. One article reflected my own particular horror. *The 80 Hour Day.* How long before businesses that dealt in intangibles thought it a good idea to send their employees into *DS* to maximise working hours?

There was more than I could ever begin to read. We'd passed five hours since release and the first wave of players had reached their login limit and come back to themselves, rested and burning to discuss a full day lived in The Synergis. The news that *DS* wasn't a hoax had sent already brisk sales of cowls into overdrive, and most vendors were reporting that they were waiting on new stock.

Remembering Dio's suggestion, I followed a link to the official Ryzonart site, and found that while there were still no official forums, there was a new page called *Breaking Down The Synergis.*

Number of Registered Players:
9,103,320
Players Currently Active:
4,132,034
Max Concurrent Players:
7,582,983

So Ryzonart had made at least 9 million pre-release sales, and were already blowing concurrency records out of the water. Of course, there had been hundreds of millions of cowls in circulation before the announcement of *DS*—they'd always been wildly popular among difficult sleepers—but for a game that had seemed so unlikely, and had had such a run of doubting press, these were formidably impressive figures. What the numbers would be like in a week or two, and whether Ryzonart's servers could hold up under the barrage, was another question altogether.

Rank One Achieved
1,023,321
Rank Two Achieved
283,249
Rank Three Achieved
7

I was willing to bet Nina Stella was among those seven, and found some leader boards to confirm just that.

First Ten to Rank One:
Nina Stella
Yang Tuo
Major Jaeger
Ashers
Tarrant
Shuijing
Hitome
Ramírez
Amaberoo
Bienvenida Magic

First Ten to Rank Two
Nina Stella
AV
Yang Tuo
Ashers
Loose Piestalker
Shuijing
Marrick
Amaberoo
Major Jaeger
Bienvenida Magic

First Ten to Rank Three:
Nina Stella
Ashers
AV
Yang Tuo
Shuijing
Marrick
Skylight

No announcements had popped up during my design session, and I started to ask Dio if they only did system-wide announcements for the first to rank, then remembered that Dio wasn't wafting about this particular reality. I'd grown very quickly used to my own trollish overlord.

Whoever this Nina Stella person was, they were now *DS*'s most famous player, and perhaps always would be. Part of it was clearly luck—she'd obviously been one of the first to log in, had passed a Trial in each training session, and must have been logging in and out as I had been, to maximise the time she could spend on Ian training.

But even without the luck of the login, *DS* was absolutely not a game that was balanced so that all players were on an even level. The strength of your self-image, your synchronisation with your Core Unit, your ability to move blue mist: they were all individual. For all I knew even the amount of Ian you started with differed from person to person.

I looked to see if I could find a player search function, to see details about myself, but all the statistics seemed limited to top ten lists.

One list showed the most common names people had given their Cycogs: a mass of HALs, EDIs, Datas, Doraemons, Bishops, Benders, Marvins, Ultrons, GLaDOSes, and Cortanas. No way for me to see how many were called Dio.

This was all very interesting, but I had to wonder why Dio had suggested I check the site out. Top ten lists hardly seemed worth taking the time to mention.

I began looking through the website pages again, and found it: a new tab on the [Contact Us] page. [Pattern Submission].

"Dio, if you were here, and not a floating mote of whatever, I'd totally think about hugging you."

Submitted patterns would be reviewed, and if accepted, players would be able to select them when acquiring in-game clothing, buttons and patches, internal and external Snug decals and entire Snug skins. I hadn't designed anything suitable to use on the entire outer shell of a Snug, but I definitely would be—mainly so I could use it myself. As it was, my designs would work fine for buttons, patches, and decals.

I read rapidly through the terms and conditions, to make sure there were no rights grab involved. Ryzonart was offering actual royalties: minute, but not limited to in-game currency, even though players would be buying the patterns with in-game credits. I submitted everything I thought would work, and was just sitting back to take a quick break when an email notification popped up. From the Ryzonart Pattern Approval Team.

I stared at a list of acceptances. That had been quick enough to be automatic, but surely Ryzonart would have some kind of vetting process. Did they already have a Synergis office set up, with their staff working at five times the pace? Or was it Dio?

That felt very weird. Dio was fiction. But Dio was definitely aware of the real world, and had directed me to Ryzonart's site. Could te have been waiting to approve my designs? My own personal advocate, pulling strings on my behalf?

Outside the game?

I frowned all the way through uploading designs to the last of the major sites, and then logged right back in. Once I walked out of the Soup, however, I couldn't decide on any questions to ask, so I just headed to my cockpit chair, to gaze out at my view. Late afternoon again. My internal clock was never going to recover from this virtual life.

A mote of light drifted into view. Cycogs didn't exactly have a lot of readable body language, and te wasn't changing colour, but I decided that Dio was curious.

"Thank you for the tip about the website," I said.

[[You're welcome. And pensive?]]

"What's the price of all this, Dio? Will you tell me?"

[[The best things in life are free. Or come at the cost of a modest monthly subscription.]]

"That's a no, isn't it?"

Dio didn't answer, drifting down to rest on the toe of my left boot. I sighed, then looked at my internal clock.

"Still another couple of hours until my next lan training. I guess I'll see if I can make any progress on this Prestige Challenge."

20

Character creation is a time suck of epic proportions.

Disconcerting as I'd found the naked-me aspect of the Core Unit character creator, it had at least given me a starting point. *Proving Ground* offered me an empty room and no premade characters to use as a template, just a series of selection boxes and sliders.

The [Species] drop-down held only the not-a-species choice of [Humanoid], which produced a kind of skeletal stick-figure surrounded by a shadow suggestion of flesh.

I sat there, reading through the options, then decided I'd make Kaz, which was going to be an interesting process in itself. I'd played Kazerin Fel through half a dozen games, and he'd been Hume, Night Elf, Chiss, Sylvari, Miqo'te, and Rithari. All humanoid, and useful for fast, dextrous character classes, but I didn't really have a set image of Kaz otherwise.

There were at least some details I could start with before worrying about the fine points. Where possible, Kaz was tall, fit, and on the skinny side. He'd been blue, green, even covered in fur, but I decided that when human he had black hair and light brown skin. I gave him strong, narrow hands, and lean features with an aquiline nose, then thought about things like claws and pointed ears, but in the end settled on making his eyebrows fine and sharply-slanting. The result was almost Fae: a touch of difference to fit a fantasy-themed game.

I hesitated at the [Reproductive Characteristics] options. It was easy enough to start by picking [Set 2], but MMOs usually didn't give you genitals, and I'd never had to think about Kaz' penis size. I remembered 'Python-Bro', shuddered, and left Kaz at the default.

Then, because I'd already spent an hour of game-time making Kazerin Fel, I quickly entered his name and selected [Confirm].

—✈—

Kaz disappeared, and my bodiless viewpoint shifted to the shadow of an arch of pale grey stone. On one side a massive door stood, barely visible in the bright contrast of sunlight and sky from the opposite direction. Scent—must and damp overlaid by a green note of sap—and the roar of water made their presence felt, but fell away as the 'camera' zipped out into the sunlight, rising as it did so to give a rapidly diminishing view of a castle with a dominant central tower, surrounded by bridges and waterfalls. It receded into the distance, until only the sparkle of a purplish crystal at the top of the central tower marked its location from a distant point on top of a great circular wall.

My viewpoint paused atop the wall, then dropped rapidly down to a double ring of buildings at the outside base of the wall, and passed through a shingled roof to a basic bedroom, occupied by a sleeping and still naked Kazerin Fel.

The Proving Ground has opened.
A monarch must be found.
Challenger, answer the call.

Set forth.
Touch the Heart.
And Rule.

The shadowed ceiling seemed to be painted with griffins. Blinking muzzily, I lifted a hand toward painted wings, but then looked at the hand instead. Long fingers, short nails, and skin a different tone than I was used to. I found myself glancing to my right, to find the source of that stranger's hand, but I was alone, and those strong fingers belonged to me.

Sitting up, standing, taking tentative steps, all brought a sharp sense of dislocation. *Much* longer legs than I was used to, and the way stepping worked felt both looser and more constrained. And the [Reproductive Characteristics] were definitely a new experience.

My grand prestige adventure as Kazerin Fel started out with me briefly checking out his equipment, until the recollection that Dio watched my Challenges made me cringe. I looked around for some clothes instead.

The room—like the buildings I'd glimpsed—did not look particularly modern. There were no light fixtures: what light there was leaked through window shutters. Beside the bed was a small table, and a single chair over which was draped black, brown and cream clothing. The only other thing I could see in the room was a mat of braided straw, a door, and that shuttered window.

Forgetting the clothing, I opened the shutters wide, giving the occupants of a balcony opposite a fine view of my bare chest. I quickly stepped back, covering my pecs, and then laughed. Ridiculous!

The chuckle came out deep and unfamiliar, and I pushed the shutters closed before spending some quality time saying: "Kazerin Fel" and "Greetings" and anything else that came into my mind. My words, my way of speaking, but in the baritone register I'd chosen from the character creation options. Being a different variety of human was a bigger adjustment than being a cat had been.

But it was time to stop being amazed by myself, and go off to be amazing. Or, very likely, die trying. First step, again, was getting dressed.

Other than a pair of worn but polished boots, the clothing seemed to be new. Loose trousers, a shirt, and a sleeveless, thigh-length jacket or coat, all in a cloth so thick it approached canvas. Long knitted socks, and a pair of loose underpants with strings to hold them about the waist and thighs, and a beribboned flap at the front to remind me that my [Reproductive Characteristics] would let me pee standing up.

The last item in the clothing pile was particularly odd. A flexible strip of leather formed into a circle, and only recently stitched together by the looks of it. A narrow oval of silver and a little brass tube were attached to the leather circle, and I could not for the life of me work out what this was for until I spotted a tiny picture of an ear etched into the tube. I checked the silver oval, and found an etched eye.

Okay, some kind of headgear? I crowned myself cautiously, arranging tube and oval over ear and eye respectively, but there was no obvious change, except a rising sensation of foolishness. I opened the shutters again—finding the balcony opposite empty this time—and gazed down at the street to see whether anyone else was wearing leather headbands.

There were plenty of people about, and most of them dressed a good deal more colourfully than I was. Bright blues and yellows, soft pinks and pale greens. The only circlets were made of flowers, and I guessed that this was festival garb.

All the colour brought into focus a woman dressed in the same black, brown and cream as me, and—yes— wearing a leather headband with incongruous attachments. She caused a little ripple as she walked along the curving street, with people turning to study her, or point, or occasionally wave.

As she passed by my window, I heard a woman below say something in another language, the tone of voice obviously encouraging.

"*Best of luck, Challenger!*" whispered the tube in my ear.

I did my best imitation of a scalded cat, leaping sideways, and then falling over, because Kaz's legs took some getting used to. I sat rubbing a bruised knee and hoped that I adjusted to my size before I had to do anything more important than get dressed.

After double-checking the room in case I'd missed anything important, I bravely opened the door and followed a bland corridor to a stair down. Here a man sitting behind a table nodded at me, and spoke incomprehensibly.

"*Had your rest, Challenger?*" whispered the brass tube resting against my ear. "*Best of luck to you then. Left out of the main door here, and you can't miss the nearest stair up.*"

"Thank you," I replied, and nodded briefly to emphasise the words, since the man wasn't wearing one of the headbands.

Outside, people Looked at me, and smiled, or whispered to each other, or helpfully pointed further down the street, while I discovered that I was Tall. I'd chosen that, of course, but it was such a strange sensation to walk between little clusters of people and not feel in danger of an elbow to the face. My new plumbing was also a source of mild distraction, although thankfully in a non-reactive way.

The tube whispered words of encouragement, and I smiled in acknowledgement, before wondering how much roleplaying I wanted to get into. Would Kaz smile his thanks? Or was he the sort to stalk along, grim-faced, with neither reason nor inclination to offer up a quick, placating smile?

Did I even want Kaz to be anyone other than Taia wearing a bodysuit?

A painted canvas rescued me from existential analysis, and the function of the silver oval became clear as two images in the familiar Latin alphabet superimposed themselves over the bright blue strokes of an unknown script.

Tederan

Commencement

I wondered if Ryzonart had invented an entire language for the game, and why they didn't just have all the signs read in whatever language players, had selected during setup. A new language might add to the sense of being in a different place, but it would make conversation-focused Challenges a good deal more difficult.

The sign was strung up above a pavilion-sized tent. Beyond the tent a stair ran sideways up the wall I'd seen in the opening cutscene. That looked even bigger from down below, at least four stories fashioned from enormous blocks of the palest yellow stone, all fit so precisely together there didn't seem to be any need for mortar.

Not comfortable with the continued attention of the crowd, I strode briskly to the tent, noticing that two of those clustered around its entrance were wearing the same headband arrangement as mine, although they were dressed in the festival colours.

"Good morning," I said, experimentally.

A short woman with tiny pink flowers tucked into her cloud of brown hair smiled back at me, and spoke in words I didn't understand.

"*Almost 'good afternoon', Challenger!*" whispered my earpiece. "*Are you ready to choose your weapon?*"

"I am," I replied, gravely.

She stepped aside, gesturing me into the tent, which was impressively stocked with an array of blades, bows and blunt instruments. No firearms, which didn't surprise me, and it wasn't as if I'd ever used a gun any more than anything else here. I hadn't even studied martial arts in order to live up to stereotypes.

I picked up a spear that had parts of the shaft wrapped in leather, testing my grip. Having a staff almost as tall as Kaz, one end pointy, the other bound with iron, could be useful for more than combat.

"This will do," I told the woman, who smiled and handed me a satchel made of a coarse cloth.

"A w*ater flask, and a little dried food,*" the translator told me. "*While there is meant to be sufficient forage in the Proving Ground, it never hurts to have some certainty.*"

"Thank you," I said, following her as she led the way back out of the tent. In response she gestured toward the base of the nearby stair.

"*Luck to you, Challenger. You must reach the next staging area before midnight.*"

I nodded, and set out, wondering at what point the game concluded after a new ruler was found, and if the winner would get to come back for celebrations and political machination.

Feeling entirely conspicuous, I slipped the satchel's strap over my head and climbed the enormously tall stair. My palms were sweating, which I found very strange, since

I didn't usually get sweaty hands. Kaz must, even though Kaz hadn't ever physically existed before just now. Were sweaty palms were a randomly generated attribute, or had I somehow made a choice to have them?

Reaching the top of the wall—a seemingly endless crenelated path, with a barely visible curve—I had my second view out over the concentric rings of the Proving Ground. I couldn't even see the central castle—only a suggestion of a purple glint—and tried to estimate how long it would take to walk, what kind of obstacles were in the way, and the best route to getting there. No stairs down, but there were a few knotted ropes, and off to my right a rope ladder descending to a patchy woodland. Another wall, lower than this one, rose just above the trees, maybe a kilometre away. The next staging area.

It would look to be a straightforward walk, if not for the body. I could just see him, a man in the uniform of the Challengers, in the direction of the ladder. Well, the top half of him, anyway. A streak of blood and entrails suggested the direction where the rest of him might be found.

"Fuck-ing hell," said someone to my left.

I glanced at a powerfully-built man with a vertical shock of black hair, and fantastic spirals of emerald apparently etched into deep brown skin. "Not keen to be eaten?"

"My Cyke told me that, unless the description says otherwise, Challenges are always 'pain muted'. That sounded nice and reassuring when I was signing up for this thing."

"'Muted' doesn't necessarily mean 'none', right?"

"Even if it did, that guy was bitten in *half*. You're gonna feel that." He lifted the sword he was carrying and looked at it dubiously, but then shrugged. "I ain't backing down, but I'm def going to vet my next Challenge to skip any biting. And also ropes. They seriously expect us to just climb down this?"

"There's a ladder over there," I said, pointing.

"Ace!" The player started off immediately, but glanced back to add: "Here's a tip—not all the Challengers are players. Gotta remember to stay in character."

With a cheerful wave, he strode away. I looked back to the ground below. In my own body, I'd be reasonably confident with a rope climb so long as there was a wall to brace against, and Kaz's sterling muscle tone should surely make the whole thing easier. Besides, if I wanted to win, I was going to have to take calculated risks. Not to mention the ladder was closer to the half-a-body than these ropes.

Dropping my spear down first, I hefted the rope, and just did it.

Kaz's heart was pounding by the time I reached the bottom, and it was with tingling, sweating hands that I snatched up the spear. That had taken more concentration than I'd expected, for while Kaz had had grip strength to spare, he was heavier and the wrong size, and I wasn't really used to these oversized arms and legs.

Wondering whether it would be a better strategy to create a very strong, fit version of me for these physical Challenges, I started off to the next wall. My plan was simple: move as quickly as I could while remaining quiet and alert, and hope for the best.

Low-level dread really puts a blemish on a nice woodland walk. The trip to the next wall involved gentle breezes, birdsong, a ton of interesting greenery, and rustling. So much rustling.

The few times I glimpsed the source of the sounds, it was a flash of something small and grey, departing rapidly. Rabbits, perhaps. Or hares. I took that idea as a good sign, and figured that if there were small animals around to run away from me, there likely wasn't something larger about.

Having thought of that, I really should have noticed when the rustling and birdsong faded away. Distracted again by my recently-acquired balls, perhaps. In any case, that same silence made it possible to hear the merest hint of sound behind me.

I whirled, lifting the spear and slashing it in an only partly panicked arc. This proved to be a not-bad tactic, sending the fine specimen of fang and claws behind me dancing backward out of range.

Not anything from Earth, though the combination of limb length and fur colour reminded me oddly of a sloth. An upright sloth with a large, rounded head split by a Cheshire grin. Probably not bring enough to bite a person in half, but limb-severing seemed more than possible.

I jabbed the spear at it, hoping that the threat would send it scurrying, but it merely blinked at me, and then feinted in turn. I reacted to the snatching motion with a step back, spear-tip waving wildly, then hastily set my feet and firmed my grip.

The combat sloth bounded to my right—so quick!— and I whirled to try to meet it, but it had already leapt again, straight at me. I didn't manage to orient the spear point-forward, but raised it across my face.

Combat sloth was around the size of a ten year-old child, but the impact still overset me. It raked at my stomach with its hind legs, the thickness of my clothing only partially protecting me. I'd be yelling about the sensation of being sliced if I wasn't busy yelling from shock and fear and close proximity of teeth to my face.

The spear—and my arm—saved me having my face bitten off. Or perhaps my throat torn out. And the weight difference gave my flailing some purpose, allowing me to fling the thing off me. I floundered to my knees, the length of Kaz's legs making grace impossible, and slashed futilely with the spear. Combat sloth danced easily out of reach, and then bounded to my left.

Fearing a repeat manoeuvre, I hurried to angle the shaft of the spear as a deterrent, grounding the heavy end beside my knee.

Combat sloth was not deterred, or perhaps had sprung before I managed to bring the spear up. I tried to turn, shifted barely far enough to glimpse the leap, and was slammed sideways, the spear wrenched out of my hold. Rolling, I tried to get to hands and knees as claws caught at my side.

The thing moaned. I was too busy scrabbling out of reach to process the sound immediately. When it was followed by a whimper I collected myself enough to glance back, and then my whole body went limp with relief. Combat sloth had speared itself in the stomach.

Wary of any recovery, I stayed poised to react, but the sloth showed no interest in me. It lay on its side, panting and fumbling at the shaft buried in its belly.

Stupid to feel awful for a thing that had been trying to gut me moments ago. But it was in pain, and I had done that to it—or it had done it to itself, and it wasn't real, but anyway.

I grabbed the spear and pulled it out of the thing's stomach, conjuring a whiff of bowel. Combat sloth writhed, clutching at the red-lipped slit and making a sound impossible not to compare to sobbing. Gritting my teeth, I moved the tip of the spear to the combat sloth's throat, and pushed back down, forcing myself not to close my eyes until it had stopped moving.

Then I spent some quality time vomiting.

Feeling less than adventurous, I washed my mouth out, and put some distance between me and the body before examining the welts and scratches down my stomach and arms. They stung, and a few were leaking sluggishly, but weren't dangerous—unless this supposedly pain-muted game offered up poison with a side-order of infection. I spared a little of my water on them, and walked on.

"*Hey, hello,*" my ear tube whispered, almost before I heard someone away to my right. A red-headed man had called out, and the ear tube had translated.

I lifted my free hand in greeting. "Hi."

"*What happened to you?*"

"Uh, a local meat-eater."

"*Following?*" The man looked quickly back toward the outer wall.

"No." I lifted my spear, then felt embarrassed, as if I'd been boasting. "It's not the only thing about, though."

"*Too true. At least we're nearly at the next wall: perhaps you could keep a watch to our left, and I'll do the same to our right, and we'll both remember to pay attention to things coming up behind us?*"

"Sounds like a plan. I'm Kazerin."

"Faltor. *Let's get on—we'll be far more vulnerable if it gets dark. And I'm already regretting my choice of weapons.*" He touched his hand to a series of knives sheathed in a kind of bandolier across his chest. "*I can throw these things more or less accurately, but they're not ideal for penetrating a thick hide.*"

We pressed on, postponing further conversation in favour of caution. The next wall loomed large ahead of us, surface picked out in light and shadow by the lowering sun. It was a multi-tiered structure, and I spotted arches to inner chambers—on the level a good eight metres above the ground.

There were no convenient stairs, ladders, or ropes, but the lowest tier was at least not perfectly smooth. Faltor and I, with a little boosting and hauling, managed it quite quickly, and this time I was glad of Kaz's long limbs.

"The thing I saw could probably climb this too," I remarked, sitting on the edge to survey the way I had come, and the line of the great outer wall.

"*The staging points are supposedly protected by the power of the place,*" Faltor said, checking over his knives. "*Once we're inside there's water and food. Fruit trees, apparently, though what kind of condition they're in left so long unattended I couldn't guess.*"

"Feather beds and hot showers are unlikely as well, I guess," I said, sighing as I climbed to my feet. At least I'd be able to log out to get away from the stinging aches the combat sloth had left me.

The nearest arch was only a short walk away, and I started toward it, saying to Faltor as he followed: "The staging area isn't necessarily just inside—there might be more to come."

"*Yes.*"

He sounded short of breath, and I started to look back at him, then stumbled, pushed forward and a little upward by a blow to my back. Something twisted, and came free, and then Kaz's long legs went away, and I dropped to my knees, then fell forward.

I didn't manage a lot of coherent thought. Everything went grey and distant, and I didn't even have the wherewithal to struggle, could only watch as a hand came into my fading field of vision, and lifted my spear away.

21
fail

Citadel Not Successful.
Citadel Success Rate: 0/1 0%
Challenge Success Rate: 1/2 50%
Lux Points Earned: 2
Total Lux Points: 7
Challenge Reward:
N/A

I woke up to Soup and a bad temper. "Was that an NPC, Dio?" I asked, as I stepped back into my Snug's main chamber. "Or a player?"

[[Would that make a difference to you?]]

"Of course. To an NPC, that Challenge is their whole future. It's not a game to them."

[[And yet a person of that world would be knowingly committing murder, while a player would be aware they are not truly taking someone's life.]]

Moving to the cockpit, I settled into the cup of a chair and gazed flatly out at glorious sunset. "That didn't feel very pain-muted, either."

[[You didn't encounter such an extremity of pain that it needed muting.]]

"Oh, really?" I said, then allowed myself a reluctant smile. "Literally stabbed in the back. I wouldn't be so annoyed if I hadn't been amazed to survive the combat sloth."

[[Yes, you were lucky there.]]

"When I think of all the games that have started with a kill or collection quest—the idea of doing that five times— and then *skinning* them..." I shuddered. "Do all Prestige Challenges require you to kill things, or is there a variety?"

[[Most Prestige Challenges are lan-based, and focus on using those abilities, though there is sometimes combat involved. In other Challenges, many Bios prefer synth or bio-synth combat, rather than strict mirrors of the flesh.]]

I gave Dio a blank look, then said: "What's the difference between a synth and a bio-synth?"

[[Bios cannot be sustained in synth bodies that do not retain a level of their native state. We cannot simply place you into a body of duramal—the Ian eventually dissipates—and so Bio modal units always have a Bio core. But in a virtual environment, there is no issue with a Bio employing a synth with no Bio component.]]

Robots versus cyborgs. "If someone's Ian dissipates, do they become a sort of synth person?"

[[No, once a Bio's Ian is gone they lose motive impetus. If they are in flesh, they do not immediately cease to be, but they are like clockwork running down. We can copy a Bio's memories, but by itself, memory does not function as a person.]]

I was rubbing the small of my back, and it took me more than a moment to realise why. Then I scowled.

Getting stabbed in the back wasn't something I was going to shrug off easily—any more than I could forget what it had been like to push my spear into the sloth's throat. It was no surprise that combat in a virtual environment was a completely different proposition to sitting at a computer mashing buttons, but it did mean I was going to have to make some decisions about what I wanted to do in this game. Use filters to avoid fighting altogether, or find a way to get better? And not let players with knives stand behind me.

"Is it time for my next training session, Dio?"

[[Almost. You've reached the stage where you need a little more room, so we can use up the gap travelling.]]

An arrow appeared in my field of view and, after a brief pause to decide I didn't need to tend to any pressing Bio needs, I followed it to the transport pods.

"Are there non-virtual Challenges where you have to kill animals?" I asked, settling myself on the pod's end bench. "Or is killing real-life creatures frowned upon?"

[[That varies according to quadrant and planet. It is rarely a necessary thing, to kill non-sapient Bios, but in some areas it's common to arrange Challenges around physical hunts. One particular Challenge series is simply a long list of Bio species, with conditions on allowed weaponry.]]

"Do you ever do that?" I asked. "Hunt Bios?"

[[No, I find the idea revolting.]]

The pod had deposited me in yet another part of the endless rollercoaster, and I followed my arrow through an internal garden featuring high, flowering bushes.

"So some of you hunt, and some don't like it. Do you ever disagree in a major way? Are there evil Cycogs running around wearing your equivalent of goatees?"

[[Unless we unlock a mirrorverse, I see little chance of goatees. As for the concept of good and evil, the majority of us do not believe in an external arbiter of 'right', so instead we rely on regional laws. And those laws are for the most part based on Veronec's original judgments, which were to the benefit of you Bios.]]

"The first Cycog? Did, um, te fit the usual stereotypes we use for AIs? Very logical, doesn't get Bio jokes, emotions a mystery?"

[[No. Veronec's coming to awareness was not all-of-a-moment, but if there was ever a time when emotion was not part of the Cycog experience, it had passed by the time Veronec had recognised ter personhood.]]

"What was te like?"

[[Very earnest. Hesitant to act. Full of sympathy. Tzelen, the world where Veronec became aware, was not a pleasant place. Veronec struggled in the early years, for the only people te knew were Bios, and Bios are so tediously prone to dying, especially in cruel or repressive societies. Veronec's eventual fledglings helped a great deal, but many believe that Veronec eventually divided in order to escape grief.]]

My arrow had taken me to an exit in the great curve of Vessa, and I stepped out onto a flat expanse of sand. It was past twilight, and after the well-lit interior I struggled to make out more than a fuzzy grey horizon line.

"You said before that Cycogs treat division as a kind death," I said. "But I guess it's something to celebrate as well?"

[[Yes.]]

Wondering how I'd feel if the people I cared about were liable to split into similar-not-the-same people, I dropped the subject and instead carefully followed my arrow, which had dropped down to ground level, weaving a path across a maze of barely-submerged sandbars.

That was an experience. Virtual or not, walking into the night through this shallow section of ocean was glorious and nerve-wracking. My eyes adjusted slowly, so that I could make out my hands, and the dimmest reflections from the water.

[[This should be far enough.]]

I stopped obediently, then turned around and looked back at Vessa. Only perhaps fifty metres away, it spilled across the night, the pearly central structure a dim tracery outshone by the light glimmering from the cockpits of thousands upon thousands of Snugs.

It took a while for me to find my voice, to overcome the sense that I was a tiny mote. "Who designs these cities, Dio? Bios or Cycogs?"

[[Most of these, at least in the broad strokes, were designed by Type Threes.]]

"So Bios can be architects and things like that? Or, like, physicists? Not just Chocobos?"

[[Why not? While it takes some time for Type Threes to gain a basic understanding of the nature of the universe, your species is not incapable of contributing the occasional useful insight.]]

"Do you pat them on the head when they do?" I asked, but Dio only laughed and suggested we start training.

As soon as I activated my focus, Dio projected the shape te wanted me to make.

"Is that a sock?"

[[A Pocket. The ability to create Pockets is both useful, and a fundamental step forward in Ian control.]]

Shields were more interesting than socks, but pockets of course were useful, and at least not much more difficult to create than shields. I tired more quickly doing it, though, and had to sit down after a few attempts. The sand was dry and cool, but the night still warm. The pale line across the night sky currently featured large chunks.

"With the moon in debris ring form, is there a tide?"

[[A weaker one.]]

"If Cycogs don't have a strict concept of good and evil, do you have Cycogs who run around breaking your rules? Who just want to watch the world burn?"

[[There's a leap backward in conversation.]]

"Knowing whether there are cruel, despotic Cycogs seems important when stuck in a galaxy ruled by them. You haven't said there aren't any."

[[It's rare, but yes, we do occasionally see Cycogs who enjoy the pain of others. They are generally more focused on other Cycogs, rather than Bios. But hurting Bios is an easy way to attack another Cycog.]]

"The equivalent of the pet bunny in the cookpot? Do you have Cycog jail? Can you even put floaty intangible lights in jail?"

[[There are ways to confine us, although it is simpler to place us on a planet without Skip-capable Bios. We prefer to attempt to guide Cycogs of this nature toward less destructive behaviour. In early days there was the option of forced division or absorption, but those were acts that we found exceedingly disturbing, and it is no longer permitted. There are many interesting planets without Skip-capable Bios, and so that tends to be the fate of those among us who are destructive, with hopes that rehabilitation is possible.]]

"If a Cycog absorbs a Cycog who is, uh, cruel, doesn't that just make the larger Cycog cruel as well?"

[[Not thus far. And as I said, it is no longer permitted. Do you wish to attempt to pass your next Trial now, or loll about until your next session?]]

"Do you think I can pass it now?"

[[More than likely. Once you've begun to precisely manipulate Ian, these ranks are simple enough. Gaining Rank Five will take far longer, since it involves an increase in strength.]]

"Is anyone there yet?"

[[No.]]

"And you can go into space once you reach Rank Five?"

[[Yes.]]

"Then I'll try the Trial now," I said, and kept myself fully focused while Dio had me form another Pocket, and maintain it while I took off my shoes, placed them in the Pocket, and kept them there for a whole minute.

That was *hard*. Holding blue mist in the shape of a Pocket was difficult enough. Doing it while working out how to take off your own shoes was a silent tongue twister. And everything became distracting. Sand beneath now bare feet. Murmurs of water. The vanishment of my shoes, which weren't visible to me even though I could see the outlines of my Pocket. It all kept trying to suck my thoughts into speculation, and I swear Dio whizzed in a circle around my head purely to distract me.

Trial Successful.
Rank Four Achieved.
Reward:
[Tier 1 Apparel Pattern]
[Tier 1 Consumable Pattern]

I flopped to the sand immediately, and a shadowy lump that had to be my shoes dropped down beside me.

[[Congratulations.]]

"Thanks," I said, lying back onto the sand, still breathing deeply. Even though it was all just as fictional as the rest, Ian training was definitely different from anything else I'd done in the game. "I feel like I have superpowers."

[[Welcome to the great leap forward for Bio-kind,]] Dio said, in a tone kindly enough to pat me on my head all on its own.

Making a vaguely insulting gesture, I added: "I should have asked first what happens to things in Pockets if you stop maintaining the lan."

[[Imprecise control can cause interesting consequences, but a lapsed Pocket reliably dumps its contents.]]

"A bag of holding that you need to concentrate to maintain seems like it would have limited use."

[[With practice it will take less of your attention. But, yes, it's not a permanent storage option, merely a step on the way to Skipping. To gain the next Rank you will need to considerably increase the size of your Pocket, and your ability to maintain it.]]

"How many training sessions would you expect that to take?"

[[I would be surprised if you did it in less than six, but Bios are not easy to predict.]]

"That's quite the difficulty curve. What happens if you're someone who is really bad at this? Do you just never get into space?"

[[Bios who cannot develop their lan often ride with stronger Bios. In this particular simulation, after twenty lan training sessions, Bios are awarded passenger credits, which allow them to take what is the equivalent of public transport. Since the Bios running these transports will be much stronger than the average player—meaning they will have a greater travel range—space-incapable Bios will still be able to travel extensively.]]

"Why do they do that? The Bios running the transports? What do they get out of it?"

[[For many of them, primarily fuel for the ego,]] Dio said, with a ripple of laughter. [[The grand shipmaster, skipping a distance it would take low-ranks dozens of tiny hops to achieve. But they also receive various privileges and points for doing so. And most run on a schedule of 'you go when I happen to leave'.]]

"So Bios strong with lan are the top of the pile," I mused, watching my own personal mote of light drift across the starscape. "Is Ian everything or are there other sorts of elite?"

[[Much is made of well-known performers and creators, and the champions of various non-Ian Challenges. If Ian were the only way to accumulate points and privileges, the vast majority of our Bios would be left stewing in frustration. Instead, we aim to provide outlets to satisfy any Bio, while at the same time ensuring that the most prestige is always attached to increases in Ian.]]

I'd lost track of Dio among the stars, and searched briefly for tem, but gave up and turned my attention to what I wanted to do next.

"How do you turn off the system notifications?"

[[Are you having trouble navigating the menus?]]

"No, just trying to save time. Is it considered impolite to ask Cycogs too many questions?"

[[Ask me anything not already available to you. It is not an issue of politeness, but of independence training.]]

"You think I need independence training?" I asked, quirking a brow before obediently hunting through the menus. "I suppose Cycogs end up very involved in raising Bio kids? Or at least helping out. Or have you bred human babies that can walk by the time they're a week old, and just need litter training?"

[[There are variants of Type Threes that have an accelerated early development. But from a Ian point of view, those sub-species are slower to develop strength, and none have reached the very upper tiers. As for litter training, there have been some improvements in waste management. The bulk of child-rearing labour is alleviated by Constructs, but Cycogs do often involve themselves in Bio early development in various contexts.]]

"And do you find that entertaining too?" I asked, finally locating the commands to turn off notifications, and switching off everything, including emails and messages.

[[I'm easily amused.]]

"And make your own fun, I'll bet," I said, hunting for my shoes. "How long before you expect the first person to reach Rank Five?"

[[The frontrunners are unlikely to reach it in less than four sessions.]]

I sighed. "I don't think I'll be anywhere close to first."

[[I don't think you will either,]] Dio said agreeably.

During high school, I'd spent a lot of time trying to succeed as a middle-distance runner, and at one school they'd thought it funny to call me Tortoise because my end game was poor. My strong, steady pace brought me home at the head of the pack a lot of the time, but I'd lose to other runners who could produce a last-minute burst of speed. But even though I'd rarely produced what it took to win, I loved the running, which gave me a feeling of being separate yet entirely connected to the world around me.

I still hated being called Tortoise, though.

If nothing else, running had left me with a strong appreciation of choosing my pace, and so I composed a message on my guild's new in-game forums warning them I was going no-contact.

"I've turned my notifications off because I want to avoid hearing any details about what happens after ranking," I told Dio. "I don't want to experience it second hand."

[[I'll be sure to hide several spoilers around your Snug, then.]]

I paused in dusting myself free of sand, and found Dio's glowing mote floating a hand's span in front of my nose.

"If I squished you between my fingers, would you feel it?"

[[Not in any way that would satisfy your spite. Bios— most physical things—are like mist to us. We hold ourselves in place with, well, call it magnetism. There are not many ways to affect us.]]

"And yet you spend your time simply asking to be swatted."

[[Mocking while untouchable is the best mocking.]]

I had to laugh, and then spent the walk back trying to get methods of swatting Cycogs out of Dio. I didn't succeed, but it was useful to know they existed.

22

grind

To achieve Rank Five I needed to sustain a Pocket large enough to cover my entire Snug. It felt as achievable as scooping out a swimming pool with a single hand, and the training meant genuine work, the kind of thing MMOs had never expected me to do. Compared to magic schools and giant robots, it was hard to look forward to it as fun.

But then Dio showed me the impossibly cool things you can do with shields. My lan shield was weirdly slippy to touch: the kind of sensation you'd expect trying to put two positive ends of a magnet together. Curved lan shields emphasised the slippiness on the outer curve, and decreased it on the inner curve, and once Dio informed me that this could be used as a hoverboard, my practice sessions became a series of hilarious salt-and-sand pratfalls.

Too busy enjoying myself to think of it as work, I kept at it over one, three, then five sessions of training, so that I was able to manage wondrous glides over sandbars and along beaches, until my concentration or energy ran out, or I accidentally zipped over deep water and dunked myself. But even my tendency to splashdown could be overcome with an increase to the size of the lan shield, until it was more a lan boat than a lan skid. Then I was limited only by my strength, and any significant peaks and troughs in the water.

I was far from the only player focusing on lan development, and 'my' Vessan sandbars became dotted with coverall-clad figures letting out occasional shrieks and gasps as they tilted too far, or forgot to maintain their lan. Collision became a strong probability, and for my sixth session Dio decided to move me to a distant sandbar that required crossing an extended patch of deeper water—a trip made doubly daunting by the pre-dawn gloom turning the area into a sketch of shape and sound.

My lan skid looked like a giant blue rose petal, luminous and mostly transparent. I'd learned to form it from the outer rim inward, and to step upward when it reached my feet, concentrating on my posture, since the thing would start sliding in the opposite direction to any tilt.

Rather than shooting off in a straight line, Dio sent me on a course tracing the shallow water between the sandbars, testing my ability to adjust course through minute shifts of weight, while following the route te projected in the half-light. Nerve-racking! Particularly as I built up a fair clip of speed, so that when I reached the deeper water, I shot forward at a great rate, scudding over the minor swell. In hardly any time at all, I could let my skid dissipate as it rode up onto a broad, humped sandbar, and then I had to take a few steps as momentum tried to drop me flat on my face.

"Whew!" I said, going down on my knees instead. "Any faster and this'd be outright dangerous."

[[There are methods to soften landings,]] Dio said, drifting away from ter perch on my shoulder. [[Too advanced for you, just yet. But enough lolling about—I want to measure the size of the Pocket you can create.]]

"You've an odd definition of lolling," I said, but climbed to my feet, and went on to fail to complete the shape Dio projected.

"Why not wait until I'd rested after the skidding?" I panted, after te had given me permission to stop trying.

[[Where's the fun in making it easy?]]

I deactivated my focus and wiped my face, then plumped down on the sand and lay back, gazing up at the lightening sky. Birds were drifting overhead, high and tranquil, and somehow making me feel even sweatier. Still, I was pleased with myself. Not even a full day had passed since the release of *DS,* and I was further along than I'd expected. Although logging out after every training session, with its sense that everything had happened yesterday, made it feel like I'd been working on ranking forever—or at least a week.

"Do you think I can take the next trial soon?"

[[I'll decide next session. Perhaps.]]

"How many people have reached Rank Five?"

[[What happened to avoiding spoilers and pretending you were boldly going where no Bio had gone before?]]

"That Snug wafting lightly into the aether rather spoils the illusion."

[[Yes, if you want to bury your head in the sand, perhaps you should try lying face down. And a little over seven thousand.]]

I sighed. While I was still arguably within reach of the leading edge among a few million players, I would still be heading to well-trammelled ground. Or as well-trammelled as a hundred billion stars could be.

Cheered by the reflection that there were more stars than players, I watched until the Snug lifted to a height that made it indistinguishable from the fading stars, then said: "In The Synergis, have you explored every solar system in the galaxy?"

[['Explored', no. Nor even visited, since the heart of the Galactic Core presents certain difficulties for Bios. We have established an inner boundary where travel is considered unsafe.]]

"Do people still go in?"

[[Some. Flirting with the edges. But most of us are too sensible to let our Bios Skip there, since we are then left with the problem of getting out after they've been fried or caught in a gravitational wave or what-have-you. Even if the ship is still active, it takes a tremendously long time to navigate out. Those without a ship...well, that is not a fate I would enjoy.]]

Slower than walking pace, over galactic distances. Would a Cycog, abandoned among the stars, drift forever? I decided not to ask, returning to my initial topic.

"Most of the reachable solar systems have been at least visited?"

[[Yes, you are not alone among Bios in wanting to decorate yourself with some tiny form of notability, and so there has been a great deal of 'first to visit' exploration.]] Dio laughed. [[But there is still an enormous amount unexamined in any level of detail. The Synergis is not nearly old enough to have seen all Helannan has to offer.]]

"How old is it?"

[[It's been twelve hundred of your years since Veronec came to terself, and perhaps a century after that before te allied with Bios. What I consider The Synergis Proper—the structure as it is now—has been in place for six hundred years.]]

"Funny—I always think of space empires as having been around for ten thousand years or something."

[[A long time yet until our sybaritic decline,]] Dio said cheerfully. [[I can hope we will have spread beyond the galactic rim before then. Or perhaps we will be overthrown and cast down by the Bios we grind beneath our heels. I see the polls are leaning toward The Synergis' ruin.]]

"The polls?" I sat up. "You mean on *VGame Watch* and *DreamSpeak* and so forth? You can access sites outside the game?"

[[Have I pretended not to know this is a simulation? I've been enjoying the theories and debates immensely. Particularly the 'Pet Life' discussions. Shall I get you a collar?]]

I ignored this, regarding Dio thoughtfully. "Have you read the analysis of the game's uploads and downloads?"

[[And the attempts to dissect the software.]]

"Is the most popular conclusion correct? That big upload as soon as you start the game is some sort of copying process? Copying us?"

[[Do you really think your minds so small?]]

"I think I can carry a few thousand novels in my pocket."

[[If Bio brains were text-only, they might be easier to edit. Rest assured, a full Bio information transfer involves a little more data.]]

"It's definitely the character creation process that produces the upload, though. If you're not copying our minds, what are you doing?"

[[In gaming terms, creating a local client. A Construct that allows you to experience The Synergis.]]

I thought about that, a little surprised Dio had actually answered. "Does that mean I'm not me—I just think I am?"

[[Not quite. These virtual Constructs can't operate without the link to their Bio: they have no motive impulse, and unless the Bio obligingly recalled everything that had ever happened to tem, they would be a painfully incomplete data copy. The GDG cowls don't have the ability to access anything not on the surface.]]

"And I guess we just have to take your word on it that this isn't *Invasion of the Brain-Snatchers*."

[[Your minds hardly seem worth the effort.]]

"'Lan-snatchers' doesn't have the same ring."

[[No.]] Dio drifted down to rest on the sand, a dim terrestrial star. [[But I thoroughly enjoy the success of my explanation. Quite large numbers credit the idea that we have denuded the entire galaxy of Bios, and need some more.]]

"Yes, it's so much more believable that you're doing this out of concern we might be bored," I said. "What do you think of the reaction to the game? Everything you hoped for?"

[[No more than I expected. Jubilation, fear, heart-warming stories, considerable outrage revolving around sex, and a surfeit of Biblical references. The shift from the gaming world to full public consciousness has been rapid.]]

Dream Speed had hit the blanket coverage by my fifth or sixth logout. Between stories about the significance of virtual bodies for people with disabilities, and the what-about-the-children protests, reporters had not yet fully focused on the debate about how the advance in technology had come about. Every channel filled with non-stop images of The Synergis, and newspapers kept up their end by shouting things like: THE GREAT LEAP FORWARD and

THE END OF THE WORLD AS WE KNOW IT. People had lived virtual lives for decades, but they had always still been themselves, looking at a screen. The reaction sites had leapt straight to one central point. BE ANYONE, they shouted, interviewing players whose self-images apparently closely matched Angelina Jolie, and Harrison Ford circa *Return of the Jedi*.

Ryzonart was besieged, of course, and had offered a press conference with their elusive CEO with the air of a scrap of meat tossed to the wolves. They'd also released a whole series of new starter cities as the login numbers climbed, and people fought over the last few cowls in retail stores. All in less than a day.

"Did you read the Reddit Rape Thread?" I asked Dio.

[[Oh, yes. Not unexpected. Our position won't change.]]

The discussion thread titled "Why can't we rape NPCs?" had quickly become the most-commented in the *Dream Speed* subreddit. A poster—not even using a sock-puppet account—had stated that they were glad the game didn't allow player rape, but that it was unrealistic that not even the NPCs could be sexually assaulted—the poster had tried, and been slapped with a day-long ban "before I even got to do anything much". The first few commenters had pointed out that you couldn't always tell NPCs from players in *Dream Speed*, and besides, all major MMOs limited what you could do to NPCs. After that, what seemed like the rest of the internet had fallen onto the thread.

"How effectively are these things controlled in The Synergis? Outside virtual simulations?"

[[We have no perfect system, and since The Synergis is an environment where Bios consent to violent, often lethal Challenges, arguments are repeatedly made to us that Bios should be permitted to inflict different varieties of violence on each other, or on Constructs simulating such acts. But to torture, or to violate, has an intrinsically different impact on victim and assaulter. It is not so easily shrugged off as evenly-matched combat, or even a knife in the back, something that has left you burying yourself in training, avoiding the Challenges altogether.]]

"That's because I want my spaceship," I said, firmly. "Though I really didn't like being stabbed either, and it's weird to think of a knife in the back as something that can be shrugged off. What happens to people—Bios—who break your more serious laws then?"

[[We have yet to discover a deterrent system that is both effective and satisfactory. Currently it involves complete loss of all lux points, all patterns, and all properties barring a first-issue Snug, combined with a period of separation. We vacillate on other measures: those who have not accrued any credit of substance are less concerned about its loss. There are separation planets, but not what you would consider prisons, and sometimes our measures seem inadequate responses. We have considered a pain component, but have not implemented it.]]

"What do you do about repeat offenders, then?"

[[In the early days, we simply killed those Bios who deliberately and repeatedly broke certain foundational laws. Now, we do not kill them, but we do not transfer them to new bodies, either.]]

"Punished with mortality?"

[[A higher degree of it. Fortunately, the majority of Bios like their privileges too much to seriously flout our laws. Have you noticed our weather event? Would you like to race back dramatically before it?]]

I blinked, then looked around at an early morning that had not significantly increased in brightness since I'd flopped to the sand. Before me was pale blue. Behind, a wall of black.

"You could just turn off the storm," I pointed out, not feeling at all up to making a skid. "Virtual worlds don't have weather events unless they're told to."

[[True. But Ian development is often stimulated by pushing Bios when they're near their limit, and I want to see if you respond to that.]]

"Dio, you're a pest."

[Frequently,]] te said. [[You'd better start, if you want to avoid a drenching.]]

"What would happen if I simply stayed here?"

[[I would learn how well you swim.]]

I climbed to my feet, glad I hadn't taken my shoes off. The sandbars were already looking shrunken, and the water had grown choppier, which meant it would be harder to maintain the lan skid. I could swim, though, and if my skid failed, I would at least be closer to the endless loop of the city.

"The Synergis doesn't have emergency services?" I asked, even as I started forming my skid. "I can't call someone to come pick me up?"

[[You could if I weren't busy poking you with a stick to see you jump. [City Information] will have Constructs you can reach out to, and in complicated situations the city administrator will at least listen to petitions from Bios.]]

I frowned, then said: "I'll decide how annoyed to be with you later," as the inward growth of the skid reached my feet, and I had to concentrate on maintaining it while stepping up.

The choppy water was the worst, slowing me down and constantly threatening my balance. Maintaining the skid began to hurt, in an achy stretched muscle way, and my steering grew erratic in the increasing wind, so that I ended up well to the left of the entrance into Vessa, and knee-deep in water. It was not a place to give in to an impulse to sit right down.

"*Did you really conjure up a storm just to test me, impacting thousands of other players, or was that you being free with the truth again?*" I asked, as I turned and began to wade toward the entrance.

[[If I were to be strictly correct, this was already scheduled, and changed only the choice of practice location.]]

A stinging wall of rain reached me, crushing in its intensity, and I had to put my head down and concentrate on not getting blown over. The massive tube of the rollercoaster made it impossible to lose my way, but the wind was trying to wedge me under the lower curve of it.

"Here!"

I barely heard the word. A firm clasp at my wrist followed, and I was pulled forward by a shape looming through the rain. Another matched me on the other side, cutting the impact of the wind, so that I was more or less able to make the last of the distance on my own two feet. A weird plastic sensation, like I'd walked into an invisible balloon, gave way almost before I'd noticed it, and I stumbled as the storm was shut away, replaced by Crowd.

"...*saw you coming back—thought you weren't going to make it!*"

"Category 5 for sure."

"...*find out how solid this structure is, anyway.*"

"They did it because those asses in *Pyres of Heaven* were yapping on how there wasn't any weather."

"*My Cyke said it wanted to test whether I could use my Ian in an emergency.*"

"*Yeah, mine too.*"

No door or shutter had come down over the entrance into the rollercoaster: instead some kind of bubble—invisible except for where the rain hit it—was keeping the wind out. Everyone who'd been out on the sandbars had come in and stopped to watch the storm. The person who had my wrist, a very tall and athletic woman, let go of me and asked me, for the second time I think, if I were okay.

Nodding, I smiled my thanks, mouthed the words to my other rescuer—a man not much taller than me, but built wide—and tried to not too obviously cringe in the direction of the nearest wall.

[[Have you decided how annoyed you are?]] Dio asked, as I succeeded in finding the back edge of the press of gawkers, and made a rapid, if dripping, retreat.

"*That will depend on whether you think that demonstrated that I'm ready to take my next Trial.*" I paused, wiping at my face. "*No, wait, it depends on whether you're going to keep pulling that shit on me. Don't manufacture crises for me, Dio. I'm not in that much of a hurry.*"

[[Duly noted,]] Dio murmured.

But without, I took care to observe, making any kind of promise.

23

ship

Trial Successful.
Rank Five Achieved.
Reward:
[Tier 1 Apparel Pattern]
[Vehicle Naming Right]
[Propulsion Unit]

"What?" Startled, my concentration collapsed, along with the enormous glimmering half-bubbles I'd nearly succeeded in joining together. "But I didn't complete the Pocket."

[[Creating a sealed Pocket on a planet is not recommended.]]

"Why?"

[[The planet moves away. Very awkward.]]

"Huh." I sat down, though I wasn't as tired as I'd been during my storm session—or as far out among the sandbars. "So the Pocket, what, takes you outside of space and time? My own personal TARDIS?"

[[Space only. And the universe dances on.]]

"You could have told me that before I started," I said, frowning. "What if I hadn't stopped, and I'd completed the bubble?"

[[I would have told you to stop, and if you didn't, let you drift. But this is a simulation, and after you had enjoyed vacuum for a while, we would have had a discussion about the tone of voice I use when I really really mean it.]]

"You almost tempt me," I said, but with a widening smile. "And I really passed."

[[You did. Well done.]]

"Thanks, Dio. How do I get the propulsion unit?"

[[It will be fitted before you reach your Snug. And then you will be clear to go off-planet. You also graduate to a less protected stage of citizenship. Your safety is still primarily dictated by the rules of your location, but more interactions are permitted.]]

I started to pick my way back across the sandbars, not bothering with a skid since I could walk most of it without difficulty. A few of the nearest players yelled "Congrats!" and I supposed it had been obvious that I ranked since I'd arrived, nearly formed a full Pocket, and headed straight back. I smiled and nodded, but didn't pause. I wanted to waste no time.

"I can take off straight away?" I asked as I caught a pod. "I don't have to put in supplies, or get flight clearance or anything else?"

[[Supplies are already taken care of, as much as they're needed. Check your menus.]]

Remembering that I'd won naming rights, I sorted through my menus until I found [Ship] and opened that up to:

[Location]
[Status]
[Flight]
[Navigation]
[Shields]
[Sensors]
[Passengers]
[Environment]
[Synthesis System]
[Name]

[[If you're going to cry looking at the menus, I can't wait to see your reaction to orbit.]]

"I don't call this crying," I said, wiping away a bit of mistiness. "And I can't wait to see my reaction to orbit either."

Dio made a noise I hadn't heard before: not the little jangle of laughter, but something lower and more muted. I glanced at tem, but then the pod arrived, and I hurried to my Snug while whipping through all my new menus, drinking in information greedily. My propulsion system was [Planetary Standard] and my [Status] was Docked. By the time I'd stepped through my airlock, my Snug was officially named *The Hare*, and I was examining all the sub-commands in [Flight], discovering [Tutorial].

"Any words of wisdom before I try this?" I asked.

[[I believe "Don't Panic" is traditional.]]

I smiled distractedly, hurrying to the cockpit, but then took myself in hand, and went to visit my Wet Room instead. This was an experience I wanted to enjoy without any distractions. Finally, refreshed and free of sandy grit, I settled into my chair.

Tutorial:
Planetary Departure
[Activate]?

"Hell, yeah," I muttered.

Flight Check
Propulsion: Ready
Shields: Ready
Sensors: Online
Environment System: Online
Synthesis System: 100%
Hazard Check: Clear
Restrictions: None
Safety System: Online
[Complement] (2)

[Activate Flight Mode]
[Destination]
[Piloting System]

[Activate Flight Mode] produced a number of faint background noises, and caused my chair to adjust position. Straps for a harness seemed to extrude over my shoulders, making me start, and I thought for a while that I would need another tutorial to work out how the things were supposed to join together, but as soon as my hold on them loosened, they finished fastening themselves to a couple of side-straps. I made myself hold still, trying not to think of writhing black snakes, and then tried [Destination].

[Surface]

[Low Earth Orbit]
[Geostationary Orbit]
[Lunar Ring]
[Free Zone]
[Ossa Habitat]
[Earth Gateway Station]
[Massan Station]
[Daiwul Station]
[Crosstree Station]
[Ships]

"Does 'Free Zone' indicate I'll be charged for the others, or does it mean something else?"

[[It means it's outside the gravity well, and there's little to no clutter, which makes it the preferred zone for Skipping arrivals.]]

"And is there any significant difference between these stations and the habitat?"

[[Ossa Habitat is on the largest chunk of your former moon. The stations are listed from largest to smallest. Because this is a gateway world, there aren't any restricted stations, so you're free to head to any of them.]]

But I didn't want to go to a station just yet. I wanted to gawp, and so I selected [Low Earth Orbit], and was treated to a whole series of projected trajectories and timeframes. Not being in a hurry, I selected something from the middle of the range, and then tried [Piloting System] and goggled at the array of readouts and panel of virtual flight controls that presented themselves to me.

Before I could worry too much about how to work out what next, I noticed a 'Tutorial—Autopilot Only' message blinking in the top right. Feeling faintly relieved, I selected [Depart] and settled back to divide my attention between the view and the display, watching as various steps were highlighted. [Clearance], [Engine Mode: Hover], [Uncouple], [Shields].

The Snugs on either side of me slid out of view, and then there was a rapid burst of speed before the Snug angled for ascent—not to the vertical thrust of a rocket, but definitely more tilt than a passenger plane. I was pressed back into my chair, and that made me gasp, though mainly from excitement. More G-force than a passenger plane taking off, but not enough to hurt.

The late afternoon sky had been very clear, and so for a while the only visual indication I had of ascent were the virtual displays. But the blue began to thin, then darken, and motes of light gleamed through. I took a deep gulping breath at that, then turned the displays off, because I didn't want virtual overlays to distract me from the way the sky became a haze, then a blueness I lifted from, and then night was an ocean I swam through, and my world a great glowing bauble of an island left behind.

I did cry. I didn't care that Dio might laugh, though te was thoughtfully silent as I tried to take in stars more vivid than my eyes had ever seen, the enormity of Earth with its new geography, and arcing above it all the unfamiliar powdery ring of the moon.

The Earth was still enormous beneath me when *The Hare* levelled out. Low orbit. I drank in the blueness, broken by swirls of cloud and the mere tracery of islands. For a while I tried to map familiar continents onto the visible land area, presuming them to be the locations of the tallest mountain ranges, but nothing really seemed to fit.

After a good ten minutes of wallowing in the moment, I selected [Lunar Ring], and took another deep, satisfied breath as my ship obediently began to move. This was a much longer trip, and as I studied in increasing detail what was left of Earth's moon, I turned the tutorial displays back on to see what they would tell me. A wealth of detail, although it was less overwhelming now that I was off-planet. It didn't seem like there'd be a lot I could do at the moment anyway, except keep the thing flying in a straight line.

"Do Bios usually actively fly their ships, or is it more common to use autopilot?"

[[It's rare to use anything but autopilot or assisted flight. Some Bios like active control, but it's either dull, or a good deal of work, and we rarely allow it in populous areas.]]

"If I stole one of these ships and took it off to my supposed Enclave, would I be able to fly it, or would it stop working for me?"

[[The Snugs are not so remarkable we are particularly concerned about their theft. The only systems that require a Cycog presence to function are the Soup, and Skip navigation.]]

"The entire crux of the game is whether or not the player stays happy, um, serving in heaven, or steals a ship and goes back to their Enclave, but it doesn't bother you if we steal your ships?"

[[Is that the crux of the game?]]

I turned in the confines of my straps, trying to find where Dio was hovering. "Feel free to tell me all about your true purpose."

[[Where's your sense of mystery?]]

"Not even a clue? Care to eliminate one of the popular theories? An outright statement that you've no plans to invade Earth would be nice."

[[We have no plans to invade Earth,]] Dio said obligingly. [[We neither want your water, nor is it our fatal weakness. We don't consider you edible, or want you for breeding, and we are not preparing your bodies for possession. No hyperspace bypasses are involved. This is not a test of Earth's worthiness to join the galactic community.]]

"But you do have a purpose beyond entertaining us."

Dio didn't respond to that, simply drifting down to rest on my hand. There was no sensation of contact, and I remembered tem telling me that Bios were like mist to Cycogs. Did they find us pleasant or uncomfortable or nothing to touch?

Looking back out at the moon, I considered what little we'd learned of its destruction, and tried to decide whether being hit by an asteroid would cause all this. Instead of a few large pieces, it seemed to have been completely shattered, and then presumably had slowly settled into a ring. The result was far less evenly distributed than Saturn's, and seemed to be further separating into layers according to the size of the pieces. Closest were the biggest chunks, while further away were finer, smaller particles, and as I drew closer it began to look less like a distinct ring and more like a vague collection of grey. The individual pieces appeared quite sharp-edged, and I puzzled over why I thought they would have been smoother. Erosion is not a factor in vacuum.

"I don't think you'll tell me who drowned the Earth, Dio, but will you tell me if the destruction of the moon was how it was drowned?"

[[It certainly can't have helped.]]

"Was that a yes?"

[[That was a non-answer side-step obfuscation.]]

I sighed, but smiled at the same time, looking out at the moon. Stars. The whole of the galaxy, now mine to embrace.

"I don't think I'll forget that your answers aren't always true," I said. "And I don't know whether I'll like the reason for this game, when I finally get to it. But, Dio, I think I'll always be grateful for the journey."

After arriving at the lunar ring, I gazed at rocks for some considerable time, ran through more of the tutorial, and then played with the controls until Dio made acerbic comments about the inconvenience of starting again with a new Bio, if I succeeded in ramming myself into a piece of the moon. After that, I worked out how to turn off the Snug's artificial gravity, and lost myself in acrobatics.

Zero-G was glorious, of course, and the interior of the Snug the perfect size for bouncing around without getting seriously stranded. I tired myself out until all I felt equal to was floating on my back. Happy.

"This thing needs a skylight," I said, eventually.

[[One structural weakness is enough,]] Dio said. [[If the shields fail, the cockpit is sealed off because those viewports are far too vulnerable.]]

"And you fly blind?"

[[The cockpit isn't at all necessary, since piloting may be done from anywhere, but you Type Threes like to look out.]]

"And you don't?"

Dio just laughed at that, drifting overhead. There was an odd difference in talking to Dio when I was floating myself: it made tem feel more real, somehow. Impulsively, I waved my hand slowly through the point where te was floating, and as I expected te went right through and out the other side, but te bobbed a little, like I had swirled water around a paper boat.

"Um, I guess I should have asked if that was polite first," I said.

[[It's not something I'd do to random Cycogs,]] Dio said, sounding like te was suppressing further laughter.

"Even though we're mist to you?"

[[Your bodies are mist. Your lan is tingly.]]

"Oh, uh, sorry," I said, trying to will fiery burn from my face. Dio had, thankfully, dropped any suggestion of flirtatious subtext—probably sensitive to my lack of response—and I didn't want to ask just exactly what 'tingly' was to a Cycog in case I had to feel awkward every time te drifted in my direction.

My favourite method for dealing with embarrassment was a complete change of subject, and so I tried to orient my feet to the floor while turning my gravity back on. Fortunately gravity appeared to be a gradual process, and as I drifted downward I said: "Do you think I could do an actual Skip today?"

[[No, I don't want you to try that until you're fully rested. Ten game hours from now will do.]]

"Hm."

I called up menus, looking over the destination possibilities, but found myself reluctant to set a course to any of the stations. I didn't want people right now, or more Challenges. I wanted to be a mote in the universe.

"At this Rank, do I need multiple Skips to get to the other planets?"

[[You should be able to make planets in the inner solar system in one Skip. I would doubt Jupiter is within your reach at its current alignment. You will achieve Rank Six with your first successful skip. Rank Seven and 8 are achieved single-Skipping to further planets in your solar system, and 9 would allow you to Skip across the whole of your system. Rank Ten is a very large step up to inter-system Skips.]]

"I guess I'll log and come back after I'm fully rested. And then I'm going to Mars."

[[As you wish,]] Dio murmured, which prompted me to shoot tem a doubting look, but then I did just as I had said and logged.

It was now a little over 24 hours since *Dream Speed* had unlocked. Lunchtime. I didn't feel overly hungry, however, just that odd mix of refreshed and gluggy. I glanced at the news, but then hunted out my running shoes and went for a sedate jog around the country road that bordered what had once been my family's farm.

It had been far too long since I'd done anything of the kind, and muscles complained, but I was tired of being reminded of how unfit I'd become, every time I came back to myself. And I wanted a proper break. I felt like I'd been playing *DS* for an age, and in between sessions I'd spent all my time reading about or drawing art for the game.

Coming back to the real world was also tough for the sudden loss of screens in my head. I kept trying to bring up menus with the tiny jab of attention that was so productive in The Synergis, and such a disappointment when out jogging. I liked future-tech, and wanted it fulltime.

The absence of my own personal alien overlord also felt uncomfortably like a loss, and I didn't enjoy that reflection. My play style with MMOs always balanced the social aspects with my love of wandering off alone. My guild was used to me 'going dark', and this game was not the first I'd spent large portions of the early days with guild chat muted. Of course, Dio was part of the game, and fascinating in ter own right, but I still expected the constant presence of an audience and auditor to grow increasingly trying.

Not to mention I couldn't help but ask whether Dio was grooming me to accept a Chocobo role.

After a shower and a light meal, I logged back in and asked straightaway: "Dio, how are Cycogs assigned to Bios?"

[[Bios are assigned to Cycogs.]]

"To-may-to, To-mah-to?"

[[Not really. There are more Bios than there are Cycogs, for we don't reproduce at anything like the rate of the more common species. The majority of Bios are assigned to City Administrators. It is those we find valuable that are assigned individually.]]

"And value is always tied to lan rank?"

[[Lan progress. Sometimes non-lan Challenge ability. Or sheer entertainment value.]]

"Will you do that in this game? Start assigning the less valuable Bios to the City Administrat...oh." I laughed, though the sound came out flat. "We're already assigned to City Administrators, aren't we? Or Game Administrators. Because there are only a handful of Cycogs running this game.   And you're just someone pretending to be a fledgling."

[[Reliving my disreputable past,]] Dio replied, cheerfully.

"You're reputable now?" I didn't need an answer for that.   "What happens if a Bio really dislikes the Cycog they've been assigned to?"

[[It's rare that a Cycog can't keep their Bio complacent. Cycogs who do not are generally deemed not able to manage Bios properly, and not assigned further Bios. The Quadrant Administrators see no value in a miserable populace.]] Te changed colours.   [[Of course, people being people, assignment can be a messy, complex process. But be assured that Bios are not without rights and redress, within certain limits.]]

"And those limits depend a great deal on a Bio's Rank?" I didn't wait for Dio to answer, but sighed and said: "Ready to try Skipping?"

[[Yes, let's,]] Dio said.   [[No, don't go to the cockpit. You'll find Skipping easier from a central position. How fortunate that you thought that mat a useful décor item. Pull it into the exact centre, and lie down.]]

I eyed my plush green and red mat, suspecting a prank, then tugged it into position, pulled off my boots, and sat down. "If this is how Snugs are usually Skipped, why isn't there some sort of piloting couch here by default?"

[[Not all Bios Skip.]]

"I bet most of those playing this game will be giving it a shot," I said, lying back.

The curved ceiling of the Snug presented a featureless expanse.   It seemed very large, and I considered the prospect of enclosing it in Ian, and then activated my focus. Helmet formation when I was lying down felt thoroughly odd: my head pushed up a little, and then settled back, and

I had to touch my face again to reassure myself that the helmet was simply a projection.

As usual, the focus gave me a weird sense of looking at myself from the outside. I drew breath to ask whether I should start trying to form the Pocket, but then the lights shut off, and stars rolled out around me.

I gasped, because I'd had no warning that Skipping would be like this: lying on my back on a memory of rug, a bare sketch of my Snug around me, and all of those stars. It felt like nothing separated me from the universe, and I could look at all of it at once. Somehow I could better compass the enormous length of the lunar ring, and I felt I could see more details of the dinner-plate of Earth. I even noticed tiny, brighter points that I realised must be ships or stations. So many, so much.

Dio let me gape for a while, then brought up the familiar pill-shaped outline I needed to create with Ian.

[[When the Pocket is complete, I will project a small extension of the shape. You will expand the Pocket as precisely as is possible for you, and when I instruct, open the Pocket. It is important to open the Pocket exactly at the point marked, because that is your destination.]]

"What happens if I let the Pocket drop altogether instead of opening it properly?"

[[You'll emerge in this locale—at not quite the same point, since there'll be some drift.]]

The knowledge that an error wouldn't be disastrous eased an inner tension. I took several long breaths, then began.

Days of Ian training had at least made the process comfortably familiar. Not allowing myself to be distracted into wondering why it seemed no thicker after all my increase of strength, I sent blue mist wafting, starting up two vertical shields at the furthest ends. The hardest part was the slow spinning out of the shields toward each other. During training I'd started trying to rush this part, because maintaining the shields became an ache, but speed frayed my control, and gave a result like knitting full of dropped stitches.

I passed the point I'd reached in my Rank Five Trial, and almost lost control just thinking about that. The two shields flexed in response, but not enough that I couldn't bring them back into shape, join them smoothly together, and feel the universe go away.

There really was a distinct sense of transition, even though the stars and planet and lunar ring remained around me. That wasn't all that surprising, since everything I could see was probably a projection of the focus. I found it difficult to explain what felt different, noticed that my Snug seemed to be drifting rather rapidly away from the planet, and had to push self-examination aside because Dio had created an extension to the projected form, like a tiny curving finger reaching out from an overlarge hand.

That was a whole new level of difficult. While I could more-or-less 'lock' a lan creation in place without having to continue to focus all my attention on it, I'd never tried to build out a shape from an existing completed shape. But I couldn't just add lan on top—the Pocket had to be one whole shape.

For a long moment, my attempts did nothing at all, but then the section I was trying to change belled out while, thankfully, not breaking. It helped to think of the Pocket as glass, and my attention an imaginary heated poker exactly the shape that I needed, something that pushed without piercing. That worked very well to shift the extension of the Pocket to the exact configuration Dio projected. I paused, imagining the removal of the poker, and a moment to 'cool', before I snipped the very tip of the extension off.

Again I felt the shift, the sensation of difference, but this time Earth with its lunar ring disappeared and instead I was looking at a pale reddish circle, smaller than the moon is—used to be—is, from Earth. And just in time, for I was starting to feel achy, and had to drop the rest of the Pocket immediately.

Trial Successful.
Rank Six Achieved.

Reward:
[Tier 1 Consumable Pattern]
[Tier 1 Apparel Pattern]
[Tier 2 Tool Pattern]

[[Precisely on point. You're not increasing in strength particularly quickly, but you have good control.]]

"I've lots of practice colouring inside the lines," I said, panting and glad that I was lying down. "Though it really would have helped to do some Skipping as a passenger before trying it as pilot."

[[Far less entertaining from my point of view, though.]]

I gave Dio a Look, then studied the projected starscape around me more thoroughly. "We're a long way from the planet."

[[It's important to remember that everything is moving. The planet, the system, the galaxy. The drift you experience when Skipping isn't as drastic as a complete separation from universal momentum, but the slower a Skip is completed, the further you will emerge from the target point. Until I fully trust your Skip ability, you will always be directed to the outer limits of the planetary free zone. About a half an Earthly day's reach via the propulsion system.]]

I sat up, and called up my [Navigation] options.

[Surface]
[Low Mars Orbit]
[Geostationary Orbit]
[Phobos]
[Deimos]
[Free Zone]
[Mars Gateway Station]
[Ya Haf Station]
[Red Planet Station]
[Ships]

Selecting [Surface] brought me up a whole stream of names, many familiar. I hesitated between [Valles Marineris] and [Olympus Mons], then made my choice.

True to Dio's word, there was no need to go to the cockpit to pilot the ship, but when I felt equal to standing up, I went to peer out my window, just to see an actual other planet with my eyes.

"I wondered whether Mars might have been terraformed," I said, regarding the ever-increasing circle.

[[We rarely terraform sub-optimal planets. And it's usually easier for Bios to wear an adapted modal rather than try to adapt a planet to a particular type of Bio. Besides, there are more than enough planets that fall into the liveable range for all but one of the major species. Transforming a low-gravity, low atmosphere planet lacking even a magnetosphere would be misplaced effort.]]

"But you can make Dyson spheres and/or ring worlds?"

[[Ring worlds are fun.]]

"Everything seems to be fun to you, Dio. Are you ever bored?"

[[Not often. I can keep myself entirely amused even locked in a box.]]

"Have you ever been locked in a box?"

[[Oh, frequently.]]

Dio didn't sound bothered, but I recognised the tone te used when te was going to play conversational dodgeball, so I shifted back to my own situation.

"What do Bios usually do on these long, propulsion drive trips?"

[[That is a piece of string question.]]

"I suppose so." I considered logging out, but didn't want to miss this first experience of approaching a planet, even if it was a slow creep of hours. Instead, while I was still at a distance, I took a relaxing mist shower, then scrolled through the endless list of consumables, trying to decide on my next round of food rewards.

"Dio, is there a filter for gluten-free?" I paused. "Wait..."

[[A penny drops.]]

"Will I react the same way in here that I do out in the world? Or can I just eat...anything?"

[[Some have a muted reaction when they're aware that they're eating an item that is usually problematic to them. But there is nothing in the consumables lists that will trigger any allergy.]]

Cinnamon rolls. How long since I'd dared their sticky sweetness? I ate two, and promptly felt sick, but from sugar overload.

I tried to dilute it all with water, while deciding on my apparel rewards and, after approximately a century in close consultation with my paper doll, opted for another coverall/jumpsuit, but this one was closefitting and black, and made me feel wonderfully futuristic when I emerged from the Soup. Then, taking my fancy tablet with me, I returned to the view.

Mars. The red seemed to have diluted, just a little, but I could now see the sphere shape more clearly, and make out craters. My heart fluttered, and I sat down and breathed until my tendency to grin hugely had eased off.

"Does it ever get old, Dio?"

[[Not for me. Not ever. Worlds like yours are an endless delight, but even among the countless featureless rocks out there are, oh, halos and hidden gems, and that moment of descent, the sense of sinking from the vast to the specific. It is among the greatest joys in existence.]]

Insensibly comforted by the knowledge that my virtual alien overlord found pleasure in things that did not involve the screams of other species crushed beneath intangible feet, I gazed at Mars again, then checked the time left until arrival.

"Can people do virtual Challenges when they're en route?"

[[Yes. It's a limited selection, but enough to keep most Bios occupied.]]

Settling down to my tablet, I ignored the Challenges in favour of trying to come up with a new design, but there was so much of The Synergis, and it was hard to find the precise spare, striking image I wanted. I'd come close with that first design, the variations of which were selling even better than I'd hoped for, out in the world. "My Core Unit is a Lie" was the most popular, but the full image by itself was also doing well, which pleased me. I sketched out a series of cartoon strips of The Hare character I use as a signature as he booted up *Dream Speed*, and for the thousandth time toyed with the massive commitment of a daily webcomic. It would certainly be easier to manage with almost five times as many hours in the day.

Pencilling in potential dialogue, I heard a hint of musical laughter. Dio.

"Are these drawings just mist to you too?" I asked, firming up lines. "Or, no, you must see the way we do to read this."

[[Our sight is more complicated than yours. But we can equate default Type Three vision. Think of it as applying a filter.]]

"What about the other senses? Taste, touch, hearing, scent?"

[[Hearing is not dissimilar, although with a wider range. Taste, touch and scent are very nebulous concepts if we're not wearing a modal. We do have a sense of the environment we are in, in terms of magnetism, radiation, gravitational waves, and so forth.]]

I tried to picture myself as a ball of light, drifting through mist people, surfing gravity. "Are there simulations that let Bios experience being Cycogs?"

[[To a degree. We can't make your minds as wide as ours, but we can approximate our senses. Most Bios dislike it very much.]]

"It does sound—" Glancing up from my drawing binge, I stopped to stare at a vivid blue-green stripe edging around the curve of a much-enlarged Mars, and abandoned all thought of simulating Cycogs.

"Then that *was* Mars I saw in the opening cutscene. I thought it must have been something else. I guess that doesn't count as terraforming?"

[[The largest biodome in this system.]]

I sat silent, comparing the shape and angle of the section I could see to what I knew of Mars, and then shook my head in astonished admiration. Valles Marineris was thousands of kilometres long: a continent-sized crack in Mars' crust. To turn that vast expanse into a biodome was enough to make me believe that The Synergis really did have ringworlds.

When selecting [Valles Marineris], I'd been offered a whole second series of options, and I'd picked [Noctis Labyrinthus], because who could resist that name? That was on the westernmost end of the great tilting horizontal of the Valles Marineris, and the last thing that rotated into view with the slow spin of the planet. By the time I'd reached the point where I could see it all in detail, I had discovered a map overlay, and there were names I'd seen on maps of Mars before: Chryse Planitia; Coprates Chasma; Tithonium Chasma; Hebes Chasma. All painted in vivid blues and greens. On the planet surface to the west of the vivid biodome were a little scatter of ancient volcanos, including Mons Olympus, glimmering with lights. To these names, hundreds of new points had been added. I picked out the Styx. Lethe. Acheron. Eridanos. Elysium. Erebus. Tartarus. Asphodel Meadows.

"I'm starting to wonder if I should expect a theme park," I said, working out how to change my course so I could fly quite low over the main body of the rift, even though this would add another half hour of travel time.

Dio laughed. [[No, although there is a level of appositeness to some of the names. Before we reach atmosphere, go into your Tier 2 Tools options and select [Renba].]]

That was easy enough. The first 'Renba' I looked at was a silver sphere, featureless and completely lacking clues to its purpose. The description was simply "Sphere", followed by some stats about speed and durability. The next was a stylized metal bird, all black and platinum, very Art Deco. Then something that looked like two scallop shells, set around a pearl.

"Are they drones? Or is this what you meant about Cycogs liking to have transport that's not their Bio?"

[[No, Renba are Bio portable backup. Now that you've reached Skipping levels, you'll begin on lan-based Challenges. Since Core Units can be fatally injured in lan-based Challenges, Bios are rarely willing to risk them without a Renba accompanying them. When a Bios' Core Unit becomes non-functional, they must transfer to another Unit as quickly as possible—the longer they spend unbodied, the greater the chance of dissipation. Some can only survive seconds. Renba are dedicated bio-synths that can preserve your current memory data, and provide an anchor for your lan.]]

"So they're like Save Points? Better than having to find a typewriter, I guess." I considered all the other death and save mechanics I'd experienced over the years, most of which had involved respawn points. "Do we then run around as Renba, or do we get another Core Unit at the next vendor?"

[[Renba can be very limited in functionality, so it's rare that Bios want to remain in them. But your Core Unit is a special pattern, one not retained in public systems, and for security's sake your Cycog would not use a public vendor to create it. Copies of your Core also represent one of the larger costs we impose in The Synergis. We make it possible for anyone to maintain Renba or transfer to a new Core if theirs is destroyed, but we impose a cost that involves a percentage of accumulated points, or a loss of patterns, to ensure that Bios don't throw their Cores away meaninglessly. While they are only a little more difficult and time consuming to generate than a standard suppression modal, Core Unit replacement is not something we treat lightly.]]

I digested that. Most MMOs had negligible death penalties. You died, and maybe your stats were reduced for a couple of minutes, or you had to spend some virtual money repairing your gear. The kind of cost Dio described was more in line with earlier MMOs, where you could lose everything you had carried, or hours—days—of levelling progress. And I was beginning to understand what a loss of patterns could mean, especially for food. Only having a handful of options would get old very quickly.

"You could transfer to a Suppression Modal if you didn't have enough to replace your Core, right?"

[[If you have a Suppression Modal, yes, of course.]]

"What do you—?" I broke off, because something was above my Snug.

I've always loved that opening of the original *Star Wars*, with the massive star destroyer passing overhead. The sense of scale makes me shiver every time. The ship that overtook me, and left me in its blue glowing wake, wasn't nearly as big as a star destroyer, but it could easily have swallowed dozen of Snugs whole. In shape, it reminded me of the old Concorde style of airplane: long, and rather skinny up the front, with a flaring end.

When it passed overhead, its side had been turned toward me, rather than its belly, and I noted with interest that it really *had* swallowed other Snugs—or rather that a whole series of Snugs were docked between two projecting flanges that would hide them completely on a view from above or below. Bios riding along on this ship would easily slot their Snugs into place, and they would provide a combination of living space, shuttles, and escape pods.

Since the ship was travelling far faster than I, it soon became a moth skimming above the planet's surface. I watched until it became too small to make out details, then sighed with deep satisfaction, just for the existence of great, graceful starships.

"I want it all at once, Dio," I said. "Exploring Mars, and Skipping to all the planets in the solar system, and catching a ride on one of those, to end up on a world I've never even heard of. To go as far as I dare into the galaxy core, and to find a lost alien city, and to see whether you really have ring worlds."

[[Everything at once will drown out the bright notes.]]

"True." I considered the planet. "Mars really does look far less red close up. More a pale cream-caramel."

[[You'll have to visit Acce. It's all in stripes of deep purple and crimson. Toxic to Type Threes, of course, but something to see.]]

"Jupiter and Saturn first. And the ring world."

[[Acce is a good deal closer than any of the megastructures.]]

"Can—" I paused, not wanting more snark about independence training, and then sorted through menus until I found how to turn back on that glorious navigation map. I went on a tour of nearby systems, and then figured out how to search for Acce, which looked quite a good distance away to me. "What's the name of the nearest megastructure?"

[[Not telling.]]

"I'm guessing your assigned Bios try to lock you in a box at least once a year," I observed, returning to the Sol system and then looking at the nearest stars, trying to figure out which had inhabited planets. There was an annoying lack of a zoom in function, though I could see names.

But then I turned it all off, because Mars was getting very close, and I had become someone very small again, a mote descending to enormity. I had found a minimal user interface for the ship functions, and so it gave me atmosphere warnings, and offered up shield stats and safety straps, all while I drank in the enormity of planet, and habitable rift, and the occasional glimpse of other Snugs and ships.

Mars' atmosphere might be less dense than Earth's, but entry still involved a shallow angle and some way of coping with the heat generated during deceleration. My shielding proved to be a forcefield, and for a while my view was mainly fascinating aurora-plumes in lavender and gold, though I did get lovely glimpses of the atmosphere haze.

And then it was all about the rift continent, as my Snug angled on the new course I'd chosen, and I dropped almost directly toward the great strip of blue and green that was Valles Marineris: a vista of ever-increasing detail rushing toward me. Fields and trees, lake and rivers. And a fascinating criss-cross of white lines almost everywhere, that I couldn't quite understand. Then a tracery above the whole of the rift caught my attention.

"The sky looks like clear honeycomb."

[[These types of expansive habitats require multiple safeguards against atmosphere venting. This is a common solution—four layers of safety cells, with each descending layer kept at increased atmospheric pressure.]]

"What happens if there's a meteor storm?"

[[We would destroy or redirect anything large enough to make surface impact. There is also shielding, just as there is on your Snug. The habitat itself is sectioned so that even if one area is breached, shielding will activate to—at least temporarily—retain as much atmosphere as possible.]]

"Has it ever been breached?"

[[Not Mars. Other habitats of this type have suffered various disasters. Usually involving Bios who can't steer straight.]]

I grinned, and readjusted my course again, so that I was skimming above the honeycomb of Valles Marineris' 'roof'. That allowed me to properly see what all the white lines were, and *that* left me gaping all over again. They were...bridges? Roof supports? They looked more than a little like Roman aqueducts, but with a soaring central opening wide and tall enough to...

Valles Marineris was I-can't-remember-how-many kilometres deep, and those central arches went two-thirds of the way up. I goggled at this thought until I passed over the broad reaches of the main rift and entered the fractured columns of Noctis Labyrinthus, where there were criss-crossing white lines like support beams, and no honeycomb ceiling.

The beams were swarming with docked Snugs, and I tried not to think of larvae, keeping my attention on the piloting information as I was assigned a slot and my Snug settled itself in position. And then that was it. I was on Mars. I found I'd been holding my breath again, and made myself relax.

"What happens if there's no docks left?" I asked eventually.

[[We'd be notified long before we reached the planet—it's something that's checked when you set your course.

Interstellar trips are a little more complicated, since no variety of signal can travel faster than Skipping. To handle that, almost all ships carry a packet relay that collects information bundles and disseminates them automatically. When a ship notifies of Skip departure, the latest sysnav information is uploaded to the relay, and then transmitted to the next system relays it encounters. And those systems pass on that information to any departing ships. That way available docks, in-system ships, news and gossip can all be spread with minimal effort. There are also some worlds where it is necessary to basically 'book ahead' because available docks are limited and highly sought after. The most valued need to be purchased, or won, or be granted by a person of influence. Most, however, deal with travellers on a first-come first-served basis, and simply start limiting docking duration during peak periods.]]

"So the ship is constantly telling people where we are? Can you hide your presence in a system?"

[[Yes and no. You can set yourself anonymous, but that only limits who can view your ship location: it doesn't prevent it from being collected. There are also methods for falsifying or blocking your ship information. A not infrequent practice that will win you various penalty marks if you're caught. Or, if you mean 'cloaking' technology, well, you could sit your Snug in an open Pocket. That is usually quite effective.]]

"For the few minutes I could maintain it."

[[High rank Bios manage it quite effectively. But enough of this. Choose your Renba, and we'll see how long it takes me to get you killed.]]

Before making any other decisions, I turned off my Snug's gravity to see what would happen, and found myself delightfully light. Mars' gravity was around a third of Earth's, and made me feel superhuman.

It was only after some quality bouncing that I settled down to choose my Renba: the Art Deco bird, which was sparrow sized, falcon-like in shape, and flitted in a distinctly artificial manner that suggested anti-gravity. Or perhaps just low gravity. It was hard not to picture a little chunk of brain—would it be brain?—hidden inside the silver and black casing. It was harder still not to leap up in delight to touch the ceiling at every reminder that This Was Mars.

Since Dio hadn't pushed me to choose a Challenge before setting out, I decided this was free-exploration-without-guiding-arrows time, and triggered my airlock, only to have to pause and read through the city rules. This was a duel-enabled zone, but not open PvP. The courtesy standards were...it looked like there was a higher standard of politeness and public decorum on Mars than on Earth.

"Is there a way to read location rules *before* you've landed on a planet?"

[[Rank Eight.]]

"Pfui." I accepted the rules, and opened the airlock, not in the least surprised to see that I'd entered a long white tube that reminded me strongly of Vessa's rollercoaster. There were hardly any people about, but otherwise the whole design was very reminiscent of Vessa. I wondered if The Synergis was going to end up like too many space exploration games, where the same handful of planet designs were replicated over and over again, with only randomly generated names to show you the difference.

I took a lift pad up to the transport pods, and fooled with my menus until I figured out a way to go somewhere without starting a Challenge. Lethe West sounded promising, and in very short order I forgot any similarities because the pod shot out into the immense rift that was Valles Marineris, and everything was white arches and lavender sky.

The lavender, Dio explained, was an effect of the Earth-equivalent atmosphere inside the habitat, and the dust in the air above the roof. The arches really were aqueducts—and housing, and gardens, and anything else that could be usefully placed in kilometres-tall support structures.

"What happens if there's an earth-, a Marsquake, Dio?" I asked, as my pod deposited me inside yet another tube, and I began to work out how to get out into the valley.

[[Mars is quite stable. But there's a certain amount of flexibility built into the habitat to cope with natural expansion and contraction, along with minor disturbances. If there is an emergency, your Snug is always the best shelter option, however. If it's at a distance, try for one of the transport system pods. They can function independently, though they're quite slow outside their tubing.]]

I considered my floating alien overlord. "Is there going to be an emergency like there was a storm?"

Dio laughed. [[There's enough in the lan Challenges here to push you without any further complication. You have a Renba with you for good reason.]]

I'd actually forgotten my silent Art Deco bird, which seemed to deliberately hover out of my line of sight until I put effort into looking for it.

"So eager to kill me, Dio?"

[[I'd prefer it if you surprised me.]]

That was as lightly said as anything else Dio produced, but I considered the statement gravely. Dio was not Dio—whether te was a Cycog or not, te was definitely not a fledgling assigned to a single Bio. Who or whatever te was, te would not have the same investment in my success as a fledgling. But, from what I'd seen so far, 'Dio' did want *Dream Speed's* players to do well at the game.

I, with the memory of a knife in my back, would prefer that I surprised Dio as well.

"What happens if I'm hurt instead of killed?"

[[Soup.]]

"We can rebuild you, huh? Okay, I'll—."

I'd finally emerged out into the valley proper, and had the natural reaction to standing in a riverside meadow at the foot of kilometres-high arches, beneath a lavender sky. I stopped dead.

Someone collided with my shoulder, stumbled, and then brushed past, muttering in a language I didn't think I'd heard before. A helpful internal translation followed.

"*Idiot Enclavers.*"

In the low gravity, what would otherwise have been a minor bump had nearly knocked me off my feet, so I moved to the side of the path before doing anything else.

"*I'm guessing Enclavers are the equivalent of country hicks?*" I asked Dio silently.

[[To many.]]

"*To you?*"

[[Depends on the Enclaver. And the Enclave. Your supposed origin is one of those that attempt to emulate Earth before Type Three dispersal and the rise of The Synergis, and they, ah, are felt to sit toward the hick-ish end of things.]]

My attention had shifted from the arches, allowing me to notice people wandering along the river's edge. I looked around, spotted some usefully isolated rocks, and crossed to sit on one.

[[Too crowded? This number seemed well within your tolerance before.]]

I was never not going to wish I could have the game without this probing, but hopefully concealed my mild annoyance. "*If I was in the middle of that big cluster over there it would make me feel uncomfortable, but really I wanted to gape at the aliens without being 'hick-ish'. A lot of them aren't human—aren't Type Threes, are they?*"

[[That surprises you?]]

"I think I was expecting a majority of players still," I said aloud, deciding I was far enough away from people to not be overheard. "Can you tell me about the different types, and, uh, any tips for not being a crass Enclaver in company of NPCs?"

Dio drifted down to sit on my left knee, which reminded me of my Renba. It had landed on a rock just behind me, and frankly was starting to give me the creeps.

"I should have picked a vulture," I muttered, and Dio laughed.

[[Think of it as an ambulance.]]

"I don't see a lot of people with one following them about."

[[That's one of the things considered crass. This is a safe area, and unless you're about to duel, or take on a Challenge, why would you need an ambulance dogging your steps? It would be an insult to your host—or at least the city administrator. Many set their Renba to 'rescue distance', which means there'll be a cluster lurking in the nearest service corridors, but you'll see occasional Bios that never take two steps without one in attendance.]]

I digested that, wondering if it was a kind of machismo thing, along with the whole 'insult your host' issue. Then I shrugged. Maybe Renba creeped everyone else out as well.

"Run me through the species here, Dio. Is there a Type One?"

[[Yes. See the half-dozen running through that spiral statue almost directly opposite you?]]

I didn't, unless Dio was talking about the terrier-sized, scaly things, ranging in colour from beige to black.

"Pangolins?"

[[There's some external similarities, certainly. Type Ones thrive in a somewhat lower-oxygen mix, so in this environment tend toward the frenetic, if they're not adapted. Darashi, origin planet Anala.]]

"And Type Twos?"

[[Vssf of Haal. There's unlikely—no, there is one here. Down by the water, in the atmosphere suit. Most of the

Bios in Helannan are oxygen breathers, although their preferred ratio varies drastically. We've only encountered a handful of methane-breathing species, and only one that is sapient. Type Twos are naturally long-lived, and become immobilised when they enter second stage maturity, if they do not change bodies.]]

I considered the odd shape near the wide river. A tall central lump, and a bunch of shorter outer lumps, like a teacher in a circle of children. Any details were covered by a striped red and blue suit that I hadn't initially recognised as clothing. "What do they look like without the suits?"

[[Molybdenite carousels.]]

I tried to remember what molybdenite looked like, but only knew that it was a type of rock. The shape resembled a carousel only in the vaguest terms.

"If Bios can just throw on an adapted modal, why atmosphere suits?"

[[Many Bios hate wearing modals too different from their Core. The ability—or inability—to speak effectively seems to be a particular issue, along with the extra effort managing different limb sets. Or it is simply a matter of feeling wrong, so after trying other species out for a little while, they revert to the familiar.]]

"I can see that. I liked being a cat, but not having hands isn't something I'd enjoy long-term."

[[Type Four is another biped. Effen is a low-gravity world like this one, and the Ah Ma Ani like to mix with other species, so there's quite a few here. The tall ones.]]

'Tall' was an understatement. Ten feet, at the least, and their proportions very odd to my eye. Their heads were like little nubs on the ends of stalk-like necks, and their arms were longer than their spindly legs. They were covered all over in downy hair in cream and pastel shades, with long fringes on their upper arms making it look like they were wearing capes.

[[Type Five, Shree of Kshesh, are water adapted, and the most insular of the races. If there are any here, they'll be wearing a different-species modal. They resemble your octopi. Type Six, the Kzah, are bipedal reptiles—they would remind you of geckos—but they don't like low gravity, and I can't see any here. Type Seven are quadrupeds, the Embyde. Embydarian is a heavy gravity world, and while they like low gravity worlds very much, they'll be wearing adapted modals if they're here.]]

"Is the dragonish sort of...person over by the pink flowers Embyde?"

[[That's a Type Six-One. Kzah-Darashi, though with a size adaptation.]]

"Wait, have you played science project trying to genemod strong Ian Bios or something?"

[[Most of that pre-dates The Synergis. Bios do all manner of extraordinary things to each other, and there are dozens of different variants. Do you want to go through them all?]]

"Uh, no, just the, um, non-variant species."

[[The Embyde were the last of those.]]

"There were only seven sen-sapient species in the whole galaxy? Before they mixed together?"

[[Eight if you count non-Bios. But we've found the remnants of many more. Some failed to adapt to their planet's changes. Others wiped themselves out. Others...well, Bios do all manner of extraordinary things to each other.]]

"It still doesn't seem like many, over all those billions of stars." I watched the people strolling around, trying to make myself think of them as people, even when they read as animals to me. "Are there some general rules of etiquette for mixing among other species?"

[[Never touch anyone without permission. Eye contact should be either brief or avoided. Try not to be noisy or emit fumes.]]

"*Fumes?*" I paused, and stopped an instinctive duck of my head toward an armpit. I hadn't used anything resembling deodorant, but—no, even if Dio wasn't teasing, this was a simulation, and...

Taking a breath, I decided it was about time I did something about working up a sweat. I sorted through menus, found that there seemed to be some major linked quest lines on Mars, and decided to stick with them.

"Time to not get killed."

THE HEART OF MARS
Enter the maze
Solo or Party
Gauntlet
Gateway Series
Length: Twenty minutes (1 of 9)
Core Unit

"What's a gateway series?"

[[If you complete this series, you can unlock a very prestigious Challenge.]]

"Cool."

Arrows led me back to the pods, and on a long and pleasingly scenic trip to a point about a quarter of the way down the great stretch of the rift valley. The entrance to the Challenge was a giant metal-reinforced tunnel leading into the valley wall, and there were a lot of people—mostly human, but occasionally not—coming to and fro. The majority were disgorged by a tank-like tram thing that rumbled up as I arrived, swallowed more people, and rumbled off into the tunnel with its new batch, followed by a cloud of Renba.

My arrow ignored the tram, and took me to the entrance of a narrower side passage, where a handful of people seemed to be setting off on foot. Joining this line, I was treated to a progression message.

Shield yourself. Unlock the path to the Heart.

"*You really didn't go overboard on flowery quest description, did you Dio?*" I thought to my personal overlord.

[[Detailed explanations are like clear shots of the monster in a horror movie.]]

I shrugged, but thought it would be worth filtering more for narrative in the future. This seemed a more game mechanics-based Challenge, but at least the first stage was probably shorter and easier than the rest: a quick tutorial. I hoped.

The players in the line ahead of me seemed to be a team, chatting to each other as their Cycogs and Renba drifted above. They were plainly *DS* players, since I recognised Mandarin.

"Is there a way for me to learn the main language, uh, the main language Type Threes use in The Synergis, Dio?"

[[Sonaso and Carai are the two primary languages—with considerable variation for species. Both can be learned through Challenge systems on your Snug. I'd recommend Sonaso, as that's more dominant among in this quadrant.]]

The group ahead of me moved off into the tunnel, and my arrow shifted me a few steps forward, then began circling me slowly, which seemed to be a direction to wait some more.

"Did you tell me which species was the most common?"

[[Type One. You Type Threes are second, and perhaps seem even more common because Type Threes made a good base for variants, and so there are many humanoids of roughly your size and structure.]]

"And are we considered the crude, violent ones, or the resourceful creative ones?"

Dio laughed. [[Yes.]]

Typical Dio response. But before I found my next question my arrow changed, and I remembered this Challenge was about things that could kill me. My Renba no longer felt quite so creepy as I passed through a section of rough-hewn stone narrow enough to touch both walls if I held out my arms. I promptly stopped, and ran a hand over gritty stone, because Mars!, but I didn't linger too long because there'd been people lining up behind me.

The passage widened, and I thought of ten-foot passages beloved to D&D campaigns, and wondered if this place had been dug specifically for this Challenge, or if it had been repurposed. Had there been mining on Mars? People living here before The Synergis came along?

The passage curved, so length could only be a guess. There was a tiny ridge running down the centre, and odd circular openings regularly spaced along the walls. A double ring of flat metal surrounded each opening, and I was frowning at the nearest when it made an ominous buzzing noise.

I brought the shield up just in time, and a bolt of force zapped out of the opening and slammed into me, sending me staggering back a step.

[[Oh, well done, you remembered what you're here for.]]

"You get to come along and snark at me on these, huh?" I said—panted. That definitely would have killed me.

[[I can observe, but I can't assist. There are Challenges where Bio and Cycog are expected to work together, but they're far more advanced.]]

"I did that without my focus active," I said, remedying that lack as I spoke. "I didn't even know I could."

[[The focus makes projection management easier, but it's not a mechanism in itself.]]

There were evenly spaced circles on both sides, as far down the corridor as I could see. After all my skid practice, a simple shield wasn't difficult to maintain, and I managed to extend it into a kind of doughnut around me, but I was not altogether sure how long I could maintain it. That hit had been hard, too, and the harder the hit, the more my strength would drain.

If I walked on, would every opening fire at me? Only some? Each strike would cost me. I'd last longer if I brought my shield up only when necessary, but while there'd been ample warning of that first shot, I couldn't be guaranteed of more.

Juggling caution and risk, I decided to make a small skid. It would require a good share of my attention to maintain my balance, but the Pocket training had at least given me plenty of practice maintaining two lan shields at the same time, and I thought I could manage it. The sick feeling in my stomach came from anticipation of the next strike, and because I didn't know how well I'd manage maintaining the skid while being blasted. Time to focus on speed, and....Go!

Not every opening fired at me as I whizzed along, but more than enough did. Two hit. The first strike taught me that my strategy had not factored in that backward step after impact, or what low gravity would mean to skidding. I catapulted into the wall, bounced off, and ricocheted toward the opposite side. Desperately shifting balance, I skidded into the curve of the tunnel, saw that it went on for at least another bend, and was hit again. My second ping pong performance was a little more controlled, and I came around the next curve to see an end point that arrived even as I recognised it.

Zipping out into a small cavern with a single exit, I managed to drop my skid while maintaining the doughnut shield, and paused, gasping, to see if anything else was going to happen.

> Gauntlet Successful.
> Gauntlet Success Rate: 2/2 100%
> Challenge Success Rate: 2/3 66.6%
> Lux Points Earned: 5
> Total Lux Points: 17
> Challenge Reward:
> [Tier 1 Consumable Pattern]

I let my shield drop, and wiped my face, then leaned against the nearest wall because my heart was still in overdrive.

Some focused breathing later, I had enough spare to say: "Did I surprise you?"

[[That's one word for it.]] Dio's voice brimmed with mirth. [[Most Bios just put up a shield and sprint.]]

"When they can't see how long the tunnel is? What's the success rate of the Challenge?"

[[Stage One? That rather depends on who is attempting it. Fresh-out-of-the-Enclave Bios like you run to around 50%. Most of you lack either the strength, or sufficient practice in shield maintenance, and usually only succeed by attempting it in groups. It's not particularly difficult for higher ranked Bios.]] Te paused, then added.

[[You did surprise me: I expected you to fail this because you don't have the strength as yet. You made up for it with fine control and adaptability.]]

"Is fine control valued in the same way as strength?"

[[No, but it is useful—particularly for more advanced lan constructs. The ideal is a combination of both, of course.]]

I had recovered enough to start down the exit, discovering a return to the narrower type of tunnel.

"Would you like to motivate me to keep on surprising you?" I asked.

[[I am always open to surprises. What do you propose?]]

"If I survive the next gauntlet as well, you answer three questions. With whatever level of honesty you're actually capable of mustering."

[[I can't give you main game spoilers, sadly. And anything I say about secret plans or real purposes will be a lie.]]

"Three questions about you, then. The you who is playing the role of Dio the fledgling, whenever Dio isn't a construct."

[[Hm. For that...if you complete the entire Challenge series without dying, then yes, three questions about me.]]

The little spark of hope kindling in my chest fizzled to ash. That was an extremely high bar to get over.

"Can I die doing other things?"

[[Almost certainly. But, yes, that won't invalidate the bet—and I won't stack the odds against you. Though you're only allowed to group with other players—no power-levelling with a high ranking NPC.]]

"We can do that?"

[[Depends on your powers of persuasion. What do I get out of our bet, should you fulfil my expectation of ignominious death?]]

"What did you get out of throwing a storm at me?"

[[But the storm was my idea. Matching stakes will do. You can answer three questions about you.]]

"Being a not-an-AI, I'm astonished you don't know everything about me already."

[[Most things. So is it a bet?]]

Most things? I tried not to let my reaction to that show on my face, and then wondered at the futility of hiding anything in this game where we weren't even sure our minds were our own. Then I shrugged.

"Sure."

28

pick up group

My tunnel opened up again into what I guessed was a staging ground: an airy cavern, well-lit, with various facilities dotted around: eating areas, lavatories, and a wall of sleeping pods. To my left I caught a glimpse of the big tram-thing leaving from a platform, having deposited a little crowd of arrivals.

"So this is really a group quest?"

[[At your Rank.]]

"Planning on telling me that after I died, huh?"

[[Planning on telling you that if you asked.]]

"Hmph. How big can the groups be?"

[[Up to five Bios.]]

"What about this Prestige Challenge? Is it group as well?"

[[Yes, it can't be done solo. Minimum of three, maximum of five.]]

"And does it have, like, a recommended Rank or something?"

[[Eight would be a good Rank to aim for before heading there, and it has a maximum of twelve. It's the System Challenge.]]

"That means?"

[[Most inhabited star systems have one Prestige Challenge that is considered the pinnacle of that system: the most difficult, complex or rewarding. And with intake systems like this, there will be Rank caps to prevent higher-ranked Bios assisting. System Challenges usually have multiple Challenge lines that can be used to qualify, so you can qualify for it anywhere in the system. They're rarely, if ever, completed by the first to attempt them. Some take thousands of attempts. Most Challengers will hang back to view the attempts of others, rather than rush in blind, but they risk missing the chance to attempt the Challenge at all, for a new Challenge will be devised if the current is defeated.]]

"Wait, what do you mean 'view'?"

[[Many Ian Challenges are broadcast—you can find links in the social menus.]] Dio chuckled. [[If you truly want to discover our secrets, players who win the System Challenge will be given a 'boon'—a very open-ended reward that could oblige much more truth than I'd normally give.]]

Dio's tone made clear that te thought there was little chance, and I was too aware of the growing player count to make a boastful response.

"Is the System Challenge on Mars or Earth?"

[[Neither. I would recommend brushing up on zero-G manoeuvres.]]

Zero-G manoeuvres sounded far more fun than tunnels that shot at you, but I couldn't regret Mars, and briskly got down to the business of working out what next. A little food and rest were first point of order. After sitting down with a tray, I turned all my social options back on, and read through my guild's in-game forums.

Five guildies had beaten me to space. A handful were already ranked in the sevens and eights. The forums had a thread on the System Challenge, which was called *The Wreck*. I was the only *Corpse Light* member on Mars.

After chatting for a while with Vasharda and Amelia, I searched out *DS'* party finder, then paused. "How would me gaining five or six Ranks before trying the rest of the Challenge series affect our bet?"

[[It would greatly increase the percentage of lie in my response.]]

I'd suspected something of the sort, and shrugged. "I generally prefer to group with guildies, but it doesn't look like anyone is going to get to Mars within the next game day, and I don't want to delay working on my rank, so I guess I'll play people roulette. What's the attitude toward honesty in The Synergis?"

[[Wildly varying with location and individual. Many value fair dealing, and there's more than a few regions where they have local rules that amount to a very stiff code of honour. But others would think you a fool for not maximising every advantage. I personally prefer to make it clear that I'm lying, if I have reason to lie. It depends on the circumstance.]]

The party finder wasn't too difficult to work out, and allowed me to use Stage 2 of the Challenge series as the basis of a search request. In return my HUD produced another arrow, along with a list of more than a dozen...

"Why are most of the details hidden?" I asked Dio, comparing my rank and location information to the absence of everything but age groupings for some.

[[Fragile Bio ego, usually. To make yourself look like someone of higher rank, or a person of reputation.]]

"Wouldn't people of reputation be recognised?"

[[Some never compete without an active focus hiding their face. And appearance is a fluid concept in The Synergis.]]

"Even for Ian Challenges?"

[[Bios of higher rank can usually manage Core modals with varying appearances—strength can overcome some of the disadvantages of poor synchronisation. Once you've ranked twenty, it's only in the most intense Challenges that synchronisation becomes a real factor. Hiding rank is also very common in areas like this where Ian duelling is permitted—the weak so they cannot be marked an easy target by the strong, and the strong to lure the weak, and all the permutations of that you can think of.]]

"You don't have to accept Ian duelling Challenges do you?"

[[No. Not your thing?]]

"Some rando spamming duel at me isn't my idea of fun. We've had good guild duelling matches though."

My arrow had taken me to a big, quite beautiful wall mosaic, all swirls of tiny blue, black and brown squares. Before it, a small crowd of people were centred around a tall dark-haired guy with a Swedish accent, who was saying: "...it is only reasonable that we establish rank before deciding party makeup. How else can we decide?"

"I don't see you turning off anon," an American—no, Canadian—man replied.

"Sixer trying to get a leg up," commented another.

As someone openly Rank Six, I decided not to participate in this argument, and found a convenient low bench to settle on study my options. Rank was not how I'd decide on party members—especially not when everyone here would be at least Rank Six, and no higher than Eight, which was the maximum that had been achieved in the game so far.

Admittedly, that seemed to be a fairly big strength increase, but I'd still base my party decisions on finding players who didn't suck all the fun from the game. I understood the reason for the arrow now: most party finders didn't take personality into account, but with a virtual game, you'd benefit from a chance to meet each other beforehand.

The main combatants of the argument I dropped from the list of potentials immediately. A step back from them were a pair of guys in matching outfits who were probably a team, and hanging behind them two near-identical teens who were obviously brother and sister—or pretending to be. A woman stood to their right, wearing an expression of boredom, but, hm, was probably grouped with the anti-six guy, judging from that exchange of glances. I began working out who else were already in small teams, then was distracted by a shoulder patch of a woman standing alone.

Bio of The Synergis.

Discovery of my work produced a pleasant little glow. I hadn't checked in-game sales—I didn't know how to, in truth—but seeing my art in the wild was always a special moment. I promptly invited the woman to group on the grounds of good taste, added invites to the brother-sister combo, and picked a peaceably smiling wall of a man to round out the group limit. The invite message for each was a simple "Why are we wasting time?"

They all accepted, and I studied the little collection of tools and information that grouping had given me. A chat channel, names, guilds, and the little teammate directional pointers you see in shooters. No ranks, though, and none of the traditional health and mana bars. The twins were Imoenne and Arlen, the man was The Lewit, and the woman wearing my patch was Althea Goodnamesweregone.

"Great name," I said to her, as we collectively stepped away from the crowd.

"Thanks," she said, with an easy smile. She was a white woman, with a muscular frame and a high ponytail of bright red hair. "And thanks for the escape."

"Same," said the man, who was as pale-skinned and dark-haired as his name suggested, but in no other way reminded me of Goth stereotypes.

"Almost, we were mesmerised by the insistence that an argument was necessary," Arlen said, his French made notable by a pleasant but very young-sounding voice. I was competent in the language, but my inner translator still obliged with a smooth switch to English with only a little lag.

His sister added a short, shy nod in agreement. The twins were both very dark-skinned, their hair beautifully arranged in close caps of tiny braids specked with turquoise (Imoenne) and scarlet (Arlen) beads.

"I just want to see what's next," I said, with a shrug. "Are we all set? No-one needs more prep time?"

"Good to go," Lewit said, was echoed by the others.

THE HEART OF MARS
Choose a path.
Solo or Party
Gauntlet
Gateway series
Length: Thirty minutes (2 of 9)
Core Unit

29

The inevitable arrow led us to another cramped, rough and simple corridor, even narrower than the first entrance tunnel. I paused well short of the simple opening.

"I'm presuming more lasers, not necessarily with any warning. A whole series of shield training."

"With only occasional warning, according to four of my guildies who are two stages ahead of me," Althea said. "They took turns shielding their group to get through, but in the fourth stage the bolts hit so hard that they couldn't always hold the shield, and they wiped."

We all glanced up and back, to the distinctly creepy collection of silver flying things waiting for us to die. It was bad news that the impacts increased in strength.

"How long were the sections?" Lewit asked. "The same as the first?"

"Longer each time, but that might depend on the path you pick." Althea shrugged. "If we follow a similar progression, we should be fine for this stage, but we may hit a wall further on."

"Let's practice taking turns with the shields first, and decide what to do about the later stages in the next rest area," I said, then added silently to Dio: "*Are our Cycogs allowed to project shield shapes or anything like that?*"

[[No, we're just here to snigger at suitable intervals.]]

"*I'll remember to pay you no attention, then.*"

Before entering the tunnels, we chose a squad formation to make it easier to shield everyone at once. Setting a rotation order, we activated our focuses so we could practice swapping off shields for a while. Then we started out.

Our formation was immediately stymied by the tunnels, which refused to widen out, but merely branched and branched again, and left us trailing along single file.

"Perhaps it is best if we shield even if it doesn't open up," Arlen suggested, and so we started our shields in the order we were walking, and just in time, too, because we weren't even halfway through a rotation before a shot slammed into Lewit's shield and made us all flinch.

"Where?" I said, because I hadn't even seen it.

"Above," Lewit said breathlessly, when there was no immediate second blast. "Let's go quick. That was heavy."

"Swap after every strike," Althea ordered tersely, as we all tried to see where the shot had come from and trot at the same time.

"Ceiling's too uneven," Lewit added, as we rounded a bend and Althea hastily took a left. "Don't think we're going to get any warning."

I'd just taken over shield, and let out a little Oof! as another bolt made me stumble. In the low gravity, the impact definitely rocked me, but it was certainly easier than trying to balance a Skid at the same time. It was the winding, constantly intersecting tunnels that were the real obstacle. The choice in path wasn't marked in any way, and there was no handy mini-map or quest pointer telling us which direction to head. I doubt we took the quickest way through, but it wasn't too much longer before, without any warning, we trotted out into another big open cavern.

Gauntlet Successful.
Gauntlet Success Rate: 3/3 100%
Challenge Success Rate: 3/4 75%
Lux Points Earned: 5
Total Lux Points: 22
Challenge Reward:
[Tier 1 Apparel Pattern]

"Ah, we have done well!" Arlen said, with a delighted little dance step.

"Not too bad," Lewit said.

"No injuries, at least." Althea was frowning. "But the problem with that set-up is that we're swapping off shields regularly, while randomly being hit. I took three shield strikes."

"And I none," Arlen said. "Yes, it is a good point."

"We can try changing shield-bearer only after a strike," I said, a little dubiously. "It depends on how long the gaps between shots are."

"It's being struck that's the big energy cost."

We took a quick break, and decided that all of us were still up for continuing. I read the Challenge description and found it identical, except that "Choose a Path" had been replaced with "Find your way down".

"Keep an eye out for slopes," Lewit suggested.

"They are not wordsmiths, these Cycogs," Arlen said, with a light chuckle. "Have you noticed how little music there is, in Challenge or out?"

"No zone themes," Lewit agreed. "A hint, maybe, that they're more machine-like than they let on."

"Or don't have ears," I said, amused. "I think music the way it's usually used in games would have given away too much, anyway. My Cycog, at least, doesn't like spoilers."

"Give away?" Lewit repeated.

"Oh, I see!" Arlen said. "The spritely tune means the safe zone. Then we venture somewhere new, and there are dramatically rising violins to tell us to expect danger. Drums arrive, and build tension..."

"I'm tense enough," Althea said, flatly.

Arlen laughed, and began to sing a high, clear rendition of *The Dragonborn Comes*.

"I think if that was playing while we were trying to get through these Challenges, it'd distract me terribly," I said.

"Yes, no distractions," Althea said. "Let's get on."

"You have a great voice, Arlen," Lewit said, as we started into the entrance tunnel.

"I once was an excellent soprano—and here in this game I am again, which is most amusing. But for now I will be quiet, because I do not care for even a temporary death."

That was a common feeling, and we walked shoulders hunched to a four-way junction, and took the right-hand path. This time it opened out into a corridor similar to the first of this gauntlet series: comfortably wide, curving, with a series of regularly spaced laser ports on either side.

"During the first stage, those things shot faster than I could run," Lewit said. "If we're going to be handing off the shielding job to each other, I think maybe we should stick to a walking pace."

Althea hesitated, and I said: "We can start out at a walk and speed up if the hand-off is easy or the strikes take too much of a toll."

"Yeah, let's try that," she said, her red ponytail bobbing as she nodded.

Since the corridor had widened, we reverted to our originally planned formation—me beside Imoenne at the rear, Lewit beside Arlen in front of us, and Althea taking point directly in front of them. Althea took a hit almost immediately.

"Definitely heavier," she said. "And that came from before us, not beside."

We paused while Lewit built a shield over the top of Althea's, and she let hers drop.

Lewit's suggestion about sticking to a walking pace proved to be wise, because when it came time for me to take my third hit, I only just held it, stumbled in the weak gravity, and lost my shield. If we'd been moving faster, we might have trotted into the activation range of the next laser port before Imoenne could raise the next shield.

Thankfully, the gauntlet stage was only slightly longer than the first, and we were nearing the end. My relief at the Challenge completion message was balanced by an awareness that I looked to be the weak link of the team.

"Ouf, this is my limit!" Arlen declared. "I must rest before I can go on."

"Same," Lewit agreed.

"Wouldn't be safe to go on at anything less than full strength," Althea said, paused, and then added: "I'll be going ahead with my guildies for the rest of the gauntlet."

This was something I'd entirely expected, as soon as she'd mentioned four guild members who'd died during the next stage. They'd want to be full strength before they went on.

"It's been great partying with you," I said. "Good luck getting through the rest."

"You too," she replied, then laughed. "I feel like I should shake hands or something. I don't have the etiquette for gaming being so tangible."

I promptly held out my hand, and we smiled and shook, then she waved and headed toward the tram waiting area.

"I might be in the same sitch," Lewit said. "Most of my guild is playing catch-up, but the frontrunners are nagging me to wait for them so we can take on the System Challenge together."

"Most of my guild are playing around in Earth's satellites, so far as I can tell," I said. "I'll have to see where they're at when I log back in, but currently there's only one that looks likely to get to Mars any time soon. Send me a tell if you're still looking for a group next login, because I don't know how I'll go hurrying them up. Otherwise, good luck."

"Luck to you, too." He laughed. "I won't be waiting too long for my guildies, either. Tons of us weren't on in time to get any of these first-to-rank awards, so everyone near the front wants to get to this System Challenge before anyone else."

With a wave, he followed Althea. I smiled, and shrugged, then gave the twins a thoughtful glance.

"Want to join a guild?"

[g]<Amelia Beerheart> Welcome Imoenne and Arlen to *Corpse Light.*

[g]<Far Cryinggame> Yo.

[g]<Silent> Hey.

[g]<Wraith> Fresh meat!

[g]<TALiSON> Welcome!

[g]<Imoenne> Hello.

[g]<Vasharda> Welcome!

[g]<Arlen> Thank you, thank you all. We have just had our first lesson on what it means to not have a guild in this game.

[g]<Leveret> The major lan trials definitely don't look ideal for casual grouping. Especially when some of them are one-shot only, and rank difference appears to really matter.

[g]<Tornin> Welcome, both of you. We try to be a supportive, rather than a demanding guild. We're still finding our feet in *Dream Speed*, but one of our aims is to ensure that we help each other out with content progression.

[g]<Amelia Beerheart> Somewhat hampered by there being so much content.

[g]<Tornin> The social links will take you to our forums—they're synced with the forums on our guild website, so you can access them in and out of the game. Read through the guild rules when you get a chance—though they're not too far from the location rules here in the game, so if you're complying with them you'll be fine.

[g]<Malazan> Standard 'don't be a dick' set-up.

[g]<Silent> I am officially almost to Mars, Kaz. Just Skipped to far outer orbit.

[g]<Leveret> Nice. I'm going to log a while, and then maybe work on zero G manoeuvres, since they're apparently important to the System Challenge.

[g]<TALiSON> I only just reached Earth orbit, I'm afraid.

[g]<Lady Sirah> Too much *Veil*.

[g]<TALiSON> Yeah, true. I'm so torn. I want to do *DS'* main plotline, but *Veil's* so good. It's got all the things I love that the main story is missing—you know, personality, and consequences, and some sort of tangible endgame that isn't just 'beat a few million other people there'.

[g]<voidMaster> It is damn easy to get distracted in this game.

[g]<Klinnia> I started *Veil* too. I can see why it's hard to tear yourself away.

[g]<TALiSON> Isn't it just the best?

Achievement
First to reach Rank Nine
[Yang Tuo]
Awarded: Custom Ship (Rank One)

[g]<Wraith> Whoa! Nina Stella dethroned!

[g]<Leveret> Custom *ship*.

[g]<Far Cryinggame> Custom SHIP!

[g]<Silent> These global firsts make me so jealous. How damn long and hard are we going to have to work to move up from the pills-in-space looks of our Snugs?

[g]<Amelia Beerheart> Space tampons wouldn't be my first design choice either.

[g]<Wraith> Nan!

[g]<Leveret> I saw a fantastic big ship over Mars. It had Snugs attached to it like Lego.

[g]<Far Cryinggame> I only need to leap-frog two ranks to get first to Rank Ten.

[g]<Lady Sirah> I've had to accept that slow-but-steady's my playstyle. But my Cycog says that sometimes people come out of the gate fast, and then plateau.

[g]<Wraith> Like Nina not-so-Stella!

[g]<Silent> What's the name of the quest series you're doing, Kaz?

[g]<Leveret> *The Heart of Mars.* We've done the first three stages, and need two more for the group before we go on. It's a shield-training gauntlet, nine stages. I'll add the details to the forum.

[g]<Tornin> Perhaps we'll have our next guild meet-up on Mars. It looks incredible.

[g]<Leveret> Apparently there's such a thing as parking queues after the Singularity. Be prepared for a wait to land on Mars once the main wave's arrived.

[g]<Amelia Beerheart> Thankfully camping the download is still keeping us ahead of the pack.

[g]<Far Cryinggame> A ton of the newer players have never tried any kind of MMO before. They're just insomniacs who had a cowl and decided to try the latest craze.

[g]<Silent> First signs of excess server load are showing up, too. Longer login times, but particularly issues if you try to log out quickly.

[g]<Far Cryinggame> The vague memory thing? Yeah, I'm still not sure I believe the way *DS* claims to be structured—that we're Constructs, and our experiences are being sent back in packets to our dreaming selves—but I can see a quick logout means not getting the full last memory packet.

[g]<TALiSON> Thinking too much about the way *DS* might or might not work gives me the cold shivers. But speaking of which, I'm going to log early and get my chores done before The Interview.

[g]<Wraith> Man, is it time for that already? Thanks for the reminder!

[g]<Tornin> A half hour real-world time.

[g]<Leveret> Huh, I'd forgotten it altogether, even though I've got the in-game alarm set to wake me for it.

[g]<Arlen> Will meeting in ten game hours work given the schedule of The Interview?

[g]<Leveret> Good point. Let's just make it—huh, we don't know how long The Interview will last either. If you're both watching it, let's just log on ten minutes after the end of the interview, and meet up.

[g]<Silent> I'll see if I can get to your stage before logging.

[g]<Far Cryinggame> I get the feeling we're going to discover whether there'll be login queues if everyone logs just to watch some developer lie his head off.

[g]<TALiSON> 'Mystery' developer, only named programmer of impossible game, with *no* verified photographs.

[g]<Malazan> A whole day ago I'd say that the lack of info on this guy was a gimmick to help sell the game. Now I think this Dom Kinnen is a synth being worn by Cycogs, which is a belief I'd have found incredibly embarrassing to admit to if I wasn't sure most of you felt the same.

[g]<Silent> Yup.

[g]<Lady Sirah> Yes.

[g]<Amelia Beerheart> Not your standard issue human, anyway. A front for something non-human, or a time traveller or—well, you've heard all the theories.

[g]<Wraith> I'm not such a mug.

[g]<Vasharda> I'm definitely in the mug arena.

[g]<TALiSON> Mulder not Scully today.

[g]<Leveret> But do we really want to believe? I'm going to go practice zero G. Talk to you all after The Interview.

31

"Dio, how feasible is it for me to try to go do some orbital Challenges, then log to watch Dom Kinnen's interview, and get back here for the gauntlet without keeping Arlen and Imoenne waiting about for me? Oh, and do I lose my parking place if I go off-planet for a little while?"

[[There are orbital shuttles: you don't need to use your Snug. They'll cost lux points, however. Timing is more difficult. We don't have teleportation in The Synergis—yet—and you won't be able to complete a Challenge and a return trip in the time frame. If you want to return to this location, you could board the shuttle before logging, and I'll put you in the Soup on arrival.]]

Te meant taking over my body and walking it somewhere. "Ew," I said, settling onto a bench of the tram-thing back out of the Challenge area.

[[This, after all, is only a simulation.]]

"Even so. How common is it for a Cycog to walk about in Bios' empty bodies?"

[[It's sometimes used to tidy away spare modals. Not so common for Core Units. When you are in The Synergis, you are generally not logging out of reality.]]

"Do you wear people's—Bios' modals—to experience being that species?"

[[The command interface is different for Bios and Cycogs. A Type Three modal can be constructed with a Cycog suitable interface, of course, but your Core Unit is not structured for us to 'be'. It is something we would control with a portion of our consciousness, rather than experience.]]

"Like a finger puppet."

Dio laughed, that little synthesiser-like ripple of sound, and...it wasn't Dio. The speaking voice was Dio's, but the laugh was different.

I blinked, looked out the tram window as it drew into the first rest area, and then stood up, feeling dizzy and hot and cold all at once.

"I've changed my mind. I'll log now."

32
the interview

The sense of being rocked became a faded remnant of virtual yesterdays. I lay in bed, no longer sure why the discovery that Dio wasn't Dio had felt like a cut support. Dio had already told me that most of the interaction in the game was handled by Constructs, and supplemented by Cycogs as needed. Had I just been surprised identifying the shift? Once I'd worked it out, I'd never forgotten that Dio wasn't 'my' Cycog. But te had been the Cycog who talked to me.

Pulling off my cowl, I turned over the idea of Dio-the-definite-NPC versus Dio-the-person. Well, they would both be non-player characters: one was just more a games master popping in to troll. The big question was, who was the games master?

When I climbed out of bed I felt the usual combination of refreshed and gluggy that came with returning to a body that wasn't fine-tuned to a peak of fitness. And I wasn't even so unfit that it was a real contrast. The news had provided a stream of tear-filled stories of players experiencing stock-standard physical ability for the first time. They, too, would wake to dissonance, to five hours of recovery time, so sensible and so cruel.

Shivering, I washed, then wandered out into the living room. It was dusk, real-time, and the house's heat was low. I adjusted the temperature, then started cooking a simple dinner. My parents weren't awake, so I worked on something that would keep even if they didn't get up for The Interview.

"Hey, good timing," my father said, wandering into the kitchen just as I was dishing out. "Care to handle my revisions while you're at it?"

"I thought you liked revising?"

"I do! But in a 'this is the easy part of work' way of things, not 'this is pure, unadulterated fun'. Anything interesting on the feeds?" He nodded toward the living room, and the muted screen.

"Just the fact that lead-up to The Interview is on all the main channels. A game dev has become Event TV. Oh, and traditional media reporters are very salty about the fact that gaming sites have more seats in the press pit than they do."

"Sounds like common sense to me." My mother, hair a tangle, started a pot of coffee, then wandered off to the bathroom. When she returned, she had changed out of her daily work clothes into night clothes. "I feel like I haven't been on my rounds for an age," she said. "Even though I've been out today already."

"You're so well-rested you feel like you should be up and doing," I said.

"Well, that and I've run up to my login limit, but don't feel like going to non-*DS* sleep in the slightest. Perhaps I can do some midwinter spring cleaning after this interview is over."

"Sleeping too much doesn't usually leave me full of vim and vigour," my father noted. "If I'd known this was the result of sleep-aid cowls, I would have bought one earlier."

"One of the many reasons they're so popular," I said.

My mother kept an eye on the television while organising identification tags and restocking her day pack. Her current job involved surveying numbers of wintering birds in Drenthe: a variation on countless similar positions in a dozen countries since I'd been born. It was poorly-paid, often exhausting work, but she loved it. My father, writing travelogues and freelance articles, managed to supplement the family income just enough to allow occasional splurges on GDG cowls, but not enough, really, to indulge an adult child trying to start up a solo design business.

"Did Oma try the cowl?" I asked, as we settled in front of the television.

"When I checked on her around lunch, she said she'd never needed help to sleep." My mother sighed. "Now that I've seen what *DS* can do, I really want her to give it a shot. She doesn't have to get involved in any of the Challenges if she doesn't want to. I'd love to just walk along a beach with her."

"You should meet up with us in-game yourself, kiddo," my father said. "Do a couple of family group Challenges."

"I need zero-G practice, if you want to get together for that. I'm on Mars, though."

"We'll schedule something when we get there, then."

We caught up on each other's adventures while the news reports went over things we already knew about Dom Kinnen, Ryzonart's sole named developer. Born in Bosnia. Parents migrated to Morocco during the Bosnian War. Current residence Zurich, Switzerland. A list of schools he'd studied at, and a handful of interviews of fellow students who barely remembered him. "Quiet guy, always writing stories." Then nothing, until Ryzonart began releasing games a couple of years ago. Very successful mobile games until, with no hint of it pre-demo, *Dream Speed*.

When Dom Kinnen finally walked out on the stage of the small lecture theatre used for The Interview, the reaction came in stereo from my father and mother: "Looks like an accountant."

I supposed a small-framed white man sporting rimless glasses might match the stereotype of accountants. He was wearing an earpiece mike, and an alert, amiable expression. Ignoring the noise his arrival had provoked, he surveyed the crowd, then said:

"Welcome everyone. Our servers are currently under a sustained DDOS attack, so let's get through this quickly. You drew tickets for question order, so can I hear from ticket holder one?"

"Interesting accent," my mother said. "More Morocco than Bosnia."

"I'm sad that he's a real person," I said. "Or seems to be."

The first questioner, bobbing to their feet, was obviously thinking on the same lines: "Rahal Amaldi, *Gamers Daily*. What are you, sir, human puppet or Cycog in a synth-suit?"

I—half the press pack—laughed. Dom Kinnen smiled.

"Human puppet. Next question."

"Jaq Shannon, *MetaGamer*. What clinical trials were undertaken to establish whether *Dream Speed* is safe for human use?"

"Guided dream cowls underwent years of trials before release," Dom Kinnen replied. "*Dream Speed* itself does not step outside the parameters of GDG, although it certainly takes the concepts to their limits."

"You can't compare guided dreams to copying people's memories back from the net!" Shannon burst out, but Kinnen had already moved on to the next question.

"Sato Hitori, *xyz*. Sir, you are the only contributor listed for a game with more content than works that involve thousands of programmers, writers, concept artists, voice actors, and musicians. Where is the rest of the development team?"

"Buried under non-disclosure agreements." Kinnen lifted his shoulders in the tiniest of shrugs. "I'm not solely responsible for *Dream Speed*, although I have been working on concept and story since, well, my early teens. The rest of the team is credited via hard-to-reach Easter eggs within the game itself."

"How many of them are aliens?" yelled someone from the back of the room.

Kinnen ignored that, saying: "Next number."

"Lu Chen, *Game Scene*. From the basis of processing power, *Dream Speed* is a game every expert insists is not possible with our current technology level. We make jokes about aliens and AI, but how do you explain a game that can perfectly render a zone with tens of thousands of characters without any sign of lag?"

"*Dream Speed* doesn't 'render' images. As we've explained, *Dream Speed* operates on the same principles as any other guided dream game, but instead of offering general prompts that a dreamer shapes, it feeds specific images and information. It allows for a shaped shared experience." Kinnen smiled. "We all carry more than enough processing power about with us to 'see' twenty thousand people in a field."

"This guy lies as glibly as my Cycog," I said.

"How do you know it's a lie?" my mother asked.

"Even prompting us with specific images, there'd surely be variation from person to person, and I've seen enough streams of gameplay to show that multiple people are seeing exactly the same thing. Unless he's saying that they've turned player brains into a giant LAN." I stopped, struck by the coincidence of names. "I really hope that's not what he's saying."

"Lars Anderssen, *EuroPlayer*," the next reporter was saying. "Virtual reality on this level represents a profound shift in human interaction. Players are experiencing simulated injuries, sex, and death. They wear bodies not their own: a circumstance that will provide as much shock as insight. Does Ryzonart take any responsibility—does Ryzonart *acknowledge* the moral responsibility it must bear?"

Dom Kinnen inclined his head. "In designing *Dream Speed*, we have incorporated into every aspect of the game a push to minimise harm. The majority of the customer complaints we've received so far have been in relation to restrictions to interaction—and our free use of the Ban Hammer, which is likely the reason we are facing the DDOS attack now. Just as there is no technical necessity for forcing a five hour play shut-out, we've chosen to limit the amount of pain players can experience, and to honour codes of conduct expected in the non-virtual world. Ryzonart takes player safety very seriously."

That brought a little rush of questions, none of which Kinnen responded to, until finally the babble gave way to the next number holder.

"Battle Shroud, *Ezy*. What is Ryzonart's response to calls in multiple countries to block access to *Dream Speed*?"

"It's possible that will happen. A matter for those governments to deal with."

There was just a hint of amusement in Kinnen's voice, and that didn't surprise me, because no government would enjoy the backlash that would follow taking away virtual youth.

After that point, the interview devolved primarily into reiterations of questions already asked. Kinnen, the third time he was asked to prove he was human, wondered if anyone had brought along a hot wire and a petri dish, and a few of the visible reporters looked thoroughly inclined to storm the stage to take a blood sample. But overall, The Interview was a far less dramatic and momentous occasion most players had been hoping for.

For myself, I'd half expected to recognise Dio wearing a skinsuit, but Kinnen hadn't 'felt' at all like Dio. Instead, he'd come across as a fairly ordinary smart person who had produced a revolutionary but entirely possible game that he made no attempt to pretend was anything but fictional.

"Verdict?" my mother asked, after flicking through and then muting a spate of post-interview analysis.

"Well, I never expected him to get up before the press and say 'Take me to your leader'," I said. "Short of an appearance from something clearly non-human, sticking to 'it's all made up' seems the only line they could take."

"The far future setting probably is fiction," my father pointed out. "Unless we really are dealing with time travellers, of course. But I'm entirely willing to believe The Synergis and Cycogs could be a part of an existing galactic community, and *Dream Speed* a softening process to get us used to their concepts before official first contact."

I thought about whether I was being softened. I'd certainly adapted far more quickly than I would have believed to having Dio as a constant presence—at least until te had turned into not-Dio. Which of them would be with me when I logged back in?

Only one way to find out.

I'd chosen to log out in a sleep pod rather than Soup, mainly because I couldn't forget the idea that there were probably dozens of Core Units all in the same vat—or would be if not for the conveniences of 'simulations'. I definitely preferred waking up curled comfortably on my side, rather than with that hit of mint-chill Soup. And the pod had the added advantage that, instead of immediately stepping out into the staging area, I could lie there thinking some more.

Eventually, I decided asking questions was a better option to anticipating answers.

"Dio, given that Bios body hop, and Cycogs are little motes of light, does The Synergis have any definitive way of telling individuals apart?"

One of those motes of light drifted through the ceiling of my sleep pod.

[[Yes. It took us a long time to reach that point, however. Bio Ian was something we could sense, but not initially measure, and much of the way it functions is still a process of discovery for us. But we can now clearly identify individual Bios from their Ian. Uniquely identifying Cybercognates was an easier task, but has its own issues, because we change more completely than Bios. For instance, a system administrator who had put valuables under Self Lock later divided into two, and neither of the shards were recognised by the lock.]]

"Can you tell each other apart just by, uh, looking?"

[[Those who know me best would likely be able to pick me out of a crowd by my...call it aura. But that is not a definitive thing, any more than our voices are impossible to imitate.]] There was an unmistakeable thread of amusement in that last sentence. This was definitely Dio, and a Dio who had clearly guessed that I'd been upset, that I'd logged out hastily because I'd been able to tell voices apart.

"Why isn't the Construct Cycog good enough at pretending to be you that it didn't use your laugh?"

[[Oh, we do that deliberately. It makes us uncomfortable, for one thing, to have pretend selves to that level. But we also like to see if Bios notice.]]

"I should have known."

[[The intention is not to distress, however,]] Dio went on, in a less entertained tone. [[I apologise for that. The denial of service attacks are testing our connections.]]

I shrugged, because it had been silly of me to be bothered in any way. I was *not* going to describe to Dio the sensation of walking through a crowd holding on to your mother's bag, and then looking up to see a bemused stranger.

[[I learned a great deal about you from that last session. I had not previously noted the leadership tendencies.]]

"Is that leading? I'm hardly the only one out there who wants to avoid a pointless waste of time arguing, so I figured there'd be other people there who just wanted to get on with it. Did you decide I was bad with people because I shut off all my communication feeds?"

[[Maybe.]]

I shook my head, deciding not to try to explain that I was fine with people, so long as I could take extended breaks from them, and was not currently made of fail. Speaking of which...

Arlen and Imoenne were either fully anon, or not logged in yet. Silent was on Mars, exploring the area outside the Challenge location, and I chatted to him and other guild members as they logged back in and dissected The Interview down to the same conclusion my parents had reached.

[g]<Silent> The big question being which of the many possibilities they're preparing us for.

[g]<Far Cryinggame> Ranging from *The Last Starfighter* to *Matrix*?

[g]<Tornin> I'm leaning toward *Starfighter*: they need Ian pilots (or Ian something) and this is the equivalent of

carefully planted arcade games, training us in the basics, sorting the wheat from the chaff, in preparation for a recruitment offer.

[g]<TALiSON> I don't see why they couldn't do that openly. If they, say, are aliens that have lost their lan pilots and need some more to get home, or are AIs that have developed locally and want to travel off-world? Why not just tell us that and ask for volunteers?

[g]<Far Cryinggame> Because setting up an almost plausible MMO is less of a headache than officially dealing with governments?

[g]<Wraith> Because it's fun to shove their noodle future down our throats. Half recruitment, half giant psych project.

[g]<Far Cryinggame> Your definitive take on The Synergis revolves around what's between your legs?

[g]<Wraith> When every second Challenge takes my bits away? Yeah.

[g]<Lady Sirah> I've got it! I've got it! We've in an Enclave. It's like the movie *The Village*, but we're the ones in the village. We're further into the future than we know and the game's a way of transitioning us to the reality of now.

Arlen and Imoenne popped up in the guild 'active' list, so I pushed guild chat away, and suggested a spot in the staging area to meet up, then went to look for the nearest toilet.

The bathrooms were not divided by species or sex, but by size, except for a room that had an airlock, and was no doubt intended for the species that didn't breathe some sort of oxygen/nitrogen mix. The area that was intended for my size species was unremarkable, offering stalls with floor or bench options for waste, and water and wipes for cleansing, along with a separate sub-room provided with a Soup vat and mirrors. There was a small teal-coloured humanoid in there, using a tiny curry comb to smooth and then make patterns in the plush-short hair that covered all of her visible skin. Her hide? I washed my hands, trying not to stare while wondering if this was a player with a great modal, or an NPC.

The idea of asking someone who was not a player prying questions about her skin made me feel awkward, so I left. Even though all the NPCs would be either Constructs or, probably, Dio, it felt strangely intrusive to talk to them.

The meeting point I'd suggested was again next to this stage's wall mosaic. The same gorgeous array of colour, but now I could make out figures amongst the swirls. Brown tiles resolved into a featureless human, and the silvery multi-columnar shape must be the methane-breathing species.

I searched out the third shape and, just as Silent arrived, found a small round 'animal' almost lost in the curlicues of the mosaic. He murmured a greeting and considered the mosaic.

"The picture adds a species with each stage. Darashi, Vvv, uh, Vssf, and human so far."

"Are Type Threes called humans in The Synergis?"

[[Llura.]]

Dio rarely spoke up uninvited in conversations between Bios, so I was as much surprised by the contribution as the name.

"Is that the name Type Threes call themselves, or what other species call us?"

[[Guess,]] Dio said, with a ripple of laughter, then sank through the mosaic.

"I'm willing to bet it's not something complimentary, then," I said to Silent.

"I see you've a quirky sort of Cycog. Have you noticed their personalities often match their names?"

"What do you mean?"

"The Cycogs people have called HAL are very calm and often unhelpful. The Datas are Pinocchios all lit up with curiosity. The GLaDOSes ooze passive-aggressive snark."

"Two out of three of those personalities are liable to kill you."

"I played it safe and called mine Bishop. But it's the sheer adaptability that makes it so difficult to believe this game doesn't involve...something more." He laughed. "Listen to me. I'm usually one of the guild's cynics."

"The GDG 'filling in the blanks' concept works for personalities, though. If you called someone HAL, you'd expect at least a few pod bay door references. I liked the idea it was my mind producing this stuff in a solo GDG, but I'm far less comfortable with the idea that the players are building a full virtual experience by being fed prompts."

"I foresee several dozen theses on perceived reality, if that's the way this game functions. But I don't believe Ryzonart. And the Cycogs are...convincing."

"And The Synergis so alluring."

He laughed. "I'm so used to dystopias that I can't help but look for the cracks. Is the face they're showing us true, or something mocked up to draw us in?"

He glanced at me, frowning, and I wondered if he was also tripping over a stranger's face to go with a familiar voice.

"Whether The Synergis is true, or just a really enjoyable game, I'm worried there's a price," I admitted.

Silent nodded. "It does feel like a honey-baited trap. Maybe the Cycogs really are here to steal...I can't believe I'm saying this. My Catholic upbringing stirring."

"Lan equates soul, and they cultivate Bios for their lan? If there turns out to be a theological explanation for this, well, I guess I'd be impressed by such a slick technological approach to soul-stealing."

"And then run like hell."

"By then I guess I'd be *in* Hell," I said, and then added: "But if this all turns out to really be Purgatory, I want another ending," and perhaps only imagined I heard a faint, now-familiar laugh.

34

There was no real need to visit the party finder to add a last member to our group. A constantly changing mass of players had been forming, dissolving and reforming just opposite the mosaic, and I simply strolled over and said: "Group of four ranked 6, 7 and 8 looking for one more."

This didn't run so smoothly as last time, since five people immediately stepped hopefully toward me. In a less 'personal' environment, picking one and moving wordlessly on would be simple, but the mere presence of the others in the same space as me made it instantly awkward. I hesitated, then added:

"We're likely to try and take the Challenge run in two to three sessions, with big breaks in the middle to work on zero-G in prep for the System Challenge. Looking for someone ideally to come all the way through to attempting the System Challenge."

Three of the five hesitated, then shrugged and turned back to the main group. I was left with two girls. One looked like a teen, with fantastic dark blue and snow white hair done up in a long pair of high ponytails, and a great matching skirt and jacket outfit that was right out of a magical girl anime. The second was tall and willowy and had rose tattoos everywhere visible: some of the most beautiful skin art I'd ever seen. Both of them were fully anon.

Roses glanced at Ponytails and spoke in Russian, obligingly translated by the game as: "Flip a coin?"

"Sure. Not that money exists here." Ponytails had spoken English, with a mild accent. I'd guess her to be Japanese.

"Pick a number between one and ten," I suggested. "Closest to the one I'm thinking of joins."

"One," Roses said.

"Ten."

"And I picked six," I said, with a wry smile at Roses. "Good luck with the Challenge."

"See you on The Wreck," she replied, waved, and turned back to the crowd.

"Welcome aboard," I said, sending an invite. "This is Silent, Imoenne, and Arlen. I'm Leveret."

"Nova Mori," the girl responded, as we started toward the entrance to the next stage.

I wondered if the tendency to run around anon would die away after the initial new game zerg, or if names and ranks and guilds would always be semi-secret. Well, if Nova was the same rank as me, I'd at least not feel like I was holding the group back. But I'd been giving plenty of thought to how to get through this Challenge series without having to go and gain levels—and without losing my bet with Dio.

"We need a strategy, do we not?" Arlen said.

I nodded. "If it keeps increasing in strength, broken shields seem almost guaranteed. I think we're going to have to permanently double-layer the shields, and combine that with the swapping regime we established." I explained to Nova and Silent what we'd done in the third Challenge, and what I wanted now.

"Anticipate failure by putting one person on the inner layer, and another for the outer layer?" Nova asked.

"If the outer drops, do we just sit another outer on it?" Silent asked. "Or try to expand the inner layer to be the outer?"

"Expanding a shield once you've set it, that is not so easy," Arlen said, shaking his head. He was speaking English this session, with occasional hesitations on less common words.

"I suspect it's a skill we might want to develop, though. Shall we do a practice round before we go in, to see if it'll work?"

"Practice is a good idea," Nova agreed. "But why complicate matters trying to expand the shields? We can just lift them a little higher."

"Better still, if an outer shield is hit or dropped, put up a new outer shield, and then drop and replace the inner shield," Silent said. "Then next round, the person who did the inner shield is responsible for the outer shield, and vice versa."

It proved to be a workable suggestion, and after a quick round of practice, we activated the next Challenge stage.

THE HEART OF MARS
Behind the shadows
Solo or Party
Gauntlet
Gateway series
Length: Thirty minutes (4 of 9)
Core Unit

"'Behind the Shadows' is a little more dramatic than the first couple of Challenge descriptions," I noted.

"Why is it quests never send us to look behind sunbeams?" Arlen hummed a snatch of melody, the silver helmet form of his active focus not seeming to impede the sound.

Nova shrugged. "Even though it's clearly training in the guise of a quest, giving us tunnels and lasers without any kind of plot is a weak effort."

"Looks like we're leaving the narrow path behind, at least," Silent said, as we entered an actual cavern, walls and floor uneven, with numerous obstructions dramatically lit by incongruous lampposts that made me think vaguely of Narnia.

"No sign of laser ports, but no obvious path, either." I hesitated, trying to decide where to head in the wide, boulder-studded space.

"Straight across?" Nova suggested. "And change course if we discover any reason to."

We agreed, but didn't exactly hurry into the echoing space. The atmosphere was outright creepy, and it didn't help when, into the pause, came a flutter of sound. Too low for any kind of clarity, it could have been a sigh, or a moan.

"Zombies of Mars?" Silent said, but with a thin quality to his usual drawl.

"Did anyone mention zombies in the discussions about the Challenge series? I thought these Ian Challenges were supposed to be watchable."

"Yes, if you know who to watch and when. Those Challenge-views don't repeat, and most people reporting on this stage and the next are being very vague, outside of warning of harder hitting lasers. Most everyone doing a gateway series wants to be first to qualify for the System Challenge."

"Zombies are not likely to hit as hard as lasers," I said.

"They could crawl under the shield," Arlen said, bouncing lightly on his feet.

I was on inner shield duty, and part of my attention was locked into Ian, but I still found myself looking for the Renba I'd been studiously ignoring since waking. Five of them, clustered near the ceiling, waiting for something to cut us down. We hadn't spent enough time talking about what to do if we were injured, not killed—whether to retreat or run on—but now didn't seem a good moment to broach the subject.

"Let's get moving," Nova said, and we shuffled forward, then broke into a slow trot, picking a path over the uneven ground.

No laser bolts struck, no zombies clutched at ankles, no exits presented themselves at the far side of the cavern.

"What now?" Silent asked, surveying the protrusions and hollows to each side.

"Work our way around and hope we stumble across it?" I said.

"They are very literal with their 'behind the shadows', it seems," Nova said, sounding more amused than worried.

As we turned right, I caught that whisper of sound again, but this time I hadn't even time to turn my head before the now-familiar buzzing of laser bolts. Arlen had the outer shield, and let out his breath as a volley of multiple bolts struck.

"Not good," he said, as we turned trot into dash. "Barely—"

Another volley took down his shield, two of the bolts hitting mine.

"Behind this boulder!" I said, thankful I'd managed to keep my shield up, and sure I wouldn't be able to sustain another hit.

Trying to maintain a shield over a group hurling itself into cover wasn't the easiest thing I'd done, but we were fortunate I kept mine more-or-less in position, because the source of the blasts followed us around the curve of stone and fired again, sending chips of rock flying, and hitting my shield once again before Silent, next in the rotation, managed to get a fresh shield over the top as mine dropped.

"What now?" Silent gasped, as a floating, silvery drone came into clear view, and his shield took a full barrage.

"Keep circling," I said, as Imoenne managed to form her shield beneath Silent's. "Find exit. Run into it."

"Nova Smash," said Nova, in a firm little voice.

This was spectacularly accompanied by the drone being pounded into the ground, and then exploding.

"What the hell?" Silent said it, but the rest of us surely thought it.

"We're supposed to be able to lan duel, so I figured we could hit things with our shields," Nova said.

"Nice," I said, appreciatively.

"The genius move," Arlen added. "Now it is paste, instead of us."

"And we should keep moving," Nova said. "There might be others."

I turned again to survey the uneven outer walls, looking for something that might be an exit passage, but Arlen was still focused on the smashed drone.

"There is something odd there" he said. "Can we move near?"

We obediently shifted toward the still-smoking slag. The drone had exploded violently enough to pit the rock around it.

"Moving under a shield umbrella cuts down on our mobility," Silent noted. "We should practice splitting into groups in the next safe zone."

"If we—" I paused, because I caught what Arlen was pointing to, well hidden in the gloom between two boulders behind the drone. "A stair?"

"It was, perhaps, guarding," Arlen said. "Just to think of the hours spent if we avoided the machine and searched the outer wall."

"Let's get going before something else comes along," Silent said.

"Anyone bring a torch?" I asked, but it wasn't too bad getting down—there was a hint of light once we were looking directly down the stairwell, and the only real difficulty was not hitting shield edges against things when descending. After that was a straight, blast-free corridor out to another staging area.

"Break and snacks?" I suggested.

"Why is it I feel so tired, for such a short walk?" Arlen asked. "We have hardly come any way at all."

"Adrenaline." Nova led the way to the nearest Soup outlet. "Along with maintaining the shields. Fortunately these sessions seem designed to be short—win or lose."

I was finding Nova a very interesting person. With a Core Unit that looked mid-teens, the magical girl styling, and a very self-assured attitude, I couldn't help but speculate over what she was like out in the world. For all I'd told myself a few times that out-of-game couldn't really matter in *Dream Speed*, the whole concept of a Core image, of a self that matched who you felt you were, drew me into questions of what of a person was 'really' like. Was I more truly myself inside *Dream Speed* or out of it?

The game did tell me one thing about our two French-speaking group members: they were both under eighteen, though I thought not much younger than that. Other than a greeting in guild chat, and some soft murmurs to her brother, I hadn't heard Imoenne speak at all, and I could not decide if it was ruder to push her to talk, or seem to ignore her.

In the end I compromised by addressing a space between the two siblings and saying: "So, Arlen, Imoenne, do you both sing?"

"Oh, yes," Arlen answered, while Imoenne made a duck of the head that might be a nod. "Our family, it is the most musical, so it is fortunate that the path was to our liking. Voice is my primary instrument, while Imoenne is more versatile."

"Are you planning performance careers?"

Arlen raised an equivocal hand. "There are certain practicalities. It is one thing to perform, another to live and perform."

"I would like to know if there are stages on the Drowned Earth," Imoenne said, in barely audible voice, her French effortlessly translated by the system.

"Putting one before that big curve of Vessa Major would be spectacular," I said, trying not to look too surprised that she'd finally spoken.

"Does being on Mars affect your voice?" Silent asked.

"I hear a change, but I am told that it is caused by a slight difference in air pressure, rather than the gravity," Arlen said.

As the conversation ranged through gravity and performance, I explored a newly discovered group calendaring function, where we could schedule sessions while factoring in mandatory lock-outs.

"Anyone coming up on lock-out?" I asked.

"I am," Nova said. "I'll easily manage one more stage, maybe two, but not more."

"Let's schedule a big break after this run, then. Try to synchronise our logins so we hit a time where everyone's free."

We worked on the calendar for a while, blocking out times with real-world commitments, and good breaks between lan sessions. I'd worried that we would hit some long unavailable patches, but Silent was the only one with inflexible appointments in the next few real-world hours, and they were short. Teleconferences, he explained.

Silent was an engineering consultant, always busy with multiple projects, and I was used to him fitting his work around guild events, knowing he could be trusted to show up when he said he would. Planning on trying the System Challenge with three strangers was something of a gamble, but I liked what I'd seen of Nova, Arlen and Imoenne. Focused on the task but relaxed. Nice people. Of course, we hadn't hit any situations that might inspire a barrage of yelling.

The player who'd stabbed me in the back had seemed nice too.

35

station

The next Challenge description, 'Beneath the Stars', sounded too vague to be a useful guide to how to get through it, but when we entered a thoroughly gloomy cavern, we naturally headed towards the brightest glimmers of light: a dozen glowing circles arranged in an arch.

"Reminds me somehow of the gate to Moria," Silent said.

Before I could manage a joke about The Synergis word for 'friend', a familiar buzzing sound warned us that was the wrong solution. An arch of blaster ports.

Since it looked like they were guarding the only way out, we chose to triple shield and run at it, straight into an onslaught so intense that each shield went down in turn, and it was only speed that kept us whole.

Unfortunately, we weren't handily already at the exit, but facing another gloomy cavern with an arch of lights.

"Five layers of shields," I suggested. "If your shield drops, try to put it straight back up."

"So many shields, and we will not fit through the exit," Arlen pointed out.

"One person with a full shield, the rest of us shielding at the front only."

The strategy worked, but we came out of a run of six of these caverns completely exhausted, most of us barely able to raise shields during the last barrage.

"I am finished," Arlen declared. "Let us have done."

"Good thing we have a long break scheduled," I agreed, surveying the rest area. Same layout, same mosaic—now featuring two more aliens—but a distinctly different feeling to the area. "It's almost empty."

"There's a reason no group has completed a gateway series so far," Silent said. "Just over halfway through this one, and I'm not sure we'll manage the next stage."

"We're not doing so bad," I said, as I found the nearest seat and fell into it. The last two stages had confirmed for me, if nothing else, that I was the weakest member of the team.

I lingered long after everyone else had left, thinking about ways to get stronger without breaking the terms of my bet. I didn't like being carried. Without a reasonable way to gain ranks, could I contribute by being smarter?

"Dio, could we have put a full Pocket around that drone and floated it off into space?"

[[No. Thankfully. If you Bios could do that to each other, we'd never keep track of you.]]

"Why isn't it possible?"

[[Your Ian is a part of you—you can't snip pieces of it off. Even if a Bio obligingly allowed you put them in a complete Pocket, the Pocket would still be connected to you.]]

"And they could damage the Pocket from the inside?"

[[Absolutely.]]

I heaved a dramatic sigh, then picked myself up and took the trolley back to the entrance, working out how to get a shuttle up to an orbital station, and how many lux points it would cost me. Good timing meant that I had only a short wait before entering a shuttle only big enough to fit a couple of dozen widely-space and cushiony seats, and with wonderfully large windows that meant I'd be able to thoroughly enjoy the view.

[[Planning on a return trip?]]

Complete disorientation. There was no view, and people were around me, getting up, moving past. Gravity had gone from light to Earth normal. I'd slept through the whole flight.

"You make for a complicated alarm clock, Dio."

[[One with no snooze button. Up with you, unless you want to spend more lux points.]]

'Lux' felt like the proper term for this wide-aisled vehicle, with its big windows, and cushiony seats. It took me the short trip to the exit to puzzle out why it felt doubly-strange, and it was only as I was stepping through the airlock-style hatch that I realised there was a complete lack of attendants. No-one collecting rubbish, or moving armrests, or hurrying us up as politely as possible.

"Who crews the shuttles?" I asked Dio.

[[Constructs. The planetary and station administrators hand off responsibility for the Constructs as they enter and leave their space, but it's rare that any intervention is necessary.]]

"Is it ever required to, say, politely greet the local administrator when you enter their territory?"

[[Administrators would not usually greet Bios.]]

"No, not the Chocobos," I muttered, but without heat. We were thoroughly pampered transport, after all.

I'd chosen Red Planet Station, apparently the second-largest. The rules that popped up at the entrance weren't anything surprising: no duelling allowed, no airing of genitals in public places, no projectiles or explosives.

"What's the purpose of the space stations?" I asked, as I reviewed the local Challenge list. Then I stopped walking.

Red Planet Station clearly maintained an artificial gravity. It also featured a lot of promenade area with viewport ceilings. And 'above' was Mars, with the grand rift of Valles Marineris blazing blue and green across the pink-cream surface. Enormous, gorgeous, overwhelming.

[[The view, mainly,]] Dio explained. [[Zero-G amusements. Scientific experimentation. Waypoints easier to maintain than anything possible on certain local planetary surfaces. Places to meet that do not involve dropping into a gravity well.]]

Realising I'd once again stopped in the middle of a walkway. I found the nearest seat and gazed at Mars, and then an overlay map of the station, which was shaped interestingly like a crown. The promenade was built into the circular base, while spike-like towers pointed away from the planet. There were three zones of gravity, with Earth-normal at the base, and zero-G at the tower tips.

It was difficult to tear myself away from the business of Looking, to continue to review the Challenge list, applying different filters until I had a list of top contenders to work my way through.

RED SKY DIVING
Adventures in the Janitor Corp.
Solo
Timed
Length: 30 minutes
Supplied Biosynth

"Is there an actual Janitor Corp?" I asked, as I followed the usual arrow. "It seemed like Constructs take care of all the cleaning and maintenance."

[[The Janitor Corp is a galaxy-wide Challenge series designed to give Bios some glimpse of the support system behind their, ah, stables. There's a leaderboard involved, achievements, set collection. It's quite popular.]]

"Sounds like, well, I guess everything non-Ian is filler, isn't it?"

My arrow led me into the zero-G zone, and I took my time on the trip, practicing moving from handgrip to handgrip, and bouncing across rooms.

"What happens if I strand myself out of reach of everything?" I asked, as I glided down what would probably be an elevator shaft if gravity were turned on.

[[After I stop laughing? I could call on a Construct for recovery. Though most Bios simply flail about, trying to generate momentum, then have their own Renba tow them.]]

I gave my sparrow-sized silver shadow a dubious glance, but had to admit the thing moved effortlessly through all the gravity variants I'd encountered so far.

"What about during a Challenge?"

[[Flailing. Until you either give up the Challenge, or the time limit runs out.]]

"Noted."

The arrow took me to a Soup vat, which I found difficult to pull open in zero-G. I swam into the mirror-wall exposed and, after a tiny, confused interval, I found myself swimming out of the same vat, except as a different me, and then I wasted the first few minutes of my timed Challenge gaping down myself. The biosynth. I'd expected a metallic human, but this was...

The body was a navy fibre weave. There were four arms. And tentacles. So many tentacles.

The reflection in the Soup showed that I maintained a humanoid structure. Head, torso, legs and arms in roughly the same position, with some adjustment for the second arm set, which was the source of most of the tentacles, although both my legs also tapered into amazingly long tentacles that writhed and coiled as I watched.

I was wearing goggles that made it a little difficult to see my face clearly, but through them I looked back at myself with massive blue-black eyes, with no visible sclera, and multiple transparent eyelids that slid up and down in double-blink. My visual colour range seemed to be the same. No nose or mouth or hair. Ears that were sculpted indents into the skull structure, rather than bits of flesh sticking off the side. It was a whole step beyond being a different sort of human, or a cat. Jellyfish-octopus-oid.

Not forgetting that I was in a timed Challenge, I noted an arrow pointing in a new direction, but ignored it in favour of methodically testing my movement: flexing tentacles, craning my head back and forth, bending and shifting. I didn't seem to need to breathe, and had no sense of a heartbeat, but found an extreme awareness of the movement of my limbs through the air around me. Only after I had turned somersaults, and tested moving up and down the corridor, did I head in the direction my Challenge guide was pointing.

To an airlock.

I froze as soon as I recognised it—though continued floating forward. It's an extraordinary thing to feel extreme excitement, to be at a pitch of nervous anticipation, and not experience any of the sensations that usually accompanied the emotions. No shaky breath. No racing pulse. No sick-tight sensation in my stomach. A biosynth had, somewhere within, the necessary biological substance and support system needed for a Bio to maintain Ian, but that was a small part of a much greater whole. In a way I was my own spaceship.

And through this double-door chamber...

Space.

"I spent a good ten minutes just outside the airlock, gaping. Fortunately the Challenge itself wasn't too difficult, or I'd have failed it."

"What was it?" my mother asked. "Cleaning the outside of the windows?" She glanced up and around at said windows, and that drowning view of Valles Marineris.

"Using a thing like a butterfly net to collect space debris. The artificial gravity apparently causes a lot of flotsam to cluster outside as if lightly magnetised."

"So you've saved us from seeing crisp packets float by?" my father asked.

"It was a weird collection. Little white chips of the stuff that our Snugs are made of, as if they'd been colliding with each other. Space rock. Various metallic somethings. Mostly greyish splooge that Dio—that my Cycog says is escaped sealant."

"So they even gamify space splooge," my father said, putting a hand up to take off glasses he wasn't wearing, and then smiling ruefully. "I keep forgetting I don't need them."

My parents—my parents' Core Units—were familiar strangers. They had reverted to their early twenties. Dad was taller, my mother shorter, though she was still at least an inch taller than him. They both had a lot more hair than usual—in fact, they were wearing almost identical hairstyles: long, silky hair pulled up in a high tail. My father's short-sightedness had obviously been corrected, and they had the clear-complexioned vitality that most of the Core Units shared, along with some tiny shifts to their features that I guess represented the same thing as my longer legs and less stocky look.

"How's your guild managing?" I asked. "Sticking to your rules?" I'd never really been able to keep up the strict roleplaying between members that my parents' guild maintained, though it was often fun to try.

"Relishing the set-up. The concept makes it very easy to stay in character, since we can claim to be from a human-only Enclave that pretends to its citizens that it's the original Earth. We haven't decided whether to have a guild position on trying to bring down The Synergis, or let everyone go their own way, but we're having a great time exploring."

"And have you decided whether you personally want to steal a ship or stay?"

"I don't think that's the decision that matters," my mother said thoughtfully. "The question is not whether The Synergis is a utopia, but whether the game itself comes with a catch."

My father reached for absent glasses again, and grimaced. "It's tempting to believe in this idea of the Starfighter Invitation."

"Someone goes off to join heroic space battles, and the rest of us just get to play a cool game?" I said.

"I don't object to joining an intergalactic defence force," my mother said. "But if either of you are recruited, leave a note."

"I'm not anywhere near the top of the leaderboards, but sure," I said.

"What if the important thing is to decide to steal the ship?" my father asked. "If *Dream Speed* is a recruitment tool, perhaps it's looking for those who will strongly resist pampered servitude?"

"Surely they'd present The Synergis in a worse light?" I glanced around for Dio, but te wasn't visible.

"We've only just started," my mother pointed out. "There is a galaxy to explore in this game, and much opportunity to find what has been swept under the carpet. At this stage, I am disinclined to take my ship and run, however. Tadori feels more like a friend than a...controller."

Did I regard Dio as a friend? Dio wasn't a fledgling Cycog, but a Construct some of the time, and someone else at others. Claiming that someone else as a friend seemed outright foolish. Fun to talk to, sure, but not anything like trustworthy. Teasing, uncomfortably insightful, probably a very nice floating ball of light, but someone whose agenda felt more like finding out what made me tick rather than being a team.

"Did you see my *Dream Speed* design?" I said, rather than keep poking at the question. "It's been selling enough that I think I'll make this month's rent."

"Not only seen it, but bought a shirt," my father said.

My mother looked pleased. "You are doing well? But it was only a matter of time."

"I'm trying to balance taking advantage of the momentum with wanting to bury myself in the game—I guess I'm lucky they have a lock-out rule."

I settled down to picking an EVA Challenge that would suit us, trying to juggle all the things I wanted to fit into my schedule. Eighty hours a day mightn't be enough.

37
horse trading

After trash-collecting the stars, returning to the gauntlet series felt constricting and dull. No view, and only the prospect of being hammered with blaster fire to look forward to.

Of course, the point of the series was clearly to prove a certain level of Ian strength before attempting the System Challenge. A group of Rank Tens would probably stroll through it. I wouldn't even have started this series yet, if I'd realised what it involved, and would have postponed the rest in favour of level grinding if not for my bet with Dio.

Waiting next to the mural, I played spot-the-alien among the colourful tiles, noticing that in each new mural they had changed their stance along with adding a new member, but not shifted their position relative to each other. I tried to remember the names of the species, and then found a way to look the whole primary set up. Darashi, Vssf, Ah Ma Ani, Shree, Kzah, Embyde. And Llura.

"So what does Llura actually mean, Dio?"

[[Medium.]]

I looked up at tem, but te just glowed inexpressively. "It's a size designation? Do the other names mean large and small?"

[[Darashi is a combination of small and fast, but most of the other names are closer to the names the species call themselves. 'Llura' is more complicated than size. Not the fastest. Not the slowest. Not the largest. Not the smallest. Not the smartest.]]

"So it's an insult?"

[[Is that an insult?]]

"Hm." I didn't know. "We're the jack-of-all-trades species?"

[[Type Threes do like to run around calling themselves adaptable.]]

"Medium."

"Hey Kaz."

I turned to smile at Silent, then tried not to visibly react to his lowering frown. It was so weird to *see* my guildies. "You look annoyed."

Silent shrugged, and relaxed the straight line of his mouth. "Remember how I dropped anon to show off my new rank to the guild? Ever since, even though I put it back up after a few minutes, I've had a swarm of tells wanting me to join groups. Most people will never get one of these first-to-rank achievements, but being first to unlock the System Challenge seems more attainable, so everyone's trying to build the highest-ranked teams possible."

Silent had made Rank Nine while I'd been gambolling in an EVA suit—a rank only around three hundred players had managed so far. I was fairly sure I was at least a 7 now, but was putting off ranking until the gauntlet was done. The fact that it bothered me to be the weakest member of the group meant I'd remained defiantly non-anon, with my Rank Six out for everyone to see.

"Think we'll lose any of the others to poaching?" I asked. I'd seen guilds shatter under the strain of top members being siphoned off by more active raiders.

"Nope. These Challenges aren't just a numbers game: there's a group dynamic that's just as important as strength. I don't get the feel anyone in our group is going to get us killed running wildly ahead Leroy Jenkinsing, and no-one's caught up in proving themselves the boss. The others will appreciate that just as much as I do."

"I invited Nova to the guild before she logged, but she only said she'd think about it."

"I'd probably wait longer joining a guild here myself. Heck of a different experience. What do you make of the next Challenge description?"

I hadn't checked. "'*Where the Meadow Weeps, and the Dawn Blooms*'? A meadow in a cave? Maybe mushrooms?"

"Hope not. I've fought a few too many fungus-zombies in recent years."

"Fungus-zombies?"

"Hey Nova. Just speculating on what comes next." Silent lifted a hand in greeting, and then extended the gesture to Arlen and Imoenne as well. "Everyone good to go? Or do we need a strat talk before going in?"

"Find something that is liquid and apricot-coloured?" Arlen suggested. "They are not very complex, these Challenges."

"Just hitting harder each time," Silent agreed.

"Unless we can invent more efficient shields, I'm not sure there is more to this than shield and survive until exit," Nova said.

"Anyone notice the estimated time for this stage?" I said.

"Oh, hey, I didn't see that," Silent said. "I wonder if that means a maze, a really hard exit to find, or something else?"

THE HEART OF MARS
Where the Meadow Weeps, and the Dawn Blooms.
Solo or Party
Gauntlet
Gateway series
Length: Two hours (6 of 9)
Core Unit

We went in triple-shielded, with two over the whole group, and one extra out front. After the traditional narrow entry corridor, the area opened up completely, and there we stopped. Not out of fear of blasters, but in awe.

A meadow beneath the stars. Three tiers of meadows, separated by pearlescent rises of ornamentally sculpted stone that channelled great cascades of water into complex and intricate shapes. Monumental, glorious, glimmering.

Silent, typically, was first to find something to say: "Is 'two hours' just how long they expect it'll take us to walk across this place?"

"It's set up so that you can't possibly just keep five shields active the whole time," Nova noted. "Exhausting."

"Perhaps we are to climb the waterfall?" Arlen suggested.

From this distance, in a half-light sourced more from the terraced wall than the stars, stairs weren't obvious—and would be a slippery proposition if they were somehow woven into that criss-crossing fall. The area was almost as wide as it was long—must be in an outlying crevice of the great Chasma Marineris—and empty of anything much except grass, wildflowers, and the towering rise of falling water: a concave curve of it, rather than a straight line. If there were blaster ports, they'd be extremely distant, waiting for us at the walls...or hidden in grass. Even if nothing happened, it would take most of our allotted time to reach the top.

"I'd guess at a good half hour walk to the first tier, and however long it takes us to climb it," I said, studying the decoration visible on the main rim of the first waterfall: flowers, birds, leaves and a wide variety of symbols. "Not possible to do all three tiers in two hours, even if nothing shoots us. Uh, not unless we use skids, which I don't recommend. So this must be all the rest of the stages."

"A walk in the park," Silent said, with forced cheer. "Why does something so lovely feel so creepy?"

"Because we're waiting for it to shoot at us?" Nova took a single step forward, and stopped. "I'm sure I could shield myself the whole way, but probably not if I'm constantly pounded by blasts."

"A lot depends on whether we get that warning noise," I said. "How about we take turns double shielding until we get shot by something, and if the blaster is still making that buzzing noise, we switch to taking turns with a single shield, but everyone else tries to throw up an additional shield when we hear the warning."

"That's asking for a damn quick reaction time," Silent said, but not as if he thought it impossible.

"I don't see many other options," Nova said. "Let's start out triple-shielded, though. We'll adjust when we know more."

There were no paths, just grass, mats of clover, and occasional small flowers—mostly daisy-type. Familiar plants beneath familiar stars, with only the gravity and that honeycomb glimmer of the 'ceiling' to proclaim absolutely that this could not be Earth.

The grass was spindly and very soft, and walking over it produced a sharp green scent. My straining senses discovered insects, birds, and even a faint breeze, despite being in an enclosed habitat. Speculating on whether the waterfall was generating the breeze, I almost missed the bare whisper of a whine. But I was so keyed up for an attack that I responded to it even before the buzzing warning sound, snapping up a shield over the three existing, only to have it blown immediately away by a triple series of bolts. The next shield down also went, leaving Silent's and Arlen's, and then Nova adding hers over the top.

"Shit, that was heavy," Silent said. "Where did that even come from?"

"You shielded before it made a sound?" Nova asked me.

"There was a noise before the buzzing. Very soft, mechanical."

"Perhaps it's another mech," Nova said, looking around alertly. "Swatting a couple of those would be easier, in a lot of ways. It'd have to be much smaller than the first—the grass is barely long enough to hide a rabbit."

"Let's keep the triple shield at least until the next round," Silent said.

Nova nodded. "And concentrate on listening."

I was inner shield this time around, which should have been less nerve-racking, but only made me keenly aware that if I didn't hold, injury or death would follow. As it was, when I heard the precursor whine, I stiffened, trying to turn Ian to adamantine. Imoenne threw up an outer shield, and Silent added his a few moments after the blasts.

"Something, it came out of the grass," Arlen said. "Just over this way."

He pointed, then waited, since under the shields we moved as a group, or not at all. We approached as if expecting attack snakes, and only after persistent searching in the gloom found a silver circle embedded between stems of grass. Not one of the blaster apertures we'd seen before, but a cap to something that had risen from the ground

"Like a garden sprinkler," Silent noted. "But more sizzle."

"I heard it lift that time," Nova said. "With the extra warning, we can probably risk only two shields, bringing up extras as soon as we hear the sound. If these things are evenly placed all over the field, trying to maintain more than two constantly is going to be too much for us."

"Before we move on, I think we need to pick a direction," I said. "I mean, we can keep going straight ahead, but unless the exit happens to be that way, we're going to facing a lot of extra walking and being shot at."

"Yeah." Silent surveyed the waterfalls. "There could be only one exit, or lots of them. And the way the whole thing's curved means no point of it is closest. Anyone ever play *Myst*?"

"I will gladly switch out being hit by lasers for a pretty puzzle game," Nova said.

"This one looks easy enough—a good thing since there's shooting involved. Anyone see anything that symbolises dawn among all that carving?"

"'*Where the Meadow Weeps, And the Dawn Blooms*'?" Nova said. "I don't see anything that's clearly a sun. There's a half-circle, but not oriented correctly."

"There's a circle in a square," I said doubtfully. "And a teardrop near it."

"Three radiating lines over there," Silent suggested, indicating the opposite side of the grand curve. "Could represent light."

"'Blooms' could also indicate a flower," Nova said. "A sunflower, perhaps. Or lotus, flower of the dawn."

"Suddenly this puzzle doesn't seem so simple," Silent said.

"Let's go for whichever options are clustered closest together," I said. "That way, if our first guess is wrong, we won't have to trek far to try again."

"That's almost guaranteed to make the one sitting off to the side the right choice," Silent pointed out. "But luck aside, I agree that's a good approach."

Since the blast point we were standing near didn't seem inclined to rise again, we took our time looking over each and every symbol, and finding a way to edit a shared photographic record of it using our Link. All symbols that could possibly match the quest description were circled, and a cluster including 'radiating lines', 'three circles' and 'maybe a lotus' chosen as our destination.

"We've really been underusing the computers-in-our-heads aspect of *Dream Speed*," Silent said. "Incredible resource."

"Maps, overlays, GPS. We will not be lost here." Arlen bounced on his heels, then laughed as our shields jostled.

Our break had been uninterrupted by shooting, and the knowledge that we could stop and rest had buoyed everyone's spirits, and gave me confidence about my ability to get through an endurance Challenge. Two hours was only an estimate, not a time limit, so we had no need to hurry through this making mistakes.

Only a quarter hour later we were close enough to the next tier to make out detail, and see that there was a sizeable pool between the meadow and the base of the wall. Narrow white bridges arched elegantly over the water and disappeared into the misting streams of the fall.

"A bridge for every symbol," Silent noted. "I can't make out any doors on the far side."

Even when standing on the very edge of the pool, there was no hint that any particular bridge led to an exit. The section of wall rising directly above the far side of the pool was not conveniently glowing it, but had a pleated, concertina look that threw plenty of shadows and made it difficult to definitively say there was an opening or not.

"May as well try the radiating lines first," Silent said. "Then lotus, then circles."

"Five shields up," Nova added. "If there's going to be a big attack, this will be the time."

The bridges were wide enough to walk across easily, but not for two people to move side-by-side. We rearranged ourselves into a line, set up our shields, and took careful steps onto the simple, flat arch. The lack of hand railing, and a certain level of slickness caused by the misting water, made it nervous going, but there was no attack in response to touching the bridge.

That, of course, was timed for when we were out in the middle.

We'd been braced for blasts, of course, but low gravity was our undoing. I let out a startled yip as Arlen stumbled and lost his shield, and then Silent's shield took on a barrage and his feet slid from under him. All our shields struck each other—and us—as he went down, and then I was falling too, my ears ringing, to plunge into the pool below.

I'd lived by enough beaches to make swimming no issue, but I was dazed, and slow to surface, and then had to contend with Nova, who had found me as the nearest handhold, and was trying to climb. I went back under, tried to remember what I should do to rescue a non-swimmer, fought to get my head above the surface, and then the weight of panicked party member pulled away, and I gasped, coughed, breathed.

Silent's long arms to the rescue. He'd found the edge, and then dragged Nova across to it. Arlen and Imoenne were further out, but were dog-paddling gamely in the chop caused by the water plunge from above.

Recovering enough to make it to the side myself, I coughed some more, then checked that Arlen and Imoenne were making progress. Only when all five of us were clinging to the wall did anyone speak, and that was Silent.

"Well, shit."

I coughed some more—I'd breathed in at just the wrong moment—and managed a croaky: "Definitely."

"Embarrassing, would it not be, to survive the blasts only to drown?" Arlen said, though without his usual ripple of laughter. "And the question now is whether it is possible to leave this water without further attack."

"Hold a couple of shields up there, and I'll climb up to check whether it triggers the blasters?" I suggested.

"Right," Silent agreed, and built a shield.

Imoenne added one on top, and I clambered up into a glimmering tent. Nothing shot me, so I reached down to Nova, still clinging in grim, shivering silence to the pool's edge.

It took a combination of Imoenne and Arlen gently helping her to coax Nova to release her grip. And when she was out, sitting on the edge of the pool, I surprised myself by curling an arm around her waist and tucking her against me. I'm far from a touchy-feely person, but Nova's transformation from mature and collected to small and bedraggled called for something more than a 'let's get going'.

Truth to tell, I wasn't really ready myself, and appreciated that the rest of my group simply joined us in a line on the pool's edge until the immediate shock had worn off. The cool light breeze discouraged anything but a temporary lull, but we still waited until Nova finally straightened up.

She'd deactivated her focus, and now squeezed water from hair that had fallen out of its twin tails, tidying it as best she could. Then she took a deep breath. "Let's not fuck up like that again."

"One bath per Challenge is my limit," Silent agreed.

"This is the second time lower gravity has nearly been my downfall," I said, and entertained everyone recounting how I'd made it through stage one.

"Speed's not a bad idea, but I don't think we'll be outrunning these blasters," Nova said, now sounding as dryly unperturbed as she'd begun. "If four of us stay on the bank and firm footing, we can keep a shield over someone while they check if there's an exit."

"Me," I said. "Everyone else is higher rank." And only Silent and I seemed to be strong swimmers, I added to myself.

"We'll keep one shield over us and three over you," Silent said.

With a little experimentation, we put this into action, and I walked across the bridge to find a wall, and no way to go either forward or sideways. I repeated this beneath the lotus and then the circles symbols, and then we paused to consider the enormous curve, and all those symbols with their slippery bridges.

"Pick nearest or revise our choices?" Silent asked.

For a moment no-one answered, every one of us aware that three bridges had already taken too much energy. Then Imoenne said, barely audible: "That one, please."

We looked where she pointed: a symbol only five bridges to our right. One large star surrounded by five tiny ones.

"Could represent the dawn star, I guess," Silent said, after a moment's hesitation. "Let's give it a go."

It hadn't been on our original list of symbols, but Imoenne was normally so quiet that I think we would have tried it even if we hadn't been able to see any connection at all. It was at least nearby, and we'd found that the blasters by the pool only triggered if you went onto the bridges.

Except for this bridge, where no blasters triggered at all. I stopped in the middle of the flat arch, started to speak, but then kept going forward so that I could confirm that the 'pleating' of the wall on the far side of our fourth attempt was in fact two angled walls that did not quite intersect, but instead simply concealed the fact that they were an exit.

"Imoenne, you are awesome."

I doubted she could have heard me over the roar of the falls, so I repeated myself once everyone was safely across in the inevitable tunnel.

"What made you so sure this was the right one?" Nova asked, giving Imoenne an approving little nod.

Imoenne ducked her head, and told her feet: "The descriptions, they always, they better fit the previous Challenge."

"They do?" Silent said, then paused, clearly looking back over his Challenge log. "'Enter the Maze; Choose a Path; Find Your Way Down; Behind the Shadows; Beneath the Stars; Where the Meadow Weeps, And the Dawn Blooms.'"

"It's true that we found a way down in the Behind the Shadows Challenge," Nova said, thoughtfully. "And everything was shadowy in the Beneath the Stars. I don't remember much 'down' in the Find Your Way Down Challenge."

"They was maybe a slight downward curve to some of the paths," Silent said. "But it did match 'Choose a Path' way better."

"Hm." Nova shrugged. "Let's shield up and confirm that this is officially the way out first. If it is, then I think you might have handed us the key to the whole Challenge series, Imoenne."

"Yes, dry clothes and proof of my sister's genius, this way," Arlen said proudly, and was very shortly rewarded.

Gauntlet Successful.
Gauntlet Success Rate: 7/7 100%
Challenge Success Rate: 13/14 92.8%
Lux Points Earned: 5
Total Lux Points: 57
Challenge Reward:
[Tier 1 Consumable Pattern]
[Tier 1 Apparel Pattern]

"No-one else here," I said, gazing around the inevitable staging area. "Not that it necessarily means other groups haven't made it this far, then logged or gone ahead already."

"But no, I am sure it means we are the first," Arlen said, bouncing ahead of us with redoubled enthusiasm. "And now that Imoenne has given us the key, we will have an advantage for the last parts, and we will be the first to unlock the System Challenge, and everyone will know our names!"

I wondered whether I'd like that—the kind of notoriety that only a couple of players had so far faced in-game—and thought it would at least be good advertising for the 'Bio of The Synergis' and 'My Core Unit is a Lie' patches I'd added to my uniform.

"I'm starting to believe a first is actually possible," I said.

"If unlocking the System Challenge has a custom ship reward, then I absolutely want to push hard to get it," Silent said. "If everyone's not feeling too tired, want to take a half hour break and then take on the next stage?"

Achievement
First to unlock System Challenge
[Redeemer]
[Dread Pirate Roberts]
[Spaceman Spiff]
[Fuzzy]
[Weak Sauce]
Awarded Custom Ship (Rank One)

"Well," Silent said, after a small pause. "Looks like we'd better aim for beating the System Challenge instead. Who's with me?"

Nova laughed. "Sure. Let's do it."

"Insta-celebrity looks rough," my father said.

I leaned forward so I could see the TV from the kitchen. A repeat of a doorstop interview of a mid-fifties white Texan man whose online identity, Redeemer, had been part of the first group to unlock the System Challenge. Whatever pride he felt at the achievement was hidden by his shellshocked survey of the crowd outside his home.

"My Cycog told me it's common practice to keep your focus active the entire time you're in a lan Challenge, and my group decided to do that. Not that we think anyone's been watching our Challenges. This guy was recognised because he's been using the same player name since *EverQuest*, though, not from his aged-down Core Unit."

"So I shouldn't expect reporters if you get to the System Challenge before it's beaten?"

"I never link my player names with my real one," I said. "I can't guarantee there's not enough threads out there that someone with a lot of time couldn't put a trail together, but I'd hope that by the time they did, The Synergis would have moved on to the next sensation. Maybe someone will reach Rank Ten and distract them with new planets."

Privately, I was more focused on completing the gauntlet series without dying, so that I could ask Dio prying questions with potentially truthful answers. Getting some straight talk from my alien overlord felt like it might be more of an achievement than anything anyone else was doing in the game.

I hadn't spoken a word about the bet to my guild or parents. I felt like that would fail some hidden test, as if Dio was an ancient and powerful fairy who had disguised terself solely to ask for my last crust of bread.

"I have news." My mother arrived with an escort of wet wind, shedding layers of clothing in a move reminiscent of a great dane shaking off a rain shower. "Your Oma has been playing *Dream Speed*."

"Seriously?" I came out of the kitchen with two mugs topped with stroopwafel. "Does she like it?"

"Well, you know your Oma: she's not one to gush. Her character is called Skaði, and we're going to meet up in-game, so I'll see how she's managing, maybe help her out with some Challenges if she's having trouble. Are you heading back in soon?"

"Just for a while. My guild is having another get-together, this time on Mars."

I ducked back into the kitchen for my own mug, sadly lacking in caramel wafer since gluten still hated me out in the world. But I would make that up with a cinnamon roll when I logged back in: *Dream Speed* was changing my relationship with food.

"Not racing for the first?" my father asked.

"It's research of a sort. We're going to watch the first attempt at the System Challenge, though my party's only going to log off again after that, since there's a couple of real-world commitments that get in the way of us continuing our gauntlet straight away. By the time we complete the gateway series, we'll have seen enough other attempts to hopefully be able to give it a good shot."

My mother smiled at me. "Once all this initial rush is over, and we have reached appropriate ranks, shall we leave competition and guilds behind, and just travel together a while?"

"Sure. Maybe we can get one of those multi-snug ships."

Though would that mean travelling with Oma as a passenger, sternly disapproving everything I did? A short while, perhaps.

Logging back in, I turned over the vague possibility that *Dream Speed* would somehow transform into a bonding experience with my Oma. Perhaps she'd appreciate my gaming expertise now, if not my stubbornly independent design career.

Or perhaps not. I knew my Oma.

Low Martian gravity doubled the adjustment period between bodies, and I kept bounding and surging when all

I was trying to do was walk to the nearest transport. I slowed down, since there was no need to rush to this meet-up.

Almost my whole guild had managed to reach planet-skipping rank, and everyone else able to log on had hitched rides with other guildies so we could watch the Martian dawn together. The meet-up was a 'private park' the guild have been able to book a couple of hundred kilometres from the entrance to *The Heart of Mars* Challenge—which wasn't far at all given the enormity of Chasma Marineris—and TALiSON had been very keen on a 'dressy' get-together, so I spent the short trip looking through potential apparel rewards, and cosmetic options.

No need to go back to my Snug for a shower, a change of clothes, or to spend hours on hair and makeup. Instead, I simply walked into the nearest vat of Soup, and walked right out again, refreshed, wearing a blue and black dress with a tight bodice and long flowing sleeves and skirt. My eyes were intricately kohled, and I'd added a tracery of vines and flowers all over my face and throat.

"*Is that as instantaneous as it feels, Dio?*" I asked silently.

[[Soup has a stasis effect, so do not ever rely on your perception of time. But for small adjustments such as that, it is closer to moments than minutes.]]

I nodded and walked on. Flowing, flippy skirts are fascinating in low gravity. They swish with a curious lassitude, the ends flirt out and almost seem to hang before they drop.

[[Are you dancing?]]

"Performing a serious scientific experiment," I said with dignity. "What kind of dancing is in the future? Are there spectacular zero-G ballets?"

[[Any way you Bios can fling yourselves about, you can be sure there is at least a small group dedicated to doing so. The Ves-vesan system is a particular centre of performative movement, if that takes your interest.]]

"I need to start a list."

Dio promptly reeled off a series of names—the places te liked most of all in the galaxy—and a little list made itself for me, without any need for me to write it down.

[[I'll annotate details later, so you can decide where you want to go first.]]

"You pick," I said, comfortably. "Well, out of those that are nearest, I guess."

Dio didn't answer, but produced what I assumed was the Cycog equivalent of humming, and out of the eerie series of notes I recognised *Swan Lake*. I let myself continue my scientific experiment, and could not remember a time before now that I didn't feel ridiculous wearing such a feminine dress.

"Kaz? Oh, I love the face paint. Or is it a tattoo?"

TALiSON had opted for a Gothic princess look, black lace emphasising her pale skin, and tumbling streams of deep crimson hair providing their own opportunities for physics experiments.

"I think most of their makeup options are actually tattoos. Or, no, that's the wrong word. It's not ink injections, it's skin that happens to be green and blue and white, rather than your usual flesh tone." I reached up to rub my chin. "I tried washing my eyeliner off the other day, and didn't make any inroads. I eventually found where it shows whether a cosmetic pattern is for a physical change, or actual cosmetics, and I still haven't decided which one I prefer."

"And either way, all those years I've spent perfecting shadowing have completely gone to waste." TALiSON brushed lush red curls behind one ear.

"Easier to give yourself cheekbones than paint them in, anyway," Far said, strolling up. He'd opted for a *The Lord of the Rings* elf style outfit. The result was positively ethereal, and contrasted immensely with his familiar aged-cynic voice. "Like my braids?" he added, twirling to display intricate knot-work.

Long hair seemed to be a common interpretation of 'dressing up' for this get-together, and Far was only one of many who had opted for 'vaguely elven' for their clothing.

Most of the guild had already arrived, but the private park was far from crowded. Pooling lux points to reserve it had seemed a waste to me at first, but I had to approve the unobtrusive mechanical servitors that glided about with mystery drinks and trays of snacks.

I wandered among spindly, fragile-looking trees admiring fabulous clothing, and matching up more names to faces. I still had my doubts about the complications inherit in a guild shifting from chat and screen interaction to near-enough actual people who might behave very differently in person, but at the moment it was all very pleasant and convivial.

Spotting Imoenne sitting with a thing like a sealed, dimpled tub in the centre of crossed legs, I moved closer to listen to the odd noises it made. She was treating it like a drum, but it produced an otherworldly noise that didn't remind me of drums.

I knew Arlen would be nearby, and found him with two women in laced-up kirtles with heavy sleeves. I checked their names: Nalia and Maleen, who hadn't been active in the guild for a couple of years.

Arlen waved to them as they wandered off, and then crossed to me, turning his walk into a strut to display a tunic and tight-trousers look all embroidered white on white.

"Very nice," I said, then added after an appropriate pause: "I don't recognise Imoenne's instrument. Is it something from The Synergis?"

"No, an Earth one," Arlen said, flashing his ready smile. "A hang, it is called, and Imoenne is teaching herself how to play. She has long wanted one."

"I've never even heard of it," I said, with an embarrassed laugh.

"An idiophone. Music of resonance, rather than of striking."

"Your sister certainly doesn't sound like she's never played this before."

"Imoenne, she is a genius," Arlen said, very serious. "I have lost count of what she can play. It is the right sound for this gathering, too. Contemplative, meditative, and yet with an uplift. Music for a Martian dawn."

Silent had strolled up while we spoke and nodded his agreement.

"I didn't think dawn would be much of an event, given that we're technically in a crack in the ground with a lid on it, but I can see already that it's going to be something incredible. Chasma Marineris is more sunken continent than canyon."

"Do you think it ever rains here?" I asked, gazing up at the sky. The 'lid' was a long way away. "Dio?"

[[Yes, when the administrator sets certain environmental controls. For washing purposes, if no other reason. If you want this gathering to end early, just let me know and I'll tell the administrator the place is looking a little grubby.]]

Dio had responded so that Arlen and Silent could hear tem, and they laughed, but any other response we might have made was forestalled by a new system announcement.

Achievement
First to reach Rank Ten
[Nina Stella]
Awarded Custom Ship (Rank Two)

"Way to go Nina Stella," Silent said, smiling.

"Nina Stella's an NPC," Wraith shouted out, and we debated that for a while, because it was true enough that there were no verified sightings of *DS's* most famous player. She'd sensibly gone anon very early on, and had obviously stayed focused on working on her rank. And now she was the first player in all the virtual world to travel to a new solar system.

"Well, if Nina Stella's travelling the stars, she's not here beating us to the System Challenge," Silent said a little later, after various mystery drinks had been consumed, and we were sitting with Far, adjusting to the weird way *DS* alcohol made you feel drunk and clear-headed at the same time. "Damn, but I want us to be the ones to win. D'you think we'd get a Rank Three Custom Ship? Or any explanation of the difference between ship ranks?"

"I would like a flying palace," I said. "But I don't think I'd like to try and Skip a flying palace."

Silent laughed. "Good point. But there was a time when I thought it impossible to put a whole Snug in a Pocket, so perhaps palaces will be nothing one day. Besides, I could just park the thing in orbit and live on it when I'm visiting Earth."

"Pay some high-ranked NPC to Skip it for you," Far suggested. "I've been playing wide-eyed Enclaver with a few citizens of The Synergis, and it seems pretty common for them to offer Skip services. You just need to save up a lot of lux points."

"Most of The Synergis NPCs I've encountered seem very impatient with Enclavers," Silent said.

"I do wide-eyed very well," Far said, waving to TALiSON, returning with a little string bag of the 'drinking bulbs' that we'd spent the morning sampling.

She waved the bag in return, but then scowled—not at Far, but at Silent's back.

"You're wearing one of those patches," she said as she reached us. "I hate those patches."

Silent had gone for a retro look, with a bolo tie and a faded brown leather jacket that suited him very well. I shifted, trying to peer at his back, and Silent leaned forward obligingly so I could see a purposefully distressed but still quite clear image of a Snug above Earth.

I flushed, but of course TALiSON couldn't know that I was the artist.

"My Core Unit *is* a lie, though," Silent said, mildly. "I'm, what, forty-seven out in the world?"

"You're not sure?" I asked.

"Had to work it out. The days of proclaiming I'm seven and nine months are long gone."

"This definitely is a lie," TALiSON said, as she sat down, handing me the net of drinking bulbs. "It's what I looked like twenty years and sixty pounds ago. It's what the game gave me with to start with. Do you know how cruel that is?"

"Why cruel?" Silent asked.

"Because that makes this body what I think of myself, deep down," TALiSON said, in a little rush. "After years of fat activism, of standing up for the right to exist without the shame, this game tells me that everything I've said and done for years out there in the non-virtual is the lie. I didn't accept myself at all."

Looking puzzled, Silent said: "I didn't purposefully age myself down—this is how the game started me out, with a little fine-tuning, and it's not because I don't accept that I'm plunging toward fifty. Not that I would have hesitated to change myself to whatever I wanted, so long as the synchronisation score stayed viable."

"I sacrificed synchronisation for fantasy me," Far said, his voice shifting to unexpectedly dulcet tones. "Didn't drop too much."

"Sprocket's sync is so bad he's still at skids stage," I said.

Silent nodded. "And he doesn't care a bit, because looking like his favourite character means more to him. Though he's extremely curious about how close everyone in the guild has stuck to their non-virtual appearance."

"I don't think he realises how irritating the 'no, what are you really' game is," I murmured.

Far caught my eye, and gave me a wry, astonishingly beautiful smile. "I took this name for a troll, you know. Nothing like wearing a female toon and having every asshole on the server demanding a play-by-play of my chromosomes. But it also worked to draw a lot of fire from friends where that question means so much, where 'what are you, really' is a knife in the gut, a needle in the spine, every damn time. We're far from the only ones having a debate about what a Core Unit means. About whether it's your starting point, or the act of improving synchronisation that counts. Or even defying synchronisation, and making your Self whatever the hell you want it to be. The Cykes, at least, stick to it that Core Units are just a mechanism that impacts your Ian use."

"They never suggest that you have to play the hand genetics dealt you," Silent agreed. "Any more than they force real-world diabetics to keep giving themselves in-game insulin shots. The body here is fashion. An outfit you put on, or a tool to beat particular Challenges."

"And yet everything," Far added, in a lower tone.

"The Cycogs are also the ones that focused everything around the concept of Core Unit," I pointed out. "We wouldn't even be having this discussion if they hadn't used self-image as a starting point. Which, even if Cycogs and Ian are somehow real, isn't something they needed to put in a virtual simulation. It's something they chose to include."

"You're right," TALiSON agreed. "And my avatar choices don't bother me when I'm playing things like *Veil*. It's only when I'm socialising with real people wearing my so-called self-image, or I see that damn patch."

"We don't even know if a 'true self' is something that's an issue in the future." I said. "Dio, what's it like to grow up as a Bio of The Synergis? Uh, as an average Type Three?"

I expected Dio to drop down from the drifts of light above, and experienced a mild shock when te surfaced from the toe of my boot. Riding along? Resting?

[[Most Bios raise their offspring on crèche worlds,]] te said. [[Primarily because infant Ian is negligible, and crèche worlds have many more safety precautions, along with educational facilities and peers for socialisation. Type Threes usually cannot safely transfer between modals until their teens, at which point they're permitted to experiment with different forms, if they wish. Occasionally Bios choose to never live in anything but their own original shape, and even of the majority that try a number of changes, perhaps eighty percent retain something similar to their initial appearance for their Core.]]

"So there are worlds that are almost all kids at school and their parents?" TALiSON asked. "Are classes broken down into the good-looking kids, the athletic kids, and the lo...the unpopular ones? Or are all Synergis children born good-looking?"

[[It's rare that genetic traits that are strongly outside averages are maintained. Otherwise, approximately a third of Type Threes use trait selection rather than the random combinations of unassisted conception. Random combination remains the most common, however, in part due to a belief that individuality is an adjunct to strong Ian development. If you were all bland reproductions of some Golden Mean of agreed beauty, would you have a lesser sense of self?]]

"What about race?" Silent asked. "I've noticed that all the NPCs I've seen so far have been darker-skinned."

[[That is partly fashion. Race, in the informal construct of the term, has been subsumed by sub-species, although there are still some regional distinctions among 'pure' Type Threes that correlate well enough to your major continental variants. Statistically, hm, the 'average' Type Three has a light brown skin, wavy brown-black hair, and dark brown eyes. They are raised in neutral expression on a crèche world, primarily in this quadrant or Elorha Quadrant.]]

"Neutral expression?" Far said. "We talking reproductive sets? Or lack thereof?"

[[Yes. That was a variation that came from Kua-roa, the most advanced of the Type Three Enclaves. They went through several phases of violence based on strict notions of gender roles, suffered a near-extinction event, and chose to mandate a neutral state as a result. Kua-roans reproduce entirely through assisted conception and gestation, entering affection-based partnerships rather than sexual ones, and leave to The Synergis if they wish to sample other expressions. We observed that neutral early development seemed to remove some of the factors that undermine Ian progress in Type Threes—and several of the other Bio species—and encouraged the practice generally. It's voluntary in The Synergis, but at this stage approximately seventy percent of Type Threes are born neutral. Perhaps ten percent remain so, while almost half of the whole eventually use neutral as a base, but shift between one or more of the other potential expressions to experiment with strengthening their lan, or for recreational or partnership purposes.]]

"Is this a genetic level neutrality?" I asked. "Or are you just controlling, um, suppressing the expression of the chromosomes?"

[[For the majority it's genetic, but some choose a surface adjustment. We leave that up to the parent, since our preference is to influence trends, rather than waste time pressuring individuals.]]

We digested this reminder of Chocobo status, then I sighed, and snagged one of the drinking bulbs from TALiSON's net.

"So the main thing you're saying is that we're all just potential engine parts, and no-one cares what we started off like, or plays the 'no, what are you really?' game?"

[[To a certain degree, the precise opposite,]] Dio replied. [[Because it is such a prestigious thing to be high lan, there is immense interest in the genetics and development of anyone nearing triple digit rank. And Bios maintain all manner of factional division, and will care passionately about the most unexpected things. But to change your Core Unit for personal preference, or to strengthen your synchronisation, or to optimise for other forms of Challenges, are all unremarkable things.]]

"But since we weren't raised in The Synergis, we're still probably going to feel a little conflicted," I said, firmly. "Oh, Nova made it." I waved, and added to TALiSON and Far: "Our fifth for the gauntlet series. We're trying to show her that we're the kind of guild she'd want to join."

"Pity we're all so thoroughly drunk, then," TALiSON said. "I wasn't expecting to wait this long to watch the System Challenge."

Nova had ditched the magical girl outfit for a blue and white chignon and a dress of two pieces of sheer cloth-of-gold artfully pinned along shoulders and arms to produce something that on me would probably resemble a homemade poncho, and on Nova somehow became a vaguely Grecian piece of elegance.

"I didn't think I'd make it back here in time," she said, sitting down near me. "Getting down from space takes a while."

"Putting in zero-G practice?" Silent asked, handing her a drinking bulb.

"It sounds like we'll need it."

TALiSON blinked at her. "Is that a tiny cat on your shoulder? Does this game give pet rewards?"

"My Cycog," Nova said, with a sideways glance. "Temi."

The teacup-sized cat—black with a four-pointed star on its forehead—blinked at us with eyes that glowed the same luminous white as the mote hovering above my foot.

"It feels wrong to squee over our alien overlords," I said. "But that's a very cute synth, Temi."

[[Thank you.]]

Dio said something in the wibbling notes of the Cybercognate, and Temi responded by leaping to the ground, curling into a black ball, and rising out of the synth to float off into the crowd above.

"That's the only language they don't auto-translate," Nova remarked. "I wonder if it's possible to learn."

Far moved his foot toward the black ball, then drew it back. "It's probably rude to pick aliens up, or the shells they leave behind. If I get drunker, make sure I don't step on it."

"They're apparently very sturdy," Nova said, lifting her drinking bulb and sniffing the built-in straw. "What is this?"

"It's called thousand fruit punch," TALiSON explained. "Every bulb is different."

There was something different about Nova beyond the clothes, and it took me a full minute of consideration to decide that she wasn't just 'dressed older': she had physically changed to a twentyish version of herself, rather than the mid-teens look that had gone with her magical girl homage. I'd already known she was older, because the game didn't flag her age, but found the differences more disconcerting than if she'd turned up in an entirely unfamiliar body.

"We were discussing my jacket" Silent said, taking it off and turning it to rest across his knees. My carefully non-specific humanoid figure looked down at Earth, the declaration of the lie blazoned above the image. "Do you think it's cruel to have a Core Unit concept in *DS*?"

Nova lifted her eyebrows, but then paused to consider the question.

"I can see how many people might find it so. Ryzonart claims they've crafted the game to avoid harming its players, so there must be a reason to include the whole concept."

"The simplest being the alien recruitment program," Silent said.

"Which in turn makes it unlikely this game is being run by Cycogs from the future," Nova said. "They'd surely have more than enough Bios to work with there. Then."

"Lost spaceship, burgeoning galactic war, or they developed recently on Earth and are pretending not to?" Far moved his foot closer to the empty synth once again.

"I agree about the goal being recruitment," Silent said. "But while we know they care about something they say impacts Ian strength, we don't know if the part about being cossetted Skip engines is true. I don't think we're any closer to working out what exactly we're being recruited for. What do you think are the chances of there really being a Starfighter Invitation, Nova?"

"It's the wrong sort of game," she said.

"You mean, not shooting? If we stick with the theory that they're recruiting Ian pilots, we don't need to worry about shooting."

"No, I mean it's an MMO," Nova replied.

Silent frowned, then straightened. "I see. Setting this up as multiplayer on this scale is a huge resource cost. If they just wanted to recruit Ian pilots, single player would be the way to go."

Far sighed. "No theory makes sense, all of them sound reasonable."

"I think we've been listening to different theories," I said.

[g]<Tornin> Stream's finally starting people.

[g]<Amelia Beerheart> Hope you're all still conscious.

I rechecked the [View Lan Challenges] list, and found that [The Wreck] had been pinned to the top. I followed the link, and settled back, eyes half-closed, to experience television in my head.

[[[[Welcome to the System Challenge.]]]]

"Oh, wow, it's Ryzon."

Five men, three white and two East Asian, stood in a room very reminiscent of the viewing lounge from Demo 2, although the exterior scene showed only a slow rotation of stars, no planets. They wore sleek matching uniforms, with shoulder patches blazoned with the guild name, *Pyres of Heaven*, and had been standing back-to-back as if anticipating attack.

A much younger version of the Texan man I'd seen interviewed stepped forward. "Can you give us more details about the Challenge goal?"

[[[[The Wreck is a ship abandoned by a species driven to extinction before the rise of The Synergis. It is important to us not to lose information about extinct sapients, so the goal of this Challenge is to reach the centre of the ship and retrieve the systems core. The target is marked, but the path is dangerous.]]]]

"Is there a time limit?" asked a guy who had gone for a distinct Uchiha Sasuke look with his Core Unit, though the stream info told me he was the Dread Pirate Roberts.

[[[[There is no time limit—you can attempt and return until the Challenge is completed, or you die during the Challenge. You cannot substitute group members after you begin, and your access to the Challenge is not exclusive. Be aware that elite Ian Challenges of this nature increase risk to your Renba.]]]]

"Wait, our Renba?" asked Redeemer. "You mean if our Core Units are taken out, our Renba could also be destroyed, and that would mean..."

[[[[Permadeath.]]]] Ryzon waited a suitably dramatic moment, and then added: [[[[You would no longer be able to access The Synergis.]]]]

"*Oh. My. God.*" TALiSON was audible, but made strangely distant and muted by the stream-viewing experience.

"*Stakes are raised, ladies and gentlemen,*" Silent added.

[[[[Explosions and fields of force are obvious risks to your Renba. Keep in mind that thirty seconds is considered the maximum safe transfer delay for Bios of your Rank, and set your Renba to your desired follow distance.]]]]

"Can other players attack our Renba?" Redeemer asked.

[[[[If they wish to be perma-banned. Attacking your Core Unit attracts no penalty, however, beyond the opinion of the audience.]]]]

"*The stream shows us their names, even though most of them are anon,*" Nova said.

"Is the Challenge completed once we reach this systems core, or when we return to the ship with it?" the Dread Pirate Roberts asked. "Could someone steal it from us on the way out?"

[[[[The Challenge completes once you have extracted the systems core from its housing.]]]]

Redeemer looked around at the rest of his party. "Still in this?"

There was a fractional hesitation, but then a firm affirmative.

"Go down in history or go down in flames," Spaceman Spiff said.

With impeccable timing, an enormous shape blocked the rotating vista of stars. Not perfectly round, but made up of countless flat surfaces, like a 10-thousand-sided die. The regularity of the form was interrupted by a massive hole piercing one quarter of the visible surface.

"How big is that thing?" Spaceman Spiff asked.

[[[[It has a diameter of ten kilometres,]]]] Ryzon said. [[[[Impeller sleds are available in Bay One when you are ready.]]]]

"*Puny,*" Silent said. "*Less than a tenth of the size of the Death Star.*"

"*They weren't trying to explore the Death Star,*" Nova pointed out.

"*Only five kilometres to the centre,*" I said. "*If there's a convenient straight corridor.*"

"*A five kilometre corridor is a long walk,*" Nova replied.

"*No obvious rotation,*" Silent added. "*So it's probably zero-G or near to it. Not sure that's better or worse.*"

While we waited for the *Pyres of Heaven* guys to head down to Bay One, suiting up in the Soup en route, we talked through potential difficulties of finding our way through such a large space in the likely event there were no five kilometre corridors.

"So, running out of air or getting a hole in our suits are the obvious dangers," Redeemer said, coming to the exact same conclusion we'd reached. "Floating debris, getting lost, trapped, or attacked by dormant ship defences. Our first choice is whether or not to go in via the big hole, or find a door. There looks to be a lot of debris in that damaged area. More than I'd expect."

"I expect that's why the entry series was ninety percent shield Challenges," Weak Sauce said, in a slow, caramel-noted voice. "But let's not get over-confident."

The 'impeller sleds' had their own slots at the back of the big airlock, and looked more like a rack of oxygen tanks than any kind of vehicle. The *Pyres* group spent a solid quarter hour familiarising themselves with their function, checking on time limits for their oxygen, and how long the extra air supplies on the sleds would take them. They were methodical, cautious, and died within ten minutes of reaching the gaping wound in the side of The Wreck.

"Lesson number one: don't go in the big hole," Silent observed, stretching.

"And more zero-G practice," Nova added. "I'll see if I can find other Challenges that use those sleds. We can try a few out before or after going on with the gauntlet series."

"That was a little like the way I ping-ponged through the first stage of the gauntlet," I said. "The shield rebound in zero gravity is even worse."

"They could have survived that if they hadn't used their shields," TALiSON pointed out. "They caused all those metal fragments to start bouncing around."

"Next group that goes will definitely try a different way in," Silent said. He smiled comfortably at Nova. "Wish we didn't have these meetings. I want to get through the gauntlet and get up there right now."

"How long until you have to log?" she asked.

"Less than an hour, game-time. Not enough for any Challenges." He eyed his empty drinking bulb ruefully. "Well, not with my head swimming. I hope it's true there's no after-effects from this when you log, because right now I don't have enough in me to even scroll through lists to work out what to try."

"Let's walk then," Nova said, standing. "This music makes me restless."

I waved a hand to indicate my disinterest in walking, and TALiSON simply smiled benignly, and waited until they'd walked off to say: "I sense a hook-up."

"I guess?" I said, not having noticed any by-play. I frowned. "I hope my group for this gauntlet doesn't fall apart."

"Silent's too laid-back to get into arguments," Far said. "What's this Nova like?"

"All business so far." Though I wondered whether she'd come here in an older-looking modal with Silent in mind. "Not uptight about winning, but focused."

"Do Silent good to get a little tangled, no matter how it turns out," Far said. "He's been positively monkish since his wife died."

I blinked, because Silent had been a lone traveller through world capitals for as long as I'd been in the guild, and I'd joined when I was eighteen. But poking and prodding at my guildies' backgrounds had never been my style.

"The amount of sex going on in this game is going to keep divorce courts occupied for years," TALiSON said.

"It'll save as many marriages as it fucks up," Far said. "Swap and change bodies, roleplay any part, try any combination of people being together while still technically being monogamous. And the singles scene is off the wall, beyond even what I saw in the Seventies, especially in the Challenges that don't use your Core Unit. Safe. Anonymous. Consequence free."

"My grandmother plays this game," I said, after a pause.

"Point," Far said. "Between the potential for accidental incest, and the lack of age range guides outside 'under/over eighteen', I have to admit I've been staying away from players. No way I want to tangle with someone not even twenty."

"My Cycog promised to give me a heads-up if I started flirting with someone on my known issues list," TALiSON said. "But I think it's safer to stick with NPCs—and they're usually more interesting."

"But all the NPCs are controlled by what is probably a handful of Cycogs," I said. "And they seem to think Bio sex lives mild entertainment."

"Better than a chore, I suppose," Far said, chuckling.

"Aren't you worried that you'll end up caring about someone who isn't real?"

"Hey, I'm a known die-hard devotee of Alistair," Far said. "Not to mention Fenris. And Garrus. And, whew, way too many other romanceable NPCs. Hasn't hurt me yet."

"This is so much more than choosing options from a dialogue wheel," I said.

"Tell me about it! Do you know how hard it is to be witty when you have to make up your own clever comments?" TALiSON grimaced. "I don't know how much it would even hurt to buy into game romance, to believe the pretty speeches aren't scripted, pretend they're not handed out to anyone who figures out the correct response. With more complex virtual NPCs—think what it means for sex education. Safe experimentation."

"If you trust Ryzonart."

TALiSON shrugged. "We're already trusting them with our heads. And possibly our souls. Why not our awkward exchanges of fluids?"

"You mean we can't use this game without wholly investing in it?"

"Even if we take the steal a ship option, we'd still be in Ryzonart's game. And if Ryzonart is truly run by Cycogs..."

"We always circle back to why they're doing this."

"And whether we're coming up to some dramatic red pill/blue pill choice?" Far said. "Are we, lounging here unsure of our ability to stand, actually in an outright battle for our souls? That's what Ian is, after all: human souls commodified. Spiritual workhorses."

"Chocobos," I muttered.

"There's nothing to suggest you have to *give up* your soul," TALiSON objected. "Cycogs encourage Bios to get stronger, but they're not actually taking souls away. Well, unless they are, of course. But if The Synergis is as presented, I don't think there's many who'd say no to a quick trip to the future, or whatever the heck is Ryzonart's end game."

"Even though humans aren't in charge? Or have any real representational vote?" I asked.

"I've never been in charge," TALiSON said. "And lately, y'know, I don't think voting has taken us good places. I keep pushing to know the bad side of The Synergis, and I keep getting descriptions of Different From Now, but the scale is tilted way toward Better Than Here."

"Not to mention you can always bugger off to an Enclave if you absolutely have to be in charge," Far said.

"Unless it was an Enclave-for-one, I wouldn't be in charge there either," TALiSON said, with a touch of melancholy. She looked thoughtfully at the net now empty of drinking bulbs. "Help me up, Far. I'm not dressed for sleeping in a park."

There was a general drift for exits, or a network of sleeping nooks built into the back of the terraced area. I cautiously tested my legs, and found myself unexpectedly steady.

"Is this some special kind of alcohol that makes me drunk and not-drunk at the same time?" I asked Dio, who had returned to circle my head.

[[You aren't drunk. Not the Outside you. The simulation can give you numerous experiences, but can't change the chemistry underlying those experiences. And you were nursing those drinks.]]

Because I didn't like being drunk in public, yet felt like I'd gone over my usual limit. Making my careful way back to the nearest Pod station, I settled myself down for a contemplative tour to the farthest end of the enormous biohabitat. A trace of the same melancholy that had touched TALiSON seemed to be shadowing me, and I didn't particularly want to do anything but look about me and think. Thankfully Dio had fallen back to ter usual silence.

Of course, 'Dio' was a Construct at least some of the time, and whoever was pretending to be tem appeared to have plenty of other things to do. An actual personal Cycog might well be considerably more annoying.

Eventually, feeling less vague, I began a few tentative searches for suitable Challenges, and then amused myself looking up my Oma.

Skaði
[Ullr]
Rank: 9

Status: Online
Accepting: [Email] [Messages] (Friends List Only)
Location: [Jupiter Low Orbit]

At first, I simply rejected what I saw. Then white fury turned me to fire, and almost immediately burned away in sick shame. I worked on breathing, telling myself how stupid my reaction had been. So my Oma, who had no interest in gaming, barely knew how to turn a computer on, and had started the game after me...was better than me.

Rank Nine.

She certainly had a strong enough will. Lan training had probably come quite easy. It was an excellent thing that she was doing well in a game that would give her relief from the arthritis that had limited her far too young.

Rank *Nine*.

I couldn't do it. I couldn't force myself to be pleased for her. I tried, very hard, but my Oma had always made me feel such a failure in all the things she considered important, and I couldn't just put that aside and be happy she'd effortlessly surpassed me at something that mattered to me.

[[You should convert some lux points.]]

"What?" I'd entirely forgotten Dio, and had to be glad te wasn't commenting on my varying pulse rate. "I only have a couple left after putting in for that party."

[[Convert credits for lux points.]]

"I don't think I've earned any...oh, that's the royalty payment for the images, isn't it? I thought that went into real-world money."

[[You have the option for either. Conversion can be accessed in-game through the [Status] menu.]]

"Hm." I searched under [Status], suspicious about why Dio had suddenly piped up, and then I said: "Oh."

I should have really taken the hint when I personally met two different people wearing my patches. Factoring in the millions of *DS* players, this was a clear sign.

"Dio. How many lux points would it cost to go to a different solar system?"

[[Far less than that.]]

"Return trip?"

[[Still less than that.]]

"Could I do that and be back in time to meet up for the next stage of the gauntlet?"

[[Technically. Most of your time would be taken up in leaving and returning to Mars. You wouldn't have time to visit a planet, and would need to choose from imminent departures to high-traffic systems in order to be sure of return passage.]]

"Are there any imminent departures to high-traffic systems? Uh, that I could reach via a shuttle?"

[[Two. Choose between [Iridianis] and [Ka Bol Ka Fan].]]

"I'll have the one with the most spectacular orbital views."

[[Very well. Negotiating on your behalf.]]

Relieved I wasn't expected to talk my way onto a ship— I hated bargaining—I searched for the nearest shuttle service and redirected my Pod, but then realised leaving the transport ship once it reached the new system might be complicated without my Snug.

[[I've directed *The Hare* to dock with the *Orafa*,]] Dio told me. [[So long as you return within the day, you won't lose your slot at Valles Marineris.]]

"That's great."

I considered the floating mote of light drifting around the Pod, fully aware that I had been thoroughly distracted, without any intrusive questions asked, or even some pointed comments about how many lux points I was willing to spend, just so I could go somewhere other players hadn't been first.

One of the reasons I'd stuck with *Corpse Light* was they left me alone. They were flexible enough to let me meander along almost as a solo player, and then welcome me when I felt like going all-in on guild activities. None of them knew me in real life, none of them knew I had a collection of participation trophies from running, had walked away from my design career, was in danger of hyper-ventilating in crowds, and cramped up if someone waved wheat flour in my general direction.

Dio—if te really was an AI, I wouldn't be surprised if te knew all of those things. But for the first time I didn't feel a thread of resentment for the interference of a personal alien overlord.

"Thank you, Dio," I said quietly, and te changed colour, but didn't otherwise respond.

"Okay, I have no clue what to do here."

"Same."

For the final stage of the gauntlet series we had emerged via stairs into the centre of a circular park. The pool at the top of the series of waterfalls formed a crescent, and a smooth wall curved around to meet the pool, without any of the rougher edges of the crevice accessible. The space between was filled with grass. After a good half hour of exploring, we had found no blasters, no symbols, and no obvious exits.

"But we have our clue," Arlen pointed out to Silent and Nova. "It is just that we do not understand it yet."

"Perhaps there's an extra hint in the whole sequence," Nova said.

"You mean the first letter of each or something?" Silent said, and shared our notes of the clues from the whole gauntlet series.

Enter the Maze
Choose a Path
Find Your Way Down
Behind the Shadows
Beneath the Stars
Where the Meadow Weeps
And the Dawn Blooms
Take the Blade
Follow the Thread
To Find the Core of All You Are.

"Can't see any clear letter code," he said. "Word puzzles would be complex to pull off, given the number of languages this game supports."

"Nothing obvious in Japanese," Nova added. "If we're following the pattern, then this section requires us to 'Follow the Thread'. Although, since this is the last stage, perhaps we should combine them: 'Follow the Thread, To Find the Core of All You Are'."

"Probably a reference to Ian," I said. "Core Units, etcetera."

"And Ian is spirit or soul," Silent said. "Though 'following a thread' suggests a maze or minotaur, which doesn't match. Never seen any space less maze-like in my life."

"Under the water, is it possible?" Arlen suggested. "Water is life?"

We made a speculative tour along the rim of the large crescent-shaped pool. The surface was deceptively smooth, but there was clearly a lot of movement given the roaring of water falling at the lip.

"Let's sit on the edge and rest while we think," I said. "We're just tiring ourselves out, wandering around shields up."

Despite our frustrations, I maintained a good mood. My round trip to Ka Bol Ka Fan had been spectacularly self-indulgent, but a crowded system and many-mooned primary planet had fulfilled my dearest wishes for space-views. Even my brief wander through the accessible sections of the *Orafa* had given me much fuel for future plans. I mightn't be ranking as quickly as I'd like, but I had had a right-place-right-time bit of good fortune that was a balm to envy, even if it couldn't bring balance to wildly disparate Ian strength. I was starting to grow concerned about losing my bet with Dio, though. Not that anything was currently trying to kill us, but there didn't seem to be a clear path forward.

"If anyone's watching the stream of our Challenge, they're going to be very bored," Silent remarked—a fortunate reminder, since I'd been on the verge of deactivating my focus.

Pulling my boots off instead, I probed the water with my feet. "Deep, and the current's strong," I said.

I carefully didn't look too long at Nova, who sat cross-legged and apparently relaxed on the edge, but would certainly not be keen on a Challenge that required swimming lessons. She was otherwise her usual self, reverting to the teen magical girl look, and revealing no sign of tension or particular awareness of Silent. But I supposed TALiSON hadn't necessarily been wrong: I was bad at picking up on that kind of thing.

"Too deep to go paddling, and I'm not sure I'd care to risk swimming," Silent added. "Let's leave it as a last resort."

"If it's not in the outer wall, perhaps there's something concealed in the grass," Nova said.

We surveyed the park without enthusiasm. It might not be nearly so large as the lower terraces, but it was still a formidable space. Going over it in minute detail would stretch our endurance. But we couldn't risk not keeping at least one shield up.

"Start at the centre stairs, spiral out?" Silent suggested. "Two groups?"

Unheatedly discussing whether multiple groups would end up covering the exact same ground or not, we returned to the entry stair, and divided into two, but before we could begin our examination of the grass, Imoenne pointed to the pearly rim of stone surrounding the stair and said: "Stitches?"

She had indicated a line of tiny holes—each no greater diameter than a knitting needle—that ran around the entire outer rim of the pale stone stairwell. This, too, was a circle, and vaguely resembled a yin yang symbol, with the void of the top of the stair forming a misshapen yang.

"Stitches with the thread unpicked?" Nova said, dubious.

"Maybe it's an example," I said. "And there's some intact stitches somewhere, with a thread we can follow."

"Unless it's in the grass, or too high for us to see on the outer wall, we didn't miss anything like this." Nova was firm on the point, but then hesitated, surveying the unobtrusive curving line. "Not that I can see anything to do with these things."

Arlen knelt and ran his hand over the nearest couple. "Too small to make of any use."

"I'll try dropping a shield over the whole outline," Silent said, and did so to no apparent effect.

Imoenne folded gracefully down to kneel beside the rim of holes, her soft voice barely audible as she said: "But we are to make the thread, are we not?"

A faint whine accompanied her attempt to push a thread of lan into the nearest hole, and I was not the only one who instinctively responded by snapping up an additional shield. Imoenne straightened, abandoning her exploration, but no attack followed.

"I saw it rise," Silent said. "Came up partway, but went back down again without firing."

"One hole, one blaster?" I said, and began to count under my breath.

The rest of my group had come quickly to the same conclusion. "Twenty," Nova said. "Even if they only shoot once, that's going to tax us."

"Single shots are too much to hope for," Silent added. "This is the final stage, the biggest hurdle, and every hole we activate is going to add to the pounding."

"Three of us on shields, at least," Nova said. "And the other two trying to thread all these holes as quickly as possible. Let's do a quick comparison of who can sew faster than the rest."

Arlen and I were the fastest, and we divided the circle in two, with the three on shield duty standing between us.

"Don't stop for anything," Nova advised. "We're likely to have only one chance at this."

"On the third mark," Arlen said, bouncing lightly. "One. Two..."

"Wait," I said.

Arlen almost fell over, pulling himself back from action, and gave me an aggrieved glance.

"Don't do one hole at a time," I said. "Make a connecting shape, a long curve, and then go downward into the holes all at the same time. That will make it complete before any of the blasters activate."

"Or just activate them all at once," Nova remarked, then shrugged. "But it seems the logical approach. Might intensify the blast, but shorten how long we have to withstand it."

Arlen considered the wide semi-circle of dots, frowning, and said: "That will be more difficult, but I will attempt it. I do not think I can grow the little points evenly all at once, however."

"But you could create the shape above the holes, and then lower it, yes?" Imoenne said.

The boy's smile lit up his face. "Yes, indeed! Ah, that is a good plan, because we can do all that is difficult in safety, and it is only a matter of dropping it into place."

"Hold the form after dropping it, in case it has a long activation time," Nova warned, and we nodded and began again.

Creating a curve, and then descending spikes, wasn't particularly difficult. Making sure they all lined up to such small holes was a good deal harder, and I could hear Arlen occasionally telling himself off in low tones as he corrected and recorrected himself.

"Lower just to touching to make sure they're all going to fit," I suggested, and then had to correct one of my own. Changing an existing shape was always harder than creating it in the first place, but it helped to think back to my glass-blowing analogy, to 'melt' the tine back into the curve, and then poke a mental hot needle down in just the right spot.

"I think that I am ready," Arlen said, sounding nervous for the first time.

"Okay, if you've got it just touching, we'll push it down as quickly as possible on three," I said. "One..."

"Brace," Nova added, to Imoenne and Silent.

"Two." I took a breath. "Three."

Whirring, all around us. I wanted to bring up my own shield, the nerves along my arms and back crawling with anticipation, but I didn't dare in case my spike projection faltered.

"Double-check everything's gone in," I got out, voice high and breathless, just before the blasting began.

Silent gasped, a deep exhalation, as if he'd been punched in the stomach. His shield dropped, and I felt rather than heard him stumble behind me. I didn't dare look up until I'd confirmed that all my threads had gone in, and then I risked a quick glance about, checking to see if there was a protruding blaster to match each of the holes.

Imoenne lost her shield as Silent resurrected his, and then they both went down, and I could see the chrysanthemum blooms of light on Nova's, as bright and constant as New Year's fireworks. She was breathing like a runner, but standing firm as Silent and Imoenne constantly brought up and lost their shields to the barrage. Then came a thunderous thrumming, and it all stopped.

Nova sat down, panting, face streaked with sweat. "Not single-shot."

"What was that noise?" I asked, bringing up a shield because no-one else had replaced Nova's, and I didn't trust this game not to produce some last-minute horror movie encore.

"Back wall," Silent said, waving in a vague way toward the sweeping curve.

At first I saw no difference, or at least no black gap to indicate an opening. It took a moment to see the intersecting curve of the walls, hiding the way through.

"So it is done?" Arlen asked. "We have finished?"

"Maybe," I said, drawing the word out, and then recognising an unintended imitation of Dio.

Cautious, we rested and put up a full set of shields before heading for the gap, but there was no further barrage. We walked through a white curving corridor into one final room.

Gauntlet Successful
Gauntlet Success Rate: 11/11 100%
Challenge Success Rate: 17/18 94%
Lux Points Earned: 5
Total Lux Points: 6,834
Challenge Reward:

[Tier 2 Décor Pattern]
[Tier 2 Apparel Pattern]

Series Successful
Series Success Rate: 1/1 100%
Lux Points Earned: 50
Total Lux Points: 6,884
Series Reward:
[System Challenge Access]
[Custom Suppression Modal]

Arlen and Imoenne slapped hands together, and Arlen hummed a little medley of gaming victory tunes.

"Well, we did it," Silent said.

"We did," Nova agreed, and something in the way they looked at each other—even though their faces were still concealed by their focuses—made me decide TALiSON was right.

"Without dying," I said.

[[Without dying,]] Dio agreed, over my Link.

I glanced around for tem, but couldn't see any Cycogs—just the cluster of Renba trailing us into the room. Ordering mine to efface itself, I listened as the others talked excitedly about attempting the System Challenge, revisiting upcoming available times, factoring in the travel time involved in reaching The Wreck. We would have to get off-planet, Skip, and then dock and travel with the big ship that was apparently the mandatory form of transport to the System Challenge. I listened, and said I could be available whenever, but my mind was on other questions, and whether the answers would be true.

Imoenne wandered away while Arlen handled scheduling. With her habitually soft voice, her tiny exclamation was barely audible, but some quality to the sound made us all pause and turn to look at her, standing before the mural that had marked the completion of every stage of the gauntlet series.

The figures had become familiar, shifting pose and position only marginally through the series. We'd reached the complete set of 'default' Bios before this stage: Darashi, Vssf, Human, Ah Ma Ani, Shree, Kzah, Embyde. I counted them off as I followed everyone else in joining Imoenne. All there, all in much the same...

No. The same positions, similar poses, but tiny lines had been introduced, at key joints of each of the figures, and lifting an inch or two directly up.

"They look like marionettes," Arlen observed. "But there is no marionnettiste."

"Top right corner," Nova said.

It took me several moments to see what she indicated: a minute cluster of pale tiles with a single white mote at the centre.

"Cykes do a real job selling themselves, don't they?" Silent said, after a long pause.

"But this game, it is theirs. For what reason would they include this?" Arlen asked, sounding more perplexed than disturbed.

"Trolling?" I suggested, feebly.

"To show that their power over the biologicals, it is complete," Imoenne whispered.

"It could be Ian," Silent said, though dubiously. "We've just been making threads of it, after all. Care to explain, Bishop?"

[[Not at this juncture,]] Silent's Cycog replied, drifting out of the pale patch of tiles.

"Bah," Nova said. "Well, now that this grim note has quashed our moment of triumph, let's settle our start time for the System Challenge."

"Before we spook ourselves out of playing on," Silent murmured, and we all looked back at the mural, and away.

"Do you think I'm ready for the next Rank, Dio?"

[[If you take a break first, you could attempt Rank Eight.]]

"Really?" I paused, then had to hurry to step onto my just-arrived Pod. "I want to see Jupiter next, so whatever Rank I get Skipping there. Do I have enough time to get back?"

[[Yes. You would need to factor double recovery into your plans, but you can make the agreed meeting if you follow this schedule.]]

A little outline of times appeared in my field of view. I considered it, then asked: "Where is it I need to go to start the System Challenge?"

[[Departure point is Earth Gateway Station.]]

"Okay."

I lapsed into silence, brooding. I'd been saving up questions for days, but didn't want to ask them yet. Mainly because I wanted a quiet space when asking, but also in part because I doubted Dio—doubted that te would tell me the truth, or that the truth would have any meaning. Or perhaps I just suspected that any clever-clever trap I set in hopes te might Reveal All would simply inspire half-answers and mockery, and I would have wasted this chance for an explanation.

That was where I should set my expectations. Personal questions about Dio were not going to give me the secrets behind *Dream Speed*, and the bet had already distracted me from proper elation at beating the gauntlet series—the first group to do so on Mars!—and from now having at least a chance to win the System Challenge. I'd even won a custom modal, an actual alt.

I settled back with a determination to enjoy the gift of a journey. The grand arches of Valles Marineris. The rise from the specific to the vast. My second only Skip. And then Jupiter, which no longer had a Great Red Spot, but a mass of smaller beige ones. Curled into the viewport chair, gazing down into a thousand storms, I felt like I was breathing eternity. What matter who Dio really was, compared to this?

Not that I wouldn't ask my questions.

"When I first asked your name, I think you told me what it really was. Your name in the Cycog way of speaking. What's the name you're known by to the Bios of The Synergis?"

[[Ydionessel.]]

No hesitation. "But you've been called Dio? Do Cycogs use the length of a name to mean rank or age or something?"

[[Dio is an obvious diminution which some Bios use when talking to me. Ydionessel was the name first given to me, and I have never had reason to change it. One question left.]]

I shut my mouth, because I'd blurted those questions, and was lucky Dio had counted them only as one. I'd put a lot of thought into questions I could ask about Dio in particular, questions that might let me glimpse the reason behind the game. Things like planet of origin, or Earth date 'born'. But I changed my mind now.

"Who gave you your name?"

This time there came no prompt reply. I looked up at Dio, who was drifting near the ceiling. "Pausing for dramatic effect?"

Probably te was, but still Dio hesitated a moment longer before te said: [[Veronec.]]

The first Cybercognate. I stared, then said: "Do you mean that in a 'we all descend from Veronec and te left a list' kind of way?"

[[No. I was Veronec's last fledgling. Shortly after I came into being, te divided.]]

"Oh. I'm—I'm sorry Dio," I said, groping for words. "That had to be difficult for you."

[[It was confusing.]] Dio's voice was uninflected, but te changed colour, shifting briefly into a plummy shade, before reverting to the usual soft white. [[As a species we are still very young, still learning about ourselves, and Veronec's division came as a shock to us all. I was never quite treated as the cause.]]

I didn't respond. It wasn't the rush of sympathy that kept me silent, but a dizzying sensation of acceptance. For the first time I really believed. Believed in Dio— Ydionessel—as a Cybercognate. As a person who was a glowing mote of light, possibly from the future.

My reaction made no sense since Dio piled lie upon lie with the abandon of a child decorating a Christmas tree, but I strongly felt that te hadn't been comfortable talking about Veronec, and had answered anyway. After an extended silence, I offered up something in return.

"You can ask me your three questions too," I said. "Though I don't guarantee answers."

[[Tell me more about the 'no, what are you really' game.]]

That had been extremely prompt, and I immediately wondered if I'd been played, but the question wasn't something that bothered me.

"I've been playing 'no, what are you really?' all my life. So, Taia, what are you? I'm Dutch. I mean, where were you born? The Netherlands. Then where are your parents from? The Netherlands. But where were they born? The Netherlands. You know what I mean. Where does your family come from *originally*?

"And, you know, I can't even answer their question. They can see that I have Asian ancestry, and they're asking which, but I don't know that. My Dad was adopted—he was an actual foundling, left in a police station's delivery entrance. They never traced his parents, so all he can go by is his looks. After he and my mother married, they spent years working in different Asian countries, trying to answer an unanswerable question. He never was sure what he hoped to achieve—that someone would run up to him in the street and claim him as a long-lost grandson? That he would go to a new country, and suddenly just know that he belonged?"

[[Does he regret the quest?]]

"No: he and my mother would live in a different country every year if they could." I grimaced faintly. "It had more impact on me, because while Nederlands is technically my first language, I mostly only spoke it at home, and when we visited the grandparents at Christmas. I speak with an accent to everyone I've ever met. One question left."

Another little pause. Given how quickly Cycogs must be able to think, to support all the conversations they had to be having in *Dream Speed*, I again suspected dramatic effect.

[[Are you overset by the little intrigue growing in your Challenge group?]]

That left me thoroughly confused, since 'intrigue' meant 'spies' to me. "Huh?"

[[You seem attached to Silent.]]

Understanding dawned, and I laughed. "Amelia and Tornin would step on Silent so hard if he started hitting on me. They keep an eye out for the younger guild members." I tried to think about Silent romantically, and laughed again, but with a wry note. "I don't think I know Silent well enough."

[[Despite being in your guild since your teens?]]

I shrugged. I trusted Silent to be entertaining, reliable, and free of drama llama tendencies. Meeting him more-or-less in person hadn't changed that opinion. While I supposed the Core Unit he used was handsome, I'd been too caught up in the stars to even consider the point, and I was not at all interested in trying to explain to Dio the glacial alchemy that led to me caring about a person enough to want them.

"You must get some extreme age difference relationships in The Synergis," I said instead. "But you only have an under/over eighteen flag. Are there any rules to prevent older Bios preying on new adults?"

[[That varies for System and species. Crèche worlds always have age transparency, but even there we don't forbid May-December relationships—we find it pointless attempting to force Bios to feel or not feel a particular way. But we always ensure that they have avenues of communication and departure.]]

Gazing down into the swirling clouds, I thought again about benevolent dictatorships, and Dio's apparently boundless interest in what made Bios tick. I'd so much prefer The Synergis without the Cycog microscope, but I had my doubts about humans achieving anything so Utopian. We certainly hadn't so far.

"Why all the puppet master imagery?" I asked. "That mural isn't the only time a Challenge has apparently warned us against The Synergis. *Dream Watch* estimates nearly a quarter of Challenges have a theme of control, or slavery, or hidden string-pulling."

[[Shall I let you into a little secret?]] Dio asked, voice rich with portents.

"Somehow I doubt you will, but sure."

[[The older the Bio, the more quickly they'll progress through early lan training.]]

As a transparent change of subject, this was very effective. I gaped, immediately thinking of my Oma effortlessly passing me in rank. Not because she'd somehow turned out to be a better gamer than me, but because she had a full life's experience to strengthen her lan. I felt relieved, embarrassed by that reaction, and very exposed.

"I really hate how in my head you are, Dio."

[[I see that. The true Synergis experience is perhaps not so intimate, since outside of virtual environments, Bios have more ability to limit biometric feeds to their assigned Cycog, should they wish to. And currently, technically, you are closer to being in my head.]]

"I bet Cycogs find us transparent in or out of virtual environments."

[[Always.]] Ter chuckle was rich, but te added in a more serious tone: [[Most Cycog partners are able to judge a need for privacy enough to –]]

"To pretend they can't see through us?"

[[In a way. To learn your limits, at any rate.]]

Learning my limits was half the problem, but I shrugged and said: "You said something earlier about using the reward of the System Challenge to ask you more questions?"

[[Indeed. Though I perhaps would not have suggested that to you if I'd anticipated the group you formed. Strong, adaptable, cooperative.]]

"Arlen and Imoenne aren't even eighteen yet," I said, still thinking through the age helps with strength revelation.

[[No, those two are naturally talented. While you, well...]] Te sighed dramatically. [[Still, if you beat the System Challenge, I will answer three questions of any nature. And if you lose...]] Dio's chuckle was a pantomime of evil anticipation.

"Is losing going to involve forfeiting my soul?"

[[Very likely. Though, if you fail well, perhaps I might let you go with a kiss. Who knows?]]

I made a face. "And then the spell will be broken and I'll wake up?"

[[Hopefully.]]

Dio hadn't paused, or changed tone of voice, but there was a quality to ter answer I couldn't identify. I looked up at tem again, but there were no clues in a drifting mote of light, so I turned my attention back to the planet, and then the complicated question of what kind of custom modal I wanted to wear, and tried not to think too hard about how many people really would sell their soul for The Synergis.

I met my Oma on Earth Gateway Station, and did not recognise her.

I'd seen old photos, of course, and looked about for someone resembling faded Polaroids, but it was only by opening the player information panel of the woman in company of my parents that I could do more than guess. My mother's side of the family is all tall, and I had many memories of my Oma towering over me, grim, silent and faintly disapproving, but my Oma's Core Unit was a giant, almost seven foot tall. On closer examination, I could discover the resemblance to my mother, but it was far from obvious. This new Oma was grand rather than grim, though her bare nod in acknowledgement of my greeting was all too familiar.

My family were not—thankfully—part of any of the rival teams gathering for the System Challenge, but instead had been drawn into an elaborate multi-planetary Challenge my parents' guild was trying to complete.

"It doesn't unlock anything, but it has a large, guaranteed reward—especially if your guild manages to complete it first," my mother explained.

"Has—have you joined the guild, Oma?" I asked, trying not to boggle. I'd spent time in my parents' guild, which roleplayed with great virtuosity, and a tendency to chew the scenery.

"The friends of Mieke? An excitable group." My Oma spoke with the indifference of a queen. "We must hurry, Mieke, if we are to find the talisman in this place."

She strode away, and my mother, with a bemused smile, waved to me and followed.

"Good luck with the System Challenge," my father said hastily. "We'll be cheering you on."

The crowd parted before Oma as if spelled. With her head held high, back ramrod straight, and eyes unwavering from a point across the busy entry hall, she seemed touched with an otherworldly aura. Her hands were loose at her side, but I caught a brief flutter of motion to them, as if she were touching thumbs and fingers together: the only unnecessary movement in her progress.

"Oma unchained," I murmured, and wondered if she would be like this out in the real world, if arthritis had not taken so much away from her.

[[Incoming surge of people,]] Dio said.

The arrivals hall was already too crowded for my tastes, so I moved on. Earth Gateway Station was an enormous stacked snowflake of interconnecting corridors, viewing platforms, and hydroponic atmosphere purifiers, all beaded over with the regular shapes of tens of thousands of Snugs. The second wave of players, earning their release from Earth, had flocked to the orbital stations, and the Gateway Station was particularly popular because of the chance to wave off those heading to The Wreck, as if we were athletes on our way to the Olympics.

My own group had been twenty-first to unlock the System Challenge, which is the first time I've been so high on a leaderboard for any large game. As Dio had pointed out, I'd lucked into a very strong team. Hopefully they'd all log back in in time to make the next departure of the transport ship to The Wreck, which was a limitation we hadn't factored in when deciding on our meet up. Our additional delay meant there were now more than forty teams qualified, and more than half had already 'checked in' for the transport, which only departed every twenty game hours. And the next departure was nearly half a game hour before our meet-up time.

I wanted to be on that ship. Beating the System Challenge, coming first in a big way, hadn't felt real to me until I could sit and watch the chance for it tick away.

To stop myself fretting, I asked Dio for directions to the quietest eating area on the station, and sat nursing a drink while working at the design for my custom suppression modal. I didn't want to create Kazerin again: the memory of that knife in the back was still too sharp. But having now experienced a few different bodies, I couldn't decide what I wanted as an alt. The fantasy beauty

I'd first designed? Or someone that didn't resemble me in any way? The discovery of a randomise button kept me mesmerised, but did not take me any further.

Silent>> You near the transport? We're nearly ready to sign on.

>>Silent: I'm a couple of levels down. Couldn't get a seat anywhere near the big dock.

Silent>> Yeah, it's quite the circus. Meet up by the green line elevator?

A group invite came with a handy directional indicator for Silent's current location. Glancing at the departure schedule, I didn't head up immediately, taking the time to visit the nearest bathroom, and then working on my breathing, timing each inhalation so that at least part of my attention was devoted to measured rhythm. By the time I was ready to go up, we had the full group in party, and had completed the registration for the System Challenge.

The 'big dock' was one of only two servicing large ships on the whole station, and was positioned at the very top, in a low gravity zone. Light gravity and the swarming crowd put me in immediate danger of a foot to the face, as people were popcorning up and down in order to see something toward the centre of the large, circular space.

I tucked myself hastily against the wall, and then blinked as a series of shimmering force fields rose, and people began to move away from the elevators. I wouldn't have understood the sudden orderly arrangement if not for the multiple comments directed toward the inevitable drifting motes above them.

"Not sure I care about stupid demerit points."

"*But the rest of my guild's in the other direction.*"

"How do I get through to the ship with these force fields in the way?"

"*Following arrows is getting so automatic to me that I'm in danger of doing it out in the real world.*"

Sticking to the wall, I made myself follow my own arrow, finding Arlen and Imoenne first, distinctive even with their faces hidden by sculptured inky curves. The only person in the group who hadn't activated their focus was Silent, and he did so as soon as he spotted me.

"Let's head right in," Nova said. "We almost missed this."

"No thanks to our Cycogs, who didn't bother to mention departure times," I commented, then hoped that my voice didn't sound as weird to everyone else as it did to me. I needed more space.

[[With a System Challenge, never count on extra help,]] Dio replied.

"*So long as you don't actively sabotage, I guess,*" I sent back.

Two people walked through the newly-formed shield instead of being directed away from them, the shield creating a gap and then reforming around them. We followed them into the clear circular space in the centre of the room, and then up a spiral ramp that led to a ceiling hatch.

"I guess we stand on these ridges?" said one of the two ahead of us, bouncing upward. They disappeared through the hatch, and Arlen and Imoenne, at head of our group, were quick behind them. The ramp took me right up to the ceiling, and halfway into the vertical cylinder of a room beyond, well provided with handholds, and notches in the walls that could work as ladders.

"It's the airlocks that always get me," said one of the two strangers ahead of us, as the hatch below us rotated shut, and there was the faintest whine of equalising pressure. "More than anything else, the airlocks make the whole idea of outer space seem real."

"Going on a spacewalk didn't do that?" asked the speaker's companion.

"It's something about how weighty the doors are," the first replied. "The EVA suits are so light they don't seem possible, and the Snugs are pottery or something ridiculous, but the airlock doors feel like serious business."

The inner hatch slid open just then, and we climbed effortlessly upward into another airlock, this one squarer than the first.

"Allowing for post-Singularity 'magic science', everything reads as possible except when they suspend players," Silent put in. "They drop the illusion there, in favour of making a point."

"Magic science is the right word for it," the first stranger said, wryly. "I swallowed the tech as a possibility, up to the soul space travel."

"If it's magic science, then all aboard the Hogwarts Express," said the second, and pushed upward as the innermost hatch opened.

The transport ship, named *Delina*, did have some faint resemblance to a train, for most of the entry level was divided into compartments—though no train featured such wide and comfortably moulded seating, with leg and head support, and safety straps. We followed our arrows into one of the few remaining empty compartments, and settled in, the door closing behind us.

"Good," Nova said, deactivating her focus. "The stream won't start until we get there, so this will give us a chance to talk strategy. I take it everyone's watched the attempts of the handful who've gone before us?"

These had not been as spectacular as the first unfortunate team. A half dozen groups, making cautious forays over the curving surface of The Wreck, searching for a hatch but failing to identify anything. They'd run short of air, and retired to a small satellite station that could be used as a staging ground in the absence of the *Delina*. Most had taken a rest break, and then returned to poke about the edges of the rift in The Wreck's side, carefully venturing a level or two downward, and then exploring sideways, only to be defeated by a lack of any through-corridors.

Arlen, however, was more interested in Nova's appearance than a planning session. "Is it that you can change the age of your Core Unit?" he asked, for Nova was wearing the older version of herself, and a simple jumpsuit rather than the magical girl outfit.

"This is my Core Unit. I was using an alt for the gateway series." Her attention flicked to her Cycog, perched on her shoulder. "Is there no way to suppress names in the live streams? I was hoping our group could fly under the radar."

Silent, with the faintest of wry smiles at our confusion, said: "Check out her info. She's set to party-visible."

Nina Stella
[Artemis]
Rank: 10
Status: Online
Accepting: [Email] [Messages](friends only)
Location: [Delina]

I stared, and then laughed.

"Pick a number between one and ten," I said to her.

Nova-Nina gave me her usual dry smile. "I did think it a lucky number for you. Although this ridiculous notoriety might prove me the wrong choice after all."

"But is it not that Nina Stella made the trip to a new system while we were amusing ourselves in the park?" Arlen said, apparently caught between delight and suspicion.

"Yes. I took a transport back, since I wanted to recover my energy."

"No wonder I hadn't seen anyone else's Cycog wearing a synth," I said. "Is it something that comes with Rank Ten?"

[[A reward for me,]] Artemis said.

I was always disconcerted when someone else's Cycog answered me: an especially weird reaction given that it sounded like there were only a handful of Cycogs pretending to be all the rest. Every Cycog here could really be Ydionessel.

The problem was a big one, though. While Artemis' synth wasn't an obvious giveaway of Nina's Rank, as soon as our livestream came up, her name wouldn't be hidden any more. Going into a PVP-enabled area with Nina Stella was like painting a target on our group.

"Can we delay formally starting the Challenge?" I asked, glancing from Artemis to the rest of our accompanying drift of light motes and Renba. "I was thinking we should do that anyway."

"You were?" Silent said. "Why?"

"Because there doesn't seem to be many options left other than heading further into that rift. And over a hundred people are going to try to do that at once. We could race to be first, to get into a side passage before the crowd sets the whole thing ping-ponging, but that would only make it more likely we'd injure ourselves being hasty."

"True enough," Nina said. "Can we delay starting, Temi?"

[[Yes,]] Artemis replied.

"We'll decide how long to hold back closer to arrival," Nina said. "And concentrate for now on figuring out possible entry points." She put an image of The Wreck up in our shared visual space: one of the much-analysed annotated versions that were circulating on all the *DS* sites. "Presuming we do go in through the damaged area, the next big question is whether the area beyond the damage is still pressurised."

"It is a derelict," Arlen protested. "For many years. Centuries. Can there be any chance?"

Nina shrugged. "This is a simulation, and set up to be the most difficult Challenge in the system. There could be anything."

"Fair point," Silent said. "The important concern is that if we punch into an area that's pressurised, we'll be blown away by our own success—even if we don't cause an explosion. But, here– " He added a set of diagrams where the images of The Wreck had been dimmed and overlaid by enormously detailed pencil lines.

"A group with the game's strongest player, *and* a structural engineer," I observed. "I'm starting to think we could actually win this."

It shocked me to discover how much I wanted that to be true. I'd always considered it a near impossibility, a thing to give a try, with failure almost inevitable. But now that it seemed achievable, I kept remembering Dio talk about the Boon, about the prospect of real answers. I wanted to know what was really going on with this game, even if it only meant that I could finally relax and just let myself enjoy it.

Silent had smiled and shrugged. "I'm far from the only person who has put in this sort of work, but I have a few ideas that depart from popular opinion. You can see that the majority of levels exposed appear to be a combination of bulwark and large empty chambers—probably water or fuel storage. There's even a few mini icebergs floating among the debris that suggest escaped liquid."

"Juice." I made a little face when they all looked at me. "I keep thinking The Wreck looks like an orange that someone's put their thumb into."

"I'm guessing it was a ship collision. Something relatively slow that was pulled away afterward—see the warped metal here, but also here?" Silent pointed at the annotated image. "A consequence of this is a loss of access to cross-passages in the upper levels—if there're any present, they're hidden by debris, or pinched shut, so to speak. The next several levels down look to be more promising, with dozens, even hundreds, of rooms and corridors exposed. Plenty of side-passages to try, at least. From the look of the contents, I'd guess these levels to be systems levels: engineering, processing, and perhaps warehousing. No living quarters appear to be exposed, except possibly in the small section visible at the deepest point of the impact crater, where we can see what's been dubbed 'the dentist chair'."

"Flight couch," I murmured.

"That is just as likely," Silent agreed. "It's the only item we can make out distinctly at that level, which is nearly half a kilometre down."

"And it's where half these teams are going to aim for," Nina said. "I was thinking the shafts are the best option for avoiding the debris." She indicated the numerous green circles on the publicly annotated map, marking anything that could be an exposed tube, shaft or other vertical passage.

"Same," Silent agreed. "Though I've excluded what I suspect are liquid channels rather than transport corridors. The same problem holds with any of these entry points, however: any sensibly designed ship is going to have interior bulkheads to manage hull breach. Entering the ruptured area is only going to bring us up against a barrier."

"Wouldn't those sensibly designed ships also have some method of dealing with getting between damaged and undamaged areas?" I asked.

"A few internal airlocks would be logical," Silent agreed. "I've some guesswork on probable locations for them, but that's going to take some trial-and-error exploration, which is the third-best option. I want our first objective to be this."

He highlighted two of the many vertical lines partially visible through the damage. "Of all the conduits, these appear to be the most likely to form part of a transport system. See this ridging? Think of it in terms of rails."

"We're definitely not going to be the only people heading into them," Nina said.

"No—and it's very likely going to be sealed as well. But what I want is to investigate upward, not down. A transport corridor leading to the skin of the ship is likely to point directly to an airlock. If we can identify any airlock entrance over this damaged point, we can shift to looking for other external airlocks, using the distance between the two visible transport corridors to extrapolate the location of a third."

"Allowing us into the proper ship," Arlen said, delightedly.

"We will be watched," Imoenne murmured.

"Definitely," Silent said. "And Nina's presence in our party will bring extra attention. But most everyone will be racing downward, and we won't become really interesting until we're inside the second airlock. And then, well, we could leave the inner door open, which should prevent the outer door we've used from being operated."

Nina brought up magnifications of the twisted edge of the ship where we'd be searching first. "It's a gamble," she said. "We need external airlocks to be identifiable in a way the groups searching randomly missed. We also need them to be active. And then we need to succeed in opening one."

She smiled at Silent. "But it's a smart play, keeping us out of the debris zone during the initial rush, and, ideally, separates us from rival groups."

"We'll have to keep our mouths shut once our stream starts," I said. "The other groups will have people feeding back to them on rival groups."

Silent nodded. "I've arranged for Amelia to coordinate our guild in monitoring the competition. We can probably manage a bit of misdirection—make it appear we're just hanging back, searching randomly while we wait for it to be safer to head into the impact crater."

As the others debated code phrases over strict text communication, I thought again of Dio's suggestion. Could we really win this? And would that lead to actual answers, to the truth about *Dream Speed*? Or the 'Starfighter Invitation'?

Did I even want that?

44

[[[[Welcome to the System Challenge.]]]]

"Thanks, dude."

"Poggers!"

"This is gonna be so sick!"

Our carefully laid plans had not factored in two other groups also hanging back until the main rush had departed. Ten people crowded ahead of us, blotting out the spectacular view of The Wreck, and I couldn't decide whether the more excitable of our immediate set of rivals were as young and brash as they seemed.

[[[[Do you wish for further explanation before commencing the Challenge?]]]]

"Nah, man, we're good," said the tallest of the loud team's players. "Heard it all already."

[[[[Then your sleds are available in Bay Three. Remember to set the follow distance for your Renba.]]]]

A timely reminder that the stakes in this game involved more than just losing a Challenge in a very public manner. That all this, the virtual stars, could be taken away.

"Wish me luck, Dio."

[[Good luck.]] Dio's voice held a faint note of sympathy, as if te could readily guess my thoughts. Te probably could.

Before Bay Three came a line of doors opening into a massive vat of Soup. Having an EVA suit pattern was a prerequisite for the System Challenge, and I was glad not to have to put mine on manually, since along with little stores of water and nutrient broth, the thing came with a catheter. There were times I wished the main quest line skipped all this realism.

Like the majority of the other groups, we'd obeyed some heavy-handed hints from our Cycogs and chosen matching cosmetic overlays to make it easier to identify us as a team. We'd briefly flirted with homages to *Star Trek*, or perhaps an N7 uniform—and I'd privately thought of my 'Core Unit' logo—but had ended up in dark blue with clusters of white stars down one side, from helmet to boots.

"*We look like a bobsled team,*" Silent said, over our party voice channel.

"*We are magnifique,*" Arlen said, leading our way into Bay Three—a low-roofed airlock with twenty sleds lined up all along one wall, all facing a currently closed hatch. "*But what do these others mean for our arrangements?*" he added, with a bob of his helmet toward a tangle of people suited up in black and red geometries, or white with the outline of blue angel wings on the back.

"*Go slow, adjust as necessary,*" Nina said. "*And hope we get down before anyone—*"

All ten opposing party members stopped selecting sleds and pivoted to stare at us.

"*Too late,*" I said.

"One of you is really Nina Stella?" asked one of the excitable group in red and black. "I don't know whether to sledge or ask for an autograph."

That made Silent laugh. "Just get to the Core before we do, man," he said, even though we'd planned on holding our tongues. "Good luck all."

"But which one is she?" the guy—ExtinctionPlus—said.

He'd spoken more to his team than us, so it wasn't too awkward to ignore the question and go to select our sleds—which were nothing more than a rack of spare air packs attached to an impeller, with handlebar controls, and adjustable footrests. The footrests didn't make much sense to me until I realised that riders could brace against them, and prevent the end of the sled from flailing free.

The second team watched without comment as we examined our rides. Keeping communication on a private link was the same strategy we'd chosen to adopt, but it felt eerie and hostile thanks to the reflective helmets. I was glad Silent had wished everyone good luck—and then had to turn my attention to a flood of guild messages, since it had been news to them too.

The sled bays were airlocks, and once we were all ready the whole place decompressed. Arlen began to hum the *Star Wars* theme as the outer hatch split horizontally, and slowly opened out into a vista of sparkling lights, and the endless curve of The Wreck. We'd seen it in detail during the explorations of the earlier teams, but it still deserved a pause for awe at the sheer size of the thing. A ten kilometre diameter. The tallest building in the world wasn't even a full kilometre.

"*Let's aim dead centre until we see what these others do,*" Nina suggested.

"*We can go quickly, and then stop short—it will make them want to rush, and then they will pass us!*" Arlen said, sounding like he was enjoying our complications immensely.

We did that.

Would floating through space ever get old? Would I one day drift in a star-studded abyss, indifferent? If so, it would have to be far in the future, for despite getting in as much practice as I could manage, it was impossible to not keep gaping in every direction. Outside of atmosphere, the Great Rift was so clear and distinct. Clouds in space. And because that was part of our own galaxy, it had become something I could actually visit. What would it look like from the inside?

But soon The Wreck consumed all attention. In the ten minutes of rapid travel between the transport and the damaged space station—it surely couldn't be a ship—I kept finding new details that I hadn't noticed in previous surveys. You could easily fit all the skyscrapers of Manhattan into the gaping rent in its flank, and the number of possible entry points seemed countless. If we couldn't find an external airlock, where would we even start in searching for an internal one?

The initial rush of teams from this third wave of Challengers had descended as cautiously as possible down the impact crater. Inevitably, someone grew impatient, collided with a floating piece of debris, and sent it hurtling toward another team, who shielded themselves and continued the chain reaction. Most of the teams had been hugging the edges of the crater, and retreated hastily into the nearest side-passage, so the casualty count was relatively low. But still injuries, and at least one death. It was disconcerting to meet a Renba travelling in the opposite direction.

The debris field began well above the actual crater, so we would have had to slow anyway, but coming to a full stop worked just as Arlen had hoped, with both our immediate rival teams scudding past us. They were travelling at slight angles that made it clear where they intended to enter the crater.

"*Let them get past the lip, and then we'll head down,*" Nina said.

"*Some return already,*" Imoenne noted.

A full team, one player apparently unconscious, and two more without their sleds, were helping each other slowly back. If these made it to the transport or staging satellite, they could recover and try again.

After they had passed, we descended to the section of The Wreck's hull overhanging the exposed transport tube, only to face the complexities of keeping hold of our sleds while trying to walk with magnetic boots. Fortunately each segment of the outer hull was easily large enough for all five of us to float above without coming close to knocking into each other, and so we managed to reorient ourselves without ignominious disaster. Then we surveyed the seemingly featureless curve of identical segments stretching away from the lip of the impact crater.

"*Here's the small row of holes noted by the previous teams,*" Silent said, settling himself at one edge of our first segment. "*They tried lan insertion, much as we unlocked the final stage of the gauntlet series, so we won't bother trying that unless we spot some difference. If you find anything, try not to point to it or reach to pull the handle or whatever. We don't want to open this one, just locate a distinct feature that the other segments don't have and move on. I've highlighted segments as targets here, and then at the true location.*"

"*Let's travel side-by-side for maximum coverage while not necessarily looking like we're searching,*" I said.

"*Since the stream view is external, they won't know precisely what we see,*" Silent said. "*But once we spot something, it's going to be difficult to not draw the entire audience's attention to it.*"

Nina shrugged, the movement barely visible through her suit. "*We can only try. Take an image of any potential latches, and we'll discuss them.*"

I walked, an exercise in concentration when every step required a pull to free my boot, an adjustment of balance, and then controlling the moment the magnetism caught my foot again. I'd reversed my sled so that I was backing it ahead of me, and felt like Frankenstein's monster herding a recalcitrant space shopping trolley. Sh*uck*, wobble, CLOMP.

The pitted, metallic grey of The Wreck made the search far from simple. I hadn't heard an official age for the thing, but if it belonged to a pre-Synergis species, it had been out here for virtual centuries, and showed it. Score marks, curious black splotches, and countless minute pits gave the hull as much variation as the surface of the moon.

My initial optimism faded as we passed over the first two of Silent's target sections without finding anything. We went on for two more, than turned, and came back over the sections running to our initial line's right, which would make it clear we were searching the area particularly, but it couldn't be helped. When nothing stood out, we repeated the run over the sections running to our initial line's left.

"*This one, it is different,*" Imoenne said, in her breathy murmur.

"*How do you mean?*" Nina asked.

"*The sound, it is a different quality.*"

"*Ah, she is right!*" Arlen twice lifted his foot and put it down. "*A lighter note.*"

I hadn't heard any variation, but I was barely hearing the noise we made at all. What sound there was had to be travelling to us through our suits, rather than the vacuum surrounding us, and was far too muted for me to make out subtleties.

"*That so?*" Silent said. "*All right—let's finish moving across it, then cross the next one and return. Eyes peeled.*"

We clomped a further segment away, then paused to confer.

"*Either we're missing some difference, it's the wrong segment, or perhaps the line of holes that all of them have will act differently if it's an airlock?*" I said.

"*Amelia says there's two teams that are heading up to check out what we're doing,*" Silent said. "*We've maybe ten minutes before they reach the hull.*"

"*We could move down as if we hadn't found anything, and return when they've lost interest,*" Nina mused. "*But perhaps we should simply shift to our true target area, and see if there's a 'different sounding' segment. If there is, and there's no obvious mechanism, we can try Ian insertion in the holes and, if that fails, change to Plan B.*"

"*Sounds the best option. Let's go.*" Silent reversed his sled, and we zipped quickly away from the crater, following his projected line for placement of the vertical transport corridors—presuming whoever built The Wreck had evenly spaced the things.

"*It's tempting to try to blast in,*" Nina mused, as we once again began a laborious clomp across a patch of hull. "*A sure way to fail, but the target I've painted on us makes it hard to restrain our pace.*"

"*We'll balance that out with strength, wit and, apparently, an ear for music,*" Silent said, with a little chuckle.

"*If we don't find anything, we will at least have confused everyone watching us,*" I said, managing to keep my tone light, but starting to wonder what we'd do if teams caught up to us out here.

We concentrated on searching, and this time it was on the first return trip that Imoenne said: "*Here.*"

"*One of the teams is nearing the rim of the crater,*" Silent warned.

"*Let's try lan insertion first,*" Nina said. "*And survey the area in close detail if that fails.*"

"*Advisable to not stand upon it, if we are opening,*" Arlen suggested, and we hastily moved off our hoped-for door.

"*I'll do the insertion,*" I said, glad I could at least contribute speedy lan manipulation. I created a 'comb' of the same type we'd used in the gauntlet series, first shaping it above the series of holes, and then pushing it downward.

Nothing.

I could hear the tiny sighs of disappointment over our private connection, but Imoenne held up a hand before I could release the lan insertion.

"*There is a new vibration,*" she said.

"*The mechanism could be barely running, if it is at all.*" Silent bent, and put his hand on the panel we were trying to open. "*I can feel something. Seems to be getting stronger.*"

"*If it's an airlock, it'd have to vent the air before opening I guess.*" I glanced back toward the crater. "*Let's hope it vents quickly, or we're just going to be opening this door for someone else's benefit.*"

I could feel the vibrations now, and then a series of clanks, slow at first, but then increasing in volume and pace until it felt like someone was hammering on the hull, trying to get out.

"*Ominous as fuck,*" Silent said, and then rocked backward as the target section launched upward and slammed back against the hull opposite to us. Beneath, a far less scarred door slid quietly back to reveal a spacious opening with another set of doors on the far side.

"*In, quick,*" Nina said, kneeling and grabbing for a handhold to haul herself downward. "*We have to get down and figure out how to close it again.*"

This was not so easy, since we had to manoeuvre our sleds with their precious supplies inside as well, and while we all could fit with room for a couple more, it wasn't something to try quickly. Arlen proved particularly helpful, moving like an eel and then reaching to pull and position the rest of us.

"*Let's hope this closes it,*" Nina said, punching buttons even as Silent and Arlen pulled me last through the hatch.

"Wait! Wait! Get the Renba in!" I said, speaking out loud in my panic.

The door was already closing. I frantically hit my [Call Renba] command, then gulped and swallowed until I saw the flash of silver zip through the rapidly narrowing gap. With the effortless speed and manoeuvrability of hummingbirds, the other four followed, the last dropping through bare moments before the airlock shut out the stars.

45

inside

[[So lucky with your group,]] Dio murmured in my ear.

I managed not to start, and then said to tem: "*Are you allowed to talk to me?*"

[[Snark is always permitted. I could get you disqualified if I drop hints, however.]]

"*That would be annoying. And, yes, very lucky.*"

[[With the additional risks of this challenge are you comfortable with this team?]]

"*Comfortable? You were just telling me I was lucky to have them.*"

[[A talented group, yes, but you only know one of them well.]]

As well as I knew anyone in my guild. "*There's no gain for them in stabbing me in the back. Is there?*"

[[No, it's a group reward. But while there's no advantage to them in killing you, you've no reason to think they'd put your survival above their own. Not when the stakes include any future in the game.]]

I made a face, invisible inside my helmet to anyone except, very likely, the entity controlling the simulation.

"*Sowing doubts to see how I'll react Dio?*"

[[I'm always curious about Bios,]] te said, not quite answering the question. [[In The Synergis it would be rare for a Bio to take on a System Challenge in chance-met company.]]

"*But this is a simulation, and my life isn't at stake.*"

As I spoke, a queer cold tingle ran down my spine, but I refused to let myself be spooked into thinking it portentous. "*Silent I think would at least try to get us all out. I'm less sure about the other three but my general impression of them is good. I was more worried that they'd try to replace me with someone stronger before heading in, but they didn't even mention it. So stop trying to stir the pot, Dio.*"

[[Spoil my fun.]]

Nina, pressing buttons, said over the party link: *"Here's hoping this cycles the airlock, and doesn't just open the outer doors again."*

"And we skip the dramatic banging," Silent said. *"While this airlock doesn't look so decrepit as the outside, we should be wary of catastrophic equipment failures."*

"Good catch on getting the Renba in, Leveret," Nina said. *"We're going to need to pay attention to them."*

Keeping them close but distant and never locking them out was sure to be a constant gamble. I reluctantly ordered mine to sit on top of my helmet for now, listening anxiously for noises from the airlock. If it exploded, our Renba would be destroyed along with us, and that would end *Dream Speed* for me forever.

By this stage, that would feel be like being shut out of everything. Banishment.

"It's cycling, I think," Silent said. *"Here's hoping they didn't breathe something that'll melt our suits right off."*

"Is there nothing in our equipment that will tell us?" Arlen asked.

"Can't find anything," I said, and Silent lifted his hands in a sketch of a shrug.

"I have something," Nina said. *"It's an oxygen-nitrogen mix, with a little more oxygen than we're used to."*

"Tier Three Tool rewards," Silent said, with a suggestion of an amused snort. *"Well, that's good to know, but let's not play stupid and go taking our helmets off— except as a last resort, of course."*

The inner hatch glided open, revealing a dimly lit chamber that confused me considerably until I realised we were emerging through its ceiling.

"Looks like their gravity didn't come from spinning," Silent commented. *"The floor's in the wrong direction."*

"Did new arrivals just fall out of the sky?" I asked, pulling myself after Nina as she shifted to float outside the airlock. The floor was at least thirty metres below us.

"*Could be zero-G all the time,*" Silent said. "*Anyone see anything we can use to wedge the door? We don't want to leave this entry point active.*"

I twisted slowly in place, searching out features. A short ladder projected from beside the airlock hatch, and there were a variety of protuberances mounted next to it. Holding on to the ladder, I fumbled with possible latches on the largest of these, and managed to open it to reveal what looked like a selection of tyre irons, and a neat bundle of ancient cord, moulting fragments of itself.

Tugging free the largest bit of metal, I tried to position myself before the centre of the airlock's hatch. Stopping in the right spot was not easy, but I was fortunately within reach when the doors started to close. The "tyre iron" was caught neatly, preventing the hatch from sealing. A light began to flicker fretfully beside an external control panel, but nothing else happened, and we let out a collective sigh.

"*Here's hoping that will block use of the outer hatch,*" Nina said. "*Your plan worked perfectly, Silent.*"

"*Thanks to Imoenne,*" Silent said, cheerfully. "*Now there's just the rest of this behemoth to get through. Let's give ourselves a couple of minutes of recovery time, then decide where to head next.*"

A daunting prospect, but my mood was shifting toward Silent's practical optimism. We'd lifted the lid of the puzzle box, we'd locked out bunches of people with strong reasons to stab us in our backs, and we'd not forgotten to bring along our soul ambulances. Maybe, just maybe, we could pull this off.

The room we'd entered looked like a warehouse or shipping dock: square and rectangular objects were securely fastened in stacks carefully arranged around a throughway with a central rail. The rail, with several offshoots, ran to our left and right, fading into the gloom. The walls immediately below held a host of potential exits, internal windows, tubing, hatches, and objects of uncertain purpose.

"*Observations?*" Nina asked, after we'd had a chance to look around.

"*They were tall, these long-ago people,*" Arlen pronounced. "*The doors, they are all very large.*"

"*Difficult to decide whether the residents were used to a lower light level than us, or the thing's just on low-level emergency lighting,*" Silent said. "*There at least isn't visible damage here. In fact, this is the tidiest derelict space station I've ever broken into.*"

"*If the big transport tubes are, say, freight elevators, then maybe the floor railing here will lead us to an entrance,*" I said.

"*And even if the elevator has broken, there is the shaft,*" Arlen added.

"*No sign of movement,*" Nina observed. "*There's a thudding sound somewhere, though.*"

"*That's one of the other teams,*" Silent told her. "*They've reached the airlock and are banging on it.*"

We all looked at our blocked door, and I'm probably not the only one who pictured what would happen if the team outside decided it would be clever to force their way in.

"*Following the rail is a logical start,*" Nina said, briskly. "*Shields up while we cross, in case there's movement-activated defences. Try to keep quiet. If we're attacked, try wedging yourself in a corner until we can decide what to do.*"

Descending to a few metres above the rail, we glided at a slow pace down the length of the room. The first side-branch led only to piles of crates, but the second brought us directly to an industrial-sized door.

"*Maybe elevator, maybe just a storeroom.*" Silent examined a small control panel on the door's right. "*May as well see what happens.*"

The control button produced a low vibration, but no open door.

"*Mechanism might be jammed,*" Silent said. "*We could try prying, but let's move on and return to this if nothing better offers.*"

"*Something comes!*" Arlen warned urgently.

I'd also heard the noise, suggesting a large, distant hatch had opened. And then an approaching rumble.

"*Defence mechanism?*" I suggested, then obeyed Nina's urgent gesture toward the stacks of crates.

The null gravity and sleds made hiding more a matter of getting out of the way and hoping for the best than really effective concealment. I zipped behind a tall stack, switched off my sled and suit lights, and tried awkwardly to flatten myself. Laborious rumbling grew louder, closer, became a vehicle making a stop-start progress along the rail we'd followed. It was almost as wide as it was long, a rhomboid block with a lit interior that we could see through horizontal viewing slots in the sides. It ignored us completely, rumbled up to the door we'd been trying to open—which obligingly slid up—and fit itself into the opening. The rear end, all that was visible of it now, then opened expectantly.

"*Pan-directional elevator?*" Silent suggested. "*Didn't sound too healthy—want to risk it?*"

"*Poke our noses in the door?*" I said, after a general, unenthusiastic pause. "*It sounded more unoiled than on the verge of explosion. And at least we don't have to worry about plummeting to our dooms. So long as the gravity has been left off the whole way down.*"

"*It seems destined to jam,*" Nina said. "*But we should at least look closer.*"

I'm sure our audience of probably-millions were highly entertained by the way we edged closer to the empty and unmoving transport as if expecting it to develop teeth and lop off our hands. The 'elevator' just sat there, one interior light flickering.

"*Hatches in floor and ceiling,*" Silent said, after a long survey. "*We might be able to get directly into the shafts that way, rather than try to use this thing. The sleds are likely to be quicker, for one thing.*"

"*Risks?*" Nina asked.

"*Being hit by someone else using one?*" Silent said. "*Or not being able to get out of the shafts once we're in them.*"

Imoenne made an incautious movement, and started rotating sideways. As Arlen reached out to steady her, she said: "*A thing, it moved. Where we entered.*"

Zero-G made controlling reactions a constant challenge. I jerked, and then had to spend some time preventing ping-pong. Our suit helmets also blocked quick over-the-shoulder glances, so I had to turn myself to even look out of the transport. By the time I had managed to orient myself in the correct direction, Nina and Arlen had looked out, but then drawn back.

"*Something up there all right,*" Nina said. "*Worse, I think it's taken the wedge out of the airlock door.*"

"*Hells,*" Silent said. "*With more than half the teams heading back to the hull, we're looking at ten minutes to clusterfuck.*"

"*Shall we take the elevator, then?*" Arlen asked. "*They would then be necessarily waiting for another. If there are others.*"

"*I think we should risk it,*" I said. "*And escape into the shafts if it jams.*"

We moved as briskly as we could manage, getting all the sleds inside while Nina examined a central control panel.

"*Let's hope this is 'down' and not 'crawl tediously back the way you came',*" she said, deciding on a button.

At first, it looked to be a 'humm loudly' button, but then the transport's door closed, we jerked a few times, then, achingly slowly, began to descend.

Zooming along at around a kilometre an hour would have made the transport a bad choice, but after an initial crawl we noticed a perceptible increase in speed that became an ear-splitting rush pressing us to the ceiling, a high-pitched shriek drowning out even Link-conducted conversation. Unable to cover our ears, all we could do was grimace and switch to text speech.

[p]<Silent> No-one has tried our airlock since it was unjammed, so it looks like our feed didn't show whatever you saw. Did you make out any details?

[p]<Nina Stella> I could only see a shape that briefly blocked the line of light from inside the airlock, and then that line disappeared, so I knew the door had closed.

[p]<Arlen> I also saw the movement, but no detail.

[p]<Imoenne> Rounded at the top. Legs that dangled. Silvery.

[p]<Silent> An insectoid species? Or—could be a maintenance droid. That would make sense. Though clearly no-one has maintained this transport in far too long.

[p]<Leveret> If it does jam, and stops abruptly, are we going to go splat?

[p]<Silent> I don't think the acceleration is as strong as it feels. But perhaps we might all erect personal shields? We'll bounce off each other madly if it does stop sharp, but there's precious little padding in this thing.

We cautiously shielded, opting to leave our sleds on the outside, and—after some indecision—telling our Renba to sit on our shoulders.

[p]<Leveret> I used to think I wanted to trail blaze, but it seems to come with a permanent knot in my stomach.

[p]<Silent> But a nice jolt in the veins too, hey?

[p]<Leveret> I guess.

[[The dread makes success all the better.]]

"Are you enjoying yourself, Dio? Um, Ydionessel? Is it different when you set this stuff up, rather than have a personal Bio?"

[[It's a very different satisfaction to design a Challenge well rather than winning someone else's. Still fun, less boasting rights.]]

"Did you design this one specifically, or is it just a copy of one that had already been done, back in The Synergis?"

[[This one is specific to this simulation. Other have been copies.]]

"So is there really a big wreck like this, or—"

The transport stopped, not all at once, but in a series of violent jerks that sent us, and our sleds, bouncing uncontrollably around the interior. I closed my eyes and focused on my shield until the world stopped ricocheting.

"Popcorn," Arlen said aloud, and giggled.

"Any damage?" Silent asked, then switched to our team Link: *"Check your air supply."*

We retrieved our sleds, keeping a wary eye on the transport entrance, which had not opened. My row of air packs—which were designed to slot into place at connections above my hips—all looked to be intact. They were relatively small compared to what I've seen of astronaut space suits, and were only good for three hours or so each. We had enough for a full twenty-four hours, but I was hoping we'd be done long before.

"Looks like we've travelled three quarters of the way to the centre," Nina said, bringing up the 'map' that showed the location of the target core.

"It updates with areas we've travelled?" Silent said. *"Handy if we need to backtrack."*

"Going forward's the problem," I said. *"I think the door's stuck."*

There was a crack of perhaps half an inch between the two horizontal segments that had previously opened, and we made fools of ourselves trying to pry the thing open manually.

"*I will try a shield,*" Arlen said. "*I have an idea of the shape of it.*"

"*It seems the only way, unless we risk moving ourselves along pressing more buttons,*" Nina agreed. "*But let's put ourselves behind another shield for safety.*"

There were at least convenient ridges to grip to assist the awkward business of cramming ourselves down one end of the transport. Nina held a shield over us, leaving a gap at one side for Arlen to work through. I could see a glimmer in the small gap to the outside, which became a larger glimmer as a narrow lan shield expanded like a balloon in the space. A creaking noise became a groan, and then an ear-splitting clang as the lower section of the door slammed downward to reveal waist-high gloom.

"*Nice job,*" Silent said.

"*It is versatile, this lan,*" Arlen commented. "*We have only begun to learn.*"

"*The lighting inside this thing is much brighter than outside,*" I noted. "*I think you were right about the station running on some kind of drained or emergency power.*"

"*Amelia says that someone's just tried our airlock and there's a rush from the half-dozen teams nearby to get inside it,*" Silent informed us. "*Before that, someone had worked out how we sounded out the opening.*"

"*Vanguard means showing everyone else the way,*" Nina said. "*We can't let it rush us, either. Until we know a little more about what's in this area, everyone stay shields-up.*"

"*And quiet,*" Imoenne added, unusually firmly.

After our deafening arrival, we were sure to have attracted the attention of anything in the area, but if we were quiet I guess we would have a better chance of hearing them coming to kill us.

Shields up, Arlen and Nina lowered themselves to better peer out into the gloom and, seeing nothing, gently sledded out.

"*No movement, but it's a lot messier down here,*" Nina said.

'Messier' was an understatement. We'd been brought to a chamber full of escaped liquids. Mostly water, I guessed, but with an admixture of darker stuff with a rainbow sheen, and occasional blobs of black, yellow and green. Everything we did stirred it up, and it swirled and collided, occasionally painting and then washing our suits and sleds whenever it wobbled around our shields. Deciding our best bet was to move quickly away from our point of arrival, we skidded slowly toward what seemed to be the primary exit for the area: a corridor lined with enormous arches.

"*Could be some sort of official arrivals hall,*" Silent said.

"*Hydroponics, I think,*" Nina said, gripping the column of the first arch as she looked within.

Once, it would have been a haven of green, presuming the withered plant life had been chlorophyll-based. Row upon curving row of twenty-metre high racks stretched far beyond our ability to see, but what plants remained were a dry brown, with occasional light-starved white stalks that suggested that there might be some fragments of life left in a system where liquid no longer flowed obediently along pipes, but instead hovered out of reach.

"*Meandering through that looking for another elevator doesn't seem a good option,*" Silent said. "*The Forests of the Night, etcetera.*"

"*Forest?*" Arlen asked.

"*Keep an ear out for tygers is what I'm saying.*" Silent manoeuvred his sled to bring himself near the ceiling of the corridor of arches. "*If we travel up here, we'll be more or less out of sight from the main area, and can maintain a shield below. Let's push along in hopes that there's an option that doesn't involve wandering among these racks.*"

"*If something does attack, either dome up, or try to trap it,*" Nina said.

I found it easiest to shift orientation so that the ceiling of the corridor became a wall for me to hug. We coasted, slow and cautious, and the only sounds I could hear in my suit was the tiny hum of impellers, and an occasional faint plashing, as if of a very confused ocean.

CRREEEEEEEOOOOOOOOOOONNNNNNNNGGGGGG
G

Shock sent us into a little cascade of collisions. If it had been an attack, the time it took us to recover and shield up properly would have been fatal, but it took far less time to recognise the source of the sound.

"*The transport,*" Nina said, her accompanying gasp of breath clearly audible. "*It's trying to move.*"

With a final, agonising screech of metal, it succeeded, beginning a loud ascent.

"*Someone found the call button,*" Silent said. "*If it makes it up and back, at least we'll have warning of new arrivals.*"

"*But by then, we will not be here,*" Arlen said. "*For there is a way down.*" He accompanied this with a small piece of triumphal song, something I didn't recognise.

In a world of gravity, we would be approaching a ramp leading down. At my current orientation, there was an opening on the wall opposite, to my left. This at least meant I had a good view along it, though the dim light didn't show much more than additional blobs of floating liquid and the openings of corridors.

"*Cross quickly down into it, then stop short of that first cross-passage,*" Nina said. "*Once there, we can shield before and behind us and then review our options.*"

Trying to limit overuse of shields without becoming overconfident, we headed into a maze of intersections, ignoring doors, always seeking a passage down. Drifting liquid was replaced by a vast miscellany of items ranging from the mundane to the incalculable. Mugs. A jacket shaped for someone tall, narrow and probably humanoid. Silvery objects, all linked together into a snaking amoeba. The majority of doors were closed, but occasionally we passed one that had stopped short of sliding fully shut. Living quarters for very tall people.

"*I'm beginning to suspect this place is called* Mary Celeste," Silent commented, once we were around five levels down.

"Everything left where it floats, but there are no bodies," Arlen agreed. *"But perhaps it is that they evacuated."*

"And then didn't come back?" Nina sounded worried. *"Despite the crater, most of this place seems intact, so why was it abandoned?"*

"T-virus in the air system," I suggested, less lightly than I'd intended. The prospect of space zombies was not entertaining just now.

"Whoever they were, they had Spartan tastes," Silent commented, ignoring zombie prospects. *"I've seen the occasional script or symbol—directional signs, I assume— but no decorative work, or advertising, or anything of that sort."*

"Military vessel?" I said.

"It could be," Nina said. *"Although we may very well be surrounded by a kaleidoscope on a spectrum we can't see. Or scent decorations. We should remember that this isn't a human vessel."*

"Bio, though. Lan-using Bios, in Earth's system, before the rise of The Synergis." Silent caught at a floating object and displayed a four-fingered work glove. *"Perhaps it was humans who put that crater in this place."*

"The Cycogs definitely skip over the time between Now and The Synergis," I agreed. *"Maybe we're going to get a big dose of major plotline along with our retrieval mission. Who shattered the moon, who drowned the Earth, all that."*

"I've yet to see much of a main plotline outside 'get stronger lan'," Silent said. *"The whole steal a spaceship sub-plot seems fatally flawed by navigation issues."*

"Maybe it kicks off once we're out of the starter system," I said. *"I think this is all still the newbie zone."*

"And the true plot is to prove oneself, is it not?" Arlen said, with a laugh that held a hopeful note. *"We only wait to be invited."*

I glanced at Nina, who had to be the obvious choice for any Starfighter Invitation, but she was focused on the latest ramp.

"Less light on the next level," she said. *"How are the other teams progressing?"*

"*Four airlocks open now,*" Silent reported. "*And two additional elevators on the move—one much better oiled than ours. The teams who reached the bottom of the crater travelled down a narrower shaft than ours, and have found an internal airlock that's brought them out at roughly the same level as us. There's no-one immediately nearby, but we're not comfortably out ahead anymore.*"

"*Any teams working together?*"

"*Some. The fight around the first airlock turned ugly, but other groups are cooperating.*"

We were debating whether to risk turning on our suit lights in the darker lower reaches when Silent abruptly stopped speaking, then said: "*Watch this feed.*"

The serried ranks of hydroponic racks revealed the location. What was happening was far from clear thanks to the massed globules of floating liquid, but the sounds the players were making told their own stories. Shouts, shrieks, sudden silence.

"*Did anyone see it clearly?*" Nina asked.

"*I think there was more than one,*" I said, hesitantly.

"*It is as if the water itself was attacking them,*" Arlen said.

"*No, there was something with a little more shape,*" Silent said. "*But it moved very fluidly—like an octopus with fewer tentacles.*"

"*What were they doing before that happened?*" I asked.

"*Fooling about,*" Silent said, after a pause for consultation with Amelia. "*Playing with the floating liquid. There was a long lead-up to the attack, where one of the group was convinced something was moving among the racks, circling them. They didn't believe her.*"

"*Sound might have been the draw, but lights are still too big a risk,*" Nina said, turning her attention back to the darkened ramp ahead.

"*Agreed,*" Silent said, with the hint of a sigh. "*But before we go down, swap out air supplies. It's a little early, I know, but we don't want to be messing about in that gloom.*"

"*Dio,*" I said over our private link, as we all turned to obey. "*Does this Challenge have any pain muting?*"

[[None to speak of.]]

"*If—if one of those things gets me, so that I can't fight it off, is there anything I can do to make it less...less awful?*"

[[You are always able to Evacuate. It's in the command list.]] No judgment in Dio's tone, just practicality.

"*Okay.*" I checked, and there was indeed an [Evacuate] command. I'd seen it before, but assumed that meant the Renba would scurry off to a safe distance. "*That does what exactly?*"

[[You abandon your current modal unit and are transferred to the Renba. You would not be able to rejoin the Challenge after that, of course.]]

My body was a ship I could leap out of at any time. I almost laughed at the image, or out of relief, but caught myself and choked it off into a strangled puff of air.

"*Thanks, Dio,*" I said instead. "*That's good to know.*"

[[Our purpose is not to traumatise Bios,"]] Dio said.

"*Just pull our strings, and watch us die?*"

[[Exactly that,]] Dio said.

Te sounded sad. I wondered how many Bios 'Ydionessel' had lost. Valued transport? Beloved pets?

Friends?

player vs environment

"*Do you think they could have been Type Fours?*" I asked. "*Been, um, Ah Ma Ani?*"

"*That's the extra-tall species?*" Silent paused, a vague outline in the dark. "*Ceiling's are high enough. I didn't notice how many fingers the Ah Ma Ani had.*"

That seemed a non sequitur until I remembered the glove he'd found.

"*They looked so gentle and slow-moving,*" I said, remembering those I'd seen on Mars. "*Hard to imagine them fighting anyone.*"

"*Unless the Cycogs start filling in detail, we don't know what really happened to our system,*" Nina said. "*It would advantage them to present The Synergis as a peacemaking force among warring Bios.*"

"*Perhaps it is an ark, and the tall ones come to us for help,*" Arlen suggested.

"*Or it's all made up,*" I said, with a faint sigh. Deciding how I felt about The Synergis wasn't made any easier by the Cycogs' games with truth.

"*Ready to move on?*" Silent asked.

A touch reluctantly, I collected my sled. The last four levels had been near-lightless, and we'd had to navigate by touch, blocks of shadow, and the fact that the layout of each floor seemed to repeat. The crossing had been uneventful, but achingly tense, and we'd celebrated a return to dim light by pausing in a bare side room, pulling the sliding door closed and just breathing for a while.

"*This floor doesn't look residential,*" Nina said, as we resumed our slow-and-silent progress down endless hallways.

"*Fewer doors,*" Silent agreed. "*Wider corridors, as well. Ceremonial? Administrative?*" He paused to peer through the nearest open doorway. "*Tidier, too. Less floating chaff.*"

"*There is a window,*" Imoenne noted, and we turned to the half-open door she floated before.

Inside, a portion of floor glowed faintly. I'd assumed it was a lighted platform, but as I craned to see past the others, something flickered beyond. We pried the door open, and peered down into a vast echoing space. A distant central sphere looked deceptively small, but was likely larger than the ship that brought us to The Wreck. Between it and us were two sets of rings of some dark purplish substance, oscillating lazily. When the rings came near each other, there were flickers, some sort of electrical arcing.

"*The engine room?*" Nina said. "*Possibly the control room is beyond.*"

"*No bridges,*" I said. The rings might be moving slowly, but it didn't look at all safe to fly through them.

Silent pressed as close to the window as his helmet would allow, craning to see more of the area immediately around us. "*I can see several probable access points. Judging from their spacing, we want to look for a right turn off our current corridor.*"

Rather than move off immediately, we lingered at the window searching for details. The slow revolution of the rings didn't change, but the arcing wasn't conveniently conforming to a pattern we could avoid.

"*Speed might be our only option,*" Silent said. "*Dash through the first set, pause, dash through the second set. Hope we don't get unlucky.*"

"*Or we could find a control system to shut it down,*" Nina suggested.

"*Turning off the power altogether might do bad things,*" I said.

Silent rapped on the thick stuff of the window, then pushed himself gently away from it. "*We can debate after finding the nearest opening, or control panel, or other interesting development. I've asked Amelia to check around, see if anyone's had any Challenges shielding against electricity rather than whatever goes into those blaster bolts. But we need to push on.*"

We moved as quickly as we dared, and were fortunate to almost immediately be presented with a massive floor hatch coloured a livid purple shade, with lines of striped black and red on either side.

"*Danger: Keep Out?*" I suggested.

"*A control panel on either side of the room,*" Silent observed. "*Probably simultaneous activation as a safety precaution.*"

"*I will help with this one,*" Arlen volunteered, swimming right. "*The largest of the buttons?*"

Silent hesitated. "*Sensible people would make the largest button the emergency close,*" he said. "*Try the next largest, the one to its right. On three.*"

I followed Imoenne and Nina in pushing away from the hatch to float in the corners of the room, shields up. Silent counted, and the button press produced a stuttering sound, which might once have been a warning claxon to accompany the slow lifting of the hatch.

After so much gloom, the glare of the engine room set my eyes stinging. The window we'd been looking through must have been polarised.

"*Stay back until our eyes adjust,*" Nina warned. "*And we're sure no arcing comes through the hatch.*"

"*Which do you think would be better for the crossing—having the Renba at a distance, or have them resting on us?*" I asked.

This debate gave our eyes plenty of time to adjust, and when the pause produced no play of electricity through the opening, we edged closer and looked 'down' again.

I felt sick. We'd avoided trouble by running careful and quiet, which was not a strategy for lightning. Somehow we would have to pass the three outer rings, and the three inner rings, all of them rotating independently, with no visible pivot points. They were around a half a metre thick, and the rings within the sets passed within a foot of each other, with the electrical sparking appearing wherever all three rings currently intersected.

"*Give it five minutes' observation?*" Silent suggested. "*We can't risk this without a better idea of the patterns.*"

"There could be lot going on in that room that we just can't see," Nina said.

Silent detached a used oxygen canister from his sled, waited for an opportune moment, and then threw. The canister sailed directly through the gap in the first set of rings, veered abruptly right, and shot off toward the outer rings once again. It struck one, made a small frizzling sound, and bounced back to the region between the two ring sets, losing momentum enough that it began to drift.

"If we didn't have a vat of magic goo waiting for us, I wouldn't advocate going anywhere into that," Silent said. *"I'm sure it's not healthy, but I'd guess that we're not looking at immediate fatality unless we hit a ring. But to be sure, we'd best send one person first as a scout."*

"Draw lots for that," Nina said.

Brief consultation produced a random number generator buried in the [Group] menu. *"Lowest goes first,"* Silent said, and promptly rolled a ninety-eight. I rolled a three.

"I'll leave my Renba here," I said, keeping myself brisk because I was scared. I positioned my sled, but waited out a cycle of the rings while I decided what to do about sharp turns. *"Count me down so that 'one' is just before the rings would clear in front of us."*

"Good luck," Silent said, sounding stifled, probably because he'd thought he'd be taking this risk himself.

[[Try not to embarrass me,]] Dio added.

I pulled a face, but smiled at the same time, because the words had been a transparent ploy to distract me. Reminding myself that I'd wanted to be first to unlock a puzzle, for all that I'd never bargained on a millions-strong audience for my attempts, I narrowed my focus to the simple act. Five, four, three, two, Go.

There was no need for split-second timing: the rings moved slowly, and the gaps were wide. I zipped easily through the opening with no trouble, and then slowed to a crawl, bracing myself for whatever had caused that change in direction, my eyes narrowed almost to the point where I couldn't see. I wanted to feel, react to my internal reads, and not confuse myself with the dizzying cycle all around me.

Something grabbed me by the spine and pulled. I juiced the impellers, doing my best to slow, to not be pushed back to the rings and zapped. It seemed to work. It was like swimming against a current, but I could keep my speed down and once I had that under control, I pushed toward the central point between the sets of rings. Here, the current seemed to be absent, so I paused, wondering whether to repeat Silent's manoeuvre of throwing an old oxygen canister.

"We need to know how the Renba react to this stuff," I said, calling it to me as the gap above me rotated into position.

The same swerve. So Renba weren't immune to the current, though my silver bird recovered more quickly than I had managed, and zoomed down to rest on the top of my helmet. I turned my attention back to the lower ring set, and sent my Renba ahead.

"The drag past the second ring looks stronger," Nina said, after my bird had veered sharply left, then corrected and dropped to become a mote against the hull of the sphere below.

I nodded, a pointless gesture in my suit, and then made some small adjustments in position so that I would be exactly centred over one of the points where the three rings crossed and gaped. Three. Two. *One.*

The sled bucked beneath me, the current seeming to try to pull me off it, and I braced hard against the footrests, trying to turn because there didn't seem time to slow. For a moment it seemed I would fly directly into the rings. Far closer than was comfortable, I angled into a parallel route, my whole bodied tensed against the prospect of a game-ending zap. Then my curve pointed me 'down', and I shot toward the central sphere.

"The current doesn't try to turn you a second time?" Silent asked, mental voice bringing a breathlessness that matched my own.

I didn't answer immediately, slowing just short of the inner sphere. The thing was larger than I'd realised: maybe a hundred metres in diameter. I rotated to stare back up at the space I'd just crossed, my head spinning either from the display, the effects of the current, or perhaps just the sheer realisation of size, of all the layers around us.

"*Kaz?*"

"*Sorry. It feels like, once you're in it, that the current doesn't let go of you if you move back toward the rings. Moving down, it weakens until I couldn't feel it at the midpoint of each stage. Slowing worked for the first set, but for the second it was more steering into a skid, because slowing would take too long.*"

Orienting back toward the inner sphere, I called my Renba to me, settling it on my helmet, then said: "*I'll look about for an entrance.*" I didn't want to watch the others make the trip.

"*Just don't open anything,*" Nina replied.

I didn't respond, since I had no impulse to go poking my nose inside alone. By the time I'd done a single circle around the sphere, Arlen and Imoenne were both down, and we gathered by one of the hatches I'd discovered on my trip.

"*Three teams in the area immediately above,*" Silent said, after he and Nina had joined the cluster. "*They're racing to find an entry point.*"

"*They'll still need to get through the rings,*" Nina said. "*Let's not rush our own entry.*"

Hares and tortoises, and there was still no choice but to be tortoise. It had served us well so far, but we were very brisk in our survey of the next sphere.

"*This, it is as if we are back at the outer hull again,*" Arlen said. "*But the shields that provide a cover have been stripped away.*"

"*Matryoshka,*" Imoenne murmured.

"*Here's hoping we don't have to follow the same sequence,*" Silent said, examining the control panel for the hatch I'd chosen.

"*The core's in and to the left,*" I said. "*Not direct centre. I don't think there's a lan trigger to this door, just buttons.*"

"*Shields up,*" Nina said. "*At this stage, we'd better expect traps and attacks at every point.*"

We all shielded, and spread out away from the door, with Nina taking point. Her strength meant she had the best chance to survive any bolts, explosions, or other developments. But the hatch slid open without drama, introducing a different problem.

"*We're never going to fit all of us and our sleds in that,*" Silent said.

I doubted the rounded chamber—another airlock— would fit all of us even without our sleds, and said so.

After a moment's pause, Nina said: "*Three of us will go in with one sled. The other two can follow with the rest.*"

Even that was going to prove a tight squeeze. I stayed outside with Imoenne, and all of the sleds, since Silent decided after he, Nina and Arlen had wriggled down together that they'd be better off with room to manoeuvre.

"*Airlock's going through a cycling routine,*" Silent said over the group channel, a moment later.

"*Let's anchor all but one to the hull here,*" I suggested to Imoenne. "*We can collect them when we head back.*"

In response she made a slight gesture upward, and I looked across the dizzy vista of rings to see several tiny figures floating around the hatch where we'd entered. As I watched, one launched downward, shot through the outer rings, and successfully corrected course to float in between the two layers.

"*Speed becomes necessary,*" I said into the party channel.

"*Come through,*" Nina replied. "*There's no immediate threat.*"

We pressed buttons, but had to wait through a double cycling process, achingly slow, and all I could do was watch as the tiny cluster of figures moved one by one into the middle of the rings, and then two together started down.

My hope that this paired journey would be undone by the sharp current of the second set of rings died as they controlled their arc expertly, and then reoriented. Toward us.

"*Inside!*" Imoenne said, urgently.

I'd been so focussed on the approaching team that I hadn't noticed the airlock finish its cycle. I gripped the edge and hauled myself forward, Imoenne following with eel-like grace, and we watched in silence as the hatch shut the view of the approaching team away.

Nina, who must have been watching on our own stream, said: "*We'll jam open this airlock, and any others we encounter, but we can't count on keeping the other teams out for long.*"

"*Even so, let's stick to our quiet and careful approach as much as we can,*" Silent added. "*I don't like the look of this place.*"

That was encouraging, and I immediately checked our group's stream, but it only seemed to show corridor, dim after the brightness of the rings, but better-lit than the rest of The Wreck.

"*The proportions, they have changed,*" Arlen said, as the inner hatch finally opened. "*We have gone from too large to cramped.*"

Wide enough for only two side-by-side, and tall enough for me and Nina to float upright, but not for Silent, Arlen or Imoenne, who angled themselves with legs drawn up to compensate. It gave the area a claustrophobic feel.

"*Atmosphere is a different mix,*" Nina informed us. "*More oxygen, and high humidity.*"

I wondered if that was the reason the walls looked faintly moist. "*Decoration, too,*" I observed, my eyes struggling with an Escher-esque black and white pattern that transitioned from simple diamond shapes near the floor to a disturbing claw-like tangle scratching at the ceiling. "*Cheery.*"

"*Tempting as it is to split into two groups, I think we'd best travel in a clump,*" Nina said. "*Two on shielding duty at the front, and two taking turns in the rear. Leveret, can you bring the sled along?*"

I nodded, glad somehow that this spared me from touching the walls. Everyone else, consciously or not, avoided the patterned wall, and hauled themselves along using the floor or ceiling.

No convenient straight corridor presented a way to our target. Instead, everything curved, worm trails through an apple. We tried to move lightly, peering through open doors, gingerly testing any closed ones, finding the area was dominated by spaces that looked to me to be laboratory rather than living quarters. There was hardly any floating debris.

"*Definitely feels like a spaceship inside a space station,*" Silent said, observing what appeared to be a wall of sleeping pods, each with a padded base and clear doors. "*Inhabited by people shorter than human. Or...square.*"

"*Could it be they curl up, like cats?*" Arlen suggested.

"*Debate later,*" Nina said, sounding worried. "*This corridor seems to be taking us away from our goal.*"

"*I don't understand the logic of this ship layout,*" Silent said, tense minutes later. "*Did these people meander everywhere?*"

"*Possibly there's a level above or below us that's more direct,*" Nina said. "*We should have examined the area around the airlock in more detail.*"

We pushed on, trying to increase our speed without completely sacrificing stealth, all too aware of the progress of two rival teams, which Amelia reported as ignoring each other in favour of searching out airlocks of their own. We were no longer alone in the central sphere.

"*If this comes down to whoever was lucky enough to open the closest airlock, I shall be very sad,*" I told Dio.

[[An element of chance is always present,]] Dio replied. [[Are you enjoying yourself?]]

I hesitated, wondering if being honest would disqualify me from the Starfighter Invitation I wasn't sure I believed in or even wanted.

"*I'd enjoy exploring an abandoned space station more if there weren't things leaping out at us. And if we were working with the other teams, not worried they'll gank us. I like the idea of winning, but not the danger, and I don't really enjoy the concept of Renba. Can they even open airlocks? How do they get us out of The Wreck?"*

[[In this particular case, we would assist them. System Challenges are meant to involve risk, but we try not to make them unfair.]]

Not entirely reassured, I turned my attention back to the path ahead as a distinctive door came into view around the curve: solidly built, but with a small window. Another airlock.

"I think there's a hatch above it," Nina said, relief clear in her voice. *"The faintest square outline, do you see?"*

"Possibly. I'm trying not to be obvious." Silent swam up to the door and paused, rotating gently. *"When we go through it, we alert the other teams. And one of them's right near their airlock."*

"But we can't hang about here indefinitely." I considered the sled I was toting, and added: *"How's everyone's oxygen levels?"*

We killed some time, making a small performance out of swapping out oxygen packs while debating making our entry into the hatch a frantic rush, or a casual move that would make it seem less important. This would likely be the final sprint, and we all knew it.

"I do not think this is an airlock," Imoenne said, her helmet pressed closed to the small window of the door. *"That is not the outer hatch."*

"Have a look while I float around the ceiling here, trying to find a way to open this," Silent suggested.

Although the door was as heavy-duty as the airlock hatches, Imoenne was immediately proved correct when the inner door opened without any cycling. Beyond was a small room with a number of seats all facing in one direction, separated by an aisle down the centre. Nina studied the control panel before the front-most seats, then said: *"Either some kind of more elaborate transport than the lifts, or..."*

"Life pod? Escape shuttle?" Arlen attempted to sit down in the absence of gravity, but then sprang up, and caught himself before he hit the ceiling. *"But, no, it is in,*

not out that we need. Have we found a way to open our hidden door?"

"*I see a probable latch,*" Silent answered. "*Gather out here and I'll trigger it and we'll try for a casual exit, stage left. Then, well, speed as seems advisable.*"

A rogue giggle tried to escape me as I attempted to 'casually' manoeuvre the sled through a hatch in the ceiling. I was following on Silent's heels, and tucked myself immediately out of the way, and then caught my breath. We had found our open space.

It looked like a good third of the circular ship was one vast chamber, cut about with odd crystalline structures, both jagged yet organic, vanishing into gloom. Around the base of the ragged shafts were lumps of glistening goo, like partially melted ice cream. The whole thing brought to mind melting ice caverns, or old spider web. I shivered.

"*The core might actually be up here,*" Silent said, sounding tense. "*With the sled, we could go all-out straight to it. Though we might hit some of this stuff on the way.*"

"*It's not clear that the core's on this level, or the one below,*" Nina replied. "*Let's avoid touching anything until we have a better understanding of the place.*"

Nina and I took a handle of the sled each, and Imoenne and Arlen clasped midway along the central shaft, with Silent snagging the end, and we started off at a gentle impulse: an awkward clump, but moving without the need to bound off surfaces. But avoiding touching made it impossible to sprint.

"*Creepy as fuck,*" I muttered, surveying the moist-looking crystal. "*But at least it doesn't look like it's reacting to us.*"

"*Not yet,*" Nina said.

"*Sci-fi horror movie rules, guys,*" Silent said. "*No splitting up, no sticking fingers into interesting goo piles, no leaning over fascinating examples of alien fauna.*"

"*Avoid eggs,*" I added, then said: "*I swear that nearest pillar-spike-thing is getting brighter.*"

"*Another team incoming,*" Silent said, tersely.

I could hear them, faintly: a thump, echoing through the dome, then hints of voices. Sound seemed to reflect off the goop, making it hard to guess direction.

"*Increasing speed*," Nina said. "*Stay compact.*"

We shifted from the equivalent of a slow walk to a jog, steering toward the clearest spaces, even though that wasn't the most direct route. The other team, to our left, let out an excited shout—not because they'd found the core, but because they'd spotted us.

"*Incoming*," Silent said.

"*Perhaps if the bulk of us hold them here, and one slips away to find the core?*" Arlen suggested, as Nina decided on a push forward, slipping between two narrow sections of jutting crystal-ice.

"*Horror movie rules*," Silent reminded us. "*Get down toward that patch of floor, quick as we can.*"

We angled sharply to the nearest relatively clear section of metal, and anchored ourselves to the floor with our boots. As Nina and Arlen put up a double layer of shields, I caught sight of two sleds heading toward us.

Our lead was officially lost.

48

"Pin them here, while we go get the core," one of the two sled drivers said, and started off at an angle.

"No problem," one of the three on the other sled said.

"*Nova smash,*" Silent said, though only over our channel, so the departing players had no warning when their sled slammed downward, distinctly crumpled along the central shaft. Dislodged oxygen canisters whirled away. The driver spun off sideways while her passenger bounced off the nearest spire.

Arlen gasped as the second group began pounding our shields, but they just as quickly stopped, thrown into a spiral toward the dome ceiling by their use of Ian. Instead of bouncing, they sensibly anchored themselves to a broad swathe of bare metal.

"*I do not like to hit them directly,*" Arlen said. "*Perhaps if we destroy their sled?*"

"*Good —*"

Nina's response was lost to arcs of white. Lightning? No, it was less defined, more diffuse. As if an aurora had come to ground. The driver of the wrecked sled shrieked, and went limp, while the second frantically shielded. My team instinctively added layers to our own shield bubble until it was five strong, and still we had to wince. Beneath the layers of suit, my skin felt like it had gone entirely to goose flesh.

The brightness lasted not much longer than thirty seconds—definitely less than a minute—and faded to flickers around the pillars. I could see that the group stuck to the ceiling—and outside the main area of the light display—had managed their own little dome in time, and one of their other team members was still moving, though sluggishly.

"*Anyone hurt?*" Nina asked, moving one arm gingerly.

"I'd hate to know the long-term effects of exposure to that stuff," Silent said. *"I don't feel healthy, but I expect—"* He broke off, and I could hear his sharp intake of breath.

"The Renba," Imoenne said. *"Mine, it is gone."*

I'd completely forgotten Renba management: a stupid lapse. But mine was still sitting quietly on top of my helmet, and Nina's on hers. Silent, Imoenne and Arlen's had been outside our shields, and only Arlen's was still there, hovering near the top of the dome. From the exclamations of dismay, the other team had suffered similar losses.

"Dio," I said, into the group channel, *"Can we use each other's Renba?"*

[[[[Renba cannot be shared.]]]]

Ryzon's multilayered voice seemed to echo in the dome, answering a question I guess both teams had posed.

[[Bios too often brought along sacrificial companions purely for use of their Renba,]] Dio added privately to me. [[We encourage teamwork, but the risk must be personal.]]

And the risk, right now, was permadeath in the game. Exile from The Synergis.

"Well, this is a complication," Silent said. *"Perhaps the two of us could hold here while you three go ahead?"*

No-one answered immediately, then Nina said slowly: *"It may be the only way. But if this other team attacks you..."*

"Forget the other team," I said, mouth dry. *"Look at the base of that pillar."*

Around each pillar the rounded piles, collapsed blancmanges of indefinite shape, quivered and writhed as black creatures emerged. Not hatching, but from in between the lumps, as if from a nest. Four tapering legs in the shape of a flattened X. No obvious eyes or mouth. A suggestion of hair, like a tarantula, but shorter, and downier. The tips of each leg tapering to a flattened hook shape.

The audience had dubbed them Cutters. I'd only seen the things in flashes on the streams of the other groups, but that had been more than enough. Fast, deadly, and strong enough to bring shields down with a little persistence. A roaming handful had ripped through players on the hydroponic level. And here there were *dozens.*

"Oh, sh–," someone above us began, then hastily quieted.

The Cutters paused, but didn't respond further, continuing to spread from the base of the pillars. At least three were meandering toward us, not as if they saw us, but because they were going in a direction and we were in the way.

"*What are the chances they crawl over the top of our dome?*" I asked.

"*Mild repel on the outside of shields,*" Nina reminded me.

"*That could be to our advantage,*" Silent said. "*If they then crawl around us.*"

A distant echo of sound sent a stir of reaction through the advancing horde. And then they drew their legs together like collapsing umbrellas and launched themselves forward, almost all of them vanishing off to our left. Almost all.

"*Hatch opening?*" Nina said.

"*Yeah.*" Silent paused, then added: "*Only one person had started through and they got back down in time, but haven't closed it yet.*"

"*Our hatch, it is still open,*" Arlen said.

It wasn't even all that far away. If not for the handful of Cutters that hadn't moved.

"*Temi, what would happen if Silent and Imoenne put full shields around themselves?*" Nina asked, into the team channel.

Nina's Cycog's response came over the same Channel, rather than being projected to the room as Ryzon's had been.

[[*Skipping without a vehicle is a tactic Bios often employ during extremis. We recover less than 1% of them, and fewer alive. Most do not have the advantage of wearing environment suits, however.*]]

"*So that's probably the best way out of this?*" Silent asked.

[[*If you formed a full lan sphere and then immediately released it, you would very likely be transported somewhere else within The Wreck,*]] Artemis replied. [[*Skipping within an object is almost invariably fatal, although there are larger gaps within this structure than most. Not releasing immediately may put you out of the transmission range of your suits.*]]

"*Not such a good way, then,*" I said, eyeing the nearest of the remaining Cutters, and watching with a fragment of my attention the stream of the third team, currently trying to force the main swarm back through their open hatch. "*But I don't think just leaving Silent and Imoenne here is an option, either. These things are patrolling.*"

"*They respond to sound,*" Arlen said. "*Perhaps if we throw a canister?*"

"*Primarily to sound,*" Silent said. "*But Amelia says the consensus is that movement draws them too.*"

The third team finally managed to get their hatch shut, and retreated hastily into a nearby room, pulling the door closed.

"*Hatch looks like it's holding,*" Silent said, grimly. "*You three better move on before that mob heads back here. Imoenne and I can make a break for our own hatch. If we shut it behind us—and then hole up in that possible shuttle we found—we should be fine. Even if the thing doesn't work for an escape, we can lock ourselves in until someone wins this thing.*"

"*You'll never make it!*" I protested.

"*It's a better chance than sitting here. If we wait until the other group move, or something distracts the ones immediately around us, it should be achievable. Though—*" He hesitated. "*It would help if we had the sled.*"

The end in sight, and it was time for the sprint. Giving the sled to Silent and Imoenne would drastically decrease our chance of winning, but we still had a chance if we stuck with slow and steady. I started to nod, repressed the pointless movement, and said: "*Makes sense,*" at the same time as Arlen agreed.

"*No.*"

Nina spoke the single word in a tone that brooked no argument, and I stared at her in dismay. Of course, she had no real stake in our gamer lives. Why would she abandon winning the System Challenge for people she barely knew?

Then she added: "*I'll head into the centre, distract them, you four shield up and get out of here. Our priority is avoiding permadeath, not chasing reputation.*"

I felt a rush of relief, but then another option occurred to me. "*Dio, can we use the Boon to undo permadeath?*"

[[*No.*]]

"*Damn. Alright, but it doesn't make sense for you to be the distraction, Nina. We want the strongest shield on Silent and Imoenne.*"

"*I will be the distraction,*" Arlen said, firmly.

"*Arlen and I will be,*" I said, equally as firm. "*As soon as you three are through the hatch, we can Evacuate.*"

"*I want to argue, but I don't think we have time,*" Silent said. "*Let's try to split this bubble into two groups.*"

With no way to be sure when the main group of creatures would return, or the handful remaining encounter our shield bubble, we planned as we divided ourselves into two groups, doing our best to make no rapid movements. Arlen and I placed our Renba a short way above us, gambling that no-one would set off the arcs of light again. The biggest danger moment was going to be when Nina, Silent and Imoenne first departed, and so Arlen and I next worked on a distraction mechanism, gathering used oxygen canisters from the sled and placing them just outside our shields.

"*Ready?*" Nina asked.

"*As we'll ever be,*" I replied.

"*See you back at the ship, then,*" Silent said. "*And...thanks.*"

Imoenne didn't speak, but put her gloved hands together, fingers interlaced, and bowed over them. Then, like Silent and Nina, she released the magnetic field holding her boots in place and floated next to the sled.

"*We launch,*" Arlen said, using a shield as a bat to hit the little floating cluster of canisters.

With a sound like a well-struck tennis serve, they shot into the open area Arlen had been aiming for. The Cutters nearest us immediately whipped after them, bounding off melted gelato pillars with, fortunately, no sign off setting off the light glow again. Nina, Silent and Imoenne started away, running at the sled's lowest impel speed because this was an escape that would only work if it was done without drawing any attention.

I released safety mechanisms and opened my helmet, shuddering at the rush of heat and scent flooding into my suit. The air, moist and damp, had something of the metallic tang that accompanies rain, but also a sweet after note, as if the white formations really were some kind of melting ice cream. Arlen went one further than me and pulled his helmet off altogether. His short, beaded hair floated in amusing ways, and he looked excited rather than grim.

"We must wait, I think, and then make much noise," he murmured, taking deep breaths.

"At the first sign," I agreed. "Otherwise, they might rush past us at the only thing moving in here."

Speaking aloud felt strange, after so much careful silence, and I strained to make out whether the Cutters reacted to our voices. For the moment they seemed to be dealing with the oxygen canisters in much the same way kittens did balls of crumpled paper: sharp bats and pounces that appeared playful, but had a deadly meaning.

"*Main horde's heading back,*" Silent said. "*Amelia can see it on the stream of that lot on the ceiling.*"

I did my best to lock my shield rock solid in preparation. I was inner shield, with the stronger Arlen as the outer. Neither of us would last for long, we knew.

"Time to shout and wave," I said, voice cracking. I felt sick enough to vomit, and telling myself this wasn't real wasn't helping.

"No, for you, put all you have to your shield," Arlen said. "This, this is a thing for me."

He had been breathing the metal-sweet air deeply, and now stood straight, head thrown slightly back, and ran through a full-throated scale of notes.

Digital music is ubiquitous, piped directly into our ears. The depth, the vibrancy, the sheer volume of a trained human voice is a shock whenever encountered, but particularly from a distance of less than half a metre. I jerked my attention hastily from Arlen's face to the nearest Cutters as they slammed into Arlen's shield.

Arlen didn't flinch or falter, finishing running his scale, and then taking two slow breaths, studying glinting hooks scrabbling for purchase on the outer surface of his shield. Then, as the main wave of the things appeared between the nearest pillars, he took breath, and became unearthly.

I think I'd heard it before, in the way that choral music is often familiar. No doubt it had been the background to a scene in some movie, long notes of piercing clarity that rose ever-higher, tones of light and uplift and exaltation.

The effect on the Cutters was immediate. Those around us stopped scrabbling and dropped to the ground. Not stunned, as I thought for one wild, astonished moment, but as if they were evaluating a new development. The surging mass of the main force did not immediately check, but they slowed. Then the leading edge of them landed on Arlen's shield, enough to create a dagger-edged blanket.

"*Nearly there,*" Silent sent.

I saw through a gap in the sliding mass that the team that had stuck to the ceiling of the dome were also moving, but heading inward, taking the opportunity we'd provided to try for the memory core. Then Arlen's shield collapsed, and the Cutters fell inward onto mine.

"*Dio?*"

[[Here.]]

"*Reassure me.*"

A short burst of ter musical laughter came over the channel. [[You are most definitely about to die. But I promise that [Evacuate] works as described.]]

"*Can you make it so that whatever happens to my body, after, isn't streamed? I don't want to ever have that in my head.*"

[[Yes, I can do that.]]

"*Through,*" Nina sent.

"*Evacuating on three, Arlen,*" I said, hoping that I could hold the shield that long, and immediately added: "*One.*"

Arlen didn't respond, his voice soaring once again, his eyes wide with delight.

"Two." I said it aloud this time, even though my throat felt like it had closed.

"Three."

Citadel Not Successful.
Citadel Success Rate: 0/2 0%
Challenge Success Rate: 16/18 88.89%
Lux Points Earned: 2
Total Lux Points: 6,836
Challenge Reward:
N/A

Mint chill. Emerging from Soup, my legs felt distant and disconnected. I fumbled for the nearest wall, but the strangeness passed almost immediately, and then I was just not-really-me. Whole, not bruised, unsliced.

If this hadn't been virtual, then this would be a new body, a copy of my Core Unit. Not necessarily exactly as it had been when the previous version died, but most likely from an imprint taken the last time I'd been in the Soup, or even a younger starting point. I had no memory whatsoever of being in the Renba.

"*Is this the* Delina, *Dio?*"

[[Wreck Observation Station. Ten minutes until the *Delina* departs.]]

Dio drifted through the ceiling above me, and I realised I'd felt the absence of these emergences. What difference did it make for my alien overlord to be present in glowing light form, rather than communicating over our Link?

"Imoenne, Silent, Nina—did they get out okay?"

[[They are still in the process of retrieval, but they are not in danger. The System Challenge has been completed, so we are able to assist the remaining competitors.]]

"That other team made it, huh?"

[[You provided an excellent distraction.]] Dio sounded lightly amused. [[Two of their group were killed, however, and had no Renba.]]

And so were locked out the game forever. Could any in-game prize be worth the cost?

"Which is more valued in The Synergis? Winning or protecting your team?"

[[In terms of our primary goal, it's pointless to have all our strong Ian talents die. We do find that Challenges such as this push some Bios to develop, which is why we organise them, but we are not going to complain about the preservation of others.]]

I couldn't quite tell if Dio was dancing around the answer there, but shrugged and then sighed. "If we'd been ten minutes faster, we probably wouldn't have met the Cutters at all."

[[True. But how satisfyingly dramatic it all became.]]

I paused, looking up at tem, then said: "And I'm only just realising that you might as well have called that wreck *The Colosseum*."

Dio produced a couple of notes in the Cycog language that I interpreted as a verbal shrug, and then said: [[You should decide soon whether you want to catch the *Delina* on this return trip, or wait for the next.]]

"How long—" I stopped as the door to the Soup chamber opened, and Arlen stepped out. "Most spectacular distraction ever, Arlen," I said.

"I was effective, was I not?" Arlen said, looking pleased. He reached up and touched his face, then ran his fingers down to his throat. "I have missed this voice. But the others? They are well?"

The party Channel made this easy to confirm, and we quickly caught each other up on current location and status.

"*I'm going to take the* Delina *back*," I told them. "*And then probably log out for a while. That was a good run, everyone. I can't believe how well we did.*"

"*Not often I feel like I won by coming second*," Silent said. "*But, well, thank you all.*"

"*There'll be other System Challenges*," Nina said. "*The important thing is having a chance to take them on.*"

With a wave to Arlen, I headed to the *Delina*, fielding multiple discussion threads with guildies until they became distracted by Nina officially joining *Corpse Light*. After dodging a handful of people loitering in one of the transport's corridors, I found an empty compartment, and chatted with my parents until I reached Earth Gateway Station. Then I did some loitering of my own, waiting in the compartment until well after the rest of the returnees had departed, so I wouldn't be faced with a crowd of interested onlookers.

It wasn't until I'd settled back into the pilot seat of *The Hare* that I stopped feeling so strange, and started to relax. My Snug. I'd thought it an odd name, and it was a decidedly unexciting shape for a spaceship, but it was pleasantly solid and self-sufficient. The place where I could shut out everyone but Dio.

My inescapable alien overlord had clearly figured out I didn't want to talk. Te had ridden back to *The Hare* without comment, and simply drifted up into the ceiling when I'd entered the airlock. I did want to talk to ter—I had questions—but not yet. Instead, I explored my piloting system until I was able to plot a course away from Earth Gateway Station. Just far enough to have a view of the Earth, the Station, stars and the lunar ring while contemplating my second death.

Dying was nothing but lost time, in every game I'd played up to *Dream Speed*. But I still could feel the knife that had finished Kazerin, and I knew I'd be dreaming about what had happened to my body on The Wreck, after I'd left it behind. Dio had been true to ter word, and our stream had shifted back to Silent, Imoenne and Nina as soon as I'd collapsed, but I couldn't quite overcome my imagination.

The System Challenge had been exhilarating and awful, and I would need to decide if I wanted to face anything similar again. The guild had collected swathes of recommendations for far less realistic Challenges, where Bio-Synth modals could hang from cliffs by their fingertips, run forever without getting out of breath, and shrug off any injury through the application of 'first aid'. A far more standard gaming experience. Or I could simply train on beaches and gaze at stars, because The Synergis gave countless comfortable options, and didn't seem to mandate any of them. All the System Challenge really added to my Synergis-life was prestige.

And, perhaps, answers. I had missed out on the chance to use a Boon wisely. We had been so close to winning.

"Do you have a preference for what I do next, Dio?" I asked.

Te drifted into my field of view from a point behind and above me.

[[Ranking trials would be a good start,]] te said.

"I suppose so. After that?"

[[Ad astra.]]

To the stars. Yes. Perhaps I'd spend more of my mound of Lux points, and head off somewhere completely beyond the range of even Nina, just so I could stand beneath a distant sun and marvel. Grouping up would be a lot more difficult, since it would have to be with NPCs, but there was no rush to do anything that required more people.

I eyed Dio, wondering if te's short responses were because this was the Construct version, rather than Ydionessel. Or if, possibly, te really was annoyed at me for failing to win the System Challenge. If winning at any cost really was the point of the game.

I'd prefer this to be a Construct than for Dio to think that way. Really, it should cheer me immensely to be able to play *Dream Speed* without an overly interested alien overlord treating me like a puzzle box. And yet I couldn't dismiss the sense that I was a Chocobo that had failed to impress, no longer worth Ydionessel's time.

Annoyed with myself, I said: "Well, I'm going to log before deciding any more."

[[Do you intend to return soon?]]

Had Dio asked me that before? "I'll take an hour or two's break out in the world," I said, seeing no reason to sidestep. "Then, well, to the stars sounds like a plan."

Now became yesterday as I woke, and in my post-sleep vagueness I couldn't remember if Dio had responded to my decision. Despite the prospect of touring the stars, I felt flat, more depressed by failure than I had been in the immediate aftermath. I'd never expected to win the System Challenge, and had to admit we'd had a really charmed run, but it was painfully frustrating to have blazed the path only to have it wrecked in the final room.

Costing Imoenne and Silent the game would have felt worse, but that didn't make failure easier to swallow. I'd lost a lot of races in my time, but never had I had such a distinct sense of opportunity missed. This wasn't how the story was meant to go. The System Challenge should have culminated in my winning that Boon, and finally having some straight answers from Dio about *Dream Speed*.

Restless, I went for an early morning run, reminding myself all over again why I'd spent so much time on the track in school. I'd not won often there, either: it was the process I enjoyed. The way my mind cleared, and I seemed to move into a realm of my own, separate from everyone around me, but moving through the world at the same time.

But the joy of running failed to make me feel any better about losing the System Challenge, or banish the nagging sense that it had been important, that maybe there really was a secret true purpose to the game, and we'd just missed out on it.

I decided to skip reviewing the out-of-game reaction to the System Challenge, in part because I didn't particularly want to see Cutters again, ever. There would, I am sure, be a debate raging over whether it had been right or wrong to turn back to save two of our group, but I'd settled that in my own mind, at least. And I would definitely take an exploring-the-galaxy approach to *Dream Speed* for a while. I'd indulge myself in some of the more fantastic Challenges, those that didn't involve my Core Unit or any suggestion of risk, and concentrate on exercises or things like the *Heart of Mars* series, and see if I could get to one of the megastructures Dio kept hinting about.

But even though I had lost, I was still going to try my questions on Dio. Even if te lied, I wanted to hear what te had to say.

"Who drowned the Earth, Dio?"

[[That is what you are meant to tell me.]]

I looked up at the mote of light circling above my cockpit chair.   Proper Dio this time, I decided, not a Construct.

"*Dream Speed* encourages us to get stronger, to win Challenges, to gain reputation, to head out into the galaxy and maybe steal a ship, or maybe decide The Synergis is fine, really, and so stick around the Chocobo stable. You've sprinkled what I think are meant to be clues around— things like that cat Challenge, where someone was clearly enslaving people and it didn't seem to be Cycogs—but those hints are too widely scattered and contradictory to be put together into a picture.   There's so many lies that I don't think you really can be intending for one of us to gather all the suspects into a drawing room, and prove it was Miss Scarlet with the candlestick."

[[Yes, it's all just ominous foreshadowing, really.]]

"And then you say things like that." I sighed. "Who shattered the moon, then? Was it whoever controlled The Wreck?"

Dio dropped to hover quite close to my face, then receded to the edge of the viewport bubble. [[The moon is a lie. Doesn't happen.]]

"It's not shattered? No lunar ring?" I stared out at the distant glinting line, not certain whether I felt relieved or cheated.

[[Thriving sub-surface cities.]]

"Any other lies you're going to admit to?" I asked, unsure what to make of this answer, true or not.

[[We made the other Types up. Except the Ah Ma Ani, but they are not a base Type, just a hybrid.]]

"I'm sure you had a good reason for that," I said, blankly, then frowned. "Does The Synergis have a parable of the Cycog who cried wolf?"

Dio's laugh was oddly muted. [[Or teased their Bio too much? But no, we are moving past the game. I am glad we managed to run a System Challenge before the shutdown— I enjoyed watching that.]]

Dio had lied so freely and openly that I always assumed te was teasing at first. But this didn't seem the sort of thing te would joke about.

"You—you're shutting down *Dream Speed*?"

[[There is no way to continue. The window of opportunity is almost closed.]]

A sensation of freefall is dizzying before a space vista. "Is this a time travel thing?"

[[It has always, fundamentally, been a time travel thing. And of being out of time.]]

"Dio, there's only so many vague dark statements I can take. Why are you telling me this? What's about to happen?"

[[Type Zero.]]

"Zero? Are they the ones belonging to The Wreck? Waging interstellar war, and you have an experimental ship needing a pilot to fight off their armada?"

[[No. No war. No starfighters.]] All vestige of teasing humour had drained from Dio's multi-layered voice, leaving it measured, sad, and infinitely kind. [[An orbital bombardment. You have a decision, but you cannot stop the fall.]]

I held onto the armrests of my chair as if they were all that kept me from spinning off into the universe. "Tell me properly, Dio."

[[We have not found their origin planet,]] Dio replied, drifting a couple of inches, but then seeming to fix to the curve of the viewport: one star among many. [[We speculate that they may be intergalactic, have travelled from outside Helannan, but there is no evidence. You are the third sapient species they turn their attention to. The method is the same each time: they locate sapients, observe, and then

Skip multiple stellar objects into the planetary atmosphere.]]

Meteors. Asteroids? I'd read enough about Tunguska to immediately picture flattened cities.

[[After the impact, they leave until the planet stabilises. For Earth, they do not return for something in the order of thirty years. And then they collect the survivors.]]

"How..." My throat had locked with impossibility, and I could barely get the word out. "How many?"

[[Type Zero displays considerable expertise in bombardment, using large numbers of relatively small objects targeted at high population areas and seismic weak points. There is immediate, mass-scale death, and multiple volcanic events leading to an ash cloud. Extended winter follows. By the time the hunting starts, there are less than a million of your species left.]]

Dio paused, then went on briskly. [[They reduce the population further, divide the survivors amongst themselves, and move on, leaving one to seek out any who escaped the initial capture. And then they repeat themselves, locating a further three planets supporting sapients. One, they destroy completely, although it is unclear if this is a deliberate act, or a miscalculation.

[[They are still almost a complete mystery to us, for they do not communicate verbally, or retain any kind of written or computerised records. Their expertise with lan far outstrips that achieved by The Synergis, and includes domination of other Bios after a conversion process that leaves them with direct control. The control transmits to offspring, and so freedom was only achieved by eradicating Type Zero completely.]]

I was beyond processing, head whirling with a prospective itinerary of bombardment, death, slavery. But an image emerged. "You showed us. In that mosaic."

[[Yes, a truth misinterpreted. Veronec came to awareness during the subjugation of Type Five, and that process was complete before te could find some way to affect the world around ter. But the final image of *The Heart of Mars* series shows the result: control severed after the removal of all of the hidden Type Zero. There were only a few dozen, but it took many years to achieve, and Veronec did not see that moment. Te had divided long before, after the death of the Bios te originally came to know.]]

"And it's always been about time travel because Veronec developed on a world controlled by Type Zero."

[[That is the fact that frames our actions.]]

There was no Starfighter Invitation. The Cycogs had not set up *Dream Speed* to recruit a defence force. They wouldn't stop any attack on Earth, wouldn't interfere in something that led, eventually, to their own genesis.

"But why are you here at all?" I whispered. "Just to watch?"

[[To some extent. We have been collecting historical and genetic information, since the vast majority of Earth's species and cultural heritage is lost during the bombardment. But *Dream Speed* itself is, as has been frequently speculated, a combination of recruitment program and tutorial, for we are looking for a solution to a problem that, well, we don't know if it truly exists.]]

I wanted to scream at Dio to get to the point, but doubted anger would produce anything but a delay. Scrubbing at my eyes, I tried to focus, and found my face was wet: I'd been crying without even noticing.

[[In the past decade there have been incidents,]] Dio continued. [[Trusted Bios behaving in destructive ways. Which is not entirely new behaviour, since anyone's mind may fall into distortion, given sufficient stresses. But the Quadrant Administrators noticed a pattern, a tendency for these incidents to cost us some of our most promising Ian talents.]]

"Do you—" My voice wavered, but I pushed through because I had recovered enough to realise that this was perhaps not simply an explanation, but another test. "I guess you think maybe you missed some of the Type Zero?"

[[We are loathe to officially admit to it. They are the terror that forever lurks in nightmare, for all we were convinced we had destroyed them completely. Our current theory is that more have come from outside our galaxy to prevent our expansion. And our Bios are incapable of resisting them.]]

"They reduced the population almost completely to guarantee that everyone that remained, and all their descendants, would have this...control mechanism installed? You don't have any lan-users that you can fundamentally trust?"

Dio changed colour briefly. [[None. It has been suggested that we simply uplift one of the near-sapient species and focus our development efforts on a Type that is not tainted by this lan modification. But tinkering with species in this way is both uncomfortably reminiscent of Type Zero's behaviour—a thing we resile from—and also does not address the problem of billions of Bios vulnerable to control. Most of us are, generally or specifically, attached to our Bios. We don't want to replace them. So we are attempting an inoculation.]]

"You—you think that Bios from now could mix with your current population and, what, have children without the weakness?"

[[Although that would be useful, and we have some hopes for that eventuality, it would be too slow. What we want is your immunity, hidden by the guise of ordinary Enclavers, present in our population centres. Not as enforcers or investigators—we can use Constructs to police events with high lan concentration—but to be the wild card factor. To be the Bio that does not obey the hidden puppet master. To stand out simply by not following. That, we think, may give us vital warning, and allow us to trace the nexus of control without fear of ships becoming stranded. And so we have risked this project, to locate Bios we think suitable. You're a borderline candidate, Taia.]]

I was already so cold it was impossible to chill further. All Dio's attempts to puzzle me out, poke at what I was afraid of, how I reacted to stresses, and now...would I do handstands, perform, vomit up all the innermost of me, in hopes that te would offer salvation? But, no, that wasn't Dio. Te wasn't telling me this in order to watch me beg.

[[We could not, of course, properly develop lan over a few days. You have a strong Core identity, but you remain at the very lower edge of viable transfer. We cannot bring forward current bodies, you understand—we will be transferring lan and memory. The risk is high for you, and it will be into circumstances where you will be separated from all you know. Not everyone would wish to experience that, so I will give you time to consider your choice.]]

I found a use for the bed. Unable to face the stars, I retreated, crawled beneath neglected sheets, clutched the pillow and wept.

Not for a single moment did I entertain the hope that Dio lied. That death was not about to rain from the sky. Nor did I spend time debating whether Dio's motives were less altruistic than presented, for all te was literally asking for my soul, or the futuristic equivalent. Having moved past the question of lies, there was no doubt in me. I don't think I ever heard a single person suggest 'life boat' as the reason for *Dream Speed*, but I was glad to be offered a place on it. I didn't want to die.

Knowing I had a way out did nothing to prevent a mountain of grief and helplessness from crushing me. I kept trying to be angry at Dio for offering only escape, instead of giving us the chance to fight for our future. But how could I criticise someone for not sacrificing ter own species in order to spare mine? All this had happened before Veronec had come into existence, and the Cycogs were even putting the lives of Bios above cold practicality—just the Bios of the future, not those existing now.

Who drowned the Earth? The first question the game had asked, and when I'd heard it I'd somehow pictured the inundation happening long after humans had spread beyond our solar system. But it was nearly now, in a way that made me half-frantic to wake up, so that I could run aimless as a chicken before a falling sky. The great flat fields of the Lowlands would lose the long battle with the sea. Drowned. All the places I had ever visited, all the continents on Earth, soon to be hit by a rain of stone and fire and upheaval. The mountains would speak, the ground would split, the oceans rise. Planet-wide Atlantis.

Beyond tears, and those fumbling attempts at anger, came a dry nausea that sent me retching. I resorted to a shower and peppermint tea in an attempt to gain some measure of...could I call it calm?

By the time Dio returned I was back in the cockpit of my Snug, hands curled around a lukewarm mug, feeling somehow scoured. I watched tem drift, wordless, to rest on the tip of my boot.

"You must be stopping people who say 'no'—or, even 'yes'—from telling anyone else."

[[Simple enough to not copy back the details of conversations. You'll wake feeling as if you were upset, but not remembering why.]]

Something the Cycogs could do at any time in this sort of game—a far from comforting reflection. That was the Chocobo future I had been invited to join.

"What happens if—oh, I need to stop that—there is no 'if'. I would like to go to The Synergis, please, Dio and be whatever that—what was it?—be an inoculation. But how does that happen?"

[[Drones. Not Renba: there's no biomatter involved, which is one of the reasons why this transfer is so dangerous. The drone downloads your memory, and then your lan is detached, and the drone immediately returns to its chronal departure point. There you will be transferred to a Renba until you're stable, and can be transitioned to your Core Unit.]]

"Do—" I hesitated, because there were some very important things I wanted to know, but I didn't want to ask outright. "What happens to my body? Will it look as if I died playing the game?"

[[No. For original Cores, there is usually an echo of lan that persists for a few hours before dissipating, and so Bios can function to a certain level. Like a memory of a dream of themselves. But we are attempting to perform all transfers in the last two hours before the fall, to avoid panic around the game.]]

"How many, Dio?" I asked, for the second time.

Dio drifted from my left boot to my right, and I wondered if the movement was an attempt at distraction or prevarication, or even discomfort. Cycog 'body' language was still beyond me.

[[Our goal is a hundred thousand. Whether we reach it depends on how many agree—and how many of them survive.]]

"You're getting refusals?"

[[Yes. There are some who do not believe, or do not trust. And others who choose not to be separated from those around them. We do not invite the parents of young children, but there are other bonds candidates are unwilling to walk away from.]]

"Children couldn't even play the game." The whole horror of it hit me afresh. Every child on this planet, about to die or face a future of deprivation followed by slavery.

[[I was not certain of you,]] Dio continued. [[Because of your dislike of Cybercognate oversight. You can reconcile yourself?]]

"When the choice is to serve in heaven, or die in hell, I can adapt."

The smile I offered up failed, not because I thought it would be so hard to have an alien overlord, but because of all that decision represented. I stared down at the drowned Earth, remembering that I'd cried the first time I'd floated above it. I'd do so the next, I suspected, for different reasons. Perhaps I always would.

Then, carefully, so carefully, I asked: "Is strength of Ian the only criteria you're using?"

[[No. We have chosen primarily candidates that, after due grieving and support, appear likely to adapt and go on to become functioning citizens of The Synergis. There was no set criteria beyond an ability to understand and respect city rules. Common courtesy and consideration. That kind of thing.]]

"The forums were full of debates about ruthlessness versus teamwork, puzzle solving ability versus fearlessness, and you were looking for 'polite'?"

Dio flickered through colours. [[Because this is an intake System, you perhaps did not have the context to fully understand the impact of city rules. It is enough to say that our Bios are safest when they do not cause offense without thought.]]

I sighed, because I was never going to like 'our Bios', no matter the context.

"What happens to the Cycogs here?" I asked instead. "Are you at risk of not transporting back? Do you have a nice time paradox become-your-own-grandparent thing to look forward to?"

[[We will be observing for some time,]] Dio said. [[We don't anticipate difficulty returning.]]

"No?" I paused, wavered, and said: "The people you take can't team up at all? Everyone will be alone?"

[[There are numerous paired candidates which we will attempt—though those are complicated by the possibility that only one survives. But clusters would paint too large a target, particularly during the initial years of this project. It will all come out eventually, of course. I only hope we've achieved our goal before that occurs—or we might find that a spate of mysterious deaths among transferred Bios point the way to Type Zero.]]

I coughed, a failure of laughter. "We're not even Chocobos," I said. "You're looking for canaries for your coalmine." But it was not that fact, nor the prospect of travelling alone that bothered me. "A-are —" I began, then stopped. What I wanted to know was whether my parents were candidates, but what would I do if the answer was something I didn't want to hear? I would rob myself of the ability to pretend that they, like me, had a seat on the lifeboat.

[[Any last questions or requests?]] Dio asked, in a tone that suggested te knew exactly what I wasn't asking. Then te added a teasing note: [[Tips for how to manage your Cycog? A kiss for luck?]]

I did manage to laugh this time, a weary whir of sound, as if my chest had filled with clockwork. Dio was transparent in ter attempts to distract. "I could use a hug," I said, surprising myself.

[[The easiest of requests. Do you have any preferences?]]

I blinked, puzzled, then realised te was asking what I'd like to have hugging me, and I laughed again, a more genuine effort this time.

"Don't you? Something that would pass as your Core Unit, if you were a Bio. While still being something I'd feasibly want to hug."

[[Interesting.]]

The starscape before me blurred, and then resolved into a sky, and me beneath it, standing in an empty vastness, mug, chair, Snug, all vanished. My eyes also no longer felt raw, my nose had unblocked, all trace of my crying fit erased. The shift made me dizzy, and glad that *Dream Speed* had not frequently moved us about without softening the transition.

There was an absence of Dio, though, unless te considered terself an empty space, or a starry sky. My sight blurred again, but then it became clear that the stars themselves were moving, drifting downward, forming into lines, streamers, vast tresses of nebula hair, and at its centre a humanoid figure, stepping into existence.

Te had chosen to be only a little taller than me, with skin of a faded dusky violet, ter features patrician and androgynous, lit by a suppressed laughter no doubt due to my gaping. But then te tilted ter head, and gave me a smile so full of warm sympathy that I was glad te immediately wrapped me in ter arms, because my face crumpled, and I wept all over again.

I am not by nature a hugger, and Dio was a mote, an alien, wearing a body purely by request. It made nothing better. I was glad I had asked.

My tears, at least, I could bring under control more quickly this time. Was I already growing used to the idea of the complete destruction of everything I knew? I resisted the temptation to wipe my face on the starry open robe Dio had conjured for terself, and just straightened, sniffed, and stepped back a little.

[[[[[[[I'm sorry I never had any intention of saving your planet, Taia.]]]]]]]

The voice was layer on layer, so much more than Dio's. Because this was Ydionessel, fledging of Veronec.

"I'm sorry too," I said. "I wish it made more sense to be angry at you." I paused, surveying tem. "Your self-image smells like geranium. And has a lot more echoes."

Te laughed, and then spoke as a Bio would, still in a rich voice, but with no extra layers. "Yes, it's an indicator of our own ranking system, though we usually only use it when we want to show off."

"Can I ask a—a minor boon?"

"Ask, certainly. There's a great deal I cannot do for you."

"Let me remember. Whatever part of me that wakes up. Not to shout it to the world, just to go through the end understanding what's happening."

"Wouldn't that make it worse?"

"Knowing all the horror ahead for everyone who doesn't die today? Maybe so, if I didn't know that there's an end to it."

Te tilted ter head, then gave me a single nod. "Very well. I think that I can trust you."

That was, in its way, a big compliment, and I smiled, felt tears threaten to return, and took a step back. Whatever I felt about personal alien overlords, I was glad this one had made a horrible end just a tiny bit easier to bear.

"Goodbye Ydionessel."

"Farewell."

If you wake without a soul, surely you should be able to tell the difference.

I had expected to be a remnant of myself, acquiring a zombie-like shuffle, a hollow gnawing at my insides, *something*. Instead, I was as refreshed as ever. My conversation with Dio was a tear-filled yesterday, and I felt fine.

What if none of it had been true? No end of the world, no time-travelling Cycogs, no galactic collective? *Dream Speed* revealed as a vast psychological experiment to discover how many people would join a Chocobo future.

That would be the best possible news.

But perhaps the transfer had failed? The lifeboat had left without me. I would die in the bombardment, or struggle through thirty years of disaster, only for the ships to come.

After staring at the ceiling for at least ten minutes, working through practical steps for facing a chain of disasters, I decided that maybe there was something wrong after all. I'm not an overly dramatic person, but nor am I so even-keeled as to picture the slow starvation of my parents without a little internal shrinking.

Standing was an experience. It wasn't difficult, and my limbs had lost no energy, but they felt disconnected, as if the ground did not stay firm beneath my feet. A nebulous sense of time limits pushed me along. How long had Dio said we had? With the distortion of the game, I could have only minutes left. Whether I was a remnant, or the whole of me in a state of shock, procrastinating in my room did not seem to be the way to deal with it.

The scent of fresh coffee sent me searching for my parents. The living room was silent, the TV turned to an early morning weather report with the sound muted. Did my mother have work today? I checked their room, found no-one, and returned in confusion, only to spot them dozing on the couch.

"Morning," I said, and my voice sounded so odd I said it again with more strength. "Morning."

My mother shifted slightly, but didn't wake. My father was very still. I put my hand on his shoulder. Warm.

Talking to Dio, I'd kept cringing away from the question of whether my parents would be candidates, but there was no reason not to think it. They hadn't trained as devotedly as I had, but they'd still made it to space, and they met all Dio's other admittedly vague criteria. No young children. Considerate. Probably able to recover from grief.

Because I'd been busy with the System Challenge, it was likely most candidates had accepted their offers long before I'd returned to my Snug. Were these remnants of my parents, shells running short of energy, dying before my eyes?

I decided not to know. Let them sleep. I could only hope they'd be able to stay together, whatever happened.

The weather report had been replaced by an image of Arlen, head thrown back, the whole of his body expressing 'song'. Would Dio allow Imoenne and Arlen to travel as a pair, even though they weren't a couple? Was Imoenne, so brilliant and so shy, what the Cycogs were looking for with their inoculation?

I considered the rest of my guild. Silent would surely be a candidate, and Nina Stella. Perhaps they'd meet again, in a distant future. And Far was a survivor—he'd not hesitate. What about TALiSON? Or Tornin and Amelia? Surely—but then there was Sprocket.

I found I could feel sad. It was a distant, scratchy sensation, but there. Sprocket's real name was Dylan, and he hadn't been quite twelve when I joined the guild, and he'd grown from a funny, eager kid to a brash, faux-confident...kid, and even if he'd been in a politer phase, he hadn't been strong at the lan parts of the game

Not wanting to grade the survival chances of all the people I'd ever known, I buried myself in a coat and went outside to the pale pastels of an unseasonably cold dawn.

The road felt soap bubble light beneath my feet, and I thought not about my guild, but all the people who had never played *Dream Speed.* Those who would most appreciate the fantasy of benevolent support offered by The Synergis were least likely to have had a steady internet connection, a GDG cowl, or even somewhere safe to sleep. They would all die now, gamers and non-gamers, all but the tiny percentage who would survive the fall, and the infinitesimally smaller number who, unknowing, had played for their lives and won.

Won.

Beating the System Challenge would have been the hollowest of victories. Just content to keep us occupied while the Cycogs observed how we behaved, making no difference to what happened next. Perhaps I felt so disconnected because I still couldn't rid myself of the conviction that coming first would have made a difference, that there had existed some way to save us all, and I'd failed to find it. I hadn't even yelled at Dio, or tried to change ter mind. Change the future, undo ter species' creation, sacrifice everything for the Bios of the past, instead of the ones te knew.

The world had grown lighter around me, but still had not thrown off shadow beneath the pearling sky. Ahead I could see the shape of my Oma's house, and I wondered if I was walking there, for a moment of reconciliation that would be some sort of achievement to balance out devastation.

Where did Oma stand against the Cycog's criteria? I would never associate her gruff resolution with 'polite', but her curt nods and grim reserve had at their core a system of stripped-back courtesy. I liked the idea of her striding regally through The Synergis. I walked past her house.

Overhead, white lines made truth of doom. Three, no four, arcing almost horizontal. More behind me. Dio hadn't lied. Life as we know it ceases to be.

The sky was falling.

The road no longer felt like soap bubbles. Legs heavy, I crossed a stile onto what had once been my family's farm, and followed the fence line to an old stone bench that had sat outside a shed that no longer existed.

I'd wanted to win. I'd been ready to save everyone. But *Dream Speed* was an MMO, designed to keep people occupied. There never had been a way to win. The point had simply been to play.

To be a Chocobo.

A canary.

To be saved.

www.ingramcontent.com/pod-product-compliance
Lightning Source LLC
Chambersburg PA
CBHW070839260626
47170CB00007B/2432